Rise of the Infernal Paladin

World Eater

Emrys Ambrosius, L.R. Monroe

Shadow Light Press

Book Cover by Ana Jade

Editing by Declan Darkmor and @niinawo

1st Edition 2025

Contents

I dedicate this book to my sister, Shannon Monroe.
We've been through a lot, but you were there with me, thick and thin.
Love you, little girl.

Chapter One

Ambrose Severen fell from a portal of fire he had opened above a giant made of red flesh, brimstone and lava. Like a falling star, Ambrose's axe of hellfire cut through the giant, parting him down the middle like a ripe fruit.

The two halves of the fire giant collided with the black earth, and shining stone that covered the land as far as the eye could see. Guts covered in slimy green ichor splooshed out of the now dead giant. Ambrose stood up, scanning the area for any more threats.

Off in the distance, a beam of crimson light could be seen. *It's like an alien tractor beam or something,* he mused to himself. Ambrose had been working on closing this Incursion for weeks now. The problem was the fire giant stronghold. It was carved with extensive wards. He couldn't teleport in, and the shield covering it prevented him from climbing it.

The average fire giant was only level one-hundred and twenty, so the experience gain was minimal. It made the whole process of coming out here very frustrating. He *wanted* to go after Eric. He needed to visit Eric's town, ransack his office or find his merchant and figure out which world-portal stone he bought.

Once he did that, he could easily buy the portal stone himself and give chase to the psychopathic bastard. Noelle sent him a feeling of eagerness. He smiled, the arcane white tiger wanted to go after him almost as much as he did, if only to give him peace.

The problem was that he had an obligation to Avalon. He couldn't leave them with the Incursions on their own, which got out of hand by the day. It was all he could do to keep them at bay. Even the forerunners, of which Ambrose knew of two, were having trouble.

The fire giants had ventured far afield from their fortress, destroying any settlements that cropped up, slaughtering people by the score, and taking resources too. Whenever he got close to the fortress, the sounds of mining could be heard.

These invaders were stripping the newly integrated planet of all it was worth, including hunting down its treasures.

In the beginning, Ambrose wouldn't have cared. He had one goal, and everything else was secondary. In some ways, that was still true, but his responsibilities now went beyond that one goal. He needed to consider how to accomplish that goal as well, and rushing in blindly with no resources would just get him killed.

The System gave people a way to grow in strength, to seize power. Eric was an old hand at such things before the System ever landed, and he had been given a huge advantage by being the first forerunner, integrated into the System before anyone else.

Ambrose felt sure that he could kill the fucker if he saw him, but now he was off in another world, doing who knew what and gaining power every day. When he faced Eric, he wanted to *crush* him. There would be no challenge, just annihilation.

That meant being patient about it. It meant building his resources.

It meant killing stupid fire giants over and over again. His hope was that the Incursion leader would come out of the fortress and face him if he killed enough of his people. He had tried slashing away at the shield, but the monster's shield was high D-Grade at least, and it held. Maybe if Ambrose brought all the Knights of Avalon here, he could do it.

That was an option he was considering. Full blown assault.

Darren's wrapped and burning corpse flashed through his mind's eye. Ambrose winced, his hands tightening, and he blew out a breath.

Only if I have to will I do that.

Seeing no other fire giants, and tiring of waiting, Ambrose opened a portal to Avalon with a wave of his hand as he tapped **[Hellfire Manipulation].** His mythic skill was beyond useful for getting around, and other things, too.

The trail of fire was like some infernal zipper on reality being pulled down, opening up a doorway for Ambrose to step through.

In the weeks since what everyone was now calling the Battle of Avalon, the island had undergone a dramatic change. It now looked like someone had taken an Arthurian medieval city, smooshed it together with a touch of modern luxury and added a dash of edgelord gothiness to it all.

Alice would have loved it.

His wife had always liked all things nerd, and the whole town was ripped right of a D&D campaign. It had also grown in population. Ambrose had never considered it before, but he could bring up the state of the town with a thought, just like his status page. Perks of having a seed.

He did so now as he walked:

Town: Avalon

Shield: D-Grade

Population: 300[Max 5000]

Taxes: N/A

Town Manager: Andrea Pender

In order to upgrade the town to a city, he would need to close the Incursions. That was part of why he wanted to close them. Having a city would allow him more people, and thus more professions, resources, SC, etc.

He had a few different stops to make. He needed to go by Troy's, Darren's Hall, and then finally the school. *Bum bum,* his heart sped up a beat. Jenny would be there. Seeing her was always a hard reminder of his failure.

Off on the western shore, Ambrose could see more people departing from boats, the Knights of Avalon escorting them to processing. He would have to visit the barracks, too.

Every day his responsibilities grew and every day Ambrose worried he would lose sight of what was truly important.

Killing Eric Delrosa.

His knuckles popped. He needed to wrap up these Incursions. Then he could go after Eric.

Troy was a person Ambrose would rather see dead, preferably by his own hand. The man looked more like a southern country singer than a merchant, with his denim over flannel, dark shades and jeans. His shop was on the western side of Avalon, what Ambrose was considering to be downtown.

When Ambrose entered, Troy looked up from a book he was reading. He moved his feet from atop the wooden counter, his throat bobbing up and down as he swallowed.

"Oh, hey Mr. Severen...uh...can I help you?"

Troy rubbed a hand on his jeans. He was right to be nervous; Ambrose sometimes beat the shit out of him on principle.

"Hey there, trash. I have things to sell."

A small flash of fire over Ambrose's raised hand, and he held a pulsating heart with black veins and ashen light in the center. Troy glanced at it.

"More fire giant hearts? I can give you two hundred SC a piece."

Ambrose narrowed his one eye, his mouth setting into a dangerous line.

Troy raised his hands. "Look man, I'm running a business here I-"

Ambrose slammed his other hand on the counter, a boom echoing throughout the small shop.

"You're a slaver piece of fucking shit is what you are. Never forget that. You sold children, you bastard. I don't care about your bottom line. Eight hundred SC, and that will keep me from breaking your jaw again."

Troy swallowed again, his hand shook as he took the heart.

Then something happened Ambrose had not expected. His jaw clenched, his gaze hardened.

Slowly, the shopkeeper put the giant heart on the counter. His voice was soft, and surprisingly devoid of fear.

"I felt every ounce of that pain I caused when you put me in that crystal. I know what a horrible person I am, Ambrose. I know it to my soul, thanks to you. But I am *trying* to be better. Who supplies your profession books? Who funds that school of yours with his profits?"

He tapped his chest.

"I do. Does that earn me forgiveness? No, maybe not. I don't think I will ever deserve it. I certainly will never forgive myself. But what else am I supposed to do? You won't let me end my life. All I can do is keep working, even if it takes all my days, to be a better man. What else do you want from me, huh, Ambrose?"

Troy spread his hands. "I'm not asking for your respect. I'm just asking for you to stop coming in here and taking me for all I'm worth because of my past. You punished me, and I am suffering for it, I promise. Let that be enough. I will give you four hundred for this, and trust me, what little I make off you will probably go back into Avalon, anyway."

His eyes were pleading, but there was a determined tick in his jaw.

Ambrose blinked, and stepped back. An angry rush was in his ears, and he got that way every time he saw the merchant. Maybe it was time to let a little bit of that go.

He sighed, rubbing the side of his face. "Fine, four hundred."

Troy nodded, completing the transaction.

Ambrose left the shop.

Time to get the school visit over with. Like ripping off a bandaid.

Chapter Two

The school was a single story building located within the same area of Avalon as Troy's shop. People went about their days as Ambrose passed by, many of them calling out to him in greeting. It reminded him of the days before the System, just normal folks doing normal things.

The Knights of Avalon were split into two groups: the Sword of Avalon and the Shield of Avalon. The latter was in its infancy, and served as the police force for Avalon. The harsh reality was that people did bad things, and now they could do bad things with super powers. With more refugees coming into Avalon every day, they were a necessary group.

There hadn't been any major issues yet, but that would change as growth increased. It was inevitable.

The school had the same gothic edginess as the rest of the town, all dark wood and darker metal. Its large double doors led into a reception area. A blonde woman was typing into a laptop. There was no internet with the System having shut it down somehow, but the laptops were still useful for storing information, writing up documents, and more.

He marvelled at how easy it was to set up everything. The System store provided all kinds of earth technology, plus more that could be done with arrays.

"Hello, Chelsea."

Chelsea Mays was a southern woman with blonde hair done up in a professional bun, wearing a pantsuit. Her features were sharp, almost bird like, but her blue eyes shined like the ocean on a sunny day. Chelsea gave him a sympathetic smile, "Mr. Severen, come to check up on us?"

He nodded. Chelsea was one of the former slaves from a town he had burned to the ground for participating in such an evil practice. She had been a secretary before the System and now chose to use her skills for the school that had been started.

She knew Ambrose was here to check up on the kids, and more importantly, Jenny. "Do you think she'll talk to you today?"

Ambrose contorted his lips until he wore a sad smile. "Probably not, Chelsea. She had good reason to think I killed her father."

Chelsea sighed, leaning forward, eyes sad. "All of us here from the start knew what Darren did for us, and we all knew you had goals beyond us and still do. Our eyes were open, Mr. Severen."

Ambrose chuckled, "And you think that matters to a pre-teen girl? All she knows is that she called out for help, and I didn't answer. That's enough for her."

Chelsea pressed her lips together, clearly wanting to say more, but then she rubbed her temples, leaning back. "You're probably right. Well, I would say good luck, but I doubt it will matter."

She flashed a smile. Ambrose nodded and went through the door on the right leading into the classroom. The teacher, a middle-aged man with honey brown skin and a black-haired crew cut, paused in his history lecture. He reached up, adjusted his glasses, and then clasped his hands together.

"Well children, it looks like we have a special visitor today! Hello Mr. Ambrose, what can we do for you?"

Ambrose smiled at the room full of children who turned to look at him.

"Whoa! That armor is so cool!" One boy breathed.

"Are you really a demon, like they say?" A girl asked.

Ambrose held up a gauntleted hand. Almost as if by magic, the room quieted at once. "I just wanted to stop by to check on all of you. Avalon is working tirelessly to bring some semblance of normalcy back into your lives. I'm glad to see you are learning, and are safe."

Ambrose meant it, even if he had to say it in his 'leader' voice. Something genuine must have come through because admiration burned in many of the children's eyes.

Except for one.

Jenny, often known as little Jenny to many, had nothing but hatred storming through her brown eyes. Her jaw was tight, her frown was so deep Ambrose wondered if it would fall right off her face. Her pencil actually bent, she was clutching it so hard.

He heard a breath of air leave her nostrils as she relaxed her shoulders. The hate never left her eyes.

Do I look like that? When it comes to Eric? More than likely he did, but the difference was that Eric had no good reasons for what he did, and was directly involved. With the kids seen to, and answering a plethora of questions, he waved to the teacher, and left.

He had hoped Jenny would want to speak to him, and would want to clear the air. Maybe it would be a good idea to stop checking. His presence likely only fanned her anger. He stopped by the barracks, which was towards the east beach, built on a clearing.

It was not only where the Knights of Avalon stayed, but also trained. Men and women hacked at dummies set up in a gated training yard filled with sand, but also shot arrows, and in one gated area, used skills.

A group was running on the beach below, and others practised martial art forms. He greeted many of the men, offered tips to some, and made sure to introduce himself to any new recruits. He didn't know much about being a leader, that had never been anything Raylen had taught him.

What he was learning, though, is that people expected you to *care*. You had to be present, you had to make an effort, to show that you had their best interests at heart. Ambrose could not spend every waking moment doing this, but whenever he returned, he made an effort to go out among the people and talk to them like regular human beings.

He inquired about one Knight's wife, and how she was holding up. He commented on the growth of one woman's child. He remembered names, and clasped hands, squeezing shoulders.

It was exhausting.

It was also necessary.

Eventually, it was time to go to Darren's Hall. Darren's Hall had evolved to be the town headquarters as well as the town hall. Andrea's office was there, and nearly all the planning and policy was discussed behind its walls.

Ambrose had a meeting with Earth's two other forerunners today.

He was excited to find out if they knew anything about Eric. He also wished to question them about the Incursions, anything they knew about it, and inquire about their settlements.

Andrea wanted to establish some kind of working alliance. He didn't care much about that as long as he got what he needed out of them. Darren's Hall was the largest building, two stories in fact, with the first story open to the public, and the second one being headquarters.

Not a lot happened on the first floor. There was artwork, and crafted pieces on display. A place to get answers to questions, and applications to start a business or have a home built. Ambrose didn't ask much from his citizens. Just do your part. Eventually he wanted to establish a free market of sorts, but he ensured everyone was housed at least.

As Avalon grew, that might become more of a problem, but it was an issue for another day.

Ambrose had arrived, and it was time to see what these forerunners knew.

CHAPTER THREE

Andrea Pender thrived on these meetings. Unlike the world outside of these four walls, it was a controlled, orderly place. Here, paperwork reigned supreme, and bureaucracy was the only superpower that mattered. It was a bastion of paperwork, a sacred place where decisions were made.

The people outside this room had no idea how much the events here affected their lives. It was a kind of power all its own that had nothing to do with skills, weapons, or the System. It was here, in this space of meetings, that Andrea reigned. There wasn't much to her place of power. A large meeting table, a simple carpet, a whiteboard behind the head of the table, and paperwork.

It wasn't her office, which was her sanctuary, but people deferred to her in this place. Even Ambrose let her be in control here. Currently, the room was filled with four people, soon five, with Ambrose on the way. A bored-looking teenage girl with hair that reminded Andrea of the ocean reflecting a night sky, pale moonlight shining on its silken waves.

Her hazel eyes were bored as she doodled with a pencil. She had on an oversized hoodie; her fingernails were painted with strokes of midnight. Across from her was a broad-shouldered bald-headed man with skin of milk chocolate, and honey-brown eyes. His features were strong, lost features of some warrior king.

He wore a suit the shade of starlight over a silver pond. Then there was Thom...who was sleeping. Thom's bronze weathered skin looked less weathered today, his long white beard was neat, and he wore flannel under blue overalls. His head was leaned back over the chair, and his snores were somewhat concerning.

The bald-headed man appeared to be trying very hard to ignore him. He wasn't succeeding. His eyes kept flicking over to him, and his face would flicker with annoyance as he adjusted his tie and cleared his throat loudly.

Andrea suppressed a chuckle. *You have more chance of waking a stone than Thom*, Andrea thought, her lips quirking in amusement.

The man sighed, "Can we please get this meeting underway? We are here to discuss linking your teleportation array with ours, Miss Pender. Not endure this man's..." he winced, "snores."

Andrea schooled her expression. *It would not do to laugh at him;* she chuckled inwardly to herself.

"I'm afraid we must wait for Mr. Severen before beginning the meeting."

The man's strong features morphed into a scowl, "And where is he? I would have expected him to show some respect by being on time."

Andrea shrugged, "Mr. Severen has always done as he wished. I'm afraid he is not a man you can rush, Mr. Akinyemi."

He crossed his arms, chest rumbling, "*I* am not a man to keep waiting. I control one of the largest towns in Africa post System. I am level on-hundred and thirty. I demand to be treated with more respect."

His eyes flashed like an angry lion that had been roused from his sleep too early.

It was true. He was the second forerunner, the leader of New Kweneng. She hadn't used [Analyze] on him as that was considered rude by many, but he had freely told her that his class was something known as a Desert Summoner.

For a moment, Andrea allowed herself to be fascinated by how quickly humanity adapted to what was quickly becoming known as the

Integration. Already new cultural norms were being implemented. New Kweneng had even managed to get the monster population in their area under control.

They roamed all of Africa, bringing them to their town, and had more merchants than any other place she had seen, which wasn't many. According to Ambrose, there were only four town seeds for four forerunners. Once one died, their seed appeared within a pre-designated spawn point by the forerunner and could be reclaimed.

That was how Ambrose had gotten his, taken from a safe once owned by Annie Hyde, the third forerunner.

Andrea allowed her eyes to land on the teenage girl. She didn't speak much, but there was a subtle aura of danger around the girl. Ambrose had said that it was the feeling of spirit. When a spiritual skill was powerful enough, it sort of 'leaked' out.

Shortly after the battle, Ambrose had gone into the island depths for spiritual control training; as his spirit had become so strong, many within half a mile around him started to feel it, their minds crawling with worms of doubt and fear, as well as finding it hard to even move.

I don't feel any of that from Akenyemi, she considered.

That either meant his spiritual skill was not powerful enough, or he had iron control. The girl hadn't offered her level or class; in fact, all she had gotten out of her was a name.

Tina Florence.

Andrea thought about the other fact about her: She was the leader of Britannia, a town established in a massive forest in France. She had even spoken with a slight french accent, when she had spoken at all.

The only reason she even knew that much was the teleportation array. It had cost a lot, but with their mining operations, it had been doable. It allowed one to teleport to other teleportation arrays controlled by System recognized towns. *If* the town leader allowed it.

Even so, you could see it, and its name, and its general location. Andrea really didn't like that because it meant anyone wishing them harm would know, but she couldn't do anything about it currently. Reigning in her annoyance, she pressed her lips together into a firm line, then addressed Akenyemi.

"While I am sorry you have been kept waiting, there really is nothing for it, Mr. Akenyemi. You're welcome to bring up your concerns with Mr. Severen when he arrives, but I cannot rush him."

Akenyemi blew a slow breath out of his nose, and he stood. "Perhaps I should simply leave then. I have no need of this place to be connected to my array, after all."

Andrea cocked her head, "Is that so? You must have all the resources you could ever need in Africa, then. Maybe you've found every treasure you need there. There is certainly no benefit then, of you having access to this area."

His jaw worked, his eyes becoming boulders. Andrea wanted to stretch like a satisfied cat who had just lapped up cream. She crushed that desire with a mental effort. It wouldn't do to gloat.

She knew she had him. Avalon was the only town in the once-great nation known as the USA. Eric Delrosa's town had not put up an array. Likely because their leader was in another world.

The System had spread out resources, treasure, and dungeons all around the world. Dungeons were recently discovered places, and idly, Andrea wondered about the team they had sent to one found on the mainland. *I hope they're okay,* she worried.

Akenyemi sat down. Tina kept doodling, unconcerned with the confrontation.

The door opened, and Ambrose Severen entered.

If you had never met him, and even after doing so for some, Ambrose was best described as a teenage nerd's fantasy character. He had a cloak of white like fresh snow, lined with midnight black lines, with a hem of fur the color of lightning during a winter storm.

His hair was wildfire, his single eye the green of fresh grass in a meadow, flecks of the sun itself within it. His features were those of an ancient Irish king, and his beard was spread out like a living flame. His left eye was covered with a black eyepatch emblazoned with runes like moonlight and powdered silver.

He wore armor that Andrea would have sworn was forged from molten lava and brimstone straight from hell. All of that would have been a sight in itself, except for the fact that he was also solid and huge. He dominated the room like a giant Viking from Norse mythology.

A pang of sympathy rang in her heart for him because a subtle cloud of loss hung around Ambrose Severen, like a lonely rain cloud in a blue sky, shunned by its cheerier brethren. It was a hard thing to notice. You saw it in the set of his shoulders, the ever so slight frown of his lips, and the ghost of it in his eye.

You felt it as he looked at the children running around, or noticed the embrace of a couple.

Here was a man haunted by profound loss.

And driven by an anger so deep it was as if it was a demon manifest.

Andrea noticed as Akenyemi went instantly on guard at his presence. His body tightened, and his feet set themselves firmly, ready for action.

Tina continued to be bored.

"You want access to our array. I want to know why you have been unable to close the Incursions in your areas. Let's hear it."

Akenyemi's response was hot iron, "No apology for being late? You just barge in and hop right to it, demanding information?" His eyes flicked to her, "You have a strange way of showing respect to your guests, Miss Pender."

"I don't show respect to adulterers and spouse killers, Kellan Akenyemi. Tell me about your Incursions, before I decide something bad should happen to you."

If Akenyemi's voice was a hot iron, Ambrose's was the far-distant rumble of thunder before a storm.

Akenyemi acted as if the Knight of Avalon had cut him down right there. His chocolate brown skin whitened, as if he had seen a ghost, his eyes widened.

"How?"

Tina began to laugh, showing the first sign of interest in the proceedings.

"Oh, I like you," she said, looking up.

Ambrose's green eye landed on her, and Andrea saw it now. A hellish gleam that burned in the center of his eye for just a moment.

"Tina Florence. Be welcome on Avalon," he said, a tinge of respect in his voice.

That gave Andrea pause. Ambrose hardly ever showed respect to anyone. Whatever he saw with the skill he had just used, it must have been something. A fey smile played on the teen girl's lips, and she inclined her head.

Ambrose turned back to Akenyemi. "I'm waiting for an answer, Kellan."

CHAPTER FOUR

Ambrose waited for an answer. In a way, he wasn't much better than the man before him. He might have been an adulterer and a murderer, but Ambrose was also a murderer and had killed many more than him. His **[Retributions Gaze]** gave him a deeper insight into the man than the previous skill. It didn't just list his crimes, but gave him a sense of why he had done them.

Kellan Akenyemi had a predator's soul. Many people think that means evil, but it doesn't, Ambrose considered. It meant a lot of things, but for Kellan, it was protecting his territory; it was power, seizing what he wanted, and protecting his own.

His wife had trampled over some of those things and hurt him in only the way family could. It didn't make his actions okay, far from it, but it did show Ambrose that he wasn't an Eric.

There was also the issue of the Incursions. Ambrose hadn't prioritized them initially, and Avalon paid for that decision. They lost Knights who had gone out on patrols to the mainland, and more and more of the land was overrun by monsters or taken for the Incursions' people.

Right now, it was the fire giants he was dealing with. At the moment, the giants were unwilling to parlay, as they attacked every time their eyes laid on Ambrose. He was forced to kill them. He did not know about the other Incursions other than where they were located, near the settlements of the two forerunners in the room.

Kellan finally recovered from the shock of Ambrose revealing information he should not have known. His throat undulated downward as he swallowed, and he cleared his throat, collecting himself as he straightened. At first, his eyes sparked with anger, and his knuckles popped, but he answered the question instead of lashing out as Ambrose had expected.

"There is a group of dwarves beneath a nearby mountain; I suspect their Incursion portal is within. A single dwarf guards the mine entrance that leads below."

Andrea raised an eyebrow, holding up a hand, "Umm, just one? Shouldn't it be a snap to get through, then?" She snapped her fingers to illustrate the point.

Ambrose wanted an answer, too, and even Tina looked interested.

Kellan rubbed his face with a weary sigh. "He's too powerful. High D-Grade, maybe even C-Grade. We can't even get close, he...he," Kellan searched for the words, "Exudes this pressure. He laughs at us, drinks from this mug, and shoos us away like unruly children."

He doesn't know about spirit, Ambrose almost breathed. Luckily, he contained the thoughts in his mind, revealing nothing. Kellan had no idea the bombshell of information he had just dropped. Spiritual skills were wielded by the most powerful beings in the multiverse, and the sooner you had one, the better.

It took a lot of training to master your spiritual skill. Training that continued indefinitely as far as Ambrose was aware because you had to know yourself. There were also Icons, which Vivienne had yet to discuss with him.

"Did it feel like this?" Ambrose unleashed his spirit, letting it leak out from his **[Infernal Aegis]** skill.

Suddenly, everyone in the room was pressed to the floor as if an anvil had been slammed into them.

Except for Tina. She grinned wolfishly, and his spirit suddenly met resistance, as if a cosmic bodybuilder was straining against the weight of his spirit. She laughed joyfully and stood up, her eyes shining with star fire.

"Haha! Yes! I love it. Hear me, le chevalier, I challenge you. Beat me in a duel, and I will tell you about my Incursion; I will even ally with you!"

Ambrose knew that look. It was the look of a person who craved battle, who thrived on challenge. The teen girl had seen a worthy foe in him, and if he didn't fight her, she would find a reason.

He sighed, stroking his beard. "Fine. I accept."

He took hold of his spirit and sealed it up again. The pressure vanished, and Kellan sucked in a breath while Andrea cursed. Thom woke up with a sputtered word.

"Shit fire, son! Do you have to go and do that? I was nappin'!"

Andrea ran a hand through her hair, "Fucking hell, I hate it when you do that."

Ambrose didn't apologize. He was studying Kellan, who was looking at him as if he were seeing him for the first time. It was a predator who had recognized another predator and one far greater than he. Ambrose met his gaze steadily.

"After this duel, I would request that you accept linking our teleportation arrays. Andrea will arrange how your people are processed coming in and out of Avalon. I want to meet this dwarf, and you're clearly incapable of dealing with him."

Kellan's face darkened at that, but he merely grunted. Ambrose turned, looking at Andrea with a raised eyebrow. "Are you good with handling that? I'll send Tina here up to do the same after the duel."

Tina laughed. "Such confidence that you shall win, le chevalier."

Thom rubbed his eyes, "More fights? Ye gods, have you children ever considered talking?"

"Fists talk more than words ever will, le vieillard."

"English, lass," Thom replied curmudgeonly.

Tina flicked a dismissive hand, her hazel eyes staring at Ambrose. In truth, he didn't want to fight her. He felt he had better things to do, but it was necessary.

"First, rules. We fight until one submits. No killing, no collateral damage. If it gets out of hand, we stop, it's a tie and we discuss from there. Fair?"

Tina nodded firmly, "Fair. You have merely to lead on to the location of our duel." She gestured at the door.

Ambrose studied the girl. He could see that she didn't have complete control of her spirit. With a thought, he used **[Retributions Gaze]** on her again.

[Tina Florence, the 4th Forerunner. She has committed no crimes and carries the burden of leading her people. Loss hangs over her, something she blames herself for, that drives her to build something lasting.]

It had been the loss and burden of leading that made him respect her. Here was someone he could understand, driven, albeit in a different way, than he was. She had a genuine battle lust, but Ambrose could see the motive behind it.

Tina Florence wanted to progress because she needed to prevent what had happened to her from ever happening again. To her core, Tina was a guardian and protector of her people. Ambrose represented a way to train, grow in strength, and use that very growth for her people's betterment.

It was a lot of responsibility for a teen girl to bear. As that thought crossed Ambrose's mind, he saw her in a new light.

She merely appeared to be a teen.

She was more than that, and Ambrose was sure she was about to show him that.

They left Darren's Hall and went to the barracks. Clearing out the training field wasn't hard, the Knights of Avalon muttering as they lined the fence, looking curiously at the two combatants standing across from one another.

A breeze drifted lazing through their hair. "Are you ready, le chevalier?"

Ambrose gestured at her. "Let's begin."

Chapter Five

Ambrose opened a portal below himself, the blazing fire rendering a hole in reality that he dropped through and directly onto the unsuspecting Tina.

Only to have his hellfire axe blocked by...fluff.

"What the..." Ambrose muttered.

A cloud made manifest absorbed his hellfire. Not all of it, but enough that it didn't cause her even a minor burn. Ambrose moved back, his eye widening as more and more fluff began to manifest itself, wrapping around the girl who was laughing.

"Behold! Cloud Manipulation!" Tina cackled as her form grew, the fluff twisting, growing, and shaping itself until what Ambrose could only refer to as a lamb warrior stood before him. It had a shield of clouds and a massive sword of the same material.

"I...what even..." Ambrose felt his mouth fall open. He shook his head.

The whole scene was comical. The sword looked more like a pillow than a deadly weapon. The shield looked much the same, not that it could block anything at all. Most of all, Tina, her head surrounded in a helm that looked very much like a lamb's head, was giving voice to mad laughter, waving the sword.

"Come le chevalier! Let us see what you have for me, eh!?"

Facing one of the more absurd opponents he had ever faced, he tapped **[Infernal Sanctuary]**, manipulating four of the chains to attempt to wrap around her. With a dash, she produced fluffy ropes that beat back at the black flames. At the same time, her sword grew dark, lightning crackled in the blade, and she slashed at him with it.

Ambrose flared **[Infernal Aegis]**, and the lightning burst against the flames.

With a roar, a cloud formed over their heads; furious and gray, lightning struck out from it.

"Baa baah!" Tina sounded at him, a wild gleam in her eyes, her smile a wild, wild thing.

The lightning could not penetrate his spirit-powered shield. He extended his spirit in an attempt to bring Tina to her knees. Her jaw worked, and her own spirit countered him. In Ambrose's mind's eye, the two energies were clasped in a brutal arm wrestling contest.

Tina's spirit was strong, but Ambrose had an advantage she did not: the advantage of experience. Tina was a teenager. He very much doubted that she had spent her entire childhood being brutally trained by a parent. Ambrose knew better now that Raylen had loved him, but he knew what was coming and had promised his mother to prepare him.

It was complicated.

Part of that complication was that Ambrose had daddy issues and a whole lot of training in how to kill things to go along with those issues. That training included lessons on focus during the heat of combat. It had been bolstered recently by Vivienne's careful attention.

Tina, right now, was standing in place, concentrating. While she was enjoying herself, she couldn't do much other than repel him.

That was a huge problem for her, and he intended to exploit it. Ambrose could do more while using his spirit. He bounded forward, forming a massive axe of flame. He slashed outward with it, the force of the fiery construct propelling her backward in a detonation of power.

Her lamb armor burned as the flames ate away at her; the spiritual pressure attempting to repel him vanished as quickly as popping a bubble. He bore his spirit upon her, imagining it as a massive gauntleted hand straight out of Hades pressing her into the ground.

Tina Florence was no longer smiling. Her teeth were flashing in a snarl of defiance, her eyes bright. New white fluff was attempting to fill in the gaps being burned away, but Ambrose had finally wrapped wraith-like chains wreathed in a stygian fire around her.

She couldn't move. She didn't stop fighting. The lighting was striking him repeatedly, the air warping, and the scent of ozone touching his nostrils. His shield of flame, powered by mana and spirit, was too much for her skill to break through.

He stalked toward her, holding out a hand, where a hellish glow began to coalesce. From it, a burnished handle of molten flames dancing with flickering otherworldly green fire, formed. From the handle, formed an axe head of the same fire.

Tina's eyes were upon it.

Ambrose stood in front of her moments later, axe raised. "I think we're done, Tina. You surprised me and fought well, too. That's more than I can say for most."

Her gaze returned to his face, her eyes narrowed, and her jaw strained. Her voice came through clenched teeth. "I...am...not done...yet."

Her spirit rose up again like a cornered animal. It clawed at his spirit, raking it and tearing at it.

"Baa baah, bastard!"

Ambrose chuckled. For all that fierceness Tina displayed, her spirit was a lion's cub compared to his full-grown tiger's spirit. All he had to do was flex it just a little more. Even then, Tina did not cease her fighting. She pressed, and pressed, a little blood trickled from her nose.

Ambrose shook his head, "Can't you see it's pointless? You're not there yet, Tina. Maybe with more training, but I've won this round."

Tina snarled, but she wasn't listening. Ambrose knew that look in her eyes.

Something in their fight had transported the girl somewhere else. She wasn't here fighting him anymore. To her, this wasn't a duel; it was a fight of life and death. Ambrose curled his lips into a sad smile.

It was the look of someone who had been hurt, hurt in such a profound way that it left wounds. These were not injuries you could see physically, maybe not even injuries you could detect within a spirit.

These were wounds of memory, of the mind. Ambrose let her strain herself, her thrashing and snarling relaxed. Her eyes fluttered. The fluffy lamb armor faded from around her like wisps of clouds blown away in a strong gale.

Her body went limp, not unlike a wet dishrag he sometimes left in the sink, much to his wife's chagrin.

Not long after, she passed out.

Ambrose dismissed his weapon, staring at her.

"What happened to you?" The question was soft; a whisper carried on the winds to nowhere.

He gestured to the ranger Dannill, who was watching nearby. He gave a huge, long-winded sigh before walking over.

"Take her to the guest house, put her in bed. Tell anyone watching over her to be careful. I don't want her waking up and destroying something."

Dannill sighed again, scratching at his rough beard. "This is a drag, you know?"

He bent down and picked the girl up, the sleeves of her over sized hoodie drooping off her arms. She did not look like a brutal warrior capable of manipulating clouds, or striking with lightning. No, in the moment, she just looked like a teenager. A kid caught up in the end of the world.

You could almost believe she wasn't a leader with hundreds of people counting on her.

"She belongs in a school, worrying about a prom date. Not here. Not fighting."

There was no one around to hear the Knight of Avalon's words.

CHAPTER SIX

Ambrose prepared to head to Eric's town. First, he saw Kellan off. The teleportation array had been set up in a large building they called the 'Arrival Hub' for now. The inside looked much like an airport checkpoint might have looked before the System. Cordoned off sections, with a few Knights guarding the area and facilitating processing.

Dannill was there as well. The ranger was quickly becoming the head of Avalon's security. Ambrose insisted on everyone contributing something. If they didn't have a business helping the economy, they had a job of some kind. Dannill, for as hard as he worked trying to be lazy, was adept at spotting possible security issues. His high analyze skill allowed him to identify most everyone and everything, too.

He stood there in his mottled cloak, scratching his beard, his face looking somewhere between profoundly bored and utterly tired. A bow was slung over his back, and wisps of yellow light trailed from the runes emblazoned on it.

Despite his expression, Ambrose didn't miss the way the ranger's eyes tracked Kellan, nor the way his stance was even, ready to spring into action. The array itself was a black obelisk, glowing with amethyst light from the runes lining its surface.

The runes brightened as Akenyemi touched its surface, vanishing back to his own array. Ambrose turned to Dannill.

"I'm off to Eric's town. What did you all call it, anyway?"

Dannill grunted, "New Miami. Rudy's probably in charge with Eric gone."

That was fine with Ambrose, he would be okay with burning the whole place to the ground. He took a breath; *most living there probably have no idea who their leaders really are,* Ambrose said to himself. He would defend himself if he had to, but he wouldn't wantonly slaughter people unless offered violence himself.

He opened a portal to his house, waving at Dannill as he stepped through, closing it with an effort of will.

His house was more accurately a large hunting cabin. He didn't stay here much, but it had an attached garage for his Hellcat. He could have used [Infernal Recall] but the car would have blazed over the town, and Ambrose had no desire to accidentally hurt anyone.

The one problem with his portals is that he needed to know the area first. Which meant he needed to be there at least once. Ambrose had never been to Eric's town, so while he could portal to the general area, he couldn't go directly there.

Besides, he liked the drive. He could coast, and just disconnect from everything. Here, he could allow it all to fall away. Just him, the car, and the path ahead. It was a simple pleasure and not many of those existed anymore.

He got in, activating [Hellfire Manipulation] transforming the car. One of the kids had purchased a set of comics from the System store, something Ambrose hadn't even known was possible, and in it there was a man a lot like Ambrose.

He transformed his bike into this demonic machine, with horns, bone and fire. His Hellcat underwent similar changes, except the metal became the darkness out of nightmares, and the fire that surrounded it, wreathing the wheels and the hood, were the same shade that he formed his axe out of. Blazing red, and eldritch green.

It wasn't just appearance, either. Ambrose pressed the gas, roaring out of the garage. His car sounded every inch a living thing, a big cat on the prowl. The vehicle could have been Noelle's kin.

She sent him an indignant jab with her thoughts. Ambrose chuckled to himself as he turned the wheel, driving over the ocean as if it were a solid road, flames trailing behind him. A few sea monsters tried to rise up to kill him, but Ambrose's [Infernal Sanctuary] combined with fireballs took care of the problem.

In other cases, he just straight up ran the creatures over. As far as he could tell, he didn't get any experience for it. A shame, but not unexpected.

The world was a changed place. Alice used to play those post apocalyptic games, one where she was a courier shot in the head and after revenge. It wasn't quite like that, but it was close enough. Buildings lay in ruins, chunks of road were missing. Everywhere he drove, it looked like a massive battle had taken place.

At one point, maybe he would have thought about rebuilding. Maybe even considered bringing some semblance of humanity back. Tina Florence was working on that goal, expanding her people, protecting them, bringing society back to life.

People like Eric just wanted a community to lord over. Kellan may have been slightly different, but the heart of it was still power, territory, for him. Following Dannill's directions, it didn't take long to find New Miami.

The town, like many he had run across, had chosen to go with a wall as the primary form of their defense. This one was far more advanced, with wards in the form of runes all over it. There were no towers, instead, battlements had been built with the wall, people walked along them.

These didn't appear to be noobs, either. They wielded bows, suggesting that they knew guns didn't do a lot of good against anyone who'd made progress within the System. The gate did have guards outside of it, and they were looking at him.

He would be too if he saw a car straight out of hell barreling towards them. They pointed, calling something out. Weapons trained on him as he pulled up, getting out.

How many times am I going to find myself in front of guards at a gate? Ambrose bit his tongue to prevent the wry smile that threatened to curl his lips. The guards were armed to the nines. Blades at hips, bows across shoulders, dressed in forest green, and honey brown leathers.

"Halt! Step any further and you'll find yourself doubling as a pin cushion."

One of the guards, a blonde haired youth with bright blue eyes and round features. His partner, a black haired, brown eyed man with a rough beard grunted in response. Ambrose crossed his arms.

"I'm here to look around Eric Delrosa's office. Let me in."

The two exchanged looks. "The boss's office? No way. Get lost."

He sighed, rubbing the bridge of his nose. "I'm trying to be nice here, so one more time. Let me in. Once I find what I need, I'll be out of your hair. Don't let me in, and I'll play hardball."

They both laughed at that, the blonde raising his hands, "Oooh! You hear that Dave?"

He hooked a thumb in Ambrose's direction, "We got a badass over here. Better roll out the red carpet."

The guards chuckled, shaking their heads. "Fuck off, Mad Max. We aren't lettin' you in, hear me?"

Ambrose nodded. "I did try."

He unleashed his hold on his spirit.

Like the fist of Almighty God himself, his spirit crushed the two before him to the ground. Plus every single person on the wall, and likely many beyond. They couldn't even groan, they were so weak that they offered not even an ounce of resistance.

"I told you, I was trying to be nice," Ambrose muttered.

It was time to find out just where Eric had gone off too.

CHAPTER SEVEN

A mbrose was having trouble with the wards. His true sight showed them as similar to the fire giants, with runes to keep him from getting in. Unlike the giants, the place did not have a top D-Grade shield array. One option was to blast the gates open. That would leave the people inside defenseless, which Ambrose was unwilling to do. His problem was with Eric, not the people here.

Even the two guards out here were doing their bit to protect the people, even if they failed to understand how outclassed they were compared to him. He walked over and searched the blonde guard. He found the key in one of his pockets.

Keeping his spirit active, he opened the gate and walked through it. Eric's town was not a murderer's paradise. It was very modern-looking, like any small town in the US before the System's arrival. Everyone in the place was flattened to the ground, Ambrose's spirit suppressing them all.

He didn't need to ask for directions to Eric's place; he knew it would be the most prominent place available, and he could see that on the hill that overlooked the whole town.

All the staff were still flat when he walked in, his spirit pressing them down. He searched many rooms before coming to an office. Eric wasn't the type to leave a journal, but he did find a notepad in a drawer with the word 'Midgard' underlined, a question mark at the end of it.

Ambrose sat down in the chair, searching through the drawers a little more. What he found were texts on mythical weapons and armor from various mythologies. In particular, there was a folder marked, Ozgood's Information Brokers

Ambrose stroked his beard as he flipped open the folder. He blinked.

It was a list of mythical weapons and where to find them. He sat back in his chair, mind boggled at the document's worth. Here was something that just told you how to find legendary treasure. It wasn't just weapons he saw but armor, shields, and more. It was broken down in sections, and Ambrose flipped to the axe section to find a whole list of axes.

There was Perun's Axe, which had lightning powers, and Labrys, which increased your wisdom. There were more he didn't recognize, either. As he flipped through, he came upon the spear section, and the word 'Gungnir' was circled. There was also armor circled as well.

It wasn't hard to put it together. Eric was going to Midgard, and he was after this spear, plus some armor.

Ambrose stood up; he had succeeded here. Walking out of the building, Ambrose made his way to what he determined to be the middle of town and let go of his spirit. Then he spoke, raising his voice so it carried. It wouldn't reach the whole town, but it would reach enough, and those who heard would tell others.

"New Miami! Hear me! I am Ambrose Severen! I won't waste any time, nor will I offer proof for my words. Either you believe me, or you don't; it's no skin off my nose. Your leader, Eric Delrosa, is a murderer, an all-around evil psychopath. He assaulted my home and killed many of my people, and he has done worse than that. Anyone staying under his thumb is in danger. Maybe some of you have had friends go missing, or maybe you've suspected something was off with him. All of that can be laid at the feet of Eric."

Ambrose paused, choosing his words carefully, "Should you wish to leave this place, I will have an ambassador show up here every day at noon. You may know him, the ranger Dannill. He will back up my words. Farewell, New Miami."

With that, Ambrose opened a portal right into the driver's seat of his car. He sped off a moment later through another portal and directly into his garage. Getting out, he evaluated what he needed to do.

He would have to talk to Troy to get a realm stone to go to Midgard. His blood still ran hot when he thought of the merchant, but he had to admit that his anger was slightly less intense since their conversation. He also wanted to check on Tina. Then he needed to make some decisions he didn't feel like making right now.

He went to the guest house first. The dark house was two stories, and Tina's room was the top floor, all the way to back and to the right. He knocked before entering.

"Come in, le chevalier." Tina was lying in bed, her skin was the gray of moldy cheese.

Ambrose paused, Tina laughed, then winced. "It turns out that straining your spirit is not good for you. Who could have figured, eh?"

"Are you going to be okay?"

Tina tried to shrug, but her shoulders merely twitched. "A few days' rest, and I should be right as rain. It is too bad you do not have a cleric here, the process would be faster."

Ambrose nodded, "Yeah, that's on the list. Your people aren't going to try storming the town to reclaim you, are they?"

Tina moved her head from side to side in the barest of head shakes. "We sent word on what happened. Besides, they are used to me getting into these little skirmishes."

"Well, that's good."

There was a moment of awkward silence, before Tina filled it.

"I have only ever been helpless like that once before. It was not a good memory for me, eh? It is why I blanked out in our fight, straining myself."

"Do you want to talk about the details?"

Tina's eyes flicked away. "I do not."

Ambrose gave an understanding nod. "I know a little something about feeling helpless if you ever want to talk."

Tina smiled, and Ambrose left. This time he headed to Troy's.

The merchant groaned as he walked into his shop. He held up his hands, "Come on, man! Not again! Look, you haven't changed your mind about kicking my ass, have you?"

Ambrose growled, shaking his head.

"You deserve it, but no. I want a realm stone, one to Midgard."

Troy blinked, then whistled, "You don't ask for small things, do you?"

Ambrose crossed his arms. "Why? It can't be that hard to get."

Troy laughed, rubbing his face with both hands. "Are you kidding? It most certainly *is* hard to get. First of all, before you start in with the intimidation, let me say that realm stones for a newly integrated planet are locked at eighty-thousand SC."

Ambrose never cared much about money. It was always a means to an end for him. But hearing that sum even caused his mouth to fall open in surprise.

"Come again?"

Troy pointed, "You heard me. I can't even lower it. The System doesn't want you to have access to the greater multiverse right now. Don't ask me why, man, it's just how it is."

Ambrose rubbed at his face, blowing a breath through his nose. "How did Eric get one, then?"

Troy shrugged, "No idea. He made a solid chunk from the slave business, but not that much."

Ambrose felt a weight set over him.

The weight of his goal slipping from his hands.

Chapter Eight

"Don't our mines cover that cost?"

Troy held up his hands, "Eventually, maybe they might. You're bringing in a steady income with it, but the people you've been selling to aren't going to be paying top dollar. Haven't paid top dollar for them. Then there is how long it takes to mine them. Thom is a miracle worker, but he's one person. Even if he went hard to the wall every single day, it would take you a year to reach that amount."

Troy shrugged, "Something tells me you don't want to wait that long."

He didn't.

"What can we do? You want to start redeeming yourself? You better start being useful."

Troy straightened; his jaw hardened. "I don't have to redeem myself to you, Mr. Severen. I have to redeem myself to the people here, the people I had a hand in harming..."

Troy sighed, holding up a hand before Ambrose could say anything in response.

"There is one thing, and coincidentally, you're probably suited for it."

Ambrose crossed his arms, raising a brow.

Troy's eyes gained a faraway cast as he looked at a screen. A moment later, he flourished a plain gray stone.

"This is a pocket realm stone, far cheaper, and sponsored."

"By who?"

"The Bounty Hunters Guild."

Ambrose snorted, "That's a thing?"

Troy flashed a quick smile, "It is, and a big thing, too. The BHG is all across the multiverse. They hunt down rogue criminals to every corner of every System integrated universe. Lucky for you, they're recruiting."

Ambrose ran his fingers through his beard, "That's good for them, but how does that help me? I doubt any bounties here on earth equal that amount, and if it does, the bounty in question is probably a lot more powerful than I."

Troy grinned, and this time, the smile stayed on his face.

"As a matter of fact, you're wrong about that. A rogue D-Grade by the name of Zane Dalewind is hiding out at the end of a local dungeon. He's wanted in connection with the murder of a prince from the world of Zinveil on the Black Rose continent."

Ambrose gave an incredulous chuckle, "What? Why, and how, did he come here?"

Troy flicked up the stone, flicking it. "Probably with one of these beauties. Newly Integrated universes are prohibitively expensive to travel to, three times as much as I just quoted you, but it is possible. That's part of why the BHG is offering so much for his bounty. Plus, they have to have someone from this world catch him."

"Okay, so what do I have to do? Can't I go to this dungeon and grab the guy?"

Troy shrugged again, his grin turning into a nonchalant expression.

"I have no idea. This information is a part of the stone description. It wants you to use this stone and register with the guild first. I highly doubt you can claim the bounty without doing that."

Ambrose bit the side of his tongue. He didn't want to join a guild. He had enough to do here on Avalon, and the most important thing was to go after Eric. However, this was a solution, albeit with extra hoops, to his money problem.

He mulled over it, chewing his tongue lightly as he lowered his head.

There were other benefits to this arrangement. Mainly, Avalon's Tree needed energy. The tree fed off the evil energy a bad person's spirit gave off. It was a complicated issue, but the tree knew who was evil and who wasn't based on the parameters set into it by its creator.

Being a bounty hunter would give him access to targets he likely would have gone after anyway. He could feed the tree via Penance Protocol One, return the person to the guild and collect the fee. Then there were the broader benefits, namely having connections outside of this world.

Ambrose wanted to find his mother. Beyond killing Eric, he wanted answers. He needed to cast the net outside his world to get them. The guild could help with that. Overall, this was good for him. A near-perfect solution beyond just having the funds readily available immediately.

"I'll take the stone, Troy. Do you know what I should expect?"

Troy shook his head, closing his eyes briefly. "Not really. The description discusses an evaluation, but that's all I know."

Ambrose nodded, studying the stone, tapping **[Retributions Gaze]**, and bringing up what the System had to say about it.

[Bounty Hunters Guild Outpost Pocket Realm Stone: Realm stones open portals keyed into a specific integrated world. Pocket realms are user-created worlds for a particular purpose.]

Rolling the stone between two fingers, Ambrose willed it to activate. Not unlike the portals he opened, just less on fire, an explicit blue vertical slit split the air, rotating open. Beyond the portal was a bar. No, that's not right, he realized. It was an old saloon. One you might have found in an old west movie.

Complete with the double wooden doors, the music, and cigarette smoke.

Ambrose laughed; he was stepping right into the old Wild West. Too bad he didn't have any spurs.

He stepped into the portal, which closed behind him. People were not dressed like the Old West; they wore things he had no idea how to describe. They were futuristic, or Alice might have called it cyberpunk. Others wore robes or a martial arts gi. As he walked through the saloon doors, no one spared him a second glance.

A man was wiping down the bar. He reminded Ambrose of Thom, with weathered skin kissed by the sun, wild white hair, beard, and a handlebar mustache. His eyes were blue waves under the light of a sunny day. He wore a chocolate brown trench coat and a white shirt with the top button undone, and Ambrose could hear his boots on the smooth wooden floors as he walked.

Ambrose walked over to him, and the man looked up. "Hmm. Newcomer. Howdy."

He spoke slowly, with a deep southern accent, which he thought was weird. This man wasn't a part of his world, was he? Why would he have an accent like that? He dismissed the thought.

"I'm here to register with the Guild."

The man nodded slowly, studying him. "S'pose you are at that. Why?"

Ambrose blinked, "Why do I want to join? Does it matter?"

"Matters to some, maybe not to you."

Ambrose suppressed a groan. He hated philosophical crap.

"To earn money. Why else would I do it? I don't mean to be rude, but I need to get through this. Who do I talk to?"

The man produced a cloth from somewhere and began to wipe down the bar. Just before Ambrose burst in anger at being ignored, he spoke.

"Talkin' to me, aren't you? You want in with the guild, that's mighty fine, but can't just let anyone in. We have a test for you."

Because, of course, you do, Ambrose groused to himself. "Fine. Let's do it."

The man nodded, throwing the cloth over his shoulder. He hooked a thumb to the back door.

"Go on through. Test is in there. Good luck."

Ambrose gave him a thumbs up and strode towards the back door.

He had never been very good at tests.

CHAPTER NINE

Ambrose entered the room to find it small. There was a single small table with an oil lamp on its surface. The only chair was pulled out slightly. On the table in front of the chair were three old leather-bound folders, and next to them was a note card. Ambrose sat down, picked up the card, and scanned it.

Determine who is guilty of stealing the Dusk Shard, an artifact that allows the user to control shadows. Bring the folder with the guilty party to the bartender. Good luck.

After reading the card, the door closed shut with a bang, and a blue light flashed downward over the door knob. Ambrose sighed, rubbing the bridge of his nose. Something told him that he wouldn't be able to leave until he had made a choice.

He opened the folder to find a dossier on Serai Graystone, divided into four categories: background, alibi, motive, and other details. There was no scratch paper, pencil, or pen to write with, so he would have to do this purely by memory.

Serai's background wasn't complicated. She was a scholar specializing in ancient System relics. She was highly respected in her field and had written several books, one on the Dusk Shard. The collector who owned the artifact hired her to study and appraise it.

Ambrose leaned back. Why bother? Just use a high-tier analysis or insight. He sighed. It didn't matter; he just had to find the guilty party.

Whether the scenario made perfect sense was irrelevant. Her alibi stated that Serai said she was conducting research at the library during the theft.

No one could confirm this since she was working alone in the private section, which had been late.

Her motive was that she would benefit from direct personal access to the artifact. It could make her career and cement her as an expert. Other details included her emotional state and the fact that she had no criminal record of any sort. She had lived her whole life obeying the law and staying out of trouble.

Ambrose nearly dismissed her as an option right away.

"She wouldn't risk it," he muttered to himself.

Being caught in a crime like this would completely unravel her career, what she had worked for her entire life. It was simply not worth it for her.

Then there was her emotional state. It detailed that she was frustrated and feeling stagnant. She longed for academic discovery but had no sense of guilt or moral compromise. She was invested in her work, but nothing there would suggest she would break the law or steal anything to obtain that, especially since, if caught, she wouldn't ever be able to achieve her goals.

Despite all of that, Ambrose wasn't ready to dismiss her. Common sense told him to consider all suspects and not hone in on just one, no matter how innocent.

Ambrose set Serai's folder to the side. The following contained information on one Torrin Vance. His background was as a mercenary, and he had a reputation for taking high-risk, high-reward jobs. The artifact's owner employed him to guard the shard during its transportation and at the locations where it stopped to be shown.

Ambrose noticed his infiltration skills. As if it were the sugar on top, Torrin had been accused of having had black market dealings in the past. Torrin's alibi was that he was guarding the vault at the time of the theft.

However, he was found outside the vault, unconscious. He claims he was struck from behind.

He stroked his beard, narrowing his eye and with Torrin's experience, being struck from behind felt like a weak excuse. His motive was clear: he could sell the artifact on the black market and make a solid profit.

Not only that, he had the skills to steal it and arrange a convincing set-up. The other details section for Torrin painted a damning picture. He had been suspected of turning on clients before, though there hadn't ever been proof. His emotions, however, were noted as panicked and fearful.

Ambrose would associate those emotions with an innocent person. He drummed his fingers on the tabletop, then set the folder aside. The final dossier contained information on Ellis Morwood. He was a wealthy rival collector who had made numerous bids on the Dusk Shard in the past. He always lost.

He had been present during the artifact's unveiling before it was stolen. His alibi was that he was meeting with a business associate in his office when it was stolen. His motive was that he wanted the shard and had the resources to hire people to get it.

He had no criminal record to speak of, but Ambrose honed in on his emotional state. The document noted him as cold and calculating. Here was a man who likely had no compunctions about stealing, likely worse than that.

Ambrose crossed his arms, bowing his head to think. He felt reasonably confident in dismissing Serai as a suspect altogether. There was just too much risk involved for her. Maybe she could do it if she thought it was a sure thing or someone pressured her, but Ambrose was positive she wouldn't steal it on her own initiative.

"It's Torrin or Ellis," Ambrose mused to himself.

Torrin seemed like the obvious choice. He had the means, the opportunity, and the motive.

Ambrose grunted because Ellis had all of that, too. It almost felt like a gamble, picking the right one.

"The emotions of these people are key here."

Had these been real people in front of him, Ambrose could have used **[Retributions Gaze]**, and that would have been that. Test over. Luckily, the emotions filled in crucial pieces he needed. Torrin felt panic and fear, and yes, you could make a case that it was the panic and fear of someone afraid to get caught, but Ambrose didn't think that was the case here.

First of all, Ellis had the stronger motive. He had repeatedly tried to get the artifact, failing every time. He was cold and calculated. It would be nothing for him to arrange this. A man like that would have no problem bribing someone to pad his alibi.

Ambrose tapped his nose and smiled. He had a way of sniffing these people out. It had been his job for many years to find deception, to see through the lies. Ellis, more than anything else, felt right. It was as if the other folders were gray scale, with Ellis's bright yellow folder.

Torrin was the red herring. It was meant to throw him off—a big target to catch your attention. Ambrose might have fallen for it had he been in a hurry to choose. He picked up Ellis's folder, standing up and moving to the door.

It unsealed in a flash of blue, allowing him to stride out of it and back to the bar.

He placed the folder in front of the white-haired man, who looked down at it. Ambrose tapped it, "Here's your guilty party."

The man picked up the folder, studying Ambrose a moment later.

Then he held out his hand, "Welcome to the Bounty Hunters Guild. Folks call me Strider."

Chapter Ten

"Why the test?" Ambrose asked.

He was sitting at the bar now as Strider turned, pulled open a drawer, rifling through it.

A moment later, he turned and presented Ambrose with an honest-to-God badge. It was a simple bronze star with BHG engraved into it. Underneath it read 'D-Grade Hunter,' it was nestled onto a black pad that could be slid on a belt or hung from a necklace.

He used **[Retributions Gaze]** on it.

[Bounty Hunter Guild D-Grade Badge. This badge designates the holder as a member of the 'Bounty Hunters Guild' and authorizes them to pursue D-Grade bounties or specially approved bounties.]

Strider nodded at the badge.

"Don't lose that. Can't claim bounties without it, you hear?"

His eyes glazed over for a moment; they cleared moments later, and he refocused on Ambrose.

"You have access to the Guild's page now. Think of it like a bounty board."

Before Ambrose could ask his question again, Strider held up the folder, tapping it.

"Lots of folks don't bother considerin' a situation. Trigger-happy idiots, who don't bother thinkin' things through, see? We don't want that in the Guild. Folks who sign up with us they gotta have know-how and some discernment. It's a simple test, ain't hard to solve, but ya'd be shocked how many don't bother looking at every folder. Pick Torrin n' move on."

Strider shook his head, "Don't need folks like that."

Ambrose couldn't disagree. "What can you tell me about the bounty on Earth, the one worth two hundred and fifty-thousand SC."

A non-committal grunt came from Strider's throat. "He has an awful lot of folks lookin' for him."

Ambrose raised an eyebrow, "Other people on Earth, you mean? How many hunters on Earth do you have?"

Strider shrugged, pouring himself a shot of golden liquid, which he downed. "Dunno. There's a few. A forerunner from your world was in here the other day."

Ambrose let out a frustrated growl, "Surely you can tell me something about this guy? Doesn't the guild get a cut of the bounty?"

Strider paused, glaring at Ambrose. "Do I look like an information broker to you, boy? The guild charges a fee to have the bounty posted. We've already gotten our cut. We aren't here to hold your hand, newly integrated. Best ask your questions a little more politely if'n you don't want to end up a red stain on the floor. As for the dungeon, it's in your world; it's called Akaroth. That's all I know."

"How do I get back?"

Strider moved a hand under the counter, flicking a small black stone at him a second later. Ambrose caught it deftly.

"Stay frosty, kid."

Ambrose shook his head, leaving the saloon and activating the portal home.

———————————

"Uhh, guessing it went well?" Troy said.

Ambrose glared at him.

Then walked out.

Andrea was rubbing her temples when Ambrose walked into her office. She looked up as her door opened. Deep bags were under her eyes.

Ambrose paused, "What's wrong?"

Andrea blinked at him as if she hadn't heard him. He repeated himself.

She let out a bone-weary sigh, slumping in her chair. "It's not that anything is wrong per se."

She gestured at the computer.

"Do you have any idea how much work is in this tiny box? Yesterday, we had one hundred new people join Avalon. We have to screen each one and do our best to make sure none of them mean any harm. Then, we have to find a place for them to stay. This isn't a huge deal; we make more housing. But some of them don't want to do anything. It turns out that when you give people everything for free, there's no incentive to work."

Ambrose shrugged, "So, use the Knights and kick them out."

Andrea glared at him, and her voice gained a mocking edge.

"Just throw them out, he says as if it is that easy. Some of these people have kids, Ambrose. Sure, those that don't are easy enough to get rid of, but it doesn't solve the other problem people. As if that weren't enough, we have people upset at those who have more than just the basics, the business owners and adventurers who go to the mainland and find things of value that they sell, etc."

Ambrose opened his mouth, but Andrea bowled over him, working herself up. "Look, I hate politics as much as the next person, but this is reality, Ambrose. We have to pick a path."

Ambrose wasn't a fan of this kind of thing. It was beyond him and straightforward to his mind.

"I like our System. Those who want to find their own way and have ambitions to earn more can. Those who want to be provided for can be; all they have to do is help. If they don't want to, kick them out, and keep their kids."

Andrea stared at him, mouth open, eyes horrified. "Separate them from their kids, Ambrose? That's horrible."

Ambrose felt his face harden, "Is it? We told them what was expected, we gave them a choice, and they chose to be this way, regardless. I'm not letting anyone hold their kids in front of them like a shield against the consequences of their decisions and then make us out to be the villains. Any parent that does that shouldn't be a parent. Give them an ultimatum and enforce it."

Andrea shook her head, slumping even more. "I guess you're right."

Ambrose chuckled, "That, and I'm a cold-hearted bastard. Is there anything else?"

Andrea flicked a hand, "There's always something, but I can handle those."

Ambrose gave her a thumbs up, "I'm going to be off exploring a local dungeon. I might be gone for a bit. I wanted to let you know."

Andrea's head bobbed in a tired nod. "Thanks. And Ambrose?"

Ambrose paused, his hand an inch away from the door knob. He turned, raising his eyebrow at her.

"Yes?"

She stared at him, compassion in her eyes. "You aren't a cold-hearted bastard, you know? You're a leader. Leaders have to make hard decisions."

Ambrose smiled at her. Darren's dead body ghosted through his mind. Alice's dead eyes. Jenny's vow to kill him echoing around him.

"Or maybe it just takes a cold-hearted bastard to be an effective leader. Take care, Andrea; I'll see you later."

Andrea watched him go, her face pensive, a thoughtful frown curling her lips.

Andrea wasn't sure if anyone else could see it, the burden on Ambrose's shoulders. Ever since the orc raid, he had been more directly involved in Avalon's affairs. He just cared more than he previously had.

He made a point to talk to people, learn their names, and inquire about their lives.

More than that, he did make the difficult decisions. He didn't shy away from doing the hard things, what needed to be done. She knew Darren's death hung around him, like a poltergeist within his mind.

He was always going to the school, trying to reach out to Jenny, and it was a stab through his heart when the girl wanted nothing to do with him.

Andrea looked at the computer, the cursor blinking on the monitor.

The work never ended.

CHAPTER ELEVEN

Little Jenny was walking through the meadow. She liked to do this after school, it helped clear her thoughts. Ambrose hadn't stopped by today, and that did nothing to melt the ice that had built up in her heart. It had frozen over as if being thrust into a frozen lake.

Ambrose wanted her to forgive him. Jenny shook her head, watching the flowers sway in the wind. That was never going to happen. Her desire to kill him was the only thing that sent a little warmth through her.

She clenched her fist, looking up at the sky. To do that, she needed power. It wasn't just the power to kill Ambrose, but the power to protect herself and her loved ones. She shook her head, remembering her conversation with Uncle Thom.

"It wasn't his fault, lass. You must know that, eh?"

She frowned, "Do we have to talk about him? Everyone always talks about him. Can't we enjoy our lunch, Uncle Thom?"

They were sitting in Uncle Thom's office near the mines. It wasn't large, and Thom hardly ever used it beyond enjoying the air conditioning and telling others what he needed done.

Thom stroked his long beard, eyeing her.

"You have a cold anger inside you, lass. It'll burn you if you aren't careful. So, yes, we have to talk about it. Ambrose wasn't responsible for your father's death."

Jenny felt her eyes become cold stone, and her voice was a winter chill. "I called out to him, Uncle. More than once, and he ignored me. I screamed until my throat tore, and then I watched my father pierced through the chest. I watched him crumple to the floor like a sack of meat. Ambrose was supposed to protect us, and instead, he left us to die."

Thom looked at her with an expression she couldn't place.

"Oh, lass." His voice was filled with heartbreak and something else. Though Jenny didn't know it at the time, what she had been hearing in his voice was the sound of acknowledgment of innocence lost.

She waved a hand, "I told you I didn't want to talk about it."

Thom sighed, "Your father wouldn't want you to be this way, lass."

Her face went blank, eyes as dead as a cold grave. "How would you know?" Her voice was a whisper, soft as silk, as sharp as a dagger's edge.

She stood up, "What did any of you know about him? Did you know his favorite ice cream was vanilla? Did you know he named me after my mother, who died giving birth to me?"

Jenny stepped towards Thom, whose eyes were watery pools. "Did you know he liked to fish and play video games? None of you bothered to ask him any of that. You didn't get to know him; you didn't take even an ounce of interest in your supposed friend."

Jenny whipped a finger upward, pointing it at Thom. "Don't tell me what my Daddy would have wanted. Don't pretend to have known him. You knew nothing about him!"

She did not wait for a response; she merely turned and stormed out of the office.

She would have to apologize; she now realized as she sat down in the grass. Uncle Thom had been good to her, and so had Auntie Andrea. She picked a white flower, poking at it with a finger.

"I miss you," she whispered, hoping her words would somehow reach her father.

Instead, they were lost upon the wind. "I could help, you know, little girl."

Jenny jerked her head up in surprise, scooting away. Before her was the devil from before. The one her Daddy had made a deal with. He wore a suit of burnished red over a vest of tawny gold. His eyes were like a viper's, a dark, glowing yellow. Horns peaked up through the red fedora he wore.

His grin was light, easy.

"Wha-What are you doing here?" Jenny stammered out.

Her cold heart fluttered like a wingbeat in her chest. A tingle ran down her spine, and her hands clenched fistfuls of grass.

The devil, Misaq, was his name, she remembered a second later, holding up a hand.

"I am not here to harm you, little one. Quite the opposite, in fact." His smile widened, and the light of the sun made his viper's eyes gleam. "How would you like the power you so seek, hmm? I can provide it, you know."

Jenny's throat was constricted, and a ball of moisture was building. She tried to clear it again before speaking, "Why would you help me? I thought you liked Ambrose."

Misaq threw his head back, and his laughter caused Jenny to shiver. It wasn't insidious; it was simply inhuman. It rang against the trees, moving the very leaves. Jenny recalled their last interaction; it would have ended with her nearly dying if it hadn't been for her father.

"Oh, child. I don't like anyone. I'm a deal maker, a wish granter, and a door opener. You want power? I can open that door for you."

Jenny still felt the cold tingle of fear but crossed her arms, stilling her heart to calm. "Can you bring my Daddy back instead?"

Misaq's grin vanished, his eyes grew serious, and he shook his head almost solemnly.

"No, dear child. If that is a power that exists, it is not mine to call. Even if I could, what came back from those doors of the great beyond would not be your father."

The hope she had kindled within her sputtered and died.

Ruthlessly, she spread the coldness of her heart, freezing the sadness that threatened to build.

"What do you want for it?" She whispered.

Misaq's grin returned in full force. "Why, nothing at all! I merely wish for you to be yourself."

Jenny narrowed her eyes at the beaming devil. "I don't believe you. You wouldn't just give me something for nothing."

Misaq placed a hand on his chest, expression hurt. "Ah! You sound as if you don't trust me, little one. Truly, I say to you, you wound me! I don't know if I can go on!"

Jenny said nothing, and Misaq tsked. "I am as trustworthy a devil as they come! I do not wish anything of you other than to pursue your desires, dear one. I mean that."

Jenny didn't believe him. She had seen the devil use deals against people before, and her Daddy would have told her not to trust or sign with him.

But she had no other way to get what she wanted. The Knights wouldn't take her to the mainland. There were no monsters to fight here. No way to grow other than a useless profession she didn't want.

Her Daddy falling to the ground, so much blood pooling around him. His eyes, lifeless before her. Her body tightened, her jaw clenching. She never wanted to feel that way again.

"I can give that to you, child. You will never have to be powerless again. You will never have to sit back and watch someone you love die ever again."

Jenny took a breath.

Never again.

"You have a deal, Mr. Misaq. Where do I sign?"

Misaq's eyes shined, and his answered grin was a Cheshire smile in her mind.

Chapter Twelve

Ambrose stopped by to see Tina again before going to the dungeon. It had slipped his mind to ask about the Incursion near her. "I might need to get a secretary," he laughed to himself. Tina was sitting up in bed when he arrived, and her skin looked much healthier—less clammy and pale.

"You're looking better," he remarked.

She smiled at him, "Indeed! I did not strain myself as much as I had first suspected. What brings you, le chevalier?"

Ambrose sat down beside her, taking a breath. "I would say I won that duel of ours."

Tina grinned at him, eyes flashing with remembrance. "So you did. Next time is not so certain, no?"

He showed her his teeth and then waved a hand. "If there is a next time. For now, I'd like to know about the Incursion near you."

Tina's smile vanished, and she looked to the side. A moment later, she took a deep breath. "They are creatures I do not understand, le chevalier."

He crossed his arms, "Surely you have analyzed or identified them, whatever skill you have for that purpose."

Tina nodded, making the gesture seem small somehow. "I have. It does not make it any easier, eh? The System refers to them as Leshi. They hail from the forest world of Hernae. They command the animals to attack us, and we cannot hunt for fear of the forest itself turning against us."

She shuddered, "They are twisted things, mon ami."

He grunted, "They have taken over the entire forest near you?"

Tina laughed, "I wish it was just the entire forest, eh? No, they've taken over all forests near us."

She turned to look at him, eyes grave, a haunted shadow over his face, "And they are spreading. Their forest is expanding; I don't know how they do it, but they are. It will not be long before it is your problem too, le chevalier."

Ambrose's chest rumbled as lightning crackled within his heart. "You were going to keep this to yourself? If I didn't win a stupid duel?"

Tina was unconcerned at his sudden anger. "Of course not. That bet was merely a way to get you to fight me."

He closed his eye, sucking in a breath. Opening his eye, he fixed her with a steady stare. "If you want to continue having a pleasant relationship with me, I suggest you not manipulate me again."

Tina pressed her lips together. "Very well le chevalier, I do swear."

Ambrose nodded, standing up. "I'm going to a dungeon. There's a man I need to collect there, after that I plan on handling these Incursions. That means visiting your town. Are you good with that?"

"I am."

With a wave, Ambrose left.

Ambrose got out of his car to regard the dungeon entrance. Ambrose didn't know much about dungeons. As near as he could figure it dungeons were not unlike the pocket dimension he had just visited.

Individual worlds with set challenges and bosses.

What was unique about them is that it was one of the very few ways the System awarded you with anything. Closing Incursions and completing dungeons were the only ways the System gave you anything beyond experience.

Which begged the question of just how this man had reached the end of the dungeon. The only way Ambrose thought he could have done it was by clearing it, and then staying in the dungeon while it reset itself.

The portal to the dungeon itself was tucked into a small cave in the cliffside of a beach here on the mainland just south of New Miami.

[This is the D-Grade Dungeon 'Akaroth.' Entering the dungeon will transport you to a System controlled pocket world. Note that any amount of users may enter, but rewards are adjusted accordingly. Also note that this dungeon will reset after being cleared in two months earth time. It is recommended not to stay in the dungeon unless you wish to re-clear it. There will be no additional rewards other than experience for clearing the dungeon twice.]

Seems to confirm what I was thinking. This Zane Dalewind must have cleared the dungeon and then stayed inside.

Idly, he wondered how many times Zane must have cleared this place.

Shaking his head Ambrose entered the dungeon. Ready to face the challenges it had for him.

He appeared in a subterranean city. It wasn't a human city, either. It was easy to figure that out because all the surrounding houses around him were made of clay, and dark rock. *Maybe houses isn't the right word,* he thought. *They were more like small huts.*

There wasn't much natural light, instead torches and oil lamps had been set up in regular intervals upon a rough, stony path. In the distance, to the north of the city, was a much larger building made of the same clay, but the stone of this particular building gleamed in the light of the fire that reflected off its shiny surface.

It was obsidian.

As he got his bearings, a notification flashed in his mind, and he opened it.

[Retrieve the Claw of Akaroth to proceed to the dungeon's next level.]

That was it. No other information was forthcoming.

"*Coi ui ulph vi munthrek, itrewic jacion!*"

Ambrose blinked, not recognizing the language. He did recognize the ten or so scaly two legged lizard creatures that rushed from around a corner and surrounded him. They wielded sharp spears. Not crude ones, either, these had looked to be of professional quality.

The creatures had various eye colors, but they were all slitted. Their scales were a light blue that ran to a much deeper blue down from the head. Their snouts were somewhat pointed, and their teeth were sharp as tiny daggers. They wore leather, all except one which had fitted plate mail and brilliant sapphire wings extending from his back.

Ambrose thought about killing them.

Until he saw a much younger creature being tucked into a house, a scared looking parent shielding it.

These are sentient beings, Ambrose breathed to himself.

He used **[Retributions Gaze]** on the winged one.

[Winged Kobold Seseth of the Bluescale Tribe Level 110]: Winged kobolds are considered among the strongest of the kobold kind. Seseth is honourable and has committed no evil. However, he is fiercely protective of his tribe. Kobolds, in general, are distrustful of humans.

Seseth said something, but Ambrose couldn't make it out. His spear prodded at him, and once again he considered killing them all. He could raze this town to the ground.

Except for a few issues. One, he didn't know if there was anyone stronger about. He would just as soon not have an enemy if he didn't have to. Secondly, it would be wrong. There were children here. Just because the kobolds weren't human didn't give him license to just slaughter them wholesale without a good reason.

That didn't mean he wouldn't. He had a goal, and he would pursue it, even if he had to hurt them. He just wasn't going to pull that trigger unless he could see no other way.

"I don't speak your language. Take me to your leader." Ambrose was hoping his raised hands and tone of voice would get the message across.

Seseth growled, gesturing for Ambrose to move forward with his spear.

Well, let's see what they have in store for me then, he almost grinned to himself.

At least things were getting interesting.

CHAPTER THIRTEEN

They took him to the big building in the distance, of course. As they walked the streets, other kobolds looked at him with wide, interested eyes. They whispered in that strange language of theirs. Some went in their huts, frightened by his presence. Ambrose saw more children, and he had to admit they looked like adorable mini dragons. One even had a tiny set of wings that fluttered in excitement.

A few appeared not to have any huts at all. As he passed through with the guards, he saw a younger kobold kicked away by a market stall owner. The stall owner hissed. At one point, Ambrose got a passing glance inside a hut they passed near, and he blinked in surprise.

It was full of random knick-knacks. Most of which shined in the torchlight. He even saw gold coins straight out of a D&D campaign. *Kobolds appear to be hoarders; who knew?* Ambrose chuckled to himself—the butt of a spear jabbed him in his back.

"*Japachi munthrek!*"

Briefly, he thought about seeing how the lizard looked when on fire, but he swallowed the anger. It wouldn't do him any good. They came upon a pond at the halfway point, and it was there that a thunderous boom shook the area.

Kobolds immediately reacted, running to their huts, screeching in fear. Another group of kobold guards led by another winged kobold marched out from another area, toward what Ambrose presumed to be the source of the noise.

What he could only think of as a large bat monster burst out from a nearby cave, rocks blasting outward, pelting the ground like raining boulders. The bat monster was bipedal with claws as large as shovels; its ears were pointed, and just like bats, if you enlarged them enough to fit on a bigger-than-human-sized skull.

A mouth full of sharp teeth shone as the ember light of the torches hit them. Its skin was black as night, brushed here and there with twilight. The creature screeched, falling upon the kobold guards that engaged it. The guards surrounding Ambrose looked to their commander, who did what no commander should ever do.

He hesitated.

It cost him, too. The creature tore the other group apart, its claws shredding through their armor as if it were paper. The air was painted crimson as their blood rained from their torn bodies. One kobold had the right idea and tried to run.

With a slash of its claws, red light lashed out and cut the kobold in two as neatly as slicing an apple. The two halves of the kobold fell to the ground, its lifeblood giving color to the dull stone.

Frankly, Ambrose was somewhat content to allow the monster to rampage. He wasn't ready to slaughter the kobolds wholesale because they were sentient creatures with lives and families and feelings. Then there was Alice, who Ambrose knew would want him to be better than a wanton murderer.

That didn't mean he had to lift a finger to help, however.

There were two reasons he ended up helping. The first was that he likely wasn't going to have a choice. That creature was going to attack anything living, and they were in its path. The second was the kobold child that had attempted to steal from the market stall earlier.

He darted from behind a corner.

The bat monster heard him, its ear twitching. It turned, and as it did, the blood from all around it started to flow like a living thing, to the creature. It flowed right into its mouth, causing it to shudder in what could only be pleasure.

Then it lifted a clawed hand toward the kobold child.

Ambrose cursed.

Then he opened a portal directly underneath himself.

As he fell through the hellfire portal, he activated **[Infernal Aegis]** funneling spirit and mana into the spiritual skill. He appeared right in front of the creature, that dark red energy lashing against him.

It could not pierce his flaming shield flaring around his armor.

It cocked its head in surprise, and Ambrose lifted an armored foot and kicked the ugly creature right in the chest with all of his D-Grade backed strength. It howled in pain as something inside of it cracked. It crashed against the stone.

He took the opportunity to flare his spirit, baring down on the creature. It screeched, but it was weak this time. No opposing spirit came from it.

Now it was Ambrose's turn to cock his head.

And then he began to walk toward it at a slow, unhurried pace. He paid no attention to the surrounding kobolds around him that had been flattened to the ground.

Seseth, Winged Kobold of the Bluescale Tribe, commander of the ninth guard patrol, knew he had messed up. He should have engaged the *Fueryon* right away. He had prioritized the human over his own people, and for that he felt shame.

Especially seeing what the human was doing now. The human, a male from what Seseth could tell, he could never be certain as humans were just weird, was a force to be reckoned with. First, he dropped through a portal straight from the depths of *Uoinota* and now he had unleashed some kind of power that was preventing any of them from moving.

Seseth tried to fight the pressure, but it was as if mighty Akaroth, blessed be her wings, had pressed her mighty claws upon him himself. All he could do was watch the situation play out.

At least it was a show.

The human man was in no hurry as he walked toward the *Fueryon*. His eye was hard, and as merciless as a dragons fury. When he finally stood looking down at the creature, he snorted. By Akaroth's tail, he was unimpressed!

The human reached down and picked up the creature with one hand, as easily as lifting a hatchling. His green eye swirled with something...*other*.

It was as if the human was an avatar of *Uoinota* himself. Whatever he was doing, the *Fueryon* did not like it. Its body was smoking, but its flesh was not burning. Even so, the scent of ash filled Seseth's nostrils, and he would have sneezed had it not been for the pressure that kept him from moving.

That same pressure kept the monster from thrashing, or even screaming. Instead, the burning scent of ashes intensified, and the smoke curling away from it grew. The light of the human's green eye blazed like a forest fire in the night.

Finally, the light of his green eye faded.

The *Fueryon* slumped as the pressure holding them all vanished as suddenly as it had come.

The human tossed it aside like it was a bag of trash. It thudded into the ground, just a sack of dead flesh now.

The human walked toward Seseth, and instinctively, the winged kobold took a step back. Glancing around for his spear. As if that would have done him any good. This human could kill them all without a second thought had he wished it.

He stood in front of Seseth, crossing his arms. A single red eyebrow over his eye rose.

"Well? I thought you were taking me somewhere? We wouldn't want to be late, would we?"

The human laughed.

What manner of horror is this human?

Chapter Fourteen

Ambrose found the inside of the building to be decidedly different from the town of huts he had just come from. Decidedly did not mean better; lining the walls of the long hallway that led up to a large dais were piles of treasures that lined the wall.

Treasure may be too generous a term. It was more like piles of 'trinkets.' Shiny baubles, coins, cups, lockets, stones, and more were in the piles. Just past the dais was a huge statue of a dragon. It was made of carved red stone, each scale painstakingly carved out.

Its eyes were sparkling sapphires, vast and luminous.

What impressed him was the dragon's wings. They were huge, expanding outward to take up most of the room. Its membrane was so thin that, for a moment, he thought it was the real thing.

There was a huge pile of trinkets just underneath it. On the dais was a throne of white oak wood. Sitting in it was a kobold that looked somehow more feminine than the others. He wasn't sure how he could tell; perhaps it was because she was sleeker than the others. Maybe it was the way her blue eyes glinted, not unlike the sapphires that served as the dragon's eyes.

Or perhaps it was the red and blue robes she wore. Either way, his suspicions were confirmed when he used **[Retributions Gaze]** on her.

[Lizella Bluescale High Priestess of Akaroth Level 128]: Lizella is devoted to her people, as they are dedicated to her. She serves

as Akaroth's voice. She feels shame for wanting to avoid the fate that awaits her.

He wasn't sure what fate awaited her, but it didn't sound good. It also wasn't his problem. He was here for a purpose. He needed the claw of Akaroth. Briefly, he wondered if he would have to get a claw off of the massive dragon statue.

It didn't take a genius to put together that Akaroth was a dragon. The colossal statue, her title, and all of it suggested Akaroth was a dragon and that these kobolds must worship it somehow.

Somehow, he doubted he needed to cut a claw off the statue. The item he needed would be an object recognized by the System.

Finally, he stood in front of the priestess. Her blue eyes regarded him as if he were a fascinating puzzle. She even put a clawed hand under her chin and squinted.

"*Tir wux renthisj dragonian?*"

Ambrose sighed, shaking his head. "I don't speak your tongue."

Her eyes narrowed further. Her claws tapped on her chin, one by one, as if drumming.

"I asked if you spoke dragonian. Apparently not. *Jaseve udoka.*"

Her voice had a strange accent, something reptilian, as if her throat had been scorched by fire. Despite that, it had an exotic hint of a melody as well.

The guards exchanged glances and then looked back at the priestess. She said nothing and didn't even look at them. Finally, they bowed, turned, and left.

When they were alone, the priestess leaned back, sighing with a sudden wave of weariness. Her shoulder dipped slightly, and Ambrose saw her arms relax.

"It is draining, the burden of leadership."

He shrugged. He had no interest in connecting with her.

"Not much of a conversationalist are you? My guards told me how you handled the *Fueryon*. You stepped in when the monster was about to kill one of our children. By doing so, you also saved the contingent of guards bringing you in. You have power. You could leave at any moment you wished, it makes one wonder why you have allowed yourself to remain in custody. It makes one wonder what you want."

Her claws drummed on the throne. She was waiting for him to respond. He obliged her.

"I have lots of questions, and ultimately, I want the claw of Akaroth."

The claws paused, hanging there in the air above the arm of the throne. Her head cocked to the side.

"You don't ask for small things, do you? I can give you what you seek, but let us address some of your questions before we get to that. Answering them is the least I can do for you since you saved my people."

He was tempted to skip the questions. At the end of the day, the only thing that mattered was getting the claw and moving on in the dungeon. His curiosity got the better of him, and he decided to ask the questions on his mind.

"Do you know that you're in a dungeon? All of my other questions stem from that one."

The priestess leaned back, lowering her head. Eventually, she looked up.

"The answer to your question is...not easy to give. The short answer is yes, *I* know we are in a dungeon."

Ambrose scrunched his eyebrows together.

"Only you're aware of it?"

"Yes."

Ambrose crossed his arms, feeling his mind walk down the paths of implication.

"I can see you turning the matter over in your mind, human. Yes, when the dungeon resets, we return just as things were when you entered it. Not everything happens the same way, but we all return here and go about our lives until some other user delves into the dungeon, killing us all or completing the dungeon in some other way."

Ambrose shook his head. "How? I thought death was final. Are you all undead?"

Lizella chuckled, "No, human, we aren't undead. Our spirits belong to the System."

Ambrose rolled his hand in a 'go on' gesture.

"When you die in the dungeon, the System claims your spirit and re-purposes you in its dungeons across the multiverse."

That caused his jaw to drop. "It does *what*?"

Lizella nodded, flashing a grin and revealing pearl-white teeth as sharp as razors.

"You heard me, human. It is the risk you take when you delve into a dungeon."

Ambrose found himself sputtering, "Why doesn't it tell you that? How did you all end up here then?"

Lizella laughed, a surprisingly light sound.

"Ah, your reaction. The System cares not whether you agree to with it, fleshling. As for how we all ended up here? I don't know. The System creates for us new bodies every time the dungeon resets, and we go about our lives ignorant of our situation. Well, most do. I always remember."

He stroked his beard. At the end of the day, he shouldn't care about this, but since there was a potential for him to end up this way, he couldn't help but ask.

"How are you aware of it then?"

Lizella sighed, rubbing her snout with a hand.

"If you choose this life, then you are aware of it. The System does not change your memories."

He gaped at her, "Why would you choose it? How did you choose it?"

She held up a clawed hand to forestall his questions, "Peace, human. I shall explain."

She seemed to settle into her throne, as if remembering.

"It was so long ago. My people entered the dungeon to serve the dragon Akaroth. We have always served dragons, gathering and hoarding wealth for them as you have seen here. It is our way. The dragon accepted our service readily enough, but she was crueler than others. She would kill us, red our flesh and burn us to a crisp when she was bored. That was how many ended up as dungeon born, as I call us. The System offered me a way out, to lead my people if I volunteered to join the dungeon. It does that sometimes. I agreed, and thus here I am."

Ambrose couldn't help but laugh at the situation the priestess was in.

He waved a hand, "Fine. Good enough for me. I have more questions, but now I want to know about the claw. Tell me where it is."

Chapter Fifteen

"If you want the claw, you must assault the Redscale clan and take it."

Ambrose raised an eyebrow, "That simple?"

Lizella shrugged, "No, they will resist of course. The claw is their sacred artifact. You don't have much choice; they will not give it to you, even in barter."

"Are these Redscales your enemies?"

Lizella flicked a claw in the affirmative.

"Convenient then. It just so happens that the item I need is held by your foes, who I will likely have to wipe out if I have any hope of getting the item I need to progress."

"Nonetheless, if you want the claw, that is your only course of action. You would have had to take it regardless of whether I pointed you in that direction."

He grunted. Truth was, he suspected there was more to this. More than that, he had to wonder why it even mattered to begin with.

"Why do you bother with these Redscales? The dungeon will just reset, no matter what progress you make."

Lizella sighed again, "It is because I do not have any choice. I would end the *xsioul* conflict if I could. The System demands it as a part of the dungeon. The System commands my spirit, so I have no choice but to obey."

"Why, though? What is the purpose of it?"

"Many have asked that question. The purpose of the System. It is a question that is beyond me. Perhaps the answer is out there, and there are certainly many theories. Some say the System desires to strengthen users and thus engineers dungeons to assist with that. Others say the System is a cruel, capricious god, and the dungeon is its torture chambers. Frankly, I care not."

He sighed, running a hand through his hair. "Fine. I guess I'll go after the claw now. What direction do I head?"

"Beyond the city where you fought the monster from earlier. The Redscales will be impossible to miss."

Ambrose nodded. Turning around, he strode out of the temple.

It was time to retrieve the claw.

A fist crashed into Ambrose's shield of flame. With a hiss and popping flare, the stone fist burned molten orange as he gritted his teeth, setting his stance.

[Stone Golem Level 148]: A stone statue animated with mana, usually meant to guard places. Some have been lost in dark places.

It has a spiritual skill! The golem was having no trouble countering the pressure of Ambrose's spirit. Its own spirit felt glacial and old. Like an unmovable wall, it didn't try to overwhelm him; it was merely a shield to prevent his own spirit from overwhelming it.

Sadly for the golem, he wasn't alone.

Noelle manifested, the cloak morphing into the arcane white tiger, her roar echoing from stone to stone. Lightning arched over her claws, and she slashed a paw outward.

Lightning the color of fresh ice blasted a chunk out of the golem. Ambrose had expected its spirit to vanish at that attack, but it didn't. In a way, that made sense. The golem wasn't human; it didn't feel pain. It had a single-minded focus, and Ambrose doubted the spirit he felt was even the golems. It might have been built in with the spell animating it, somehow.

Summoning an axe of hellfire, Ambrose slammed it down onto its shoulder. It did nothing. Nothing that mattered anyway, except for the stone heating to molten gold. Grinding stone rumbled throughout the cave as the golem brought its fist down upon him like an oversized hammer.

His shield brightened, succeeding in repelling the attack. However, for the first time in a long time, Ambrose felt the shield of fire waver.

Is this thing going to break through? It hadn't been a concern for a long time. His shield, at a far lower rank than it was now, had repelled a lake of lava. Yet the stone monstrosity was punching with the full power of a falling building, maybe even greater.

Luckily, he had a plan. He sent that plan to Noelle, who flicked an ear in acknowledgment. Once again, he tapped [**Hellfire Manipulation**] and summoned a portal.

Right beneath Noelle. As the white tiger fell through the portal, the golem rocked another punch into his shield, the rock and stone of the cave around him vibrating from its force. Ambrose pulled on his core, pouring more mana into his skill.

Good thing, too, since the fire of his shield flickered, sputtered, and nearly died. The moment he used more mana, it rekindled in force, protecting him again.

At that very moment, Noelle fell upon the stone golem's head. She roared, her tail swished, and she placed her two front paws on the side of the monster's head, her back legs bunching inward, those claws digging into the golem.

Lightning crackled, sparked, and flared violently into the stone golem's head. Stone split, veins of lightning glowed, pulsing, and the monster's head exploded in a detonation of black and gray stone shards with a destructive crack like booming thunder.

The golem crashed into the ground, shaking the very earth.

[You have defeated a Stone Golem Level 148! For defeating a foe beyond your level, you have earned increased experience and advanced to level 143!]

Noelle fell on her feet with effortless grace. She licked her paw with a satisfied chuff.

He strode over and scratched her ears. "Thank you, girl."

A blue eye regarded him, and she sent him a wave of self-satisfaction.

He chuckled. After that, he turned his attention to his progression. It had been an age since he had looked at his full character sheet, so he brought it up now.

Name: Ambrose Severen

Level: 143

Race: Human (D-Grade)

Traits: Ruthless (Uncommon), Giant Slayer (Uncommon), Reforged-Legendary, Infernal (Mythic)

Class: Infernal Paladin (Epic)

Profession: Knight Of Avalon (Level 35)

Skills: [Hellfire Manipulation-Mythic], [Retributions Gaze-Epic], [Infernal Sanctuary-Legendary], [Infernal Aegis-Legendary (Spiritual Skill)], [Infernal Recall-Rare], [Infernal Dimension-Epic]

Constitution: 223

Strength: 242

Intellect: 254

Wisdom: 258

Willpower: 284

SC: 40

Attribute Points: 8

He scratched his beard, studying the screen. His progression had slowed quite a bit. He remembered when he was flying through the levels. The System seemed to reward defeating higher-level foes the most.

Once again, he had to admit that made sense, especially with his class, spiritual skill, and power. Defeating foes his level or below wasn't doing it. Also, it highlighted the danger of the System and the multiverse as a whole. You needed to seek out ever greater dangers to grow in power.

You had to grow in power if you didn't want to end up under someone else's rule or thumb. Or maybe many choose that life anyway. It was safer that way, and you could progress with a profession.

For a moment, Ambrose studied the stone as if it were the most exciting thing in the world. *What if it had been different?* It could have been. He and Alice could have gone to one of the other forerunners, he could have found a profession, relative peace. It wouldn't have been as good as his life might have been before the System, but it wouldn't have mattered as long as he had Alice.

Alice. Who had been taken from him by Eric, who was in another world doing who knew what. He blew out a breath. Quickly, he assigned his eight points to constitution since it was falling behind.

There was nothing to do but move forward.

He had a claw to obtain and a bounty to claim.

CHAPTER SIXTEEN

Tina Florence shook Andrea's hand.

"Thank you, mon ami, for your hospitality. I will remember this. Britannia will remember this."

Andrea smiled and nodded at the other woman.

"Of course. Are you sure you wouldn't rather rest up a little more? There's no rush."

Tina shook her head, "I thank you for the offer, but no. I must return to my own town before my people grow restless."

"Very well. Should you wish to return, you have access to the array, and you're always welcome here."

With a last smile, Tina activated the array, vanishing in a puff of blackness.

She appeared a moment later in her own array room. It was a tiny space with nothing but the array and a single guard. Dressed in a green and gold form-fitting plate mail, the guard smiled at her. She had long hair like corn silk on a moonlit night. Her elfin face was proud when her warm brown eyes looked at Tina.

"Welcome home, madame."

Tina hugged the guard, whose name was Lenaia. "I am happy to be home, mon ami. Tell me of the news of the town."

She and Lenaia walked out of the room and onto the wooden platform. As always, Tina was proud of the town they had built here in the trees. Rope bridges connected to platforms as far as the eye could see, leading to tree houses built within them.

There were a few huts on the forest floor below, but they were for lookouts more than anything else. A group of four large trees housed their market, and all the buildings within them were interconnected.

The same was true for Tina's headquarters. A shield array was within another tree, and it was enough to cover the whole of their little town in the forest.

As they walked, Tina asked for updates. Lenaia closed her eyes briefly, a little color leaving her cheeks. "We lost another patrol to the Leshi, madame."

Tina bowed her head, rubbing her hoodie covered hands against her face. It was always a blow when they lost people. If she had her way, none of her people would go out into the forest beyond their town limits.

"I wish we didn't have to send out patrols in the first place, Lena."

Lenaia nodded sadly, "I know. But if we want to survive..." Lenaia trailed off.

She didn't need to explain what Tina already knew. They had to go into the forest, explore and progress. It was the only way to get resources to sell. The only way to gain levels.

"What of this Avalon you went to. Can they help?"

Tina smiled at that, "Yes, I believe they can."

She explained all that had transpired in Avalon.

Lena blinked, her mouth falling open. "Truly, he is so strong?"

Tina couldn't keep down the bubbling laugh that escaped her, "The strongest I have ever faced," she sobered, her expression growing serious.

"But there is something in him, Lena. A dark passion."

Lenaia frowned, "Why should that matter as long as he can help?"

Tina shrugged, "It doesn't, we have to hope that whatever it is doesn't prevent him from providing aid to us."

For all their sakes.

Kellan Akenyemi had chosen to establish New Kweneng in what was once the Sahara Desert for many reasons. The first was that you had to be strong in the desert. The place did not abide the weak.

Kellan Akenyemi had never felt weak, not since he had been a babe.

Not until he met Ambrose Severen. He held up a fist, curling his fingers slowly, building up strength with each one until they and his knuckles were white. He gritted his teeth.

Every part of him wanted to find Ambrose Severen and show him just what real power looked like. Except it would be futile. Whatever power that man had gathered to him, it was too much for him to overcome.

He would die.

And that fact pissed him off. His desert lion tore into the large cobra with claws glowing with desert fire. Kellan dismissed the experience he had gained and with a wave, unsummoned his lion.

The desert sun baked the sands beneath it, but he was unconcerned with the heat. Not a bead of sweat formed on his forehead. Some ways away were mountains that loomed over the desert, the sun making them appear warped, like a mirage.

There was an Incursion in that mountain. An Incursion of dwarves. If you got close enough, you could hear the sounds of mining and the rings of hammer blows.

At the mountain's entrance was a particular dwarf that also made him tighten his grip. His power was not unlike Ambrose's.

With a sigh, Kellan returned home.

New Kweneng was a town of tents. Large and ornate, they covered a large area of the desert. His shield array and teleportation array had their own tent. He would have to put the teleportation array in a bigger tent for visitors.

It grated on him to allow others to teleport into his town. He didn't want to allow it, but he also had no choice.

The dwarves were claiming resource after resource and he wanted what was in that mountain. If he had to use Ambrose to accomplish that, he would.

A group of children ran past, laughing. Pride bloomed within his chest. He had done this. Provided a place of safety for these people.

His guards, spears sparkling in their hands, slapped fists to bright chest plates. It was a good thing stats staved off the sun or they would have been cooking in that armor.

His tent wasn't the largest. What he did have was luxurious, but no massive tent mansion for him. That was the burden of leadership.

Men respected you more when you didn't flaunt your wealth. Not that he had much of it.

He had no doubt there was endless wealth in that mountain, but so long as the dwarves were there, it was not for him.

Sitting in his comfortable chair, Kellan poured himself a shot of gold liquid. He needed to relax after the day he had.

"Enjoying yourself, hmm?"

Kellan swore, spitting out the precious liquid in his mouth. "Blood of the prophet! Who are you? Guards!!!"

The red skinned, red suited man smiled, revealing a single fang.

"Oh, I'm afraid they can't hear us at the moment. Tell me, Mr. Akenyemi, are you suffering from a case of not enough power?"

"What?"

"Are you feeling a little impotent today? A case of 'someone's more powerful than me-itis'? Well look no further for I have the cure! A steal of a deal with your savior, moi!"

The red skinned man with devil horns poking out from a fedora gave a flamboyant bow.

"Who the fuck are you?"

He beamed, "I, the fuck, am Misaq."

Kellan narrowed his eyes, his voice was a growl, "I don't appreciate sarcasm."

Misaq put a hand to his chest, "Me? I would never! I'm a mere salesman, sir. Sarcasm is wit beyond me, sadly."

He sounded perfectly serious. Kellan took a deep breath.

"What do you want? Why are you here?"

Misaq's eyes shone with devil may care light.

"Why? I'm here to make a deal with you, Kellan Akenyemi. A deal that will allow you to handle your small dwarf problem, and perhaps, even, your other problem, hmm?"

Kellan sat forward, "Go on, I'm listening."

Misaq's answering smile reminded him of a crocodiles grin.

Chapter Seventeen

A mbrose stood on the path leading to the Redscales city. It looked nearly the same as the Bluescales city, complete with the same temple. There was a difference, each hut had a red hue to it. The Redscales themselves also had, well, red scales. They went about their business, unaware of Ambrose's attention on them.

Noelle was sitting beside him, cleaning her paws. The big cat showed not the faintest hint of concern at anything that was going on. Ambrose scratched her ears as he thought about his options. First option was violence.

He couldn't prevent a wry smile from curling his lips.

Violence doesn't have to be your go to solution, boy.

That little nugget had always been interesting to him. His father had exclusively trained him to be violent, after all. In fact, when he asked his old man what other options he may have had, he appeared stumped.

Scratching his chin, he had told his son, "Well, you could try talking. For what that's worth."

Given how the Bluescales had reacted to his presence, he didn't think the Redscales would be willing to entertain conversation, and further, he doubted they would even understand him. Likely, they had a priestess like Lizella, but he didn't think she would be willing to talk if he slaughtered scores of her people just to get to her.

Then there was option two, which he was leaning towards. Tempered violence. That was often the best answer. Not a lot of violence, nor too little. You needed just the right amount. None of the kobolds here could match his spirit. It would be easy to suppress them all, stroll on through and collect the item he needed.

The one and only issue with that route was what would happen after. Yes, he would be able to walk on in and take what he wanted, but it would leave him with enemies.

It doesn't matter. If they could follow me out of the dungeon, maybe, but that isn't so, Ambrose mused to himself. In fact, no matter what he did, the kobolds couldn't retaliate in any meaningful way. He was just...beyond them. Maybe some of them registered as D-Grade but he knew that it went beyond just stats. You had to condense your core.

Beyond that, there was his spiritual skill and training with it to consider. Ambrose had rigid control of his spirit, and all it had cost him was a painful understanding of himself. It had led to power. Not only could his spiritual skill be used to defend himself as a shield, but he could bring the full pressure of himself down upon anyone within a decently sized area.

Even if the kobolds had all been true D-Grades, it didn't matter even one whisker. With no one among them having a spiritual skill or the control to match him, Ambrose may as well have been a god amongst them.

He looked at Noelle.

"It feels wrong, though. Like I'm taking candy from a baby."

Noelle flicked an ear at him, chuffing.

A predator doesn't care about such things, she seemed to tell him.

Rolling his neck from side to side, he sighed and with little fanfare, released the mental hold he had on his spiritual skill.

When you reached a certain understanding of yourself, your spirit began to leak from the skill. Like a bad faucet. If you let it go fully, it begins to spray uncontrollably.

It resulted in a mountain of pressure that bore down on everything around himself stretching a couple miles out. He didn't doubt the Bluescales may have felt it at the fringe of their territory.

Ambrose could immediately make out the Redscales, pressed flat against the ground like a giant spatula pressing down on cooking meat. With Noelle by his side, he began his walk to the temple. Eyes swiveled to regard him, filled with utter horror at what he was managing to do. Noelle's tail swished from side to side as she walked beside him.

Striding through the temple, he found a priestess not unlike Lizella, on a throne not unlike hers, except her throne was the red, found in freshly spilled blood, and her attire was the same.

Carefully controlling his spirit, he removed the pressure from her. She gasped, as if he had just saved her from drowning. Her eyes moved to stare at him, they were the red of a sun baked desert.

Ambrose held up a hand before she could speak, shaking his head. "I don't speak your language, just so you know. I am here for the claw of Akaroth. Give it to me."

Her jaw snapped closed, not unlike an alligator snapping up prey.

Then she spoke, sounding much like Lizella. "I am the high priestess Deira Swiftclaw. Who are you, human?"

Ambrose shrugged, "Impatient."

To punctuate the statement, Noelle roared, lightning playing across her sharp teeth. Her roar shook the very stones, and shadows danced over the room from the flash of the lightning in her jaws.

Deira's red scales turned white for a moment.

"The claw isn't an item!" She squeaked out.

Ambrose blinked. Even Noelle cocked her head, ears twitching.

"Explain," he stated.

Deira rubbed her snout, sitting up in her throne.

"It's not an item. The claw is a kobold, a high priestess of the Bluescales. She is known as the Claw of Akaroth."

Ambrose crossed his arms. He waited.

She went on hurriedly, "In order to summon Akaroth, you need her claw, her chosen priestess. You sacrifice her at her alter, and the dragon will appear."

"Why can't I sacrifice you? Why does it have to be Lizella?"

"How do you-of course. She sent you here, didn't she?"

Deira muttered to herself, shooting him a look she went on, a hitch in her voice.

"Look, it switches every cycle, okay? I don't know why. Take it up with the System. Every cycle, or every dungeon reset, who the claw is between us changes."

Ambrose looked at Noelle. She laid down, putting her head between her paws. He snorted. Lizella had manipulated him. A heat bubbled in his chest, causing his very blood to boil. She had tried to use him like a tool, and he hated that. Hated it more than anything.

Eric had used him, had manipulated him in such a way as to give Eric an excuse to kill him. His fists clenched. He was tired of being used, of people thinking they were cleverer than he was. Of using him like some kind of blunt weapon. Luckily, he had taken a step back and didn't just start cutting into them.

She wanted a hammer to solve her problems? He was going to give her one.

"So you know you're in a dungeon, too. Very well, it seems Lizella and I need to have another long talk."

A portal of hellfire split the very air, a vertical tear in reality.

Noelle's blue eyes were narrowed in a dangerous way that a predator does when ready to pounce on prey. Her tail swished, her paws flexing. A hungry gleam was in her blue eyes, and the smell of lightning filled the air.

Both of them went through the portal.

CHAPTER EIGHTEEN

Ambrose did not unleash his spirit upon the Bluescale guards that rallied around their priestess. Instead he gestured at Noelle and the arcane white tiger unleashed lightning upon them.

Their ashes coated the floor a moment later.

A part of him lamented at killing the guards. They were merely doing their jobs, after all. However, they were not deaths that he laid at his feet but rather at Lizella's.

She had manipulated him. Now her people reaped the consequences of her choices. Ambrose knew how that felt and he didn't mind her feeling it at all.

He could see it in her eyes, the streak of sadness that appeared within them. The muscles in her jaw worked as she regarded him.

"You used me. I don't like being used, priestess."

"I did. I would do it again, too."

At least she doesn't deny it. A symphony of rage still sung within him. He couldn't kill her. He needed her. She was the claw of Akaroth.

"Why? You can't tell me it was just because the System demands your conflict with them."

Lizella shook her head, eyes closing briefly. "That is precisely why. You have no idea what it's like to watch your people die over and over again in a conflict without end."

She shuddered, "My own death reoccurring repeatedly is bad enough. I remember each one, vividly, human. It doesn't go away, not even when I sleep, when I can sleep. But my people? Oh, stars above, the *hatchlings*. It haunts me. And I can do nothing about it."

She hissed, spitting to the side. "We cannot leave, and even if I tried, my tribe would abandon me as a heretic. The System pushes at you, pushes and pushes, and it doesn't stop. Not ever. If I do not seek the conflict, the Redscales certainly will. That *fueryon* you defeated? Woken up by their spies. They knew it would be in a rage, and that it would attack the nearest living beings. Us."

She pointed at single claw at him, eyes ablaze.

"So, yes, human. I used you. I saw a way to be spared watching my people die for the hundredth time. Spared from their screams and dying pains."

His anger did not abate at her passionate words. He understood, could even empathize with Lizella and Deira's plight.

But it didn't change what she had done even after Ambrose had saved her people. It did change his perspective on the System.

For the first time, he began to think of the System as more than just a faceless, neutral force of nature. It was evil, what it was doing here. Sure, Lizella made this choice willingly, but no one could be prepared for what she had gone through.

No one would fully understand what that choice entailed, not until you experienced it. Not even he could be sure at the anguish and despair she must feel.

Ambrose was no stranger to cruel torture, but this went deeper than mere physical pain. It was the first truly evil thing he felt could be blamed directly on the System.

None of that changed what he had to do. His bottom line was going after Eric, and for that he needed the money that the bounty would provide.

In order to get that, he needed the claw of Akaroth, and that was Lizella.

He spoke slowly, making sure each word pierced her and as he did, he encased his heart in a sphere of numbing ice. This had to be done.

"You're coming with me. We are going to summon this dragon of yours, and I'm going to get what I came here for. If you resist, I will bring you back here, and I will force you to watch as I butcher your people in front of your eyes in the most violent ways I can conceive of. Is there any doubt in your mind, any at all, that I can do this?"

Lizella's scaly throat worked up and down. A tear fell from one eye. She shook her head as her shoulder slumped; her voice resigned. "I'll come with you. Just don't hurt anyone."

Ambrose wouldn't have done that. There were children here, and he wouldn't leave them to starve to death. However, he didn't want to drag a struggling priestess along with him, having to keep his spirit active.

It would be much easier if she cooperated, and the threat, even baseless, ensured that happened. Especially because Ambrose knew how to deliver threats.

You didn't get loud; you didn't go into detail. You spoke low, with direct eye contact, and you left much to their imagination.

There was no doubt in her mind that Ambrose would carry out his threat, because he conveyed not a single hint of deception in his intimidation tactic.

Nodding tersely, he laid a hand on Noelle's head. "My friend will make sure you stay obedient. Now, let's go."

Another portal opened up. The group stepped through it.

"Tell me about Akaroth, and where this alter is. Is it a lair, how much room is there?"

"Akaroth is a storm dragon," Lizella stated as if that explained everything.

Ambrose was just behind her as they walked, going ever deeper. Noelle kept a lazy blue eye on her. If she bolted, they'd see it.

She couldn't see his look, so he said, "That doesn't explain anything. What do you mean?"

She looked back at him, eyes widening slightly. "You don't know about storm dragons?"

Ambrose blew out an impatient breath, annoyance coating his tone like a bad coat of paint.

"No, I'm just asking to make conversation. Again, what are storm dragons?"

She made a clicking sound, "You're already going to kill me, do you have to be rude, too? Storm dragons are...cruel beings. They love treasure with a passion as hot as their lightning. Which is very hot by the way," she tossed the last part out with a snort.

Ambrose didn't bother responding to the clear sarcasm in her voice. Tit for tat, he figured.

"So, what does her lair look like?"

"It's a big wide cavern filled with treasure. The altar is on a platform that overlooks it all. You sacrifice me on the altar and Akaroth comes."

Ambrose frowned, "Is the sacrifice necessary? What if I just try to take some treasure and go?"

Lizella laughed, "Do that and Akaroth will appear alright. Except her treasure madness skill will activate and you'll be facing a vastly empowered red dragon."

Ambrose eyed her, "Why not lie? I could have done that and probably have been killed."

Lizella rubbed at her face.

"Or you could portal away, put two and two together and slaughter my people in revenge. Besides, I don't really blame you. Adventurers like you can't be expected to do any different in these dungeons. And,"

She added, "I hate the dragon more."

"Seems weird for a priestess of Akaroth."

"That's my title because it has to be if I want to lead my people."

"Why?"

She turned her head back to look at him, "Why what?"

Ambrose gestured at her, "Why lead your people? Let someone else do it."

She laughed loudly, and still chuckling as she said, "Because I am the best one for the job. Who else would do it better? No, it has to be me."

The cave rounded another corner. Before long, Ambrose and Lizella found themselves before a raised platform.

Just as she had said, there was an alter upon it.

"Well now, human. We have come to it. Time for you to kill me."

Chapter Nineteen

"What, big bad human can't do it now that you've realized I'm not some mindless beast?"

Lizella was kneeling at the altar, looking back at him with scorn-filled eyes. The altar itself was made of obsidian, carved in the shape of a dragon's tooth. Shifting red glyphs had been emblazoned on it. Ambrose stood before her, head cocked.

After she spoke, he couldn't help but laugh. If Lizella had eyebrows, they would have furrowed. Instead, her eyes just shifted a bit.

"I have killed people I love, priestess. People who, unlike yourself, won't be coming back. I admit, I regret the necessity of your death, but it must happen if I am to get what I want. I was just thinking."

Her tongue flicked in and out of her mouth. "About what?"

He crossed his arms, "Does it matter? I'm about to kill you, after all."

"Call it a last request."

He scratched his chin, "Hmm. Is it really a last request? Your death isn't permanent."

She glared at him.

He just stared.

"How about a trade? You tell me what you were thinking about, and I'll give you some interesting information on Akaroth."

Ambrose frowned, his eye glinting dangerously.

"Why didn't you tell me everything already? I thought you hated the dragon."

A reptilian smile split her lips.

"You're still going to kill me, human. This death will haunt me like all the others, am I not entitled to even a small form of comeuppance?"

He blew out a breath, letting the hot flash of wrath go with it.

"No, I guess I can't. Fine, if you must know, I was thinking about my wife. I usually am, at any given moment."

"Your 'wife'? Is this a term for a human mate?"

He flicked a hand, "Yes. Anyway, now you know. Tell me about the dragon."

Lizella stared at him for a second, and then her eyes widened slightly. "She is gone, isn't she? Your wife."

Ambrose went cold, and Noelle let out a warning growl. "You should drop the subject, priestess."

She shrugged her shoulders, "Or what? You'll kill me? What more can you do to me, human? I think I shall bring up whatever subject I wish."

He felt his knuckles pop. Noelle stood up, blue eyes sparking with lightning.

"I could flay the skin from your body. I wonder how your scales would look as a coat, or maybe a cloak?"

He saw her swallow, and then she looked away, "Every colored dragon embodies an element. They are immune to it and attack with it. Blue dragons embody lightning. Your companion there will not do any good against Akaroth."

Ambrose looked at Noelle, whose ear flicked and eyes filled with determination.

He sighed, "Sorry, girl. You know I can't risk you. Especially against something you cannot do anything against."

Noelle chuffed, ears swiveling. Her claws kneaded into the stone, the scraping sound echoing slightly around them. She wasn't afraid. He knelt down and scratched her cheeks.

"My brave girl. I know you want to do more, I know. But I won't risk you, I won't lose you."

Briefly, he put his forehead to hers. She chuffed, nuzzling him.

He unmanifested her, and moments later, she settled over his shoulders, a cloak once again. Regarding Lizelle, he took a deep breath.

"I will say this much, priestess, I respect you. I know a little something about leadership. You do your duty, no matter what it is. For that, I admire you. If it were different, I would have never taken this course of action. Sadly, I have a goal, and you're a means to an end."

He didn't give her a chance to respond; with a flare of hellish flame, he formed an axe of blazing fire, swept it outward, and cut the head from her shoulders.

Her corpse fell to the ground, her neck a blackened, charred stump. Her head tumbled from the platform, disturbing the treasure below, its clinking cascading from stone to stone.

The glyphs on the black dragon tooth altar shone with carmine light. A roar shook the cavern, and the treasure vibrated, moved, and parted. A huge form rose from it.

A creature from myth and forgotten stories appeared before Ambrose. It was as if a god had taken the very storms, forming scales from them and weaving them into the creature's body. It went from dark blue to blue-gray, to the precise shade of lightning on a black sky. Its wings were huge, and even as wide and large as they were, the cavern was still big enough for it to fly if it wished.

The membranes of the dragon's wings crackled with lightning, and its claws were as big as his. Somehow, the dragon managed to look feminine. It was the curve of her jaw, the glint in her storm-gray eyes, and the pride of her majesty that hung around her like a personal cloud.

To look upon her was to see the fury of a hurricane, to behold the beautiful destruction nature was capable of. Here was a force of nature brought to life.

A black collar, with green runes shining and rotating around it, was around her neck. A black-haired man in a dark robe, his dark eyes alight with excitement, was in a saddle on her back.

"You think I'm an easy bounty to claim, eh bounty hunter?! Think again! I am Zane Dalewind! I am this dragon's master, and I am your death!"

He laughed maniacally. Akaroth's eyes burned with sudden hatred. She roared, blowing Ambrose's hair away from his face. Air warped around the dragon, as electricity arched over her claws and wings.

Strangely, he didn't feel scared when looking at this creature. As always, his mind sharpened, focusing itself, and his heart started to slow. Training, ingrained in him long a go by a father who sacrificed everything, even the love of his only son, to give him the tools he needed to survive in this world, came to him.

As always, the first step was assessing the threat.

He tapped **[Retributions Gaze]** and used it on the dragon.

[Akaroth, the Mother of Storms Level 195 (Dominated by Zane Dalewind)]: Some say Akaroth was hatched from the very first blue dragon ever. Many believe blue dragons to be cruel, capricious, but Akaroth only cared about the freedom of flight. As a hatchling, she enjoyed watching the storms. She had one desire, to make storms of her own.]

Dominated? Ambrose thought to himself. He filed that information away, it could be useful. Next, he turned his skill on Zane.

[Zane Dalewind Artificer Rogue Level 185]: A murderer, rapist and selfish to his core, Zane has never once thought of anyone other than himself. He is wanted for killing a prince he claimed was his friend.

As he did all of this, the sound of thunder rumbled across the cavern, treasure shifting, as if it were a golden sea.

"It's mine! All of this treasure, this dragon, all mine!"

Zane's face was a contorted, twisted thing.

He's mad, utterly bonkers.

Even as he thought it, clouds formed in the air above, painted a dark gray found in river stone, lightning struck in several places around the cavern. Akaroth's wings flapped, sending powerful gusts outward as she rose into the air.

She opened her impressive maw, lightning built within her throat.

It was directed right at him.

CHAPTER TWENTY

A beam of concentrated lightning shot toward him. Calling upon [Infernal Aegis], he wreathed himself in a shield of fire. Lightning crashed into him, and the fire and lightning went to war with one another. Ambrose was pushed back, his eye widening in alarm as mana drained from his core.

Whatever Akaroth had hit him with, it was powerful. He couldn't just tank the attack like he normally would. Even his spiritual pressure that he brought down like a divine hammer did nothing to the dragon. She just flexed her own spirit because, of course, she was a proper D-Grade being, and his vanished.

Gritting his teeth, he opened a portal beneath himself, dropped into it, and exited some ways away. Lightning bore into the stone where he had been standing, blasting it into chunks. He forged hellfire into a mighty axe, swinging it at the dragon.

Zane laughed and held up a hand. A lime green shield of mana spiraled outward in front of him. His axe collided with it in a detonation of power that rocked throughout the cavern. The pure force caused treasure to fly in every direction.

"Weak! I shall cast your bones across this lair, hunter!"

Noelle fluttered behind him, sending him supportive determination.

"Okay, let's see how you handle this," Ambrose muttered to himself.

His mana surging within him, he formed as many needles of hellfire in the air as he could. With a thought, he sent them flying toward the dragon, intending on shredding it with a thousand fiery burns.

Akaroth had other plans. She lifted a mighty claw, roaring, and tore lightning from the air, clouds above her booming in time as the needles of hell flame were brushed aside.

Zane laughed, shooting a lance of green energy at him. It did nothing to him.

Akaroth apparently grew tired of hovering there; her wings crackled with lightning, and she shot toward him faster than she had any right to be, claw slashing. Zane's mad laughter accompanied her in her wake.

Knowing he couldn't take a direct hit like that; he fell through another portal he opened beneath himself just in time. Claws raked the wall he had been standing by, flashing teeth gnashing. Akaroth roared in anger, whirling her massive body around.

The storm that hung in the cavern air swirled, rotating, with more lightning and thunder shaking the space around them. Ambrose couldn't keep his jaw from dropping as an honest-to-God tornado dropped from the sky, picking up treasure in its powerful winds.

Akaroth opened her maw, and lightning traveled up her throat, glistening with iridescent blue light. She thrust her head forward, and the lightning spilled out in another beam.

He did not just sit there waiting for all this power to hit him; he thought fast and then acted. Using his spirit, he did something with **[Infernal Aegis]** he had never done before; he spun it around himself. Faster, then faster still, he spun it.

A vortex of sanguine and eldritch green fire spun around him like a mini cyclone.

Akaroth's tornado, powerful winds born from the dragon's wrathful power, hit him. At the same time, her lightning fell upon him like a hungry, living thing.

All of it, every ounce of power directed at Ambrose Severen burned away. Like a flaming siphon, the air was lit aflame, and as suddenly as it had come, it was gone. Her lightning could not find purchase, no matter its howling as if it were an angry beast.

Akaroth cut off the beam with a snap of her jaws.

"Not bad, hunter. Not bad at all. This will be fun! If power does not work, we shall tear you apart with tooth and claw!"

Akaroth flew toward him, her great claws ready to rend his flesh.

Ambrose had no intention of becoming a chew toy for this beast. He summoned another axe of hellfire, slashing at Akaroth with it. She was mid-leap, and he knew Zane would form a shield to block it.

Sure enough, the lime green shield reappeared. Knowing it was coming, Ambrose had formed another axe of fire from behind the blue dragon, bringing it down like a crashing tide of fire. Akaroth was cut out of the air, sent crashing to the treasure below as it sprayed into the air, glittering gold shrapnel, flickering like fireflies.

Zane let out a string of curses as he was sent flying from the saddle.

Quickly, Ambrose enacted the next part of his plan. Opening a portal, he stepped through the doorway he had burned into reality. He was in front of Zane Dalewind, who sputtered, and close up, Ambrose could make out his features more clearly.

He was a rat-faced man; even his eyes were beady, filled with insanity. He tried to shoot Ambrose with a green orb of energy, but his shield held firm.

Ambrose's spirit wouldn't do much good against Akaroth, but he was willing to bet it would work on Zane just fine. To his surprise, Zane had a spirit of his own. He laughed, his spirit repelling Ambrose's.

"You think I am some newly integrated trash with no spiritual skill? Pathetic!" Zane spat at him.

The globule of spittle burned away against his shield.

Even with that setback, Ambrose could see that Zane had to concentrate on maintaining his spirit. He hadn't had much practice maintaining it while remaining focused. While Ambrose had spent his whole life learning how to focus in combat situations where his life was on the line.

He reached down, lifting Zane up by his robes. Zane snarled, "Let me go, fucker! You goat fucker! You shit fuck, bastard!"

He trailed off into expletives, a bead of sweat falling from his brow, his spirit wavering.

Ambrose ignored it, activating **[Retributions Gaze]** not to see his information but its other effect.

As Vivienne put it, every spirit carried guilt within it. All their selfish deeds, petty anger, and evil acts reside within a person. Even if they couldn't feel it, it was there. As far as Ambrose could tell, it stained you, and no one was immune from that.

His skill took all of that and made it into kindling. Kindling that would burn, a transcendent flame that forced the being to experience all the pain they had caused, all of it a thousandfold.

Zane Dalewind screamed, and Ambrose could see his throat tearing. Blood poured from his eyes as his capitularies burst. His body writhed, his spirit utterly vanishing. With his skill, Ambrose was making him relive everything he had done to others, but this time, it was being done to him.

Do unto others as you would wish done unto yourself, after all. Zane experienced all the rape, all the murder, all the torture, all the wounds, everything, all at once. His madness had been a controlled emotion before, a source of power from the man.

Now it became madness in truth, as his mind fell upon itself like a ravenous monster, shredding itself into pieces. His mouth was foaming, his eyes rolled into the back of his head.

And then he was limp. Ambrose tossed him aside.

Slowly, he turned around to regard the dragon that was getting up. The collar around her neck pulsed, and she reared up, roaring as a bolt of lightning descended towards Ambrose's head.

Chapter Twenty-One

E ric Delorsa walked a jaunty jig into Nidaros. He paid little attention to the groups that went about their business. Nidaros was a town of length. Buildings and walls made with vertical logs and intertwined planks. Runes gleamed on some of the buildings.

Dirt roads wound throughout the little town, and the scent of ocean spray carried on a slight breeze. A large cliff overlooked the town, atop it could only be Lord Elgin's castle. It was a circular design, almost like a fort to Eric's eyes. Planks made up the walls, but they weren't ruddy to look upon, instead the planks had been polished smooth, runes shining upon them.

It took up most of the cliff and a singular path led up to it. A seagull drifted lazily above it. Even from here, on the main road, Eric could see the two guards at the gate that barred the way up to the castle proper.

Conversation drifted to his ears.

"Adventurers Guild has put up a bounty for a werewolf in the forest! They say it could be high D-Grade, maybe even C-Grade! They need a gold class adventurer to take it on."

A robed pink haired woman was saying excitedly to a pasty-faced youth in silver chain mail. Her white robes were touched here and there with blue lining, and she held a brown-gold sceptre. Her green eyes sparkled in the light of the sun.

She might have been pretty, if Eric bothered to notice that sort of thing. The youth had strong features, but his brown eyes were dull. He shrugged at his companion's words, "What does it matter? We aren't going to have anything to do with it."

Pink haired girl slapped his shoulder, the chain mail ringing. "Dummy! Gold rank adventurers are a rare sight! Think of the questions we could ask! Lord Elgin is only silver!"

Eric rubbed his hands. *There appear to be ranks separated by metals here, good to know,* he acknowledged to himself. He had no idea what they meant, but it wouldn't be hard to find out.

Finding a nearby tavern wasn't hard, and he slid into a table near the very back moments later. A plump blonde woman in serving attire came over to him flashing a dimpled smile.

'What can I get for you, hon? Our specialty is a pork roast right now, and we have a nice honey mead to go with it."

He gave her an easy grin. He might have missed it if he hadn't been used to picking up on it, but an ever so slight shudder went through the woman, her smile suddenly looking slightly strained.

"I'll take that. Sounds delicious."

She nodded, writing it down on a notepad. "Right then, that's 25 SC."

Eric willed the System to give her some of his SC and it was taken from his account. Her eyes glazed over for a moment as she verified, nodded politely, and walked away.

Eric was here for a purpose, of course. To observe and to listen. He could have attempted walking right up to the castle, using his legendary skill to take over, killing everyone inside.

However, he couldn't be sure it would work out that way. Lord Elgin could be very powerful for all he knew and his skill might be useless.

He snorted softly, that hadn't been the case yet, but it didn't pay for him to take stupid chances.

He sat. He waited.

He did that for most of the day, picking up lots of information. He had to piece it all together like a puzzle, but he managed it.

What he came away with was incomplete, but gave him a good grasp of how things worked here in Midgard. The Adventurers Guild could be considered the main organization of this world.

It worked much like a mercenary organization worked. You paid them a fee to put up a job, and an appropriately ranked adventurer, or group of adventurers picked it up and did it, collecting their pay from the people who offered the job.

It usually came with experience because more often than not it involved fighting monsters, or a group of bandits. Sometimes it was collecting dangerous ingredients from a dungeon, or other such places. Regardless, Eric had also learned a lot about the rankings.

It was more than just your grade, but also how many jobs you had completed. How dangerous a job was or ended up being was also considered. Then you had to take an assessment, based on how well you did in that test, you ranked up.

What was crucial to Eric, was your ranking determined where you could go in Midgard. A tin ranked adventure, basically an E-Grade with no jobs completed, was stuck in town, hardly better than a civilian. If a civilian wanted to move out of town they had to get approval from the town's lord, and then a group of appropriately ranked adventurers escorted them.

Eric had wondered why this was so, but no one had talked about it yet. He had only figured that out because an elderly couple had talked about moving to Laragos, and they had to have a jade ranked adventurer party of three to do that.

Currently, he was frowning, rubbing his hands absently. No one had revealed anything in particular about Lord Elgin. He was able to confirm that the forerunner used a spear. *But is it the spear I'm looking for?* He sipped at his mead.

It was fine, certainly nothing to write home about. A little too sweet for him.

Moving around would be a problem, because Eric didn't want to leave a trail of bodies in his wake wherever he went. Those he had killed in the forest were going to draw attention enough already if and when they were discovered.

Not that he was worried about it. It would appear as if they killed each other, unless someone was smart enough to think it was a skill, those deaths would remain a perplexing mystery. If found out, it could bring dangers upon him that he may not be ready for.

He drummed his fingers lightly on the table top, mulling over his options as his viper brown eyes trailed over the room. It had grown considerably bigger, with parties of adventurers discussing their plans, or going over loot they had found.

The blonde serving woman was still present, bustling from table to table with practiced efficiency. Another woman had joined her, a matronly woman with silver white hair, and a warm smile. Scents of cooking food, mead, and well traveled adventurers were in the air.

What Eric wanted to do was get involved with this town's less reputable people. That they existed was not something he doubted. Where there was society, there were criminals. It was a multi-universal fact as far as he was concerned.

If he could get a grip on the town's underworld, that was sure to open doors for him.

There was Ambrose to think about, too. He was sure to come after Eric. It wouldn't be all that hard for him to figure out where he had gone. Getting the cash together would be difficult, but Eric knew Ambrose Severen. He would find a way as surely as the sun rose.

It would be nice to have resources in place to slow him down when that happened.

Eric had felt that pressure from him, that overwhelming unseen force that threatened to crush everyone in its radius. That was part of why he had left for Midgard. He had nothing to counter that. He had no spiritual skill of his own, and that was very quickly becoming a problem.

This spear though, if the information dossier he had bought was accurate, and it had been so far, would help with that.

I will have that spear. After that...then we'll see.

CHAPTER TWENTY-TWO

Ambrose rolled out of the way on the bolt of lightning, treasure parting around him in a clinking, ringing sound as he stood up. Akaroth roared, building up more lightning in her throat. Quickly, he opened a portal at the last minute, directed just in front of the dragon. Her lightning breath passed through the portal, only to slam into herself.

It didn't really damage her, since she was immune to lightning, but the force of it did push her back. Akaroth's wings flapped, the clouds above her swirled. He could see her building up power within them, readying another tornado more than likely.

He could counter it as he had last time, but all of this defense was draining his core. It had been a long time since he had to worry about a lack of mana, but this fight was taxing him. He needed to do the same thing, in a cheaper way.

She blasted more lightning at him. This time, he formed his hellfire axe, and with a grunt, split the lightning down the middle with it. Parted lightning hit the treasure, sending clouds of the bright metal flying to the sides.

Powerful tornadoes descended from the clouds above, picking treasure, turning into a deadly whirlwind of metal.

Ambrose used [Infernal Aegis] so he had a shield around himself, then he tapped [Infernal Sanctuary], producing spectral chains, black fire coating them. With a small effort of will, he began to spin them in front of himself.

Faster still, the chains blurred, a vortex of abyssal flame. Both tornadoes slammed into him, winds so powerful he thought Noelle was going to fly off his back. His hair was a crimson mess, slapping him in the face, and his ears rang. Bits of metal burned to molten liquid as they pelted his shield.

Unfortunately, this took all of his concentration, and Akaroth wasn't in the mood to sit around waiting for him to fend off her attacks. She pounced on him like a cat waiting in ambush. His chains lashed her scaly body, but she simply did not care.

Her large claws pressed him down, so sharp they would have rent the flesh from his body if it weren't for his shield.

However powerful his shield, the dragon must have weighed more than some houses, and he wasn't so powerful yet to counter all the pressure. Treasure parted around him as he was *pushed* into it. Akaroth roared in triumph, jaws opening, she attempted to bite his head off.

Idly, Ambrose thought about how weird his life had become. He had faced down drug lords, more guns of various types than he could count or name, squirrel monsters that shot acid, a devil, plant monsters, including a mutated mushroom, bears, a lich, and more besides.

Now he was being gnawed on by a huge dragon straight out of mythology. She hadn't gotten through his shield just yet, but she would. He could open a portal, vanishing through it, but there were problems with that. He recalled more words of wisdom from his late father.

If you do the same thing over and over again expecting a different result, you're not just insane boy, you're an idiot. Nothing worse than an idiot, boy.

Teleporting away would save him, but it would also use up mana. Mana that was very quickly becoming scarce. If he ran out, he would have no defenses, no way to attack. He would die, that would be that.

Game over. No respawn.

Consider all the information you have in front of you, boy. Then act.

His dad's advice echoed in his mind. This time, he didn't ignore it.

As Akaroth chewed him like an old bone, albeit one on fire, he allowed his thoughts to race. His goal was to find Zane Dalewind. He had done so, and put him out of commission. He wasn't dead, just unconscious from the pain of his skill. Ambrose had very deliberately cut it off before killing him.

He could just leave. However, if he wanted rewards, he needed to complete the dungeon. If he didn't, he would walk away with nothing to show for the venture other than the bounty. That wasn't enough. He assumed he had to kill the dragon to complete the dungeon, but was that really true?

The System hadn't told him he needed to kill the dragon, merely obtain the claw of Akaroth. It wasn't enough, because if it had been, he would be gone by now. Still, nothing said he had to kill the legendary beast.

A plan began to form within his mind then. A way to end the fight, and possibly complete the dungeon.

Let's see how this goes, then.

He opened a portal below himself, but this time when he fell through, he did so onto the dragon's back, directly onto the saddle there. Akaroth reared up, roaring as lightning struck all around. He wasted no time, sending his chains forth, he struck the domination collar around her neck. Akaroth thrashed from side to side, wings flapping.

Treasure was shifting, the mountains of it flattening. Ambrose willed the chains to slide under the collar, looping the chains under the collar and around, he willed them to flow to his hands, where he began to pull with all his might.

His muscles strained, Akaroth roared her fury, the collar screeched, glyphs flaring.

Metal tearing filled the air in a painful cacophony.

With a snap, the collar came apart, falling to the treasure below with a clang.

As quickly as snuffing out a candle, silence reigned in the cavern. Akaroth stopped moving, dark clouds above dissipating, vanishing as quickly as they had come. The blue dragon settled onto the pile of treasure, and her voice, as loud and melodious as mountain wind on chimes, boomed throughout the cavern.

"*DESCEND FROM MY BACK, HUMAN. LET US TALK, YOU AND I.*"

Uncertain, but curious, Ambrose did so, sliding out of the saddle and onto the treasure below, his armoured boots ringing as metal struck metal.

Akaroth's head snaked around, until one huge eye regarded him, a living jewel. She blinked, her voice booming once more.

"*YOU HAVE FREED ME FROM THE WILL-TAKING COLLAR AROUND MY NECK.*"

A statement, not a question. Ambrose nodded once.

Another blink.

"*WHY? WHY NOT JUST KILL ME? YOU COULD HAVE DONE SO, CHOKING THE LIFE FROM ME AS EASILY AS BREAKING THE COLLAR.*"

It was a fair question. Ambrose could have done that, in all honesty, he probably should have.

Yet he couldn't help but think of Avalon. Many of the townsfolk on his island had once been slaves, meant to be sold to some unknown force in the multi-verse. He had taken exception to that, killing everyone involved.

There was something about another living thing being enslaved that really bothered him. In the end, he didn't feel like justifying it. Enslaving another living thing was wrong, and ending it needed no justification.

To the dragon, he said, "No living thing should be enslaved against their will. Not unless they really, really deserve it. If I must kill you, at least you will die free."

In a way, it was a lie. Akaroth had already died, likely long ago, and now the System used her spirit for this dungeon. She would always be a slave from a certain perspective.

However, as of right now he could do nothing about that.

Akaroth made a chuffing, growling sound in the back of her throat.

Is she going to spit up a huge hairball? He hoped not. A moment later he put it together. *She's laughing!*

"I BELIEVE YOU TO HAVE THE HEART OF A DRAGON, HUMAN. THUS, I HAVE A PROPOSAL FOR YOU."

CHAPTER TWENTY-THREE

A mbrose gave the dragon a wary look, "I'm listening."

A part of him still expected her to pounce on him. He hadn't lived this long by taking unnecessary risks, and he was ready to use his skills at a moment's notice. Akaroth raised a single claw, ***"BE AT EASE, I WILL NOT ATTACK YOU."***

With a single claw, she traced a line in the air, and as she did, a slit not unlike Ambrose's portal split open the air. Beyond the small portal was a vast space filled with even more treasure than was in the room. Akaroth reached in with her claw, removing it a second later; she parted the claw in front of him to reveal an item.

It looked like a jewel, and an inner blue light shone within it. Ambrose used **[Retributions Gaze]** on it.

[Blue Dragon's Heart-Akaroth (Mythic)]: Akaroth, the Mother of Storms, was once an A-Grade Blue Dragon. This is her heart. A Dragon Heart contains the totality of their being, including their spirit. It can be used to create a powerful mythical item. Note, doing so will trap all that Akaroth is within the item.

Ambrose looked up at the dragon, whose huge eye blinked at him. "No way you're giving this to me?"

"INDEED I AM, MORTAL."

He shook his head, more than a little baffled. "Why?"

Her other claws needed the treasure below her. *"THERE ARE MANY REASONS. I AM TIRED OF BEING TRAPPED HERE, ENDLESSLY KILLED AND REBORN. USING THAT ITEM WOULD GIVE ME BACK A SEMBLANCE OF THE FREEDOM I ONCE HAD."*

He blinked, "You know about what the System is doing to you? I thought only the priestesses knew."

The great dragon shook her head, *"OF COURSE I KNOW. THE SYSTEM FORCES ME DOWN TO D-GRADE WITHIN THIS ACCURSED PLACE, BUT I REACHED A-GRADE IN MY FORMER LIFE, HUMAN. I KNEW WHAT WOULD HAPPEN SHOULD I PERISH WITHIN A DUNGEON. THE SYSTEM BOTHERS NOT WITH ALTERING MEMORIES OF THOSE THAT ALREADY POSSESS THE KNOWLEDGE AND DO NOT CONTEST ITS WILL."*

He scratched at his chin, eyeing the heart. He was very tempted, but he wasn't about to jump into anything. "That still doesn't fully explain why."

"DOES IT MATTER? YOU WILL GAIN A POWERFUL ITEM FROM THIS."

Ambrose laughed, "Yeah, maybe I would. Yet the description says you will be trapped in it. What does that mean? What level of control will you have? Last thing I need is to be in a dangerous situation only to have an item I have come to count on for survival turn on me."

Akaroth's body shook, and a coughing sound came from her throat. It took him a moment to understand that she was laughing. *"SO CYNICAL FOR ONE SO YOUNG. NOT UNLIKE THE CLOAK YOU WEAR, WHATEVER ITEM I BECOME, I WILL BE BOUND TO YOU. BETRAYING YOU AT THAT POINT WOULD BE COUNTERPRODUCTIVE. AS TO THE WHY OF IT...OTHER THAN MY FREEDOM FROM THIS PLACE, I WILL ASK A*

BOON FROM YOU. A TASK I WILL WISH YOU TO COM-PLETE."

He crossed his arms. He didn't have time to complete random tasks. He said as much to the dragon and then added, "I have my own goal that I will complete. Anything else, everything else, is secondary to that goal."

Akaroth rumbled her eye regarding him with intensity. *"A STORM RAGES IN YOUR HEART, MORTAL. IT YEARNS TO FREE ITSELF, TO RAGE ACROSS THE LAND UN-SHACKLED BY YOUR WILL THAT CHAINS IT. I WILL RELISH SEEING THAT. FEAR NOT; THE BOON I ASK IS BEYOND YOU FOR NOW. IT WILL LIKELY BE AN AGE BEFORE YOU COULD COMPLETE IT."*

Ambrose felt his arms tighten, and his eyes narrowed in suspicion. "Sounds like you're not even sure I can get this task done. Why not anyone else? Surely, you've been spoiled for choices."

Akaroth shook her head, snorting. A tiny bolt of lightning struck a pile of treasure.

"THAT IS NOT SO. EVERY WOULD-BE ADVENTUR-ER THAT COMES BEFORE ME MERELY TRIES TO KILL ME. THERE IS NO TALK, NO DISCUSSION. USUALLY, THEY ARE WEAK. THE ROGUE YOU DEFEATED OVER THERE, HE SLAUGHTERED A PRIESTESS, VANISHED, AND BEFORE I KNEW IT, MANAGED TO GET THAT AC-CURSED COLLAR AROUND MY NECK. RATHER THAN JUST KILLING ME, YOU FREED ME. YOU'RE THE FIRST TO TAKE ANY ACTION AGAINST ME THAT WAS NOT VIOLENT OR SELF-SERVING."

He took a deep breath. So far, the dragon had been very forthcoming with her answers. He had more questions, but he allowed the edge of suspicion he held within his mind to deflate. He could understand her desire to get away from this place if it was anything like the priestesses had explained.

He had one more pointed question to ask, however. "What happens to everyone else? Lizella, the kobolds, all of them? When you vanish, the whole point of this dungeon goes with it."

Akaroth cocked her head, her tail swishing and her wings ruffling.

"I KNOW NOT. I CARE NOT. THE SYSTEM WILL LIKE-LY RE-PURPOSE THEM."

He closed his eyes, rubbing the bridge of his nose as he thought. If he could, he'd free them too. Yet he only had one dragon heart, and it worked only for the dragon. "Is there any way to address the System directly? Lizella said she accepted a deal with it."

Akaroth rumbled. *"THE SYSTEM IS NOT A SENTIENT BE-ING IN THE WAY YOU ARE THINKING, MORTAL. THERE ARE MANY THEORIES SURROUNDING IT, BUT IT IS WIDELY ACCEPTED THAT IT OPERATES BASED ON PA-RAMETERS KNOWN ONLY TO IT. YOU CANNOT SPEAK TO IT LIKE YOU WOULD YOU OR I. IF IT OFFERS A PACT, IT IS NOT SOMETHING YOU CAN NEGOTIATE. IT IS A YES OR NO."*

That was that, then. He couldn't free them, and even if he did, where would he take them? Avalon had room, but something told him they wouldn't be happy there. Accepting it as impossible, he looked at the dragon. "I accept your proposal then, Akaroth. What item will you be?"

"THAT IS UP TO YOU, MORTAL. YOU WILL BE ABLE TO CHOOSE. YOU ALREADY WEAR ARMOR AND A CLOAK. PERHAPS I SHALL BE A WEAPON FOR YOU? OR MAYBE A HELMET, HMM?"

He tugged his lips downward, "Not really a helmet, fan," he muttered to himself.

Maybe an axe? There was an argument to be made that an axe would be a waste. He could already form an axe out of hellfire. The problem with that was any situation where he either ran out of mana or was in a place where he couldn't use mana. There could also be beings that were resistant to it, like Akaroth, who was resistant to lightning.

Plus, he just liked the feel of a weapon in his hands, of having something physical he could hold and use. As he thought about it, he grew warmer and warmer to the idea. His basic axe had been with him for a long time, and now it was gone. Surprisingly, he found himself missing it.

He nodded to himself, "Very well then. Give me the heart. I hope you like being an axe, Akaroth. It's about to be your permanent form."

He took the heart from her claw, focusing on it.

[Would you like to use the Dragon Heart? Think of the item you wish as you do. Note that this will bind Akaroth's consciousness and spirit to the item permanently. The item will be bound to you.

Y/N?]

He willed his answer to the System and watched as Akaroth burst into a cloud of gray-blue light. The heart in his hand, as if pulled by an invisible force, lifted into the air. It began to elongate and twist as the storm light wrapped around it, delving into it and becoming one with it.

Before long, an axe settled into his hands.

It was a marvel to look at. He had never been an art person, but the weapon he held was as much art as it was a tool of violence. There was a deadly beauty to it. The blade was curved, not unlike a dragon's tooth, with jagged edges like mini fangs taken directly from the great dragon's mouth.

Its handle was carved from obsidian, wrapped in scales that shift from dark blue to the gray of lightning. At the center of the blade is a glowing sapphire embedded in a spiral of runes that constantly crackled with blue and white energy. The axe hummed with latent power, not unlike a brewing storm.

Lightning arced around it, jumping over its surface like a living thing. He could feel Akaroth's mind within it, giving the new weapon an ancient feel.

Smiling to himself, he used **[Retributions Gaze]**. Time to see what it could do.

Chapter Twenty-Four

[Akaroth-Mythic]: Once a mighty A-Grade blue dragon, this axe now embodies everything the dragon once was. Known as the mother of storms, this weapon reflects that title and has been enchanted with unique effects. First among these is the ability to channel Akaroth's power into a storm, causing bolts of lightning to rain down against your foes. Note, this ability is indiscriminate. Secondly, Akaroth may absorb lightning, thunder and wind, turning these elements into usable mana. Finally, using Akaroth's spirit within the axe you may summon the dragon's true form for a limited duration. Note the dragon's grade is locked at your current grade. This weapon is alive, and grows alongside you.

Ambrose let out a low whistle. Akaroth's voice filled his mind like a concert and he was in front of the stage.

I'M GLAD YOU APPROVE, HATCHLING. I SEE THAT YOU HAVE ANOTHER COMPANION BOUND TO YOU. HELLO LITTLE CUB.

Ambrose hissed, almost dropping the axe as he clenched at his head with his other hand.

"God above, that *hurts*. Can you quiet your voice? Otherwise, you'll need to not talk. Ever."

The dragon's answering thought was a distant rumble of thunder on the wind. He grimaced, but when she spoke next, he sighed, unclenching his hand.

You should embrace the pain, as a dragon would, hatchling. Out of respect, I shall...lower the noise of my thoughts.

Noelle sent feelings of concern to him, and a dismissive flick of her ears and tail to the dragon. Akaroth's thoughts carried an amused edge.

Careful little cub, or I may decide you're a snack.

Noelle's response was to send an image of a tiny unthreatening blue lizard. Ambrose growled before the dragon could respond.

Enough, you two. I have better things to do than be a baby sitter.

Akaroth's answer was a snort within his mind, and Noelle an image of her flicking tail. That exchange done, he turned his attention to the notification that was screaming for his attention.

[You have cleared this dungeon! For clearing a System dungeon, and doing so in a unique way, you have earned increased experience. You have advanced to level 150. You may choose one new skill at this level. Since you have received a mythic item, further rewards will not be rewarded.]

He was slightly miffed he wasn't getting anything else, but eight levels was nothing to sneeze at. It gave him a solid sixty-four points to spend on his stats.

With a thought, he pulled up his attribute points.

Constitution: 223
Strength: 242
Intellect: 254
Wisdom: 258
Willpower: 284

You should put those points into strength.

Ambrose ignored the dragon's thoughts. He would put points into strength, not on her say so, but because it was growing a little behind.

He wasn't sure what threshold he needed for C-Grade, however, he had to have balance. He knew that much. With constitution being the lowest, he dumped thirty-two points into it.

He rubbed the bridge of his nose. That brought it to two hundred and fifty-five. It also left him with thirty-two more points to spend.

Thirteen points went into strength, making it equal to his constitution stat. Ten more for wisdom and the final nine for his intellect.

He looked over his new stats.

Constitution: 255

Strength: 255

Intellect: 267

Wisdom: 268

Willpower: 284

Strength should be dominant, but it appears you understand the need for balance. Another seventy levels and you will reach the next threshold for C-Grade.

Akaroth mused to him. He appreciated the information. Even so, that was far off. *Seventy levels.* Knowing the kinds of things he got into, that would likely come sooner than later. Opening up his **[Infernal Dimension]** he put Akaroth inside of it. His connection to the dragon axe was still present, but she still complained.

What are you doing? I demand you do not put me away like some common object!

He gave a mental approximation of a shrug and closed the realm. Akaroth growled within his mind.

I will eat your bones, hatchling!

Ambrose chuckled, *With what teeth?*

No answer from the dragon. Noelle sent smug feelings toward the axe. Akaroth grumbled, but said nothing else.

Ambrose shook his head, and opened up the options for his new skills.

[Infernal Aegis-Unique (Spiritual Skill)]: Through constant use of your spirit, this skill has been offered as a unique and evolved form of the skill. You may now weave your spirit through your body, and objects. This will offer the same protections and abilities as the previous skill, but you will no longer be able to manipulate the size of the shield. However, your spirit will be less strained with this skill.

[Infernal Shroud-Epic]: Protect your identity through this skill. It will take legendary analytical abilities to pierce through this skill.

[Infernal Resistance-Legendary]: Resist the element of fire, becoming immune to it. It would take a mythic level of fire to break through this skill.

He wasn't thrilled with these options. First was the unique version of infernal aegis. He didn't feel like he needed it. His spirit was doing well enough. *But* how he felt may not matter.

You will need to take this skill, hatchling.

Ambrose frowned at the dragon's words, but Akaroth explained before he could voice his question.

Fire smolders before it rages, hatchling. Spiritual strain is the same.

Solve the small problem before it grows, Ambrose stroked his beard. If spiritual strain becomes an issue, and from what he saw Tina go through, it was certainly a big deal.

The other skills were worth considering even if he wasn't thrilled about them. Infernal shroud for example was one he wouldn't have minded picking instead.

People not being able to tell who he was or his level of strength was useful. Being underestimated was always good. It gave a certain element of surprise. It had already happened to him a couple of times, and he'd been able to leverage it.

Infernal resistance seemed redundant to him. He didn't really need resistances when infernal aegis could block most anything.

Careful not to have your wings clipped by a single arrow, hatchling.

That was true. Having the resistances and not needing them was better than not having them and needing them. Despite that, Ambrose could only pick one skill for right now. It had to be the spiritual skill.

Spirit was the game changer. It created a huge disparity between him and anyone who didn't have it. He wasn't about to let it fall behind.

He selected the skill, feeling it change within himself.

Change made, it was time to return to Avalon.

With a flick of his hand, a portal of hellfire split the air. Avalon was beyond it. Light played across grass, and the smoldering fire of the portal mixed with the idyllic scene was a study in contrasts.

So, this is Avalon. I have heard stories, but never been. I am interested in seeing it. Noelle too sent a flutter of excitement.

It did feel a little like coming home. Sure, he had responsibilities there, stresses there, but what home didn't have that?

Picking up the unconscious form of Zane, he stepped through the portal.

He had Incursions to deal with.

CHAPTER TWENTY-FIVE

First, Ambrose appeared beneath the tree of Avalon. Every time he came here, he was struck by its beauty. Its canopy spread outward like an ocean of crystalline color. His noose hung from a branch, swaying slightly in the breeze that carried forth from the lake that lapped gently against the shore.

It was a place of peace as much as it was a place of justice. Vivienne appeared moments later, head bowed. Vivienne was the mythical Lady of the Lake. She was the island's spirit made manifest.

Her hair was the setting sun on the water, her face as ethereal as the moon's pale light on a starless night.

"You have returned, Sir Knight. With a new weapon, an axe of great power I see. Ah, it was once a dragon. You have had an interesting adventure."

Akaroth rumbled within his mind. *This spirit is dangerous.*

She's a friend, be nice, he thought at her.

"I have one for the tree, but then I need to take him to the bounty hunters guild."

Ambrose dropped Zane's unconscious form to the ground. Vivienne's eyes glittered, matching the tree's leaves.

"This one is barely alive, Sir Knight."

Ambrose shrugged. **[Retributions Gaze]** might have killed him had he not cut off the skill's power in time.

"What protocol shall he suffer?"

Ambrose rubbed his nose. He had already endured the pain he had inflicted on everyone else. Yet the tree demanded a punishment as it drained the ones contained within it.

He perused the options in his mind before selecting the quickest one.

"Protocol five, Vivienne."

"As you wish, Sir Knight, it shall be so."

She held up a single hand, and crystal encased the wanted man. He did not turn away as it sank into the ground moments later. He did not allow himself to feel any empathy or sympathy for the man, he was a rapist and worse.

What is protocol five? Akaroth questioned.

Pain. Was all he said in reply.

"Shall we discuss Icons while we wait, Sir Knight? You have been putting the discussion off."

He had been. Not because he wanted to but rather because he had been moving non-stop. From managing the town's needs to fighting or dealing with the other Forerunners, he hadn't had much of a break. When he had been training, he had been focused on the spirit part of it.

Icons are important, hatchling. One should not ignore sharpening their claws.

"Alright. What are Icons, Vivienne? Let's start there."

"They are embodiments of a concept, Sir Knight. These embodiments manifest when a being's spirit has enough connection to that concept."

Vivienne laid a hand on the tree, "Take this tree as an example. Were it living in the same way you were, it would likely be able to manifest the Tree Icon."

He crossed his arms, "I thought you need a spiritual skill to access your spirit?"

Vivienne nodded, "Indeed you do,"

"So in order to manifest your Icon, you first have to have a spiritual skill?"

Vivienne simply nodded.

He allowed his expression to turn thoughtful, "What do these Icons do for you? What is the point?"

Vivienne smiled,

"Manifesting an Icon would grant you a new class, a special Unique class known as a Sage."

Ambrose frowned, gesturing for her to continue.

"Arthur was the Knight Sage. His Icon embodied strength, honor, justice, and more besides."

"This still doesn't tell me what the benefits actually are. What would this new class give me?"

Vivienne did not react to his rushing of her. Akaroth did, *rushing out of the nest leads to disaster, hatchling. Give her time to answer.*

"Other than a powerful evolution of your class, it would grant you Authority related to your Icon. Authority... it is hard to explain, hmm." Vivienne tapped her cheek with a finger, cocking her head. Ambrose crushed his impatience.

"Authority is a measure of control over reality. That is the best way to put it. In another way, you might better understand that it gives weight to your attacks, to your presence. Think of it as existing beyond a mortal level. Should you wish to advance to C-Grade, properly, you will need to manifest an Icon. That is the first step of the process."

He leaned his head back, looking at the canopy, and took a deep breath. He already had so much he needed to do. First, the Incursions needed to be dealt with. That meant the fire giants, the dwarves, and Leshi Tina talked about.

His fists clenched because, of course, there was Eric he would pursue.

Calm your storm, hatchling. Or it will overcome you.

He didn't need the dragon's advice; he had perfect control over his anger.

"I don't have time to do all of that, Vivienne. How would I even begin? What Icon would I even manifest?"

She made a thoughtful sound, "Mm. Icons are deeply personal things, dear Knight. Like your spirit, it comes from knowing yourself and what symbol you feel most represents you. Some take years, decades even, to manifest an Icon. It is careful meditation and deep reflection. Even so, I think I know the Icon that fits you."

He arched a brow at her, "Well?"

Vivienne laughed, "Oh, I will not be telling you, dear Knight. Understanding yourself and your connection to a symbol is a part of the process of manifesting an Icon. I suggest taking some time out of every day and considering it. Like now, perhaps. The tree needs at least another hour before you may retrieve the evil-doer below."

Ambrose sat down, muttering to himself. "Evil-doer. You sound like a caricature."

Vivienne gave no answer. She just turned and walked onto the waters of the lake. Briefly, he wondered what she did when not talking to him. Vivienne was Avalon's spirit, but she had a mind of her own. Did that come with goals and desires? He made a note to ask her one day.

He sat cross-legged and considered Icons. The first problem was that he wasn't sure where to even start. In his spiritual training, he needed to know himself. Now, it sounded as if he needed to connect himself to a symbol—an Icon that he closely embodied.

Admittedly, he wasn't great at self-reflection. He had used memories, trying to study them like an outside observer, almost like a character discussion you might have in an English class. Sighing, he closed his single eye and started there.

What first came to him was the idea of a phoenix. After all, Ambrose certainly rose from the ashes enough times in his life. *I'm powerful, too, and I do a lot with fire*, he mused. *Both are true things.*

Except it didn't fit. He didn't feel reborn; he wasn't a new person. He wasn't all that changed of a man when you got down to it. He had done terrible things, but he wasn't trying to be a champion of good. If he were, he would abandon his quest for revenge and focus solely on the people who counted on him.

He wouldn't do that. His knuckles popped.

No, that wasn't an option.

That symbol was discarded, and he moved through more of them. With each option, he tried to make it fit within himself like a puzzle piece. Was he a sword? A shield? A dragon?

Akaroth snorted in his mind, and even Noelle sent an image of her swishing her tail in amusement.

Sometime later, after a dozen or more symbols had been thrown in the mental trash, Vivienne reappeared before him. "The tree is done, Sir Knight. You may retrieve your captive should you wish it."

He stood up, running a hand through his hair, "Good. Time to collect that bounty."

One step closer to Eric.

CHAPTER TWENTY-SIX

*D*o I have to buy a stone every time? Ambrose frowned as he walked the streets of Avalon to Troy's shop. He entered and the reformed merchant groaned. "Please tell me you aren't here to hurt me again; I'm telling you I am try-"

Ambrose held up a hand to cut off his bumbling, "I need another stone to return to the guild."

Troy frowned, "They didn't give you a way to get back?"

Ambrose crossed his arms. "Right. You wouldn't be here if they had."

Troy face-palmed. "Fine. Here." The merchant produced a stone, and Ambrose turned over the required SC before taking it. Zane was slung over his shoulder, still knocked out. He had woken up screaming his agony for all to hear, so Ambrose had bonked him on the temple with Akaroth.

I do not bonk, growled the dragon.

Noelle sent smug amusement to Akaroth, who sent her own image back to the tiger of her munching on a tiger. Noelle replied with a bring it on feeling and a swish of her tail.

Ambrose clutched at his head, "It's like a daycare in my head," he muttered.

"Pardon?"

He ignored the shopkeeper and left, using the stone as he did.

The Bounty Hunters Guild was unchanged from last time. With the same old man at the counter. He looked at Ambrose with amusement as he set Zane on the counter of the bar.

"One Zane Dalewind. Intact."

"Well now, that was quicker than expected. You have a knack for this, eh?"

He shrugged in reply, not interested in the banter. "Two-hundred and fifty-thousand SC is what he's worth, I think."

The man smiled, fingering one side of his handlebar mustache. "Yes indeed, he is. Payment comin' on through via the System."

Ambrose glanced at his status page, confirming the man's words. He turned to leave, but the bartender called after him, "Hey now, did you use a stone to get here?"

He nodded.

"Lemme see your badge for a second," the old man requested.

Ambrose turned it over, and the man muttered, tapping the center.

"There, now. You can use this like a stone to appear here. Indefinitely."

He eyed the badge and then nodded before tossing it back into his infernal dimension.

"Thank you."

The barman nodded.

Ambrose left.

Ambrose rolled the stone to Midgard in his fingers. *Eric is just a stones throw away,* he thought in grim amusement.

Yet he couldn't go there yet. No, instead he needed to deal with Incursions.

Andrea stepped through her office door moments later, pausing when she saw him. She took a sip of her morning coffee.

"Just gonna wait for you to explain why you're chilling in my office this early."

Ambrose threw the stone into a small hole he made to his infernal dimension.

"I need you to send someone to Britannia and tell Tina I will be over after I deal with the New Kweneng Incursion. Tina's Incursion will probably take more of a coordinated effort, I think."

Andrea sighed, drinking more coffee. "When did I get demoted to secretary?"

She flicked her hand, cutting off his response before he could give it.

"I'll get it done, Dannill has been helping with that sort of thing lately. Is there anything else?"

Ambrose stared at her. "What's wrong now?"

Andrea sat her coffee down on the table and rubbed her temples. "Bunch of whiners, that's what's wrong. We have several groups of people complaining that we, namely me, weren't elected. That we shouldn't have any authority over them. They demand an election. I've explained that this isn't a democracy, and that they are welcome to leave if they want to complain, but they denounce me as being a tyrant if I do that."

Ambrose narrowed his eyes, his eye patch crinkling. "Do you want me to talk to them?"

She stared at him, as if he had just spoken gibberish. "And do what? Flex your awesome power? The problem is that they've put me in a catch twenty-two, Ambrose. If I have you come in and lay down the law, I look like a tyrant. Which means more people will want to leave or come around to their way of thinking. Right now it's just a few small groups, but that could change."

He shrugged, "So what if they leave?"

Andrea laughed, then took a sip of coffee shaking her head. "I love how that's your response to everything. Who will work in the mines? Did you know we have people refining those crystals now? Don't bother answering, I know you don't. We even have alchemists, weavers, smiths, and enchanters now. People rely on the town now, Ambrose. They have a way of life here."

She was working herself up now, "We can't just kick people out. Remember when you suggested that last time? Well, we did it and it was a real blow to morality. People lost faith in our ability to solve problems without resorting to force. So no, Ambrose, that won't work." She huffed out a breath.

Ambrose raised an eyebrow at her. A faint blush appeared on her cheeks.

"Sorry," she mumbled.

"I see you're dealing with a lot. I know I haven't exactly been around..." He trailed off.

Andrea gave him a small smile. "No, you haven't. But you never pretended you would be. No, I need to earn my keep with this. It comes with levels at least. Whenever I solve a crisis or do anything involving the managing of the town, I get experience. It's just draining. Mentally I mean."

"Put a few points into intellect," Ambrose suggested helpfully.

Andrea glared at him. "Don't you have some Incursions to close or something?"

Laughing, he left.

"Welcome to New Kweneng, Mr. Severen."

A man in sand colored robes said to him as he appeared in a large tent. It was sparse, with two guards and the array.

The guard was bald, and dark of skin. A scimitar was in a sheath on his belt.

Ambrose nodded at him, "I'd like to see Kellan Akenyemi, please."

The guard nodded, gesturing at him to follow.

He led Ambrose to a huge tent on the far right side of what Ambrose could only call a tent town. There were tents everywhere, glyphs shining on their surface.

The sun above baked the sand like golden rice. A camel with his robed rider walked the street. It was like a desert town was ripped straight out of a fantasy book and placed here.

The huge tent had several guards at front, who nodded to Ambrose's escort as they walked through the flap.

Opulent rugs covered the ground, and on a couch was Kellan Akenyemi, this time dressed in gold and brown robes shifting with shining glyphs.

He stood as Ambrose entered. "Ah, Mr. Severen. Welcome."

There was a weariness to Kellan's eyes, as if he was encountering a dangerous predator and couldn't be certain what it was about to do.

Ambrose nodded at him, and they shook hands.

Kellan's hands were warm, and rough. No stranger to work.

"I'm here to hopefully help you deal with your Incursion. Anything more you want to tell me about it?"

Kellan's eyes flashed. "I'll tell all I know. Please, sit. Let us begin."

CHAPTER TWENTY-SEVEN

Andrea Pender wanted nothing more than to go back to her tiny home Darren had built for her in what felt like ages ago, and soak in a nice hot bath.

She crushed the urge to rub her temples as Cassius Dex waxed on.

"We have no say in the day to day! We toil under threat of eviction! What do we get for the sweat off our brows? A standard home and subpar wage? Bah! I say things need to change. We need democracy! An election. We have a right to choose our own leaders, and have a say in the laws that directly affect our lives!"

There were mutters of agreement across those seated here in the designated town meeting room of Darren's Hall. Cassius Dex was not an imposing man.

Andrea couldn't help but be reminded of a light pole every time she looked at him. His bright blonde hair even looked like a light. His dark eyes looked like tiny square chocolates.

Andrea had to admit that his speaking voice was enrapturing. Velvet smooth, rich and carried easily. He could have been a decent audio book narrator if he wished.

It was the kind of voice that brought people around to a person's way of thinking just by being heard.

It infuriated her.

Cassius went on, and all of it was sweet, impassioned poison. None of it was actually true when you considered the full context.

He said that no one was fully aware of what to expect of life here, and that now they have settled here, they deserved to have a say.

He even tried to sound reasonable by saying he would be okay with electing a council. He was even fine with not taking a seat on that council himself as long as there was one.

Imagine that.

Finally, when he was done speaking, Andrea was able to reply. She had a few ways she could do so. She picked a path, and went with it.

"Mr. Dex. First, we hear your concerns. It's understandable that you would feel this way. Let me address some of them directly, and respectfully as possible. Many of you were brought to this place by Mr. Severen. He saved you, fought for you, and provided for your needs. More importantly, he gave you homes."

Andrea swept her gaze around the room, doing her best to meet each pair of eyes with her own. She wanted to ram the point home.

"Bottom line is that many of you owe him your lives. I and many on this council before you owe him our lives. We are all here at his forbearance. He wants things to stay the way they are."

She spread her hands, "And are they really so bad? Ask yourselves, do you truly believe we are tyrants? That we abuse our power? Was it abuse of power when we opened the school. Was it abuse when we allowed small businesses to open. When we built homes for you all."

She didn't phrase them like questions. They were challenges. Statements. She designed it to force people to think past their initial anger.

She saw it working, too. Expressions turned thoughtful, some turned away, looking slightly ashamed.

[Due to actions in line with your profession, you have gained experienced and advanced to level 56.]

Nice. Cassius was not an idiot. He knew how to play this game, and that was clear in the way he didn't interrupt her.

Then it was his turn, and he took a surgical knife to her words.

"Mr. Severen saved us, indeed. There is no doubt about that. But does that mean we lose all of our basic human rights. Does it mean that we bow to him like some kind of God King."

Cassius shook his head, "Friends, I ask you, do we change one slave owner for another? I say to you, an unseen collar is a collar all the same. I do not think Mr. Severen would want that for us. In fact, I ask that he come here now to answer that very question."

Even Dannill raised an eyebrow at this. Thom, who was next to her, rubbed at his face.

Andrea had to fight off a grimace. Cassius had neatly played his counter card, and it was a doozy.

Faces twisted, people nodded, one person grunted and patted Cassius on the back.

Cassius knew as well as she did that Ambrose wasn't around to answer questions. In fact, he had hardly been around lately. There was a reason for that, a good logical reason.

But it also didn't matter. When you were seen as a leader, there was just no replacement for being *here*. Cassius *knew* that and so he played off it. He knew Ambrose wasn't around to correct him, and even if he was, he'd likely be forced to acknowledge their feelings.

In addition, he had neatly slipped that collar back around their necks himself, and it was now an unseen chafe they couldn't get rid of unless they had some form of control.

There wasn't much Andrea could do about it, either. There was no getting rid of it, not now that the idea was there.

Cassius gave her a ghost of a smile, his eyes holding a subtle smug light.

Andrea took a deep breath. "This meeting is adjourned for now, but rest assured, we will discuss the possibility of an election and reopen discussions next week."

People filed out of the room, already talking. They were dark, angry mutterings. She briefly closed her eyes.

She couldn't see a way around this now.

Thom placed a weathered hand on her shoulder after everyone had left. "We'll get through this, lass. You helped build this town into what it is, no way that snake in the grass is outsin' you."

Andrea squeezed his hand fondly. She showed him a tired smile, "I don't know, Thom. You saw them. They were all looking at me like I was the enemy at the end."

Thom grunted in acknowledgment. "Ambrose will set this right. They can't argue with that lad, he's the real master of this place and everyone knows it."

Andrea shook her head, "Maybe, Thom. If he were here. You know he's off dealing with these Incursions, and who knows how long that will take? Besides, can we really get rid of all of these people just because they don't agree with us? What does that make us then, Thom?"

She combed fingers through her hair, "Like it or not, this isn't something we can brute force away. Still, I prefer to get a head start on this."

She flicked her gaze to Dannill. The ranger was scratching his chin, looking profoundly bored. His bow was slung over one shoulder.

He looked for all the world not to be paying attention. Andrea knew better. The ranger wanted to be underestimated.

"Dannill, I want you to dig up everything you can on Cassius Dex. He wants an election? We'll give him one. Thom, I'm going to visit Vathwin. Maybe he can help somehow."

Thom shuddered. Vathwin gave him the creeps.

Dannill let out a giant sigh. "Do I have to? Fine. What a drag."

CHAPTER TWENTY-EIGHT

"So these dwarves just stay in their mountain?" Ambrose questioned.

Kellan nodded, "They do. So long as no one tries to enter, they're peaceful. If you get close enough, you can hear the clangs of their hammers."

Dwarves have always been craftsmen, and treasure hoarders. It is why dragons often take over their dwellings, Akaroth provided.

He leaned back on the couch, "Have you attempted to talk to them? To establish an alliance?"

Kellan's face twisted, a mixture of confusion and anger suffusing his features.

"Why would I do such a thing? The Incursions need to be closed. They are invaders upon our world. Our only option is to wipe them out."

This one is much like a wild flame, he seeks to consume all. Like a hatchling, he has no concept of control.

He had to agree with the dragon's assessment of Kellan.

"You know you can close the Incursion just through an alliance? Or even just a mutual agreement."

Akenyemi scowled, "I will not do this with these bearded aliens. That would be giving up."

Ambrose sighed, pinching his nose. He was all for violence when a situation called for it. In fact, Ambrose tended to feel like it was usually the quickest way to get what he needed. But he wasn't a butcher, he was willing to at least try talking.

Kellan was acting like Ambrose was suggesting they try bargaining with a cockroach instead of a living, thinking being. Not to mention the fact that if he tried talking, he wouldn't have to sacrifice men.

He put that aside for now with a sigh. "How far have you gotten?"

Kellan's jaw ticked, "Not far. There is a dwarf at the entrance, and whenever we get close, he unleashes something similar to what you can do."

Kellan smacked his hands together, "We are all pressed flat, and can do nothing. I am hoping you have some way to counter this, yes?"

He did.

Kellan beamed, "Perfect. I shall prepare my men for a frontal assault. If you can counter the dwarf-what?"

Ambrose was shaking his head. "I want to try talking, first. If that goes poorly, *then* we can assault them."

The other man stared at Ambrose, rubbing a hand across his bald pate. "You want to negotiate with these invaders? To possibly give up land to them? To allow them to keep the treasures that they have stolen from below those mountains? I am not okay with this, Mr. Severen."

Ambrose shrugged, allowing a bit of fire to touch his voice, "Frankly, I don't care what you're okay with. I'm going to give you some free knowledge. I'm going to tell you why you can't face that dwarf and why your opinion doesn't matter to me."

Ambrose held up a single finger and unleashed a tiny bit of his spirit from his spiritual skill. Akenyemi felt it like a giant hand pressing down slightly on his head. "What you are feeling is spiritual pressure. You see, at some point the System offers you what is known as a 'spiritual skill.' Some people don't take it, I know I almost didn't. I can't say whether it offers it to you again, I don't know. But if you don't take it, you're at a serious disadvantage. It's a serious disparity, because you have no way to counter anyone who can use that skill properly. Your advancement may as well be crippled. *That* is what the dwarf is doing to you."

Ambrose sealed his spiritual skill once more and the pressure vanished. Kellan's eyes were hot coals. Ambrose met them calmly with his own one-eyed gaze.

"That's why I'm going to do whatever I want. You can't stop me, and I'm not about to let people needlessly die if we can solve the situation through mutual understanding. Honestly, it astounds me that you haven't tried to have a discussion before this point."

He stood, leashing his anger. Kellan could have already dealt with this, and likely just by talking. Instead, his greed and prejudice blinded him. Ambrose had to remind himself that his house was made of glass.

He didn't always do the smartest or morally correct thing. Often enough he actively chose not to. Yet, usually in those situations he had reasons that were at least understandable. Kellan Akenyemi wasn't stupid, he was just selfish and it showed. He could have forgiven that, but not when it put everyone at risk.

"I'm going to go see this dwarf. If he'll talk, I will attempt to close the Incursion with an alliance. If he won't talk, only then will I use violence."

"Should it come to that, I want the first pick of any loot you come across," Kellan said, his voice strained.

Ambrose arched a brow. "Why in the world would I agree to that?"

Kellan's body tensed, his jaw worked, and his nostrils flared. "This is not a good way to have a working relationship with me, Mr. Severen. You cannot just bully me."

The fire you start could consume your own hoard, hatchling.

Personally, Ambrose didn't care about making an enemy of Kellan. Something about the man rubbed him the wrong way. Maybe it was because he was an adulterer. It wasn't so much the specific act of cheating on a spouse that bothered him, it was more to being disloyal that did chafed at him.

No matter what someone could say about Ambrose Severen, it could always be said he was loyal to those he made promises to, and at least he was open with them, even if he sometimes prioritized his own wants.

Kellan was a snake. He projected a warrior's honor, but it felt slimy, fabricated. This was a man after power not for any sort of goal, but just for the sake of having it.

However, did he want him for an enemy? Akaroth was right in that Akenyemi could prove troublesome. Avalon just dealt with a major attack, and Ambrose didn't want to have to deal with another. Except for two things.

Kellan and his forces were here, thousands of miles away. That hadn't been the case for Eric, and Ambrose highly doubted that Kellan would have a way to teleport close to Avalon any time soon.

I don't owe him anything, and I won't bow to threats, Ambrose growled in his mind.

"I don't want you as an enemy, Kellan. I would prefer we maintain mutual respect, and a part of that means keeping what you earn. I'm not about to give you anything I earn through battle just because you have some twisted perception that you're owed it."

Kellan's face became ugly, "Fine. Get out."

Ambrose obliged.

It was, in fact, a dwarf at the entrance of the mountain's depths. He looked like what you might expect a dwarf to look like, with a few differences. He was short, but not the kind of short that made you look small. In fact, he looked almost like a bear cub might, covered in black fur, with gleaming silver-blue chain mail. A pickaxe made of the same metal as his chain mail was at his side.

His beard was impressive, black that had gone to silver early, and his pale blue eyes twinkled in the light. *How is he not burning up under all that fur?* Ambrose thought. His right ear had three golden rings lining it. His hair was a mane of midnight, and he had been sitting on an elevated rock near the entrance of the mountain as Ambrose came into view.

As soon as he spotted Ambrose, he hopped off his rock, and a spiritual pressure descended like a falling building upon him.

CHAPTER TWENTY-NINE

This dwarf is powerful, Ambrose acknowledged. Focusing his mind to a sharp edge, he unleashed the spirit from his spiritual skill. The dwarf's eyes widened in surprise as his spirit met resistance. He stood up from his rock, a smile curling his lips, beard quivering as his spirit pressed against Ambrose's own.

This was not a being new to this, not some newly integrated like Ambrose, who had just unlocked his spirit. The dwarf had the focus and training needed to be formidable. He was running a thumb over his pickaxe, eyes now narrowed as he regarded the human before him with new interest.

He said something to Ambrose, but he had no idea what it meant. Knuckles whitening, Ambrose took a step forward. He snarled with defiance, but the dwarf may as have been a mountain. It was a feat all its own that he was still standing.

The dwarf before him knew this because a light of respect twinkled in his blue eyes. As suddenly at it had come, the pressure vanished.

"Ah must say, ah'm impressed human! Yer the first ah've encountered with access to spirit. Ah was growin' bored!"

His voice was as deep as the mountain's depths must have been. To Ambrose's surprise, the dwarf sounded Russian. From out of nowhere, the dwarf produced a small silver flask that he took a sip from. He smacked his lips and held out to Ambrose. "Bit oh snifter for ya?"

A little bemused, Ambrose shook his head.

Shrugging, the stout warrior took another sip before closing the flask and making it vanish.

Deciding to take stock of the situation, he used **[Retributions Gaze]** on the dwarf.

[Aleksei Strongpick Level 170]: Dwarves are known as the craftsmen of the multiverse. They spend their days mining, smithing, enchanting, jewel working, and perfecting many other crafts. Aleksei harbors a secret guilt, something that isn't truly his fault.

"Done analyzing me, human?" Aleksei arched a brow.

Ambrose brushed the notification away. He didn't answer the question. Instead, he said, "I want to discuss an alliance between your people and mine. I'm sure you know that we can't allow the Incursion to remain open. But neither do I want violence if it can be avoided."

Aleskei rubbed the point of the pickaxe as he arched a brow, "Ah wasn't expectin' a negotiation, to be sure. Hmm."

The dwarf seemed to mull over something for a bit, his mouth working like he was chewing on a piece of gristle.

"Tell ya what, human. We dwarves are craftsmen to our bones. All we want is to live in this mountain and practice our craft. We do trade from time to time and have sent out a few patrols. There's a dungeon nearby, in this place called the Valley o' Kings or some such. Information we have says the dungeon rewards ya with valuable resources we need for our craftin'. Go complete that dungeon, bring us back half o' the rewards, and ah'll get you a sit down with the King. What do ya think o' that?"

He almost groaned. *Another dungeon? Really?* It made some sense, dungeons were one of the few ways you could get direct rewards from the System.

Aleskei was surprisingly reasonable. He could have demanded the full reward from the dungeon, but instead, he asked for half. Part of Ambrose considered saying no, however. It was more time he had to dedicate here instead of going after Eric.

It would be far easier to just kill of them. Aleskei's spirit was powerful, and it was a worry for him. It wasn't insurmountable. Especially as he had other abilities to call on. A quick portal to behind the unsuspecting dwarf, or even in front of him, grab him and activate **[Retributions Gaze]** and it would be over.

He rubbed a hand through his hair. Aleskei appeared perfectly content to let the human take all the time he needed to think.

Not all fires start with a roar. Akaroth was right again. He didn't know how strong the dwarves were. Aleskei spoke as if others held more authority than he did. At least a king.

He highly doubted the King would place his most powerful warrior at the entrance. Oh, Ambrose had no doubt the dwarf in front of him had lots of power.

Level one hundred and seventy with a powerful spirit like that meant he was no slouch.

He also had to consider the long game. If these dwarves were as good as craftsmen as Aleskei claimed, then their people would make better allies than enemies.

Something hot built within him, a pressure built in his ears. *More delays,* he growled to himself. It was as if someone out there wanted to drag things out and were arranging things to make it happen.

"Fine. I'll take on the dungeon and bring back your rewards. I want that audience right after, though."

Aleksei produced his flask again with a beaming smile. "Ah knew you you'd agree! I have good feelings about you, human!"

He drank, as Ambrose turned and stalked away.

The Valley of Kings wasn't hard to find. It had been a tourist area in the old world. The Systems arrival had changed a lot.

Avalon towns folk talked about it. Ambrose had been freeing Avalon's curse at the time, but there had been great earthquakes, and portals, with monsters pouring out of them, and the weather going wonky.

It altered a lot of areas.

This meant the Valley of Kings was no longer a tourist area. Instead it was a place of ruin.

It was also guarded by a giant monster. A huge wolf creature in ancient egyptian attire wielded a gargantuan spear. Its fur was the black found in ink stains on parchment. The eyes were golden, glowing with avarice light.

Behind its massive legs was a small cavern that Ambrose just knew was the dungeon. To get an idea of what he was dealing with, he tossed a [Retriþutions Gaze] at the creature.

[Anubian Guard (Sector Lord) Level 182]: Sector Lords are elite creatures designed to truly test an areas inhabitants. Defeating them will grant a special reward.

Akaroth, do you know anything about Sector Lords?

Her reply came quickly, *Defeating them usually grants a spiritual skill, or vast experience if you already have one. They are dangerous foes, hatchling. But dragons do not back down from a challenge.*

He sighed, looking at the stationary monster. If he didn't know better, he would have sworn it was just a statue with how still it was.

It was interesting that it offered a spiritual skill. It was one of the few ways to correct your advancement if that were true, and he had no reason to doubt the dragons words.

He would just gain increased experience, probably more than increased, but he didn't have much of a choice. It wasn't going to just let him waltz into the dungeon.

He *could* portal past it, but that was leavings threat behind for later. He didn't want anyone else gaining power from this thing. Especially an enemy. *Nothing for it, then.*

He summoned Akaroth from his infernal dimension.

Noelle sent an image of her stretching her claws.

"Okay then, big guy. Let's see what you got."

CHAPTER THIRTY

Ambrose opened combat up by imbuing Akaroth using his [Hellfire Manipulation] skill and throwing it at the Anubian guardian. A spinning vortex of blazing fire, shining with arching blue lightning, slammed into the guardian's chest.

He expected a burst of blood or at least knock it off balance, but nothing of the sort happened. Instead, he raised its spear and took a single lumbering step toward him, clearing more than half the distance between them. It thrust its spear at him, and it was as if it were thrusting an entire building. That was how big it was.

He tapped his newly upgraded [Infernal Aegis] skill, and instead of a barrier of flame surrounding him like he was used to, mana poured into his armor from his core, and the metal lit up like living lava. Heat poured off of him as his armor became like a living creature of hell, blazing bright like a crimson star.

Slamming into him like a sharpened battering ram, Ambrose was flung back, and as he was, he opened a hellfire portal behind him...right into his Hellcat Challenger. Rocking back against the seats, he closed the portal and opened another one.

At the same time, he tapped his skill once more, pulling the required mana from his core. He infused the Challenger, and like a living thing, he roared through the portal and onto the sand and rock of the ruins that once was the Valley of Kings.

Roaring like the creature it was named for, the car was wreathed in spectral flames of burning red and eldritch green.

Give me some storms, Akaroth.

Responding with a growl in his mind, the axe flew up from his grip, and in time with her mental roar, the sky itself answered. Clouds of blackened gray swirled above, thunder rumbled, and a boom echoed throughout the sky as if an angry god was hammering on the anvil that was the world.

Looking up, the Anubian guardian raised a hand. A shining yellow barrier seemingly formed of golden sand wove into existence before it just as lightning shattered into it with an electrifying detonation. Unharmed, the spear swept forward to slash Ambrose and his car to scrap.

His core flared as he pushed his mana into the car. Metal glowed with carmine light as the spear tip made contact. He felt his skill strain, but more mana took care of it, successfully repelling the attack. Above, Akaroth's storm raged, lightning crashing all around like bolts thrown from the Almighty himself in an attempt to smite the monster.

The Anubian guard's shield splintered but held against the onslaught.

Ambrose frowned as he unleashed his spirit upon the creature, only to find it didn't do anything to it. He encountered no spiritual resistance, and yet clear as the day was before the storm above, his spirit did nothing.

He couldn't exactly stop and analyze why, either.

Turning the wheel sharply, he avoided another slash. With its other hand, the creature began to form what Ambrose could only call a ball. It was swirling wind and dark power.

It was also huge, like a model globe but perhaps a hundred times larger. So big in fact, he wasn't sure he could avoid it.

Luckily, he didn't think he needed to.

As the Sector Lord threw the globe of wind and darkness at him, he pulled on his connection to Akaroth through his mana. Rotating through the air, Akaroth slashed through the ball and promptly absorbed all the wind within it.

This did take nearly all the power out of the attack, but not all of it.

He couldn't do anything about whatever aspect the darkness that made up the globe was.

He allowed the attack to hit him, his spiritual skill shielding him from the worst of it.

Deciding on a different approach, Ambrose used **[Hellfire Manipulation]**, and this time, he flooded the mana through Akaroth and into the storm above. A swirling gate of hell opened in the air above and lit the sky aflame.

It was beautiful, in a way, as if the dawn had mixed with the storm, creating a living pastel of dark gray, iridescent blue lightning, sanguine flame, dark green light, and subtle pink veins highlighting it all. With it came a deluge of power.

Lightning straight from Hades blasted the golden shield apart as fire rolled down from the sky in a tide sent forth from the very heavens.

The Guardian wasn't done; with a wave of its massive paw, rubble and stone lifted of their own accord, and they flew together like massive puzzle pieces. It managed to block some of the fire, but it was simply too much power for it to ignore.

Ambrose wasn't idle as he did all of this, either. He pressed the accelerator and tapped **[Infernal Sanctuary]**, sending out spectral chains of gleaming dark fire. He flew through the Anubian guardian's legs and, turning the wheel to the right, he willed the chains to wrap around the legs of the monster.

More stones rocketed up, but this time seeking him out like homing missiles. It blasted itself apart like shattering glass upon his enhanced vehicle.

Chains continuously wrapped themselves around the monster as Ambrose opened a hellfire portal, roaring through it just as a truly massive stone head of some ancient pharaoh collided with the earth where he had just been.

Writhing like tentacles, the chains dug into the monster.

Sometimes, even in a world like this one, physics has its say. With a thunderous crash, the Anubian guard was brought to its knees, sending a wave of sand and air in all directions.

Ambrose turned the wheel again and blazed from the right and right up the Anubian's back. Sending his chains forward, he wrapped the spectral chains around the Sector Lord's neck as the car launched itself into the air off of its head and to the right.

At the same time, Ambrose tapped another ability of Akaroth's, and the axe pulsed with power. Suddenly, it shifted and Akaroth was an axe no more. Instead, she was in her true dragon form, the massive blue dragon, the mother of storms.

She roared with fury, and the hollow of her throat lit up with electric blue power as she opened her mouth. A beam of destructive lightning arched out in a concentrated force that blew through the Anubian guardian's head like a rotting pumpkin that had found itself in a hurricane.

Blood, brain matter, and other viscera coated the ground like droplets of rain. Above, the storm abated, the lightning died, and Akaroth returned to her axe form, whirling into Ambrose's hand.

[You have defeated the Sector Lord and, as a reward, have earned enough experience to advance to level 165.]

Ambrose stopped the car in front of the monster's corpse and stepped out.

That was well-fought, hatchling. I do not mind having been in my true form, either.

Noelle sent an image of her stretching in satisfaction at a job well done.

He had many points to spend, but before he got to that, he opened a portal, returned his Challenger, and then returned to the dungeon. He took a deep breath and entered the dungeon, taking a step down the path of closing another Incursion.

CHAPTER THIRTY-ONE

When Ambrose entered the dungeon, a notification popped up.

[Welcome to the "Pharaohs Pyramid." Find The Djinn's Heart.]

He dismissed the notification and took in his surroundings, which were a whole lot of nothing. All around him was a sea of sand and rock. There were no trees or mountains that he could see, nothing but sand. A wind picked up the grains, blowing them against his flesh.

He was D-Grade, but even with that, the sand still bothered him a bit. For now, he used **[Infernal Aegis]** to protect himself from the mini sandstorm. It was just a trickle of mana, but over time, it would add up if he wasn't careful.

Sighing, he picked a direction and then began walking. As he did, he manifested Noelle, giving her time to roam. The Arcane White Tiger rubbed her furry cheek against his palm, chuffed, and frolicked in the sand some ways ahead of him.

As he walked, he tended to his advancement. Fifteen levels meant a whopping one hundred and twenty points for him to spend on his stats. To get an idea of where he wanted to put them, he brought them up.

Constitution: 255
Strength: 255

Intellect: 267
Wisdom: 268
Willpower: 284

I spoke in jest before, but your strength does need shoring up hatchling.

Akaroth was correct. First, he brought constitution and strength to two-hundred and eighty. That was twenty-five points a piece for a total of fifty points. That was nearly half the points he had to spend. He had seventy points left. Thirteen points went into intellect, and twelve went into wisdom.

Forty-five points spent with forty-five left to spend. He stroked his beard and wanted to make sure his core had more mana; he plopped the sixteen points needed to bring his willpower to three hundred. With his final points, he put ten into constitution and strength and the final nine into intellect.

Advancement seen to, he thought about what he needed to do here in this dungeon. Looking around, there was just nothing. What he needed was a way to track his progress. He could easily find himself looping around with no idea of where he was if he wasn't careful.

The best way he could do that was with landmarks.

He paused, and Noelle's ears flicked up as he bent down. She bounded over to him, cocking her head. Ambrose began to push sand together in a massive mound. He sent an image to Noelle of her using her lightning on the mound.

She blinked pale blue eyes at him but did as he said. Just as he thought, the lightning turned the mound into fulgurite with a crackling sound. It was noticeable but not from afar. He piled more and more sand atop the fulgurite mound, having Noelle do the same.

Before long, he had a tower slightly taller than him built entirely of fulgurite. He would have preferred to be able to see it from way afar, but he didn't have any way to get up higher. Using Akaroth, he scratched in the best approximation of a one he could manage.

That went on for a long time. Every so often, he'd make another tower of fulgurite. During this period, he let his skill go, choosing instead to deal with the sand without it. He had no idea what he was looking for, but at this point, he would settle for anything. Anything at all.

Eventually, he did come back around to his first fulgurite tower. He gritted his teeth, sucking a breath through his nose. Slowly, he let it out, draining the frustration with it.

Thinking there must be something hidden, something he couldn't see, he used his eyepatch of true sight and swept it around the area. Almost as if to mock him, a portion of the sand in a wide area around the fulgurite tower vanished, revealing a staircase of sandstone leading downward.

He threw his head back and laughed, his body shaking with mirth.

You have found the scales in the clouds, hatchling.

He brushed off the dragon's words. He'd been wandering for hours upon hours by now, and all he had to do was use his eyepatch. It just reaffirmed that one needed to stop to think and use everything available to him before moving on.

As he descended the steps, he came before a massive dais, stone doors behind it. On the dais was a large sphynx.

The creature's creepy face, with the golden furred body of a lion and the wings of an eagle, the sphinx eyed him with huge green eyes. He used a **[Retributions Gaze]** on the creature.

[Pharaoh's Sphinx Level 175]: Sphinx's are often the guardians of sacred temples. Each holds a code of offering riddles before devouring any who get their questions wrong.

Ambrose unmanifested Noelle, who settled around him. A purr emanated from the sphinx in a rumble.

"Ah, a visitor to the Pharaoh's temple. If you wish to enter unchallenged, you must answer my riddle's three, adventurer."

He thought about it for a moment. Truth was, he already felt delayed. This whole venture was something he wanted to square away as quickly as possible, not spend all of his time-solving riddles he couldn't be sure he would know the answer to. If he got it wrong, the sphinx would try to eat him, regardless.

Summoning Akaroth through his dimension, he infused it with **[Hellfire Manipulation]** and threw it hard at the sphinx. Perhaps it was the surprise of the attack, or maybe the ferocity of it did it. Either way, Akaroth, blazing with sanguine eldritch flame, cut through the Sphinx's neck like it was butter.

In a burst of viscera, the head plopped to the ground like a falling apple with a sickening squelch. It rolled away slightly as the body twitched for a second before it fell to the side like a toppling sand tower, wings still undulating.

[You have defeated a Sphinx Level 175. You have earned increased experience for defeating a foe beyond your level. You have advanced to level 166.]

Ambrose nodded and quickly assigned the points. One went into intellect, bringing it to two hundred and ninety. The last seven went into wisdom. The doors beyond the dais where the now dead sphinx lay, ground open to reveal an utterly dark room beyond.

Ambrose didn't feel bad about killing the sphinx. Likely, he would have had to fight the creature no matter what. He wasn't very good with riddles, even if he could work them out. Plus, the monster was a dungeon creature. The System would bring it back, if not here, elsewhere.

A decisive blow, I approve.

Ambrose rolled his eye. Of course she did.

Before he could enter the utter blackness of the room beyond, a notification appeared before him.

[Go straight no matter what.]

He paused, reading the System's message a second time. It must be a part of the dungeon. A little more warily, he eyed the now ominous darkness. There was nothing for it but to press on. With a tight grip on Akaroth, he stepped into the next room, the darkness eagerly swallowing him whole.

CHAPTER THIRTY-TWO

Ambrose was surrounded by a darkness that was so all-encompassing he thought for a moment that he was in the void. It didn't feel like he was blind or had entered a particularly dark cave. Instead, it was as if he could actually see the darkness itself as if it were a physical thing.

"You've come back to me."

Ambrose stopped. A flutter went through him, and his face went slack as he went white as fresh snow on a moonlit night.

"Alice." His voice was a whisper of a hope. Yet the back of his mind was screaming at him even now. He needed to stay on the path. This was a trick designed to get him to stray. He knew it.

But.

"I've been here so long. I don't know how I got here, but I knew. I knew you'd find me, my tarnished knight."

His eye closed, his fingers dug into his palms, and he felt his shoulder tremble as his heart beat like a furious chorus. Almost against his will, he turned towards the sound.

Noelle screeched at him, a tiger roar in his mind. He stopped, taking a breath.

Which is when Alice appeared before him. She floated there, a ghost-given flesh once again.

Just as beautiful as the day he first laid eyes on her.

Their relationship had never been very traditional, but as he looked at her, he recalled a conversation he had had with her on one of their early dates.

A conversation about flowers.

They were walking through the Kampong, a botanical garden in Miami, Florida. His hand was clasped in hers. Sunlight played in her green eyes, making them look like an ocean of glittering green. She wasn't pregnant yet, but even despite that, to Ambrose, she glowed.

"Flowers, eh? I bet you take me to see some roses. Just like every man." Her voice was wry, her lips curving as she shifted her eyes to look at him, not turning her head.

Well, that had been my plan. "No, of course not. I just thought we'd enjoy the walk. I'm still thinking about what flower encapsulates you."

Her brow moved upward, "Oh, really. Any ideas?"

No, in fact, he had none. "I'm not spoiling the surprise. A complicated woman like you means you deserve a complicated flower."

"I'm complicated now, am I?" She had a slight edge in her voice, but she was still amused.

"Hey, there's a squirrel," Ambrose pointed.

Alice laughed, playfully bumping his shoulder with her own. "Nice save, mister."

That day, he looked up a bunch of flowers, trying to find something that fit her. He learned way more about them than he ever wanted to know. Even so, he found one that especially fit her, he felt. He bought it, and when it was delivered a few days later, he called Alice in.

"What's up?" She said, running a comb through her dark tresses.

Ambrose gestured to the 'Before the Storm' black irises he had bought for her. These irises were as dark as painted midnight, with just a slight subtle hint of purple within them. Even he found the flowers to be mesmerizingly beautiful.

"I present to you your flower!"

Alice walked forward, reaching out. She picked up one and brought it to her nose, caressing the petals. Her eyes closed, her face softening, a small smile playing across her lips. A moment later her eyes opened, "What are they called?"

He grinned. "'Before the Storm Irises'. Supposedly, these represent power, mystery, and beauty. All traits I think fit you perfectly well."

She placed the flower down and took his head in her hands, placing a soft kiss on his lips. "You're sweet. Thank you."

Ambrose cupped her chin, running a thumb along her lips gently. "The perfect flower for my perfect princess," he grinned as she shook her head.

As quickly as it had come, the memory faded, and Ambrose found himself reaching out to his dead wife before him, looking as real as that day.

Not all that glitters is gold, hatchling. Some burn with false fire. If you touch that thing, you will die as surely as if I had eaten you back in the dungeon.

Ambrose ripped his hand away. A hurt expression crossed the Alice he knew was fake.

"Why do you reject me?"

Hand opening and closing, Ambrose forced himself to walk straight. *This is too far, System.* He raged inside his mind. It was never simple; there was always a challenge. Usually, it was monsters or a puzzle, but this time, the System was making it personal.

Or maybe it was a creature? Ambrose activated his true sight, but he saw nothing but the same physical darkness. No monster out there, no illusions to pierce. Or, if there were, it was beyond his item's ability to undo.

"Daddy? You came for us, Daddy!"

Something tightened in his throat, a ball of moisture that he tried to swallow.

"No. Not that," he said.

He closed his eye, not daring to turn around.

The child's voice, small, vulnerable, spoke as if directly into his ears. "Where are you going, Daddy? Don't you miss us? Don't you want us, Daddy?"

He kept walking. Noelle sent him waves of concern, trying to wrap her thoughts around him as a layer of protection. The voice didn't care.

"I've missed you so much, Daddy! Don't go! I want you to play with me!"

With a fist, he knocked himself in the jaw. Not too hard, but hard enough that he felt the lance of pain shoot through his face. *She isn't real, it's a distraction, an illusion to make you wander off the path.* He repeated this over and over.

"I named her Jennifer, just like we talked about. Little Jenny, remember?"

Oh, light. I do. He swallowed again. The damnable lump wouldn't go away. He turned to techniques his father had taught him long ago. Within his mind, he constructed a flame, a bonfire that he fed everything to his emotions, his distracting thoughts, and the memories playing through his mind like an unwanted ghost.

All of it went to the fire he formed in the center of his mind.

He did this until all that remained was the goal—one foot in front of the other until he could make it to the end. *Stay on the path. Go straight, do not deviate.* With his battle focus came clarity. In the moments before the flame, he had been Ambrose, the grieving father.

The father who would have done anything to have his family back.

But now? Now, he was Ambrose, the killer. He was the cold SOB that people used to call in to fix their problems. He was the one who got it done, and he would not be deterred.

It was easy, now, to ignore the plights of the voices and the images that flashed before his eyes. Even when his "daughter" started sobbing his name, and Alice began to plead and belittle him. He walked on.

Finally, the surrounding darkness around him broke, and he emerged into dusty light. Before him was a throne, and all around him was treasure and ancient hieroglyphs. On the throne was a small golden lamp.

A feeling settled over him then.

A feeling that this was the dungeon's end.

CHAPTER THIRTY-THREE

As Ambrose took a step inside the room, the lamp on the throne pulsed with sanguine carmine light and rose into the air. Ambrose prepared himself, poking his *[Infernal Aegis]* skill with a mental finger to activate it. A swirl of black smoke poured out of the lamp, twirling and swishing like a wind being shaped by an unseen hand.

Flame as red as a glowing ember of a cigarette butt smoldered into existence, flowing along with the smoke as if being threaded like a needle. An angular, devilish skull formed in the air, solidifying from the air itself.

Coals of dark fire were its eyes, its gaping maw gnashing with jagged teeth of golden orange flame. From the black air, armor formed, forged from nothing, like sleek, polished obsidian in the sunlight. Crimson flames shone from the armor as if it were kindling, and a whip of dark fire lashed into the air.

Ambrose tossed a **[Retributions Gaze]** at the monster.

[Fire Djinn Level 188]: Djinns are elemental spirits. There are four types: earth, wind, fire, and water. They are collected by being trapped in magical artifacts and can usually grant three wishes to those who capture them. This Djinn's master died before it could grant its third wish and has been trapped here since. The Djinn cannot be recaptured until returning to its realm after being freed from its current captivity.

"It's going to get a lawsuit, is what's going to happen," he muttered.

Like striking lightning, it attacked, air whooshing and warping as the fiery whip blazed toward him with an eagerness to consume and burn. Luckily, his skill was enough to repel it. However, his skill was contained to his armor, and now, it no longer expanded around him.

It was an important fact to note because the whip was able to wrap around him and yank him towards the Djinn at flashing speed. Anyone else might have allowed it just to happen, but as he spun towards the being of fire and smoke, he opened a hellfire portal just in front of him.

He flew through it as the Djinn let out a roar like the cackling blaze of a bonfire during a starlit night. He appeared just above it, Akaroth in hand. Noelle billowed behind him, and Akaroth was roaring in his mind as he brought her down in an overhead slash.

Lightning arched, adding the scent of ozone to the burning scent of dust and ash to the air. The blade bit into the armor and was knocked away, sparking like he had struck a stone.

He landed with a clang of steel on stone and pushed himself back away from the Djinn as it lashed out with a clawed hand.

Its eyes smoldered, tracking his movements.

Then it launched fireballs at him. Dark balls of sanguine crimson, hunger followed in their wake.

Ambrose merely flexed a hand, opening a portal in front of himself once more. Sailing through it, the elemental attacks detonated not against him but the Djinn.

Explosions rocked the room, dust and rocks falling to the ground. Treasure fell, the noise echoing around them, mixing with the sounds of the detonating fire to create a cacophony of chaos.

Unharmed, it moved its arm upward and then down, sending the whip of darkness and flame his way.

However, Ambrose was ready and grabbed the elemental weapon with his left hand. Using all of his D-Grade strength, he pulled. Roaring, it was pulled off the dais.

He could almost see it put more mana into the whip as its fire tried to burn through his shield and eat him. Ambrose did the same, making sure his shield held.

Hefting Akaroth, lightning danced around her, and he threw the axe, after infusing it right into the Djinn's face. Its head reared back, and the gleaming stone that formed its face cracked.

Fire blazed in.

Noelle exalted him and urged him to finish it. Ambrose recalled Akaroth and attempted to yank the whip from its hands.

A cackling sound came from the thing.

It's laughing, Ambrose thought.

Vanishing into smoke, his hands closed around empty air, no longer holding the whip. Another whip threaded itself into the air, rolling outward in a fast attack that would have taken his head off if not for his quick thinking.

He brought Akaroth up in a parrying slash that kept the whip from his face.

Maybe I should get a helmet; Ambrose smiled a wry, grim smile.

Right now, he needed to take a different approach. It was a lot of back and forth, it wasn't going anywhere. Deciding to test the waters, he unleashed his spirit from **[Infernal Aegis]** and the pressure blanketed the room.

He expected the Djinn to have access to spirit, and so it wasn't much of a surprise when the creature unleashed a blazing spirit of its own to counter his.

For a moment the battle turned away from the mere physical.

The Djinn's spirit was truly an unchecked fire. However, Ambrose knew a little about fire, and his spirit was a match. He pushed, trying to overcome, but no, he couldn't.

Gritting his teeth, he flooded the ground around it with his mana, and used an ability he hadn't used for a while in a tactic he had developed ages ago.

Jaw working, Ambrose used **[Infernal Recall]** to pull the stone around the room directly upward with a boom like exploding rockets. Stone spun, shards ripping through the air.

And Ambrose fell along with the Djinn into utter darkness. It's whip struck toward him, a living serpent of flame that hissed and spat fire. He batted it away with the flat edge of Akaroth.

Falling through the utter black, lit only by the flames that swirled around them, Ambrose couldn't help but think they looked like falling meteors in the night. Using Akaroth's ability, he sent tendrils of lightning towards the Djinn.

It roared as the dangerous electricity did battle with its flaming form.

Ambrose summoned axes of flame, but the fire did nothing to the Djinn.

It must have an immunity; he thought with a frustrated growl.

He was tempted to send in Noelle to claw at it as they fell, but again he was worried about losing her to such a powerful foe. Instead, he leaned into Akaroth, blasting it with bolts of iridescent blue electricity. That proved to be most effective, but the Djinn quickly put a stop to it with a shield of dark fire it called into existence.

They fell for an age, fighting back and forth until Ambrose decided he needed to go all in. Raising Akaroth, he willed her into her true form as a storm brewed in the surrounding darkness.

Akaroth roared, lightning billowing around her like clouds formed of pure lightning. Ambrose fell onto her back as she opened her maw and let loose a beam of destructive electricity as thunder echoed around them.

Akaroth's wings flapped as some kind of solid surface of yellow rock came into view, quickly approaching. Its shield of fire repelled his dragon's beam, but it shattered into smoke and fire as it hit the ground in a detonation of darkness.

Begone spirit of fire! Akaroth echoed in his head.

He doubted it could hear her words, but almost in response to them, the Djinn began to morph.

This battle was just getting started.

Chapter Thirty-Four

Dark smoke and sanguine fire mixed, undulated, and morphed, changing and growing. Wings of shining stone lit ablaze, with membranes of shadow catching the sandy wind. Before him was what looked like a dragon of shadow and flame.

All around them was nothing but golden sand, broken stone, and darkness above, lit only by the dim light of the hole they had fallen through. Heat from the flames made the sand glow a molten cherry color. Akaroth roared, the hallow of her throat lit up with iridescent blue, the smell of ozone, ash, and molten sand hanging in the air.

She opened her maw, and lightning struck forth in a concentrated breath of arcing destruction.

But the Djinn wasn't out of tricks, yet. Its now serpentine head with burning coals for eyes swung around, and from its own maw, it unleashed umbric flame.

With a sound like tearing rock, and sundering flame, the two elements clashed. Lightning, shadow, and fire mixed to create a truly mythological image of power.

For a moment, it looked as if the Djinn might win the exchange, its beam pushing the lightning back. But Akaroth was no longer truly a dragon. She was an object, an axe with a consciousness, yes, but still an object.

That meant he could infuse it.

[Hellfire Manipulation] activated, and infernal mana rushed out of his core into Akaroth. Fires of acrid flame and gloom wreathed the blue lightning, giving it a rush of power. Ambrose could feel it when the Djinn put more mana into its attack, but it just wasn't enough as Akaroth's attack split through the shadow fire like an arrow splitting another arrow down the middle.

A detonation of thundering boom and wildfire shook the ground as the attack landed. Blasted away, the Djinn skidded against the sand, creating a molten trail across the ground. Akaroth leaped onto the Djinn, raking with her claws.

Like being shredded away, Akaroth's claws rended shadow and smoke. Moving like an eel, the Djinn turned, biting at Akaroth with smoldering teeth.

Akaroth pushed away, wings flapping, she rose into the air. Roaring, Akaroth breathed more lightning onto the Djinn, who rolled away and pushed into the air itself, wings of shadow creating a halo of darkness around it.

Flying through the air, Ambrose tightened his legs around Akaroth as the two exchanged blows. She lashed out with a claw, and the Djinn ducked its head, avoiding the blow.

Ambrose felt a little useless here, and the longer the battle raged on, the more mana he burned. Using [Infernal Sanctuary], he sent out chains of silver coated in a murky fire that he willed to wrap around the Djinn's wings.

He yanked on the chains with his will, and the Djinn cried out in a rumbling roar. Sending his thoughts to Akaroth, she enacted his plan, crashing into the Djinn and bringing it to the ground once more.

It tried to slash out with its claws, but the mother of storms ignored it, pressing all of her weight into the creature. Using her front two claws, she grabbed the snout and jaw of the Djinn, yanking them apart.

As she did, lightning built up in her throat, the ominous glow dancing with the shadow as Akaroth bent her head forward and unleashed devastation into the mouth of the Djinn.

Like a vase shattering in slow motion, the fire, shadow, and gleaming stone of the Djinn's body began to fracture, crack, and flake apart.

The Djinn didn't cry out in pain or rage. Instead, it let out a sigh. A sigh of something laying down a great burden. A sigh of relief.

A final pulse of darkness echoed around them as the Djinn burned itself out into ashes on the sandy wind.

Ambrose dismissed Akaroth's form, landing on the ground, and the axe settled into his grip.

[You have defeated a Fire Djinn Level 188. Due to defeating a foe beyond your level, you have earned increased experience. You have advanced to level 173.]

A satisfying battle Akaroth projected into his mind. She sounded utterly smug. Noelle was a grumbling feeling in the back of his mind. She was upset with him, and he knew why.

Consistently, Ambrose chose not to involve her in fights. He had a lot to get to and chose to give her some space for now. He rolled his neck and warily eyed the swirling darkness that coalesced where the Djinn's body had been.

Like the material of the body that had made up the Djinn, a dark stone with a center of burnished ember formed in the air. A notification appeared in front of him.

[Claim the Djinn's heart to clear the dungeon.]

Ambrose waved the notification away and focused on the heart, tapping his **[Retributions Gaze]** skill.

[Fire Djinn Heart-Epic]: The hearts of Djinn appear after the elementals have been defeated. It is an epic ingredient used for smithing, enchanting, or alchemy. It is said these hearts are formed from the leftover essence the spirits must leave behind when leaving the material realm.

He deposited the heart into his infernal realm. I've overcome another obstacle. One step closer to Eric. Having this, he had a real shot of allying with the dwarves and putting an end to this Incursion.

Looking at his advancement, Ambrose had fifty-six points to spend. Some might say it is better to leave it alone for now. He hated doing that.

He brought up his stats.

Constitution: 290
Strength: 290
Intellect: 290
Wisdom: 287
Willpower: 300

The first thing he did was bring all of his stats to three hundred. This cost him forty-three points. He assigned the final thirteen to his willpower. He looked over his stats with a nod. So far, he has maintained a fairly balanced advancement.

Soon, he needed to think more about his Icon. Maybe an axe? He ran his fingers through his beard. He used an axe often, but did he most identify with one? No, not really. He was more than just a weapon, even if he didn't feel it sometimes.

[Would you like to teleport out of the dungeon?
Y/N?]

He mentally selected yes, and in a flash of darkness, he appeared at the entrance of the dungeon. Now, he needed to return to the dwarf. He was eager to do so, and at the same time, he wasn't. He had been going at what felt like full-speed. Alice deserved that from him.

But a weariness had slithered into his mind and settled onto his shoulders. Fight after fight, problem after problem. He needed to take that next step, but that weariness was holding him back.

So, he took a break and sat down in front of the cave. He cleared his thoughts and allowed some images to come to him.

Was he like a hammer? No, I'm not. Maybe he was an inferno, but again, that didn't feel quite right. It wasn't wrong, though. That thread of thought called to him. He focused his mind, like he would in battle, and let himself follow it. Hammers and fire, was something there?

Yes, but what? He thought. A frown had curled his lips. He could feel the connection, just out of reach.

It was sometime before he decided to give it up and open a portal back to Aleksei.

A council with the dwarven king awaited him.

Chapter Thirty-Five

"You've returned." The dwarf took a sip of his silver flask, "Ah was wonderin' if you would."

Ambrose lifted up the Djinn's heart. "I have what you asked for. One epic ingredient. Are you going to keep your word?"

Aleksei raised an eyebrow, studying the heart. Finally, he let out a low whistle and spat to one side. "Ah would say you've done better than ah could have hoped. Alright, human, let's go see the king."

He followed Aleksei into the mountain's depths.

Under the mountain looked like how you might expect a mining operation to look, except with less modern equipment. Rail carts had been set up, with glowing stone-like flickering embers set up in sconces at various key points in the walls.

Somehow the dwarves had managed to hollow out the place, if the System hadn't done it for them. Dwarves mined in what Ambrose could only call a merry fashion. Tuneless, joyful whistling carried through the air, drowned out by the sound of pickaxes striking stone.

As they walked, he saw a few of the dwarves place ore in the carts, and then touch a glyph on the side of it. A flash of bright green light and the cart would zip down the railways deeper into the mountain.

"Aren't you worried someone will try to get in while you aren't up there?" He asked Aleksei.

Aleksei shook his head, "Baltair is takin' mah place for now."

Ambrose nodded, assuming Baltair was another dwarf. As they walked, going ever deeper, he decided to fish for information, "Where do you all come from?"

Aleksei fingered his beard, "We hail from Dweverheim."

"Surely not all of you came here," he stated to the dwarf.

Aleksei laughed, "O' course not! This is one o' our Incursion forces. One of our nobles becomes king of the force and leads it into the new world."

Ambrose grunted. He supposed that made sense to do if you were already an established world. "How many of you are there?"

If Aleksei had noticed the probing nature of his questions, he either didn't care or didn't see Ambrose as a threat. Maybe it was both. "There's a few hundred o' us. A solid portion o' us is D-Grade, too."

Finally, they came to a chamber with a solid path made of smooth red stone that led to a large set of golden double doors adorned with images. Dwarves were fighting winged serpentine creatures.

Dragons! They're fighting dragons! He realized.

Your kind fought the dwarves? He thought at Akaroth.

She gave the mental equivalent of a snort.

It was more like breaking twigs with iron claws.

The images unfolded almost like a story, from the bottom of the doors outward towards the top. They showed dwarves in mountains with piles of treasure and on thrones. Dragons would come against them, burning and slaughtering. They would settle into the treasure themselves, pushing the dwarves out.

Not to be deterred, the dwarves built massive ballistas with special stone-tipped projectiles specifically designed to pierce dragon scale.

We called them wing-clippers. The dwarves would shoot them through our membranes, ending our flight. Akaroth's voice was filled with pained anguish.

According to this, the dwarves were just taking back what dragons stole from them, Ambrose responded mentally.

Even the calmest lake reflects the storm, hatchling.

Her thoughts died off after that. Aleksei pushed the doors open to reveal more red stone leading up to a dais. On that dais was a round throne of gold with an emerald sheen. Countless jewels were inlaid into the seat. Frankly, to Ambrose, it looked somewhat uncomfortable.

On the throne sat a dwarf in gleaming silver armor with a simple iron crown. His features were as noble as a dwarves could be, with gray eyes holding within them a sea of wisdom. His black beard had touches of silver, and beaded through it were rings of iron. He was the tallest dwarf he had seen yet.

Smile lines were on his face, and his ringed fingers drummed on his throne armrests. His gray eyes flicked to Ambrose as he entered. Aleksei bowed low, but Ambrose merely nodded his head in respect.

Amusement twinkled in the dwarf king's eyes. "Not one inclined toward accepting any authority but your own, are you, boy?"

His voice was a river flowing over stone, merry, free, and touched with a hint of cold.

He shrugged, "I'm here to discuss a possible alliance between our peoples."

The dwarf king smiled, "It is customary to exchange introductions upon meeting someone new in my world. Is that not the same here in yours, boy?"

Ambrose frowned. He tried to push past the boy comments. "It is. I apologize; I am eager to be done with this. My name is Ambrose Severen."

"'Tis forgiven. I am Herne Throrvin, known as the Hunter King."

Akaroth growled within his mind, and he felt mental claws tense in anticipation of a fight.

Forget this alliance, hatchling. Let us raze this place to the ground and mount that murderer's head upon a spike for all the world to see!

He nearly blinked at the ferocity of her words but chose to ignore them for now. He'd dig into that at a later time.

"Aleksei informs me you have brought me the heart of a Djinn," Herne said.

Ambrose produced the heart, holding it out to the dwarf king. Aleksei took it from him and brought it toward his leader. Herne picked it up, studying it with a critical eye. He grunted in satisfaction, "A valuable gift. Very well, boy. Let us discuss this alliance."

Ambrose suppressed a sigh of relief. Finally, he was getting somewhere. He would close this obstacle and would be one step closer to pursuing Eric. "I have simple terms that boil down to live and let live. You can have this mountain, have the surrounding land, and in exchange you help me close the other Incursions. Once that's done, we live our lives. Maybe even set up teleportation arrays to visit one another."

Herne let loose a booming laugh that echoed throughout the throne room like rolling thunder. "It is not so simple as a verbal agreement, boy. I'm afraid we will need scribes. Aleksei?"

The dwarf made a strange rolling gesture with his hand, "At once, sire."

Aleksei turned and walked from the chamber. Presumably, to go and fetch this scribe.

"I've done verbal agreements before, the System backs them," Ambrose said.

Herne waved a hand, "Of course it does. However, it only backs the letter of the agreement. We must make sure to get everything in writing to cover the most ground. I will have my people fetch you a chair; I'm afraid you'll be here a while."

Internally, he groaned. He was hoping for a simple deal. Agree to help each other and not to kill one another, and move on. Briefly, he lamented not bringing Andrea along for this. Maybe he could go get her and bring her here? No, he dismissed the idea. She was dealing with Avalon's affairs; closing these Incursions was his responsibility.

Herne leaned forward, eyes flashing like lightning, "In the meantime, why don't you tell me why you have brought a sky slug in my presence, human."

Chapter Thirty-Six

"I'm curious how you know," Ambrose said, arching an eyebrow.

Herne growled, "What matters is your explanation, boy."

Ambrose resisted the urge to unleash his spirit and show this dwarf just how much of a boy he was. He never did respond well to threats or challenges. He blew out a breath through his nose, and his voice came out in a crackling growl of kindling embers.

"Let's make something really clear. I am not a boy. Among my people, I am a man. I have fought a man's battles, tooth and nail since the System arrived. I am a leader of my own settlement, and more importantly, I am a guest here who has given you a gift."

Ambrose bore his gaze into the dwarf's gray eyes, almost as if he were trying to drill a hole.

"You will show me the respect I am owed."

Herne leaned back in his throne, his knuckles whitening as he gripped the armrests. "I see there is good metal in you. You are right, of course, and I am sorry. I must still insist on an explanation before these negotiations continue."

Ambrose nodded curtly; he took a breath, calming his mind, and he relaxed his muscles.

"If it isn't obvious, I am unfamiliar with your culture. I had no idea your people and the dragons were at odds with one another. Besides, the dragon I brought with me is really a mythical item now, an axe with a consciousness of what was once a dragon, in truth. It was a reward for completing a dungeon."

Herne appeared to relax himself, grip loosening on the arms of his throne; tension bled from his eyes, replaced by that merry twinkle. "I see. This makes sense, and as you said, you were unaware of our history."

Moments later, scribes came into the room, some carrying a table and chair for Ambrose to sit down. The dwarves had also brought a map, which impressed Ambrose. He had yet to see one of those.

Negotiations began in earnest at that point, with scribes logging their words and preparing what would be the main document. There were many small details, things Ambrose frankly didn't care about, down to a guest finding objects on each other's land.

One discussion was very important because it involved Kellan and his people.

"This pact would not bind him, nor any other leader amongst your people. Unless they are on board, the Incursion will not be considered closed."

Ambrose ran his fingers through his beard, annoyed. He wanted to be done with this.

"How about this: you consider hostilities over with them through me. If anyone claiming to be a leader among my people attacks you or takes any hostile action, I will deal with it or support you in dealing with it."

Herne eyed him, "You would do this thing? Side with a foreign people over your own?"

Ambrose was already shaking his head, "I don't see it that way, first of all. Closing these Incursions is a priority, and besides yours, I have two more to handle that likely will not be as peaceful. My people shouldn't be fighting if they don't have to be. Anyone that can't see that is no ally of mine and endangers the whole. I will gladly correct that stupidity if it comes down to it."

Herne didn't look convinced, "Loyalty is important, especially among dwarves. I must say, you aren't showing much of it here."

Ambrose crossed his arms, scowling. "With all due respect, Your Majesty, you do not know me or what loyalty I've shown. I am loyal to the people of Avalon, and I am loyal to the goal I have set myself. Everything else, everyone else, is secondary to that goal."

Herne lowered his head before looking up, "Very well, I shall agree to that. I suspect that particular agreement will come due sooner than later. Those of your people living in this desert are led by a man determined to see us ousted from this land."

Ambrose silently agreed, even though it irritated him. Kellan wanted this mountain and had been willing to part as allies to see it done. He had an idea for that in mind: a show of strength. It would come later.

There were agreements about trade, land, what would happen when conflict arose, and more besides. It was so dense and boring that Ambrose considered the violent approach more than once. Water and food were brought at one point, even though he insisted he didn't need any.

It was traditional, so Ambrose didn't have much of a choice.

He managed to work on crafting agreements into the deal so Avalon could commission from the dwarves. He felt fairly proud about that one. More than once, he seriously wished he had brought Andrea along. Finally, they ratified a treaty.

There was so much to it; Ambrose wasn't sure the dwarves hadn't managed to add something sneaky to the document. He read it over many times just to make sure. He felt a little better after that. It boiled down to what he had wanted. Mutual peace, neither attacking the other unless provoked, with options to peacefully trade and teleportation arrays being connected.

Herne would also send a contingent of dwarven warriors to help close the other two Incursions. Ambrose stretched, feeling happy he had accomplished everything he had set out to.

[**You have closed an Incursion through an alliance. Two reward options offered due to recent choices. Would you like insight into a resonating Icon or experience?**]

"What?"

Ambrose couldn't help but say aloud. Herne looked at him, head cocking, "Did you receive an interesting notification?"

Ambrose was a little hesitant to share with the dwarf king, but finally he shrugged. Maybe he could tell him something about it. He told Herne about the notification.

Herne...looked shocked.

"Insight from the System on an Icon is invaluable, human. People have died seeking out such a reward. I would take it, were I you. You are safe here, so I would do it now."

I do not like agreeing with the dwarf, but he is correct. Akaroth grumbled in his mind.

Shrugging, Ambrose confirmed his option, and suddenly, he was no longer in the room.

Hammer blows echoed throughout the darkness. Above, set in a starless night was a full moon, ever bright, its pale light shown on the embers that sparked below with each strike of the hammer that echoed in the night.

A man was hammering something on an anvil as black as the starless night above. Ambrose realized the man was him, and what he was hammering was also him.

Bang! Clang!

Hammer blow, after hammer blow. The smith, Ambrose, was trying to put something inside of the version of him being hammered on. Or maybe he was trying to enhance it.

On the anvil, he glowed with inner fire. A storm of flame that wanted to be unleashed.

In this place, he was the forge, and the forge was him.

Like smoke, the scene faded away, Ambrose was blinking.

"Ah, you're back. Good. I hope you're ready, human. Already you must keep your agreement, for your fellow humans are here, and they bay for blood," Herne told him grimly.

CHAPTER THIRTY-SEVEN

Surrounding the entrance of the mountain were Kellan and ten others. All mounted on horses. All wore a combination of what Ambrose would call desert-style robes and gleaming armor. Scimitars were belted on, and Kellan himself wielded a staff.

The staff was made of wood and curled at the top like a question mark. It did not have glyphs or designs, nothing at all adorning it. Unmistakable power radiated from the staff. Ambrose would have sworn that the staff itself had a spirit of its own. Aleksei was frowning, staring hard at Kellan.

Ambrose knew why, too. Aleksei's spirit had fallen over the area like a canopy. It wasn't focused on Ambrose this time; instead, Aleksei's spirit was fully concentrated on the mounted warriors surrounding the mountain entrance.

Aleksei was frowning because it had no effect. Kellan was beaming, his rich voice echoing around them all.

"Now that we are all on even playing field, it is time for you to hear my proposal."

Kellan's voice became as hard as granite, "Surrender to me, and give me everything in this mountain, and I'll let you live. Don't, and I'll be forced to take more...drastic measures."

Aleksei's frown turned into a full-blown scowl. Herne stayed silent, sweeping his gaze around. No other reaction was forthcoming from the dwarf king. He was waiting for Ambrose's response.

The Infernal Paladin was still weighing his options. His instinct was to kill Kellan and everyone there. Even with the power of the staff he currently wielded, Ambrose was fairly confident he could take him down. Kellan was a forerunner, and he was dangerous.

But he wouldn't be expecting an attack, so he felt confident he would have the element of surprise. He wanted to go after Eric, and he had finally taken a step closer to that goal by closing an Incursion.

Just because he had closed it didn't mean he could walk away. He had an agreement he was now System-bound to keep. This was his mess, in other words. He wanted to clean it up through his most effective tool: brutal violence.

Part of him also felt that Kellan deserved it. The man was far too willing to butcher people just to get some wealth. Not even certain wealth, either, as Kellan could have no idea what was in the mountain. Even Ambrose didn't really know. He had no idea how to measure how good the metal the dwarves mined was.

He assumed it was very good since the dwarves were not willing to leave the mountain. Despite this, he tried talking first. Stepping forward, Ambrose said, "Kellan, I've closed this Incursion. Dwarves and I have an alliance. If you attack them, you're attacking Avalon, too."

Kellan's voice was hot, burning as he responded, "So what? Your little island wasn't very hospitable to me when I was there. I'm not afraid of you, Mr. Severen."

Ambrose shook his head, a little bemused. "You think you can take on both the dwarves and my people? The dwarves alone are probably enough of a match for you."

Kellan smiled. It wasn't a pleasant smile. "I'm far more powerful than you think. Here's my ultimatum. Three months. Three months to gather to resources you want and then to clear the mountain. If you help them, Ambrose, consider your people and mine to be in conflict with one another."

With that, Kellan and his people turned and left. Herne turned to Ambrose. "Well then, it looks like you have your deadline, human."

Since hitting D-Grade, Ambrose had yet ever to experience a headache.

He certainly had one now.

Ambrose returned to Avalon, but not to see Andrea, but rather Vivienne. So he appeared under the tree, closing the portal behind him.

"Welcome back, Sir Knight. I believe there are events transpiring on the island you should be apprised of."

As always, Vivienne stood beneath the tree, her hands at her sides.

He raised an eyebrow, manifesting Noelle moments later. The Arcane White Tiger promptly strayed away from him, lying near the water. Ambrose frowned slightly at the tiger. Her mind was walled off from him. She licked a paw, acting like he didn't exist.

He turned his head to look at Vivienne. "Well, hit me with it, then."

"It involves Andrea Pender, and a certain man named Cassius. They are at odds."

Vivienne filled him in on the recent town hall.

He leaned against the tree, feeling the rough bark beneath his fingers. He could go up to the island's surface and take care of it. It was his island; what Cassius wanted meant very little. He had put Andrea in charge; he trusted her.

This political nonsense was just that, nonsense. He would never let Cassius remain in charge.

Sadly, if he stepped in, it would just worsen the situation with Andrea, really. She would be seen as incompetent, unable to keep control. On any other day, Ambrose wouldn't have cared a wink about what people thought, but he was building a society here.

It was important for her to show she could handle things. Especially since Ambrose intended to go off on his own to another world. He didn't want to worry constantly about Avalon and what was going on here. He needed to know Andrea wouldn't need him every five minutes.

It meant that the people needed to trust her, too, and look up to her. If he solved every problem, it would be clear who the real leader was. He didn't want that. He wanted Andrea to lead; he wanted to be in the background, helping and investing, but not leading.

Ambrose had never had what one would call a real job, but he knew he hated micro-managers and wouldn't be one.

"Thank you, Vivienne. Keep an eye on it, but I have other things I want to talk to you about." He told her about the vision the System had shown him.

Unlike the dwarves, Vivienne did not act surprised. "System insight is very valuable. It also isn't cryptic, it was showing you a forge. How that connects to yourself and your spirit is for you to decide. You will know because your spirit will resonate with it. You will feel it as you feel your own hand."

"That's it? All I need to do? There must be more to this Icon stuff."

Vivienne nodded, "There is, but the first step, which leads to C-Grade is understanding what Icon fits you best. It's more than just knowing the right Icon; it's also understanding why it is the right Icon."

Ambrose leaned his head against the tree. *Why does a forge fit me, then?*

Obviously, he was forging himself. That was clear, but that didn't feel totally correct, either. There was more to it. He just wasn't sure how much more. Was it Avalon? Yes. He felt a click, but it was just a single puzzle piece.

He needed the other puzzle pieces. He just wasn't sure what those were. What else was there about a forge that connected to him? There was the hammer, and he wasn't sure how that fit in. It was a tool used to shape the metal in the forging process, so maybe that was it.

No click.

Sitting against the tree, Ambrose allowed his mind to drift, thoughts filled with the sound of a hammer on an anvil and the roar of a fire.

CHAPTER THIRTY-EIGHT

Andrea had come to the cemetery to check out Vathwin. It was almost as if she had been transported to a different world—a world straight out of a gothic fantasy novel. Dark stone had been carved into buildings, and a well of dark blue and black had been built in the center. Cold light shone from it.

Vathwin himself was within a small building tucked between some dark trees. Andrea wasn't sure how it worked, but what little she did know, she would say the area had been suffused with dark mana. Vathwin himself was tinkering at some kind of alter. On top of it were bones, crystals, and a knife painted with strokes of midnight.

"What is this? Because it looks creepy as fuck, Vathwin. You know you don't have to lean into the edge lord vibe, right?"

Vathwin, looked up. He really did look like an edge lord. Andrea had never been much of a gamer, but she remembered having a boyfriend who loved to play an online game, which he had a character that looked almost identical to Vathwin. "Miss Pender. I haven't seen many Avalon officials lately. What can I do for you?"

She shuddered as a black spider crawled up Vathwin's arm. A thin layer of dust hung around the room, mixing with the smell of old bones and dried blood.

"I'm dealing with an issue. A man named Cassius is trying to force an election. He says that we have no right to be tyrants."

Vathwin shrugged, "What does this have to do with me, hmm?"

Andrea crossed her arms, "Anyone in power that wasn't me could oust you from here, you know? Banish you from the island if they wanted."

Vathwin snorted, examining a bone before placing it gently next to a crystal. "My agreement is with Ambrose Severen. We both know he is the real master of this island, and the System enforces our understanding."

Andrea sucked a breath in through her nose, flaring her nostrils.

"Maybe, but do you think he'd be happy if he found out how unhelpful you've been with me?"

Vathwin shrugged, "I do not care. I held up my end."

Andrea felt her pulse quicken, a hot flash pulsing in her chest. "You live here, Vathwin. Does any part of you have any loyalty to us?"

Vathwin leaned back in his chair, finally looking at her. "Was my loyalty not proven when my draugr fought for this island? I do not mind fighting when an enemy shows up or helping with burying your dead and ensuring their souls pass on safely. I even provide healing, something else you have overlooked. But political machinations?"

Vathwin shook his head, "How do you humans say it? It is not my scene. Besides-" Vathwin waved a hand, "What do you expect me actually to do to help you? I raise the dead and tinker with souls. I am no spymaster, no politician. How did you expect this to go?"

Andrea's foot tapped. He had a point, and she knew it coming here. It was just that she didn't have many other options, and Vathwin was the only other magical type she knew of on Avalon.

"I was hoping for some spell, something that would give me information, anything about Cassius that might help put this to rest."

Vathwin stared at her. Then he sighed and picked up a bowl. He then picked up a small bottle on his work surface and handed both items to Andrea.

"The bowl is enchanted. All you need is mana-infused water, and it will let you search for people and locations you know or have been to. This is the best help I can offer. It is the only help I can offer, clear, hmm?"

Andrea nodded mutely. It was more than she had prior.

It would have to be enough.

Ambrose appeared in an honest-to-God tree house. It was high up, with a wooden bridge connecting it to other tree houses that extended across a large area of forest. A guard lifted a spear and lowered it when he saw Ambrose.

"You must be Ambrose. Tina has told us to expect you at some point."

Ambrose nodded, "That's me. I'd like to see her?"

He gestures for Ambrose to follow. "Follow me, then."

He did, over several bridges, before coming to a treehouse at what felt like the center of the forest. Instead of being constructed like a large square, it was like the people had pulled inspiration from a Viking long house and built it in the trees. Glyphs glowed on the wood, multicolored and bright.

How did they even manage to build this? Ambrose dismissed this as he entered the house.

In the center was a truly massive table that many people sat around, including Tina at its head.

Still, in her oversized hoodie, the teen was pointing at a map. She looked up as Ambrose entered and grinned, waving at him, hoodie sleeves waving in the air.

"Le chevalier! You made it!"

"As promised."

Some of the people exchanged glances but stayed silent. As Ambrose walked over, he looked down at the map. Several "X's" had been placed in what looked like key positions at the forest edge.

"This is our wall. It's massive, but these are the key points along its edge and where the Leshi tends to attack the most."

Ambrose crossed his arms. "You get attacked a lot?"

Tina nodded, "More and more every day."

Tina closed her eyes briefly, then opened them. "We've lost a lot of good people. But we're still here," her voice hardened, "And we will always be here."

"Are they planning a bigger attack?"

A woman with hair like moonlight on corn-silk spoke up from beside Tina. "Our scouts suggest that they are mobilizing, yes. Each attack has gotten bigger than the last, and it is getting harder and harder to repel them."

Ambrose flicked his gaze to hers. "Do you have a plan?"

Tina waggled a hoodie sleeve. "Yes, but it isn't a good one."

Ambrose cocked his head. "Well, what is it?"

She told him.

"You're insane," Ambrose said bluntly.

"It is the only way. Leshi will keep coming back otherwise."

It is wise to strike when the scales turn silver, I like this plan, hatchling.

Of course she would. It wasn't that Ambrose was against the proposal, it just had a lot of risk.

"Let me go alone. I have the best chance of survival, anyway."

Tina was shaking her head. "We are not your people, le chevalier. You owe us nothing."

"But we are in an alliance."

Tina frowned, "Maybe so. But you aren't the only worthy warrior here. A small team will go."

Ambrose sighed, "The more that go, the greater the risk. No, let me go alone. At least, if I die, you aren't risking any of your own people."

Tina's face turned troubled at that. She clearly wanted to say yes, the loss of her people weighed on her, visible bags under her eyes. Yet, the warrior in her didn't want to back away. Ambrose knew that feeling. So he gave her the push she needed.

"If it makes you feel better, I am not alone. I have my items, and they turn into powerful beings."

Tina took a deep breath, schooling her expression. "Fine, but only because I know how capable you are. Let's hash out the details. We don't have long before the next attack."

Chapter Thirty-Nine

Moonlight like crushed pears, played amongst the swaying leaves like a faerie out of a fantasy. An eerie breeze kissed his skin, and he could see his breath. A long time ago, when Ambrose was just a child, he liked to pretend he was a dragon out of myth, able to breathe frost to devastate his enemies.

Raylen had told him to quit acting like a fool.

The wyrm hoards what it should nurture.

Ambrose rubbed his face, shaking himself from the memory. Raylen hadn't allowed him to have a childhood, this was true. Except Ambrose knew why, *now*. He had been preparing him for what was to come. Somehow, Raylen knew the System would descend. He had known his Mother was integrated, and had promised her to prepare Ambrose.

There hadn't been time for a childhood.

Did Ambrose lament that? How can I grieve for something I never knew?

He brushed aside a tree branch as he walked. He headed into the heart of Leshi territory, and he could feel it. Silence could be a physical thing, sometimes. There was a weight to it, a subtle edge of wariness that all humans felt at some point.

Taking out the trash at night, that sense that warned you something was out there and to get back to safety as fast as you can. Walking into a bad neighborhood, shooting furtive glances because you know predators are nearby.

There was a tingle across his neck, like a light touch. Ambrose constructed the flame in his mind, feeding all of that to it. Calm focus replaced those feelings, his mind becoming a blade, a weapon he wielded and controlled instead of it controlling him.

Before him was a truly massive tree. The tree was a study in contrast with the tree of Avalon Ambrose knew so well. The tree of Avalon was a fantastical, otherworldly sight. You would find it in a world of light and beauty.

This tree was altogether different.

There were people in the world who carried with them a presence of wisdom. It was there in their eyes, in the way they walked, in the set of their face. You could tell that here was someone who knew a thing or two about life.

The tree before him was like that. Old. Wise.

And much like Avalon once had been, corrupted. Not in the same way, of course, but a wrongness hung around it. Permeating with that ancientness, it radiated around it like a spirit of its own. Seemingly carved into its trunk was a dark entrance that descended.

This tree was the heart of the Incursion. Months prior, a few parties had scouted it and attempted to infiltrate its depths and find a way to end it.

They had not succeeded.

It was a simple yet deadly plan; Ambrose thought it a little crazy at first. While the main attack was underway, a small team would infiltrate the tree in the hopes of finding it less guarded and finding a way to close the Incursion.

He had felt it was a dangerous, crazy idea because the few that remained were sure to be powerful. Fighting the enemy on its home turf was just a bad idea. He volunteered to go it alone because for this to work, the fewer people involved, the better. Further, he was the most pow-erful among them.

He had the best chance of success, and more importantly, he could portal out if he needed to.

At first, the original plan had been to go beneath the tree, kill any Leshi he came across, and find a way to close the Incursion.

As he looked at the tree, a different idea was occurring to him. You could cut a tree down if you wanted, but a tree's real weakness was something altogether more devastating.

Fire.

A fire could wipe out most of the forest, and Leshi were, from what Tina had told him, creatures made from nature. If it didn't work, he could still descend into the aftermath and enact his original plan. Either way, he didn't have much to lose.

Rubbing his hands, Ambrose held them out to the side. In his mind, he held the image of what he wanted to happen.

Using his core, Ambrose called on his skill [**Hellfire Manipulation**] and on each side of the tree, hands the size of huge boulders appeared.

Flames the color of crushed red berries, blood and spitting acid served as the flesh of the hands. As if Hades himself were reaching out from his realm into our reality, the hands of fire clasped the tree.

Up until now, Ambrose had used his skill in a straightforward way, creating weapons, infusing objects, and creating portals, but this was a mythic level skill for a reason. He could do so much more with it than he did. He was limited by a few things, his imagination being one of them.

A sound like tearing wood and hissing flame filled the air as the tree was set afire and the hands attempted to pull it from the ground like ripping up weeds from a garden.

All around him, the forest floor groaned as roots strained. Moon-light danced in the dark embers that flared in the air. The flaming hands tightened, yanking harder in response to his will.

Not unlike kindling, the bark of the ancient tree was set ablaze, and a howl of rage, and pain split the air like the sound of a chainsaw roaring to life.

In that moment, he knew that what he had done hadn't just hurt the tree, it had hurt the Leshi connected to it. Leshi were made from nature, and thus they were connected to it. Connected to the tree they had bound themselves to, they all felt what Ambrose had done.

And they were coming for him.

From the ground beneath the tree, vines shot up, forming into abominations with gleaming eyes of glowing green. He had flash backs to the root knights he had fought so long a go, but these things were more than that. They had an intelligence, and a connection to nature those root knights hadn't had.

Howls echoed in time with the rage and pain of the burning tree and the Leshi that poured from it.

Wolves bounded into the area, snarling, fangs gleaming with saliva in the light of the full moon above. Their amber eyes reflecting the dark fire of the flaming hands that even now tore at the tree.

A wolf leaped at him, claws flashing. Ambrose manifested Noelle who roared, sending out a claw of lightning that struck with wolf, turning its snarls into rage.

In the same instant, Ambrose pulled Akaroth out from his infernal dimension and cut a wolf in half, viscera raining onto the ground, the two halves of its body splooshing to the forest floor like limp, soggy meat.

Through it all, he kept a part of his focus on ripping up the tree. Leshi sent lashes of sharp vines toward him, and Ambrose activated **[Infernal Sanctuary]** sending out spectral chains of black fire to repel the attacks.

A sound of tearing thunder, sundering earth and a burning tree boomed across the forest as Ambrose's hands of hellfire succeeded in ripping the tree up from the ground.

With it came the wrath of the forest itself.

CHAPTER FORTY

Like roaches exposed to the light, Leshi poured out of the gaping hole exposed by the trees uprooting. Noelle roared her fury, and with it came a surge of lightning that burned and electrocuted any Leshi and wolves close by.

Flashing claws threatened to tear Ambrose's flesh, but a twirl of Akaroth ended the threat. As he fought, Ambrose sent ropes of wraith like chains coated in black fire swirling around him.

His **[Infernal Sanctuary]** wrapped around many of his foes, making it easy for him to end their lives. Noelle ended them with lightning wreathed claws.

It wasn't just wolves that poured into the area from the surrounding forest, there were insects and even a giant grizzly bear.

Its growl of wrath shook the ground, and its eyes held a wild light within them.

Akaroth sparked with arching lightning, and he blasted, slashed and hacked any enemy that got close.

Within the melee he found a rhythm.

His father used to call it "The Song of Battle," and spent many hours trying to get Ambrose to feel it. More than the clarity of focus, notes could be felt more than heard. His heart added its own beat, and his rushing blood gave it all depth.

Sounds of rending flesh, roars of rage, splitting air, all became like the rift of a natural guitar. Movements in time to it all added an ethereal beauty to the carnage.

Hanging over all of them was the weight of the Old Man's shadow, for he waited to use his scythe once again.

Attacks and unknown skills sought to end the Infernal Paladin, but his **[Infernal Aegis]** infused his armor, protecting him as the skill caused his armor to shed smoldering sanguine amber light like lava come to life.

He tried to use his spirit to suppress his enemies, but something met him every time. It wasn't the spirit of a single foe, but more like the collected spirit of every Leshi present.

Ambrose didn't have time to wonder how that was even possible as the bear engaged him.

Grizzlies were fierce, and huge. If that wasn't enough, this one was being enhanced somehow. Lightning that should have ended the animals life then and there, did nothing.

The bear just did not *care*.

Its massive paws batted at Ambrose, who flowed like liquid fire underneath the attack and slashed out with Akaroth as a counter.

Guts and blood should have been spilling from the animal after that, but yellow glyphs lit up the beast's fur, and his attack glanced off as if striking armor.

Ambrose furrowed his brow. He took a breath, and more spectral chains lashed out at the bear, wrapping around it.

Roaring in defiance the bear struggled against the chains, but it was no good. If not for the glyphs, the bear would be dead already.

At least, that was Ambrose's initial thought.

It was quickly disabused as Leshi began to flow towards the bear. A mass of bark, vines, and branches pierced the grizzly bear as it howled in pain.

Muscles undulated, sick popping sounds came from the bear's bones as its form elongated and grew.

Before long, what stood before Ambrose was an abomination of tree and bear. Two times larger than before, the bear had become a titanic tree monster.

To Ambrose's mind it looked like a tree ent that was vaguely bear shaped. Spirit poured from it like water from a hydrant.

He used **[Retributions Gaze]** to get some idea of what he was dealing with.

[Leshi Bear Horror Level 195]: Altered by the collective will and mana of the Leshi, this bear is now a titan of their race. It defends its home from intruders.

It's almost level two-hundred, fuck! Ambrose almost let the thought shatter his focus. The battle rhythm shook, and he nearly fell out of tune with it.

Lifting a massive leg covered in fur, bark and lime green vines, the bear horror tried to stomp on him.

In response, Ambrose opened a portal that he intended on stepping through and reappearing behind the beast.

Except it didn't work out that way. A vine lashed out, pulsing with acidic mana, and cut through his portal, shutting it closed in a burst of embers and falling ash.

All of his training came to bare to keep him in focus, and not standing there in absolute shock at what just happened.

Instead, he flooded more mana into **[Infernal Aegis]** so his spiritual skill would better protect him. Just in time as the massive limb descended with the inevitability of a crashing building.

He was smashed into the ground and if it wasn't for his quick thinking, he would have experienced what an empty soda can experienced in a trash compactor.

Dirt exploded around him as if he had fallen from orbit. Infernal mana infusing his armor flared as the limb lifted off him, allowing moonlight to shine on his currently prone form.

The limb lifted up once more, and Ambrose knew he probably couldn't withstand another attack like that.

Pale chains like molten silver and starlight painted with a brush of twilight flame, wrapped around the limb and yanked to the side.

Pulled off its intended trajectory, the Leshi horror roared as it was sent falling. Vines burst from its back, holding it upward and preventing its massive fall.

It was enough for Ambrose to stumble upward.

Hefting Akaroth, the sky above turned, churning with dark clouds of gray and blue. Thunder detonated with an almighty boom across the vast sky, leaves rippling from the surge of air.

From the wingbeat of a dragon, comes a storm! Akaroth roared in his head as lightning answered her call.

Noelle's form was a shadow of the storm as she leaped onto the bear, tearing fur and bark flesh, sending pulses of lightning into the creature.

Acid light popped through the night like a bubble from the horror as it howled, vines wrapping around Noelle and flinging her into the air.

Ambrose unmanifested her before she could impact the ground and the Arcane Tiger sent him a wave of anger at the action.

Glyphs lit up along the creatures form as lightning struck it. Opening its maw, acidic liquid poured from it in a tidal wave headed straight for him.

Using **[Hellfire Manipulation]** Ambrose created a shield of fire that he placed in front of himself. Acid met dark carmine flame, and the air warped and shook with power as the resulting explosion of sound added to the cacophony of the storm and chaos around them.

Some droplets still managed to touch him, sizzling as it burned away. His skill kept him safe, but a whole wave of the stuff might have gotten through.

Which was why he was worried as the bear monstrosity unleashed another wave of the acidic liquid towards him.

His fire flickered, and Ambrose put more mana into it, gritting his teeth. Vines from the forest struck out toward him like striking vipers.

Lightning collided into the vines, turning them to charred remains. But the grizzly wasn't done.

Like a rising tide, the acid flooded over the fire, and directly towards Ambrose's head.

CHAPTER FORTY-ONE

Everything slowed down as Ambrose's mind raced for options. His **[Infernal Aegis]** was likely not going to be enough, and he couldn't teleport away. Not with whatever the bear horror was doing to shut that down. More hellfire was likely his best bet, even with the acid going over it like a wave over a building.

Grimly, he set his jaw and, with a tendril of thought, pulled mana from his core to further power his spiritual skill. At the same time, he began to call more fire. Even as he did, he saw the bear's eyes flash, its jaw flexing as more acid poured from it.

It felt endless, like a dam had been burst open. Some part of him knew that he wouldn't be able to avoid or block this attack. There was something behind the acid, giving it a life, a weight, that Ambrose simply couldn't match.

Then he saw it, a faint outline behind the bear, something spiritual and yet beyond even that. Just behind it, an image of a tree shimmered. Barely visible, the tree was hard to make out, but it was there, and it was *doing something* to the monster's attack, lending it far more power than it otherwise would have had.

So, this is it then, Ambrose thought. He had nothing for this kind of power. No constructs of fire he created, no portal he could open, no spectral chains, no car he could infuse in time, there was nothing he could do in the face of whatever the Leshi Bear was doing.

He could infuse the ground, using the same trick he had used time and again, but there was no time. Plus, the acid was still coming, like an inevitable tide, it was coming, and it was backed by what he suspected was an Icon.

This thing was on the cusp of C-Grade, and it was a power he couldn't hope to match. He had to consider it an achievement that he had done as well as he had so far.

Ambrose didn't feel fear, he didn't feel anger either. Instead, a calmness surrounded him, clearing his mind not like the flame, but a wave of peace.

It was the brush of acceptance.

It was the knowledge that he was finally going to rest.

In his mind, he reached out to Noelle.

Thank you, girl. You were there for me when I needed you.

Noelle howled in his mind, a howl of utter brokenness.

Thank you for your help, I am sorry I won't be able to keep my agreement.

Akaroth did not reply.

Finally, his thoughts turned to where they always belonged.

Alice.

He had never been worthy of her. She had always called him her tarnished knight, and there was a reason for that. He *was* tarnished. Ambrose Severen had been a killer of men. He had spent his life in violence, inflicting nothing but cruelty and evil upon the world.

Yes, he saved some people, and yes he had tried to do some good in the end. But he was trying to serve clean water from a filthy cup. He had no idea where he was going, but either way, he was going whether he wanted it or not.

So, in his last moments he thought of his wife. Her wry smile, her sparkling green eyes.

Her lips on his, hands on his face.

The...fluff of her pillow? What is that?

Ambrose eyes rose as a wall of fluff like clouds erupted in front of him, his hellfire lighting them ablaze. The acid crashed into the wall of fluff and flame, and to his shock, held.

Oh, the fluff was burning down at an alarming rate, but more would just replace it. It gave Ambrose enough breathing room to move away, creating distance between himself and the monster.

As he did, his eyes widened. Off to the side was Tina, armored in her fluff armor like that of a lamb. Her eyes were shining in the moonlight, her jaw clenched, and a spear apparently made of clouds raised high.

"To me! For Britannia! For our home! *Attaque!*"

From the trees and bushes surrounding them, figures rushed out, swords, axes, halberds, and weapons of every kind raised. Arrows poured out from on high, striking the Leshi horror.

It roared, paws out, head shaking as air reverberated.

The wall of fluff morphed, and a giant goat creature stood there moments later.

It cocked a fluffy fist and slugged the abomination of nature right in the face.

"Yeah! Taste my fluffy fist of righteousness!" Tina called, pumping a cloud wreathed fist.

Ambrose shook his head, and then his body followed. He opened his mouth and crowed with laughter. He raised Akaroth in salute to the girl, no, the *woman* in front of him.

"I thought I asked you to stay behind?" He called out his question to her.

Tina shrugged, "My mother always used to say that the best way to deal with a stubborn man is to make him think he's won."

He tried to fight the grin threatening to overcome his lips and failed. He turned, twirled Akaroth once and set his mind to focus once more.

"Alright then. Let's get this show on the road."

He raised Akaroth high, and the storm above boomed its fury as he willed his axe into its true form.

Akaroth rose into the air, lightning dancing around her, she shimmered, and a moment later, the dragon's wings beat the air.

Behold, the mother of storms! She called, her mental voice touching all near her.

Combatants roared their excitement and hacked at the bear.

Tapping his skill, Ambrose fed infernal mana into Akaroth, and the dragon began to change. Almost like his armor, molten fire covered the dragon, highlighting each scale with smoldering ember.

The Leshi horror opened its maw to spray more acid, but Akaroth was ready, and the beam of hellish lightning she unleashed was touched with infernal flames that smashed into the bear's jaw.

It growled with pain as it was pushed back, more arrows peppering it. The goat warrior fell upon it, punching it with fluffy fists like a prize fighter in the ring.

"Fear the floof!" Tina yelled.

Acting on an idea, Ambrose flooded the goat warrior with mana.

The result was a demon born of fire and clouds. Sanguine and eldritch flame wreathed the fluffy warrior.

The newborn demon grabbed the bear's lower and top jaw, positioning itself around at the head of the beast.

Akaroth descended and pressed her weight down on the monster. It writhed, trying to free itself. Acid tried to build up, but the cloud demon didn't let it happen. With more force than he would have thought possible from a creature made of fluff, it ripped the jaw apart.

A sickening snapping sound echoed throughout the night, and Akaroth bent her head down to unleash a destructive fury upon it.

Fire, lightning, and the power of fluff itself was the monster's downfall.

It may have been nearly C-Grade, but it wasn't C-Grade yet, and whatever Icon it was using didn't fully come into play until one had reached C-Grade in truth.

Ambrose and his surprising allies brought too much power to bare upon it.

A moment later, it twitched and then went still.

A notification trumpeted in his mind.

They had done it.

Chapter Forty-Two

Mug slapped against mug in a slosh of golden liquid that splattered wetly to the wooden floor below as a triumphant "Hurrah!" boomed throughout the room.

"We have done it, mon ami!" Tina called, her eyes bright, lips spread wide in a bright grin.

Ambrose grunted, and sipped his...*what is this?* It tasted of some kind of berry, and honey. Normally, he didn't enjoy alcohol much, but Tina had pressed the issue and he gave in. Whatever this was, it was good, and he allowed himself to enjoy it. Just a little bit.

Tina was grinning like a mad cat, soldiers all around her laughing, jostling each other and pouring golden liquid down their throats.

Ambrose had manifested Noelle, and a group of fighters were pouring the alcohol down her throat, screaming their delight. The result was.. entertaining. Noelle stumbled away, looking for all the world like a newborn kitten. Her tongue snaked outward, licking the air, and her bright blue eyes whirled this way and that.

Then she promptly tripped over her own tail, giving rise to giggling laughter.

Smiling slightly, Ambrose checked his notifications.

[You have defeated a level 195 Leshi Bear Horror and closed an Incursion into your world. Experience shared with allies. You have advanced to level 185. Note that no more skills or skill upgrades

will be offered until C-Grade is reached and your class has been upgraded.]

Twenty-two levels was nothing to sneeze at. One-hundred and seventy-six points to spend. Since he hadn't looked at his character sheet in a while, he brought it up now.

Name: Ambrose Severen

Level: 185

Race: Human (D-Grade)

Traits: Ruthless (Uncommon), Giant Slayer (Uncommon), Reforged-Legendary, Infernal (Mythic)

Class: Infernal Paladin (Epic)

Profession: Knight Of Avalon (Level 35)

Skills: [Hellfire Manipulation-Mythic], [Retributions Gaze-Epic], [Infernal Sanctuary-Legendary], [Infernal Aegis-Legendary (Spiritual Skill)], [Infernal Recall-Rare], [Infernal Dimension-Epic]

Constitution: 300

Strength: 300

Intellect: 300

Wisdom: 300

Willpower: 313

SC: 9040

Attribute Points:176

His character sheet was looking solid to him. He had one mythic skill, and one mythic trait. That was probably way more than most people had, so he couldn't complain. His fingers tightened nonetheless. He had struggled against the Leshi, and for a moment, he genuinely thought that was going to be the end of him.

He hated feeling like he had given up, but his bag of tricks had run out at the time. If it hadn't been for Tina...he shook his head. He was still here, they had won.

But it highlighted a problem that Ambrose hadn't wanted to admit to himself.

He needed to slow down. He had noticed it back in the dungeon with Lizella, and Akaroth. He didn't ask the questions he should ask, he didn't gather the information he needed to. He just kept pressing on. He had access to people and beings that knew things.

He could have talked to Vivienne about the Leshi, or talked to Troy about buying relevant information on them. He may not have been blindsided had he done that.

Ambrose blew a breath out through his nose and bit the side of his tongue. If he just took the time to do some serious meditation on his Icon, he may not have had to have been saved by Tina. There were lots of things the tree of Avalon could do if he spent some time hunting down evil souls.

Instead, he rushed headlong into task after task. Not stopping to ask relevant questions, not stopping to consolidate power, or even find weaknesses of his enemies. For his whole life Raylen had been teaching him that knowledge was an important weapon like any other.

He hadn't even asked the dwarves for help, and they had promised to do so.

Ambrose sipped at his drink. He couldn't make it to Eric if he was dead.

He didn't want to, but acknowledging the necessity, Ambrose resolved to slow down. Grumbling, he addressed his advancement.

He dropped thirty five points into every attribute. He had one point left over. He took a sip of his drink, savouring the sweetness on his tongue and the warm tang in his throat.

Shrugging, he put the final point into willpower. He felt his core grow within him. Newfound strength rushed through him, causing goosebumps to break out over his skin. He clenched his fist and resisted the urge to shout at the zing of power.

Yes. He had made mistakes. Yes. He needed to slow down.

But the results were clear.

He chuckled, the sound lost in the cacophony of the party around him.

His stupidity had been rewarded. Anyone else might have been incentivised to keep being stupid.

Noelle stumbled over to him, chuffing and pressing her head underneath his hand. Her anger at him had abated somewhat since the battle.

He scratched her ears and she wobbled, slumping against him.

He still had one more Incursion to deal with.

But true to his word, Ambrose slowed down.

And allowed himself to enjoy the victory he had fought for.

Tina's palm slapped into his, shaking vigorously. "Thank you, le chevalier. Without you, my home would be no more."

Ambrose nodded. "Keep in touch, Tina."

She smiled at him. "But of course. We are allies, after all."

Like a bolt of lightning, a thought struck Ambrose.

They were allies.

For a while now he had been wondering how to help Andrea without compromising and making sure she could deal with things on her own.

But she didn't have to be on her own.

"Hey, Tina. Could I ask a favor?"

Her eyebrow rose, "Name it."

He told her what he wanted.

Her answering grin was all the answer he needed to see. Waving, he opened a portal beneath the tree of Avalon and stepped through it.

Vivienne stood before him here as she always did.

"Vivienne."

She inclined her head. "Sir Knight."

Ambrose took a breath.

No more rushing.

He had two things he needed to accomplish. He wanted to work on understanding his Icon, and he had a way to go about that, though it was unpleasant.

Secondly, he wanted to know everything he could about Fire Giants.

He decided to pursue the Icon option first. "I'd like you to replay some old memories for me. It's time I reviewed some of Dad's old lessons."

Vivienne inclined her head. "As you wish, Sir Knight." She raised her hand and Ambrose's world became an ocean of white.

Memory after memory played through his mind, not unlike when he was first exploring himself and his spirit. But this time he tried to connect it to his Icon, the Forge.

He tried to find out how he fit in it.

Already he had established that he was forging himself, already he had connected himself to fire.

It took many memories of his past self for Ambrose to understand another piece.

He wasn't the only forger. It wasn't just him forging himself, it was his past, and the people in it.

His father.

His mother.

His Alice.

These were the fires, the anvil, the hammer, and the blacksmiths. They made him what he was and drove his actions even to this day.

Just like that, another puzzle piece clicked into place.

CHAPTER FORTY-THREE

Eric Delrosa had been probing the Nidaros underworld for a while now. It turned out there wasn't anything organized at all about Nidaro's crime. There were criminals, something close to what you might call gangs, except the locals called them dark guilds.

They were adventurers unaffiliated with the adventurers' guild who had turned to banditry. The town didn't have an official slums, nor was it very dangerous. Eric was able to learn of a dark guild headquarters in town, an open secret.

Eric sauntered into the western part of town, moonlight and warm ember torches casting shadows on the road and buildings that looked like eldritch monsters.

A blonde-haired elven ranger in green leather was casually rolling dice on a small wooden table directly outside the door to a two-story wooden building. Amber eyes flicked upward, and a frown appeared on the elf's narrow features.

"Keep walking if you don't want to get hurt, human."

The elves melodious voice was touched with a dark undertone.

Eric smiled at the elf. "Take me inside."

Immediately, the elf rose and opened the door, leading Eric inside.

Inside the building there were displays of various monster and animal heads. Display cases held weapons inside them, and rugs with various abstract patterns were lain across the wooden floors. Orbs of soft light hung from the ceiling, giving the whole building a warm feeling.

Not at all what you might expect the lair of a vicious group of murderous adventurers to look like. In the main room, adventurers lounged, tossing cards onto the table. Voices could be heard before even entering the room.

"We need a score, supplies are runnin' low."

A grunt was the reply, "Could always set up a toll road, tha' usually works."

They didn't get much farther as the elf led Eric into the room. The three bandits looked up. One was clearly a mage, wearing robes and a staff leaning against the chair he sat on. He was human, thin and tall, with a mop of brown hair, and a scarred face.

His eyes were a dark brown, and currently they were wide with surprise at Eric's presence.

The second was a woman, ashen haired and wearing bright chain mail, a massive sword leaning against the wall near her. She would have been lovely if it wasn't for the fact that one side of her face had a nasty burn scar across it.

The third was also human, in dark leathers and two daggers on his belt. His hair was like tree bark, and his face was like a beaten plumb. A hood laid around his head, ready to be pulled up at a moments notice.

Before any of them could move, Eric tapped his skill.

"Do not move." Eric smiled as each of the adventurers in the room froze, faces morphing into deep scowls.

Eric looked around and found a cup and a wine bottle on a table; he filled the cup up with the dark red liquid and took a sip. He smacked his lips experimentally, "Cheap stuff. You might be wondering what I'm doing here. It's okay, I would be too," Eric rubbed his hands together before pressing his glasses closer to his face, "Suffice to say, I am your new leader. Don't bother disagreeing; you can't."

Eric chuckled wryly. He settled into an open seat and leaned back, swirling the wine in the cup.

"You serve me now. See? Just like that. Now that we've settled that, I have a task for you all. I want to know everything you can tell me about the forerunner in this town and the castle he resides in."

It turned out there was a way into the castle. A few days of digging turned up the blueprints, which weren't easy to find, but the elf, whose name turned out to be Eledin Fairbright, had turned them up in an old book he found in the library.

There was a tunnel that led to the castle's library. Getting to it was the problem, as you had to dive into the ocean on the beach below the castle. Then, emerge through an underwater tunnel. Unfortunately, the tunnel had been sealed off at the back of the library by stone.

What he needed was a skill to get through the stone without causing a huge ruckus. This too, proved easily solved through spell scrolls. Eric hadn't known it was possible, but there was a profession where you could imbue paper with certain skill effects for a one-time use.

The usefulness of these was that anybody could use the scroll. They also tended to be expensive depending on the grade and the skill imbued. Rock shaping at D-Grade costs a decent chunk of SC. Despite that, he bought two of them.

Luckily, Eric had gotten a huge amount of SC from his deal with Misaq before the System descended.

Buying the scroll was easy, and Eric did it through the elf. Just in case things went awry, Eric wanted to do as much as he could through proxies.

He also bought scrolls of water breathing, one for each of them. He wanted the others as shields more than anything, and he doubted he would need them.

The plan was simple: They would take the underwater tunnel to the castle library, use a scroll of rock shaping to get into the library and make their way to the forerunner chamber to deal with him.

There were a couple of hangups to this plan. First, he had no idea what this forerunner could do. That bothered him. He didn't like not knowing, not at all. He used a spear, and he felt like it was the one he needed, but he wasn't sure.

He had confirmed that Elgin was D-Grade, if at its peak. With that, he wasn't worried at all about taking him. His skill would work on him just fine. The spear did worry him.

Some mythical items had their own spirit and were bound with those that didn't actually have a spiritual skill. The caveat was that if you ever got access to a spiritual skill, you could no longer use the item.

Eric wanted that spear. But he had no spirit of his own, and if he wanted to have a chance, he needed to catch Elgin by surprise. This plan was the best way to do that.

He pushed his glasses up the bridge of his nose again, sighing. If this didn't work, he was in real danger of death, and that troubled him.

Eric had learned one fact about life long ago, even before the System cemented it: With no risk came no reward. Eric had no other options.

Ambrose Severen would come for him, and without that spear, Eric had little chance of defeating him. Such was the disparity between those with a spiritual skill and those without. If he had known this sooner, he would have never turned down the spiritual skill that had been offered to him earlier.

But guides to the System were guarded treasures, and those offered for sale were beyond his means. Mistakes happened; he had made one.

Now was the time to rectify them.

CHAPTER FORTY-FOUR

Obsidian is formed when volcanic lava cools so quickly that crystals don't have time to grow. It is shiny, holding a hint of the fire it once was. There was a reason it was called fire glass. The ocean Eric Delrosa looked out at reminded him of obsidian.

Black as obsidian, it reflected the twin full moons that hung in the sky, and the waters rolled gently. It would have been beautiful if Eric could feel such an emotion. Activating the scrolls of water breathing, he and the others dove in.

His experience with swimming beneath the ocean weaves was limited, but he was D-Grade, and those stats helped him now as he swam easily through the water. The tunnel wasn't hard to see, especially since Eric had taken care to purchase goggles. Getting into the cave mouth, they all emerged on the banks of wet gray stone, as sleek as an otter.

He was careful not to lose his balance. The last thing he wanted was to perish here, on the jagged rocks of this unknown cave. Ahead was a narrow path that they would need to follow to the library. First, he had the mage use a skill to dry their clothes.

The mage was interesting, as classes went. He had an elemental manipulation skill at epic rank. It gave him some control over basic elements. Sadly, he could do nothing about stone. Hence the scrolls.

None of them said much, which was a result of Eric's skill. They were in a trance-like state, aware and not aware of their goings on. They did possess some autonomy, but it was fairly limited. Eric was lucky none of them had access to a spiritual skill.

He had grilled them about it, trying to shore up his knowledge and he learned some interesting things. Apparently, spiritual skills were rare and when they were offered, very few tended to take them because usually they weren't great to start out with.

Eric had asked why no one knew this, given how they were essential to advance, and found the answer very interesting indeed, although it was nothing new.

The answer was power, of course.

Those at the top didn't want competition. The more people who had access to spirit, the more people who could challenge them. This meant that the information about spirit was guarded and rarely given out. The only reason the mage knew was because of an old book he had found in a dungeon written on the subject.

He had since sold it, of course.

He remembered most of the knowledge, though, and Eric had made sure to get as much of it from him as he could. There were two ways to get another spiritual skill. Either you could hope the System offered another later down the line, which was rare but possible, or you could defeat a sector boss.

Sector bosses were powerful opponents, especially if you were taking one without spirit.

Eric had considered pursuing one but chose not to. He was going the third route, finding a mythical weapon with a spirit of its own.

Mythical, spiritual weapons allowed a wielder access to its spirit, and Eric was resolved to possess one. The spear, Gungnir was said to be one of the more powerful versions of these weapons.

Eric resisted the urge to rub his hands as they emerged from the path, finding themselves in front of a massive wall. Using stone shaping, they morphed the stone until it was open, revealing the library beyond. It was a silent process.

Eric had made sure of that before buying the spell. It would defeat the purpose if he let everyone in the castle know they were there. The stone closed behind them, leaving nothing but a smooth gray wall.

The library itself was lit by orange lamplight that cast long shadows over the old shelves filled with tomes. Near the front was a desk area, probably for the librarian. It was quiet, likely because everyone was in bed.

Or he hoped so anyway.

The corridor was lit by more faint light, along with the moonlight that drifted in from the windows.

They did run across a pair of guards as they made their way to Lord Elgin's chambers, but Eric merely used his skill: "Be silent, forget you ever saw us. Go sleep in your room."

The temptation to end the guard was strong. It had been so long since he had felt that zinging thrill he so loved. But leaving a trail of dead bodies in his wake was precisely what he had been trying to avoid with this venture.

After that, they came upon Elgin's rooms. Two more guards in front of the door were taken care of much the same as the first. Eric had the mage scan for any glyphs protecting the door, and he turned up nothing.

Eric did rub his hands then. After what felt like an eternity, this was it. He was finally going to get the weapon he had came for. Everything pointed to this Elgin having the spear.

He took a breath, and slowly, with practiced ease, Eric opened the door.

The chamber beyond was a large room, with a massive bed, a desk area, a few dressers, adorned with pieces of art and expensive looking rugs.

Eric wasted no time, tapping his skill, he spoke the words he was sure would bring him victory.

"Wake up, you serve me now. Come, and stand before me."

Eric rubbed his hands, as from the bed, a figure got out. He was a lithe man, with a large brown beard touched with silver, and bright blue eyes. A scar stood out on his right cheek. He was dressed in green and gold silk night clothes. His bearing was straight, carrying himself with all the confidence you would expect from a lord.

He walked over to Eric, standing at attention, eyes glazed over.

Eric smiled, "Finally. Do you know how long I've been waiting for this, Mr. Lord Elgin? Go and fetch Gungnir."

Instead of going to a chest or anywhere else the spear might be, Elgin held out a hand. There was a pulse of black and silver gray light and in his hand was a spear.

Eric had expected it to look majestic, to be mythical in appearance.

Instead, the spear was made of a black wood, with silver font adorning it. The blade itself shone like molten silver, crushed pearls and captured moonlight. Glyphs like burnished gold shifted and moved along the blade.

That was the most fantastical thing about it. Eric's eyes shone with undisguised avarice.

He used **[Identify]** on the spear:

[Gungnir-Mythis Spiritual Weapon]: Said to have once been owned by the god, Odin, Gungnir never misses its target. This weapon levels with its wielder and can be blocked by anyone equal or above in power to it. Anyone wielding this spear may access its spirit, wielding it as their own. In addition, grants lightning resistance. Additional effects unlock at higher grades. Currently soul bound to Lord Elgin.

Not for long, it won't be.

Eric could see Lord Elgin attempting to fight off Eric's skill. Honestly, Eric felt a little disappointed. Elgin would be no match for Ambrose. He had expected more from this world. More from a forerunner.

"Take this spear and impale it through your throat."

A flash of sanguine liquid and pale silver, a gurgle, the scent of iron and then the thud of a body dropping to the ground.

Just like that, Eric leveled and achieved his goal.

Gungnir was his.

CHAPTER FORTY-FIVE

Ambrose now only had one Incursion to deal with. The fire giants. The dwarves had a solution, but the king was being difficult.

"We have a counter to the array covering the fire giants, but if you want it, you must solve the issue of these desert people that plague us."

Ambrose scowled, "We have three months to deal with that."

A booming laugh was the dwarf king's answer, "That man may have given you three months, but I will shave my beard and eat it if he has any intention of peace, even if we did agree to his demands."

"Kellan is mostly honorable. He'd honor his word."

Throrvin was already shaking his head, his beard like a moving bush on his chest. "I do not trust him. Honorable he may be, I will not sit idly while he gathers strength and prepares to attack my people. Not when you are bound to do something about it."

One should not allow a hoard to grow teeth. Akaroth mused within his mind.

She had a point. Ambrose took a breath. He had resolved himself to slow down, and yet even now his impatience prodded him to deal with the fire giants.

He nodded to himself. "If I deal with Kellan, you'll help me take down the fire giants' array?"

Throrvin stroked his beard, "More than that, we shall fight beside you."

Ambrose nodded, "Okay then. Deal."

With that, Ambrose opened a portal back to his car. Settling into the leather seats, he considered how he wanted to handle the striation.

The problem was not Kellan's people. No, it was Kellan himself that was the issue. He didn't need to remove the forerunners town or his people.

He just had to take care of Kellan himself.

So how do I do that? He drummed his fingers against the car. While he thought, he manifested Noelle who appeared in the passenger seat.

Reaching over, he stroked the big cats ears. She chuffed, licking a paw. Her blue eyes were like living sapphires, reflecting the desert sun and brimming with mischief.

For a little while she had been upset with him for not using her in critical battles. But when he'd almost died, her attitude had reverted.

"I know you want to come out more, but I can't lose you, girl. You're all I have left."

Noelle's blue eyes bored into his. Images flashed through his mind, a cub, and then a grown tiger hunting her prey.

He smiled. The message was clear. "I know you're not a cub but..."

She put a paw on his nose, practically covering his whole face.

The Arcane White Tiger shook her head. More images of her, and fierce lightning, fighting alongside him. Then a cock of her head, a questioning light in her eyes.

Ambrose sighed, "Yes. You're my partner."

She let out a soft "Moo" and chuff. Her eyes were firm, determined.

He rubbed her cheeks and bit his tongue before closing his eye. "Okay. Okay. I'll start trying to treat you like it. I guess it's the time for self-reflection and change, isn't it?"

Noelle snorted, going back to cleaning a paw.

What about you, Akaroth? You want to get in on this?

The cat said enough. Adequate for a kitten.

Noelle growled, lighting sparking in her eyes.

The dragon ignored her.

Ambrose turned his thoughts back to Kellan.

Any ideas? He thought at the dragon.

A dragon does not use deception. A dragon advances.

Ambrose grunted. Where had he heard that before? He blinked, suddenly getting it.

"Lions are proud."

A trait I find most disagreeable.

Ambrose snorted. *Pot. Kettle. Black.*

Akaroth huffed in his mind.

Turning on the car, he appreciated the growl of the engine that rumbled over the desert sand.

A bit of mana and the car thrummed with power and fire like some ancient beast from hell itself.

"I have a plan," Ambrose stated aloud. Now, he just had to hope it worked.

He put his foot to pedal and blazed across the desert.

Ambrose stood in the center of the tent town, and he infused his voice with mana, allowing it to boom across the city. "Kellan Akenyemi! Come and face me! I have a challenge for you!"

His words rolled like thunder, stirring the sand and tent flaps. People began to pour out of their tents, faces holding curious expressions.

Kellan appeared moments later, staff in hand, flanked by two men. His strong features were bent in a scowl. "Have an answer for me already, Mr. Severen? That was quick. It seems I have misjudged you."

His voice was thick with saccharine. It reminded him of maple syrup.

Ambrose crossed his arms and swept his eye around the area. *Yeah, plenty of people now*, he thought.

Lions were proud, they couldn't allow challenges to go uncontested.

"I challenge you to a duel. Either until death or one of us submits."

Kellan's brow arched, and Ambrose saw his hand tighten around the staff.

"I see. What is at stake?"

Ambrose shrugged, "I think you know, but I'll spell it out for you, I guess. If I win, you'll promise, under the System, to leave the dwarves alone. Permanently. If you win...well, I'm no longer in your way at that point and Avalon will be free for the taking."

He was risking a lot putting Avalon on the line. It was one thing for him to risk his own life, quite another to risk the lives of his people. But it had to be done. Ambrose uncrossed his arms, flexing his hand. He had never shied away from doing what was necessary, and he wasn't about to start now.

Kellan pretended to think about it, but Ambrose knew he had him. People were muttering, casting glances his way. One of his men stepped forward, a nasty sneer curling his lips.

"Our leader will tear you apart, foreigner."

Ambrose ignored him, merely looking at Kellan. He allowed a tiny, mocking smile to curl his lips.

That did it. His pride was too great to ignore an insult like that. His face went as blank as a slate, but his eyes shone with sudden smoldering hatred.

He gestured sharply, "Follow me, to our arena."

Ambrose did so, and they wound through tents until they came to a mostly clear area of sand. It was well away from the town itself. A crowd had come with, and they fanned out, keeping enough distance to hopefully not be in any danger, but still able to see the fight that was to follow.

Tension hung in the air like a thick soup, Ambrose was sure that he could cut it with a knife.

Kellan stood across from him, staff in hand. "Your terms are acceptable, Severen. Are you ready?"

Ambrose opened his infernal dimension, a small hellish tear in reality. He reached through and pulled out Akaroth, twirling her once in his hands. Sunlight reflected off the axe, and Ambrose put just a trickle of mana into her, causing a faint rumble of to echo across the plains.

All around, people shuffled nervously, looking upward.

"The question is, Kellan, are *you* ready?"

Chapter Forty-Six

A cobra the size of a large boat and the color of hot sand and burnished gold struck out at Ambrose. Silver chains formed of the mist of a moonlit night bathed in flames of darkest shadow, wrapped around the large snake and yanked it to the side before it could make contact with him.

Ambrose flared his spirit, but as expected, his spirit met resistance. Ambrose frowned because the opposing spiritual force wasn't coming precisely from Kellan himself; instead, it felt like the staff in his hands was pulsing with it.

Kellan lifted the staff, and the sand itself responded to his call, a pillar of it rocketing toward him like an oncoming train. Ambrose opened a portal right in front of him, sending the pillar through it and directly on top of Kellan.

Kellan's face twisted into a grimace, but he held up a hand, and instead of the sand crashing down on him with the force of a landslide, it parted around him in a cloud of golden brown rain.

Ambrose took the opportunity to form an axe of hellfire, cleaving through the cobra, which vanished in a burst of sand-colored mana. Kellan raised his staff, and sand began to coalesce around him.

Ambrose sent a blast of hellfire at him, but a shield of sand formed in the air, blocking it. This gave Kellan enough time to finish what he was doing, and a huge...creature of sand was before him. It was a giant lion creature with a swirling tail and glyphs of pale blue shown on its body.

Spirit flared from it as Kellan's voice roared, "YOU THINK YOU'RE THE ONLY ONE WITH POWER?!"

Ambrose didn't respond. Instead, he allowed Akaroth to draw on his mana and the clouds above began to rotate, growing and turning gray like an eldritch monster was forming in the sky. Kellan did not wait for the storm to finish forming but instead pounced on him with claws of sand extending.

Ambrose didn't try to dodge. Instead, he opened a portal, and falling into it, he fell through the air, throwing Akaroth forward. She took her true form, and Ambrose fell onto her back. With an effort of will, he manifested Noelle, and she roared her fury as her white form, suffused with radiant lightning, fell onto the sand lion.

Her claws began to rake at the sand, the lightning creating furrows of fulgurite.

Akaroth opened her maw, gathering power to unleash upon Kellan, the towering lion.

But the leader of Kweneng was not interested in just sitting there. He let out a thundering roar, reared up a massive paw of sand, and struck a blow against Akaroth; her face pushed to the side from the force of it, she prematurely unleashed the beam she had been building, and the surrounding crowd around us screamed and scattered.

Turns out, they had not created enough distance after all.

Destructive lightning, crackling, and spitting turned the very sand black. Kellan's maw opened and he tried to go for Akaroth's throat.

But Noelle was not idle, she had been running up the lion's body and bounded upward, falling like a flashing bolt of white, she smashed into his head. Akaroth reared, and Ambrose flooded infernal mana into her. As he did, he unmanifested Noelle as she was falling from Kellan's head.

Akaroth began to warp as stygian eldritch veins of liquid flame shot through her form. Her eyes glowed as her pupils gained a subtle hint of carmine light. Her wings became wreathed in the same fire, and she breathed lightning and hellfire upon Kellan.

It was at this point that Ambrose pulled out his trump card.

Before visiting Kellan, and after dealing with the Leshi incursion, he had gone to the tree of Avalon and meditated on his Icon. Another piece of the puzzle had slid into place, and now...now he could call upon it.

Akaroth's power, fueled by his infernal mana, blasted into Kellan, and the moment it did, Ambrose called upon his Icon.

The Forge Icon was faint; Ambrose still needed to do more work meditating and understanding how he was connected with it, but it was a power Kellan couldn't match. Not as he was, not even with his staff.

It was almost an afterimage, straight out of a fantasy story, and drawn by an amazing illustrator of shadow and light. Ambrose wasn't quite sure what the Icon did, but calling upon it was as easy as tapping his mana with his will.

The Forge, though not fully in focus, gave weight and power to his attack that Kellan couldn't match. It was as if Ambrose's attack was more real, more present than Kellan. Blasting through the sand as if it weren't there, the hellfire and lightning stripped the sand bare to reveal Kellan at its core.

His eyes widened, and his mouth opened in a scream of fury and pain.

Spirit flared, lashing out like a whip, but Ambrose's own spirit, backed by the power, as faint as it was, of his Icon, quickly crushed it like a bug.

Ambrose watched as Kellan screamed, eyes wild, as his flesh began to turn to ash before his very eyes.

"NOT LIKE THIS!" Kellan bellowed.

Ambrose said nothing in reply; he poured on the power, and it wasn't long before the forerunner, leader of Kwenang, was nothing more than ashes on a desert wind. Surprisingly, Ambrose gained nothing for his death.

He had thought that Kellan might decide to submit, but proud till the end, he had refused.

Ambrose had no desire to lead Kwenang and didn't even bother trying to help the town find a new leader. Nor did he even try to look for the System Seed. Instead, he poured mana into his voice and allowed it to roll forth, carrying to every ear in the area.

"Your leader is dead. Slain in a formal System-recognized duel. You will no longer be able to threaten the dwarves. I will be sending ambassadors from Avalon to discuss new terms with your people and help establish a new leader if you so desire. It didn't have to be this way, but it is. Let it be a lesson not to cross me."

Ambrose left through a portal, Akaroth retaking her axe form.

A dragon does not suffer fools, and neither, it seems, do you, Knight.

Noelle sent him feelings of satisfaction as he reappeared at the dwarven entrance. Aleksei greeted him by offering him alcohol, which he turned down. Aleksei led him down, and before long, he was once again before Throrvin, the dwarven king.

Throrvin fingered his beard, "It appears you return victorious."

Ambrose nodded, "Yes, Kellan Akenyemi will no longer be troubling you. Or anyone, for that matter."

Throrvin did not react jubilantly at his words, instead he merely grunted.

"Now, it's your turn. I want your help with the fire giants. You said you had a way to deal with their array."

Thorvin smiled, "Indeed, human. But I will offer more than that." He clapped his hands, and Aleksei came in with a map.

Throrvin unrolled the scroll, gesturing at Ambrose to come forward.

When he laid his eye on the scroll, he blinked.

Throrvin's smile grew.

Chapter Forty-Seven

T ina looked bored as Ambrose, the contingent of dwarves given to him by Throrvin, and the other fighters went over the plan.

"We will use our dwarven friends earth shaping ability to create a tunnel from this point here, just outside the start of fire giant territory, and use that tunnel to get underneath their base. Another use of the ability should allow us to launch a surprise assault. Any questions?"

Tina raised a hand, the sleeve of her hoodie drooping down her forearm.

Ambrose pointed at her, rolling his eye at the exaggerated way she wove her arm.

"Have you tried talking to them, le chevalier? After all, you managed to convince our bearded fellows here to join in on an alliance."

Ambrose nodded, "I have. They won't bother even saying anything to me; they simply attack."

Tina frowned, and Aleksei grunted. "Ah haven't had a good fight in a while, but perhaps we should conduct some observations first, eh?"

Ambrose was already shaking his head, "I've tried that, too. As I said when I first approached you about this, I cannot get past their shield, and the walls cover their activity. I will say that most I have encountered haven't been much of an issue for me so far."

Throrvin stroked his beard. "Maybe so, but do not underestimate them. They are powerful foes."

Ambrose eyed the dwarf king. "Have you fought them before?"

Throrvin inclined his head. "Yes, I have. They force they sent here will not be too powerful; the System places limitations, but there will be at least one close to C-Grade."

Ambrose wasn't that worried about that, as he could manifest his Icon. It was the weakest version of an Icon one could have, but it gave him a power unmatched by any foe he had yet to meet.

The quiet hunter brings down the bold dragon, Akaroth mused in his mind. He had to acknowledge the dragon's point. He couldn't grow too cocky. Despite that, he couldn't help but feel a little excited. This was the last Incursion, and then, finally, he could pursue Eric.

"Is anyone from Avalon going to be joining us?" Tina asked.

Ambrose shook his head, "No. It's just me. I said I would handle the Incursions on my own, and this is me doing that."

Tina pursed her lips, looking as if she wanted to say something but choosing not to.

Ambrose didn't ask for her thoughts. He had told her she didn't need to bring anyone else along, and she had chosen to bring them anyway. Not that it was a problem, he was merely speculating.

After going over some of the fire giants' abilities Ambrose had seen in action, and a loose plan involving keeping a lookout for each other, it was time to move out.

Ambrose closed his fingers into a fist.

Soon.

Charging forward from the tunnel, Ambrose exploded into a little slice of hell made manifest in the world. All around him was black stone, a mini mountain with a waterfall of lava into a basin of liquid fire that warped the air.

Huge houses were made from obsidian and dark wood. Fire giants, tall creatures with hair of flowing fire, dark armor and molten-colored skin, walked around, living what Ambrose presumed to be normal lives for them.

When they saw intruders, they bellowed and summoned weapons wrought from black metal and flame. They charged, shaking the earth with their steps.

Tina called fluff to her, turning her into a giant ram made of clouds. She engaged a fire giant with a massive cloud hammer.

"BEHOLD, YOUR FLUFFY DOOM APPROACHES!" Tina called, a mad grin suffusing her face.

Her hammer swung with the force of a thunderclap, smashing into the fire giant and creating an impression on the hammer like a tempurpedic bed. The giant's face contorted, and red saliva spurted from its mouth.

Arrows began to pepper other giants as Tina's people let loose. Aleksei shaped earth into massive boulders of dark stone that he hurled at giants. Ambrose used [Infernal Sanctuary] and his wraith-like chains writhing with ghostly black fire wrapped around giants, pulling them downward as they cried out in anguish.

Dwarves hacked and slashed at the fallen giants, killing them in sprays of blood and cries of pain.

A roar like a burning fire shocked through the air. Emerging from a larger building was a massive fire giant, holding an axe that was black as night and burning with scarlet flame. His eyes, filled with hatred, locked onto Ambrose, and he hefted his axe. Muscles bulging, he threw the massive axe at him.

Ambrose felt his mouth twitch as he considered the irony of someone else attacking him in a similar fashion he attacked others. Calling on his skill, he willed his chains to block the axe, which detonated in an explosion of crimson and abyssal fire.

Bellowing, the giant rushed forward, holding his massive hand out. The giant recalled his axe, and it slapped into his palm with a boom like a crashing boulder.

Deciding to respond in kind, Ambrose hefted Akaroth and flung it at the giant's head, hellfire and lightning surrounding the axe like a cloak. The fire giant struck his axe out of the air with his own, but Ambrose responded instantly by recalling it before it could hit the ground.

A spark of fire in the giant's left hand grew, twisting and blowing until a tornado of flame was between them. Ambrose was already using [Infernal Aegis], and his spiritual skill was already protecting him, though the giant before him was countering his spirit.

However, it was here that he used his connection to his Icon. Ambrose didn't fully understand how he connected to the Forge. He understood enough to use the Icon in its absolute weakest form, but how exactly that power expressed itself wasn't fully known to him.

One thing Ambrose was certain of was that the Forge built things, improved them, and supported them. Like adding support structures to his skill, [Infernal Aegis] became deeper, became more connected to reality.

As best as he could figure it, the giants attack had become more of a fantasy, on a different realm than he was.

He had nothing to fear from the tornado, but his allies certainly did. Sadly, he could only worry about himself. Luckily, his allies had eyes and worked to protect themselves. Tina called up a wall of fluff that burned like marshmallow in a campfire. Aleksei used a shield of stone, but he brought it up some ways away from him so as not to have the heated rock burn him.

Ambrose rolled through the tornado, not even feeling the fire, thanks to his spirit and Icon. With a slash of Akaroth, he sent forward a slash of lightning.

The giant was not expecting his own attack to do absolutely nothing, and thus he hadn't prepared a defense. Lightning tore into his skin, and pain tore from his throat in a scream of fury. Thrusting his hands forward, the giant sent forth a tide of flame from his fingers.

Ambrose used **[Hellfire Manipulation]**, and a portal split the air.

It was time to end this.

CHAPTER FORTY-EIGHT

Blazing flame passed through Ambrose's portal of hellfire and directly on top of the fire giant. Sadly, the fire didn't appear to harm the giant much at all, his flesh unburnt. His eyes burned with annoyance, and he flung his axe at Ambrose once more, but he was already gone, stepping through a portal.

Ambrose had won this fight. Unfortunately for this giant, he couldn't harm the Infernal Paladin, not with the access he had to his Icon. There was only one question, and that was how to finish this fight. He had appeared behind the giant, and Tina and his allies were easily mopping up the other giants.

Tina's hammer of fluff was wrecking giant after giant, her eyes flashing with mirth and satisfaction. Aleksei and his fellow dwarves were bringing the giants low, finishing them off with their weapons and abilities.

Ambrose manifested Noelle to assist, the arcane white tiger bounding forward in flashes of viridian blue lightning, striking out at the giants with sharp, gleaming claws. She tore into tendons, sent blasts of lightning, and raked fallen giants with the ferocity of a storm.

He had a few options for how to deal with this giant, to finish the battle. He could use [**Infernal Recall**] to sink the giant into the earth, but a sudden thought struck him, he flicked his eyes upward and then nodded to himself.

With a gesture, and a surge of mana into **[Hellfire Manipulation]** Ambrose opened a portal of hellfire below the giant. With the second portal opening at least one-hundred and fifty feet in the air.

No one was expecting orbital giant, and everyone present paused for a moment to see the huge giant fall like a meteor to the ground.

The result was...interesting to say the least. The fire giant was at least high D-Grade, so the fall didn't kill him. However, it was still a massive fall, and apparently the monster didn't have a gravity defying skill as the impact with the ground sent an explosive, thundering rumble all across the area, the ground cracking outward as if the giant had preformed a super hero landing.

A sickening crack split the air as the giants legs crunched, twisting to an awkward angle. The giants roar was like that of lightning striking a tree. His body writhed, and even as he tried to pick himself up.

Ambrose walked forward, and with a boot, he pushed the giant over, who growled in pain.

He looked into the giants eyes, and activated **[Retributions Gaze]**.

Within the giant, his soul lit flame, and for the first time, the giant felt what it was like to burn. He thrashed, saliva foaming up from his mouth, his eyes unable to tear away from Ambrose's gaze, his skill holding him hostage as it turned the giants soul into ashes.

It wasn't long before the fire giant was nothing more than an empty husk.

Tina swore softly, having come near him to watch. "Remind me to never tangle with you, le chevalier. You are terrifying."

When she finished speaking, a notification dinged within him mind.

[You have closed Earth's final Incursion! Those involved have gained experience, but as you were the one to defeat this Incursions leader, you have earned an increased amount. You have advanced to level 220. You are now a C-Grade Being! Note, you

**have a class upgrade available. You have earned one Word of Power.
Make selections now?**

Y/N?]

Ambrose dismissed the notification for now, briefly wondering what a Word of Power was. He turned to his allies, who appeared to be reading their own notification.

"How interesting, I have earned insight into my icon?"

Tina flicked her eyes to him. "I believe we are even, mon ami, yes?"

Ambrose nodded, "Thank you for your help. All of you."

Aleksei nodded, flicking a hand, "Yah helped us, only right to return the favor, methinks." He stroked his beard.

After that, they looted the area, but Ambrose found nothing he cared about. He was eager to get a move on. Eric was waiting, and Ambrose didn't want to disappoint him. He hadn't forgotten his resolve to be more patient, and he had questions for Vivienne.

After returning everyone via portal to their homes and wishing them well, Ambrose went to the Tree of Avalon.

———————————

Vivienne greeted him as she normally did, with an inclination of her head. Ambrose cocked his head at her, struck with a sudden thought.

"Hey, Viv?"

"Yes, Sir Knight?"

"What do you do? Surely your entire existence isn't to just hang around and answer my questions whenever I have them."

Vivienne's lips twitched. "As I have always done, I maintain the island, Sir Knight. The limited defenses, the ones contained beneath, the protocols they go through, all of it. I also watch those on Avalon, acting as what your society referred to as a surveillance system."

Ambrose stroked his beard. "Okay, that makes sense. Anyway, as it happens, I do have questions."

Vivienne did smile then. "Of course."

"What are Words of Power?"

"Words of Power are...think of them as command words for reality. Except that is not quite right, as it goes beyond language."

She cocked her head, putting a finger on the side of her cheek. Above, the Tree of Avalon swayed, multicolored lights broke and danced.

"Words of Power are related to an Icon, and contained within the word are certain ways of commanding reality. This is the best explanation I can give that your mind would understand."

"What do you mean about it being related to my Icon?"

"Just what I said, Sir Knight. Say one's Icon is water, Words of Power available to that Icon would have something to do with water. Drain, for example, might be a Word that one might use."

Ambrose frowned, trying to understand, "But that's vague. Drain could mean anything."

"This is why will and Icon are important. The word might be used to drain a human being of all their water, or perhaps evaporate the moisture from some land."

Ambrose felt his mouth fall open. "That is...almost terrifying."

"Indeed. Words of Power are powerful. Having access to one at C-Grade...the System has rewarded you handsomely, Sir Knight."

Ambrose leaned against the tree. All the power he could gather would only help him. At this point, he didn't think Eric had much of a chance. When he found him, and he would find him...there would be novels written about what happened to him.

That didn't mean he could underestimate Eric, but the last time they had met, Eric hadn't even had access to spirit, that alone would leave him so disadvantaged, he may as well be a child.

However, Ambrose now knew that items could give you access to spirit, such as Kellan's staff. Idly, he kicked himself for not picking up his staff, but at the time he hadn't been concerned about it. He had spirit, but he could have sold the staff.

Eric could get access to a similar item, and in fact, due to what he had found in his office weeks ago, he was certain that was what Eric was going after.

Taking a deep breath, he turned his attention to his progression.

Time to upgrade his class.

CHAPTER FORTY-NINE

Ambrose sat down against the tree. Class upgrades felt serious to him, it would establish his path further and how he progressed in the world. It informed the skills he would later receive, and likely shape how his existing skills upgraded. Before he got down to it, he wanted to see his character sheet now before he did anything to it:

Name: Ambrose Severen
Level: 225
Race: Human (D-Grade)
Traits: Ruthless (Uncommon), Giant Slayer (Uncommon), Reforged-Legendary, Infernal (Mythic)
Class: Infernal Paladin (Epic)
Profession: Knight Of Avalon (Level 35)
Skills: [Hellfire Manipulation-Mythic], [Retributions Gaze-Epic], [Infernal Sanctuary-Legendary], [Infernal Aegis-Legendary (Spiritual Skill)], [Infernal Recall-Rare], [Infernal Dimension-Epic]
Constitution: 335
Strength: 335
Intellect: 335
Wisdom: 335
Willpower: 349
SC: 9400

Attribute Points: 320

Studying his sheet, he summoned Noelle, and the white arcane tiger settled down next to him, head in his lap. She was due an upgrade as well, and Ambrose felt fairly sure that would come after he selected his class upgrades.

Idly, he scratched Noelle's ears. He decided to assign his points before he looked at his potential classes. He had gained forty levels for closing the final Incursion, which was wild to him, but he wasn't the one deciding. More power was welcome, since it served his goals.

Assigning his points was easy, he just put sixty-four points into each of his five stats. When he was done, he brought up just his new stats:

Constitution: 399
Strength: 399
Intellect: 399
Wisdom: 399
Willpower: 413

He was beginning to feel truly powerful, and he wasn't even done progressing yet. Willing his answer to the System, he brought up his class choices:

[Infernal Crusader of Realm Walking-Legendary (Sage)]: Infernal Crusaders bring their will and fight to all realms. They use portals not just as a means of travel, but of attack. With this class you are able to freely manipulate portals, and are able to open up multiple portals. +10 attribute points per level up.

Ambrose liked the class. The portals he currently used allowed him a lot of tactical freedom. He could use them to get around the battlefield, redirect attacks, and even dodge if need be. This class would also give him the freedom to go wherever he wished.

That was useful in more ways than one. First of all, he would need to start hunting down criminals again. His profession was falling behind, and Avalon needed energy. He had neglected it so far, and though he had gotten away with it so far, he felt like it wouldn't be long before that might bite him in the ass.

Being able to realm walk, as the class called it, would give him options.

He pulled up another class:

[Infernal Paladin-Legendary (Sage)]: Continue down the same path you have walked so far. Being farther down the path, you grow in power. +10 attributes per level.

It wouldn't be a bad idea to continue as he had been. There was something to be said for not fixing what wasn't broken. It just felt stagnate, like he wasn't moving forward.

Marking it with a mental maybe, he moved on:

[Infernal Lumberjack-Legendary (Sage)]: Your power with an axe is unmatched. Wield infernal powers related to the axe and-

Ambrose dismissed the notification, not bothering to read it further. He wasn't interested in focusing on a single weapon. He moved on to the last option:

[Infernal Wizard-Legendary (Sage)]: Wizards use skills through incantations and lean into using Words of Power. People on this path are on the path to power and some would say is even beyond the System. +10 to attributes per level.

Ambrose paused in scratching Noelle, who chuffed at him, letting out a little mooing sound. She batted his hand for him to keep going, and after a moment, he did. The class offered looked simple on the surface, but he knew it was anything but.

He wasn't interested in a pure skill path, which this seemed to be. What he *was* interested in was the Words of Power. Something told him that selecting this class would make using, and acquiring Words of Power a lot easier.

However, the problem was that he didn't want to be a wizard. Wizards were squishy, as one of his very first encounters had shown. If Words of Power were locked behind the class, then that would decide the matter for him. But that wasn't so, because he had already gained access to one.

Clearly, that meant he didn't need the class. Power beyond the System was alluring, but Ambrose felt like that was because of the Words of Power.

Infernal Crusader and Infernal Paladin appealed to him more. Infernal Paladin was just an upgraded version of the class he already had. Infernal Crusader though really opened up his options. It felt like a continuation of his path, like an apprentice becoming a journeyman or expert.

Yes, it was a little more...niche than what he was doing now, but that was okay. Specializing your craft was a path people often took. A blade smith, for example, obviously focused on blades. Whilst a farrier focused on shoeing horses.

Specializing wasn't a bad thing.

Portals gave him a tactical advantage, and expanding on that was something he really wanted to do.

He thought about it for a while longer as he allowed his fingers to glide through Noelle's soft white fur. He had promised not to rush into things any longer, and he wasn't about to do that here.

After a few moments, he realized he had already made his decision. Taking a breath, he willed his answer to the System.

[You are now an Infernal Crusader. As a C-Grade being with an upgraded class, Noelle will be upgraded, Merlin's Grimoire will be upgraded. Standby...]

White light enveloped Noelle, and the grimoire within his Infernal Realm pulsed with radiant crimson light. Noelle rose in the air, and her form shimmered, twisting, and changing.

Ambrose felt his eyes widen as Noelle was changed from a tiger, to a young woman.

A smattering of white and black freckles dusted her face, and her eyes were like lightning crafted into crystalline orbs. Her white hair was wild, frizzy and with no sense of style. Black and white furred ears poked through her hair, twitching back and forth.

She wore an oversized shirt with stripes of white, blue and black decorating it. A tail swished from her back almost as if it had a mind of its own. Noelle lifted her delicate hands, looking at them while Ambrose openly gaped.

Ambrose would have placed her at maybe twenty-years old, small and lithe, the shirt she wore went past her knees. Lightning arched around her hands, and she made a fist.

Her eyes glanced downward, meeting Ambrose's own. She beamed, and promptly threw herself into his arms.

She tried to chuff like she had before, but what came out was a squeak. She frowned, and opened her mouth, trying again. Her frown deepened, she poked at her throat.

Opening her mouth, she attempted to speak, "A-ah-ah."

Another frown.

Ambrose couldn't help it, he laughed. He held his hands at his sides, air leaving his body as laughter bubbled out of him in an uncontrollable burst. He tried to suck in air, couldn't, and rolled over into the ground.

Noelle was not amused, fist on hips, she puffed out her cheeks, and her glare could split a tree.

"You're-ah.. Hahaha! C-aat girl, ah!"

Somehow, he should have saw that coming.

CHAPTER FIFTY

"**I** promise I'll talk later, okay?" Noelle nodded at him, and he brought up her stats, pleasantly surprised to see she had changed significantly.

> **Name: Noelle**
> **Race: Nekomi (C-Grade) (Mythic Item-Soulbound)**
> **Attributes: Shared with Ambrose Severen**
> **Traits: Soul-Bound- Strength, skills, and level based on soul-bound partner. Grants +20 to all of Ambrose's stats.**
> **Skills: [Lightning Manipulation-Legendary], [Arcane Shift-Legendary]**

It was a simple sheet, and it looked like the lightning manipulation had been upgraded. He pulled up more details on it, scanning it, then nodding. It made her immune to lightning and allowed her to do practically anything with lightning like he could with **[Hellfire Manipulation]**.

Plus, now that she was C-Grade she boosted his own stats up by twenty. Finally, he pulled out Merlin's Grimoire. For a long time the book had just sat in his inventory, doing nothing. He gained benefits from it, the book granting him a trait that completely shaped his path thus far.

The book had changed. Black with crimson veins, a slight golden light suffused the pages. Heat radiated from the book, a subtle power thrummed within it like the beat of a heart.

[Merlin's Grimoire-Mythic]: This grimoire is a mythical item that contains all of Merlin's power. Bonding to this item will grant you the [Infernal-Mythic] Trait. This trait will alter class selection and skills upon advancement to any grade. It passively grants +50 to all attributes and strengthens your mana core. These effects will increase at A-Grade.

It was a good item. In a moment he was going to look at his updated character sheet, but before that, he looked at his evolved skill.

[Hellfire Manipulation-Mythic has changed to Hellfire Portal Manipulation-Mythic]: All previous effects of this skill have been retained. Using this skill in conjunction with this class, you may now freely manipulate portals you create. Edges of portals can cut through nearly everything at the same grade or below.

It was an amazing skill. He allowed his mind to race with possibilities. Maybe he could portal an entire mountain of rocks over his opponents? Open portals inside of them? He could set them spinning like shurikens maybe.

Pushing the combat potentials aside, he pulled up his character sheet one more time.

Name: Ambrose Severen
Level: 225
Race: Human (C-Grade)

Traits: Ruthless (Uncommon), Giant Slayer (Uncommon), Reforged-Legendary, Infernal (Mythic)

Class: Infernal Crusader-Legendary (Sage)

Profession: Knight Of Avalon (Level 35)

Skills: [Hellfire Portal Manipulation-Mythic], [Retributions Gaze-Epic], [Infernal Sanctuary-Legendary], [Infernal Aegis-Legendary (Spiritual Skill)], [Infernal Recall-Rare], [Infernal Dimension-Epic]

Constitution: 429

Strength: 429

Intellect: 429

Wisdom: 429

Willpower: 443

SC: 9400

Attribute Points:

Noelle was opening her mouth, attempting to sound out words. She crossed her arms, pouting when she failed. Ambrose laughed. "Don't be too hard on yourself. You spent most of your life as a tiger, and you spend even a part of that as a cloak. I promise, we'll work on it."

"I could teach her, if you like, Sir Knight."

Ambrose turned to Vivienne, raising an eyebrow. "Didn't take you for a teacher, Viv."

Vivienne waved a hand. "I am not. But I know the theory."

Ambrose nodded. "Okay, well, I still have a Word of Power I have to select. Why don't you two get started on that?"

Noelle skipped over to Vivienne, ears twitching, tail swishing as she beamed, eyes wide. She and Vivienne went around the tree for some privacy. He willed the System to bring up his Word of Power choices.

[*Break*]: As with all Words of Power, the intention you put behind the Word is important. However, meaning is as well. This Word is designed to do one thing-break. Trying to use the Word outside of its established meaning will likely fail.

He liked this word, he could see a lot of potential uses for it. For example, he could likely break a skill's effects with it. Or wards and enchantments. Hell, he could probably use it to straight up break enemies.

He brought up another word.

[*Enforce*]: As with all Words of Power, the intention you put behind the Word is important. However, meaning is as well. This Word is designed to do one thing-enforce. Trying to use the Word outside of its established meaning will likely fail.]

Like with break, Ambrose imagined a lot of options with this word. He likely wasn't going to pick it, though. He had defense fairly well covered, and he was always able to empower his skills further with more mana. He wanted something more...active.

[Enforce] would be good for defense, maybe even for adding more oomph to his skills. But that wasn't what he wanted.

He moved on to the next word.

[*Empty*]: As with all Words of Power, the intention you put behind the Word is important. However, meaning is as well. This Word is designed to do one thing-empty. Trying to use the Word outside of its established meaning will likely fail.

This word felt a little more vague. A few ways to use it came to mind, but there were lots of ways he could 'Empty' something. This was the last word he could pick, and ultimately he dismissed it as a choice. It was simply too vague, and he didn't want to try and use it in a fight only to have it fail.

With that in mind, he picked [**Break**]. It was straight forward in its meaning, and he felt like it was just versatile enough to give him an array of tactical options.

Standing up, he stretched. After a moment he regarded his armor. It wasn't bad armor, but at this point it felt more like he was wearing it for fashion rather than actually protecting him. His skills did that.

He added new armor to the list of things he wanted to get.

But more important than that was moving on. It was time to go after Eric. He produced a stone, rolling it between his fingers. It was to take him to a different world.

Midgard.

He didn't know much about it, but there was a way to learn more. An information packet. He could buy one from Troy. Part of him wanted to just disregard the thought and jump right into the world.

Except he would be doing so with next to no information about it. That was a bad idea. Every time he had rushed himself, things hadn't gone as well as they could have. No, it would be better to gather information, to think about what he wanted to do, to have some idea of what to expect.

With a wave of his hand, he opened a portal to Troy's shop and stepped through it.

The shop keeper looked up, put his book on the counter, then sighed. "I thought you were going to a different world. Here to beat me up one last time?"

Ambrose ignored him. "I need an information packet on Midgard."

Troy pursed his lips, and his eyes glazed over as he looked at options only he could see.

"If it will get you out of here quicker, I can sell it for twenty thousand SC."

It was a steep price, but Ambrose had it. "Let's have it, then."

A small book popped into existence, Ambrose transferred over the SC and picked it up.

Ambrose went back to the tree.

He was going to educate himself on Midgard, and then he was pursuing Eric.

When he found him, he would kill him.

Nothing more than that needed to be said.

CHAPTER FIFTY-ONE

E ric Delrosa had no trouble getting the badge he needed to move to the next section of Midgard. He just took the one Elgin had. After leaving the same way he had come, he showed his badge to the guards at the gate, and stepped onto the path that winded through the forest beyond.

He traveled most of the night and killed many monsters. The spear's power was incredible. With it he was able to unleash its spirit to combat another's.

However, it wasn't long before he was able to select a skill upgrade, and it was a game changer.

[Divine Voice-Mythic]: You speak and others listen. Any who hear your words must obey them. Now, your voice affects even skills and Words of Power.

Eric had no idea what Words of Power were, but he had a nagging feeling he had just earned a crucial ability for his continued survival.

He was headed to Fenraheim. A forest said to contain the armor of Loki at its heart. The armor would offer him defensive power and a powerful summonable companion.

If the information he had gotten was correct, at any rate.

He felt the ambush before he saw it. Call it instinct, or years spent around criminals, but he knew when danger was on the air. It allowed him to pick out the moving figures in the trees. He swept his gaze upward, picking out the archers on the branches.

Smiling to himself, he whirled Gungnir, and with a fluid, yet unpracticed motion, he flung it at the nearest archer on the tree branch. As it turned out, practice wasn't needed. The mythical spear flew as true as if thrown by a master.

It took the surprised archer in the throat in a spray of sanguine blood.

The light of surprise faded from the archers eyes as his lifeless body crashed to the forest ground below.

With a splitting hiss, the spear flew back to Eric's hands, and before the surrounding enemies could unleash skills or weapons upon him, he spoke, flooding his voice with mana.

"All of you come out and freeze."

Four people emerged from the forest. They were clothed in mottled greens and brown. Cheap swords were at their hips, and bows were slung over shoulders. Two of them were human women, one blonde, and one brunette.

Their brown eyes glared at him, along with the gruff looking men with wild beards and broad shoulders.

It didn't take much for Eric to put together that these were bandits. There wasn't any other reason to attack him on the road. He didn't take it personally, it was half-shod and a poorly organized ambush, but it would have likely worked on anyone else.

One of the women tried to unleash spiritual pressure, but Eric called upon Gungnir's spirit and easily countered the spiritual attack. He waggled his finger at the woman, "That's not nice."

He transitioned his finger wagging into rubbing his hands together. "You know, there are better ways to earn than ambushes. But who am I to judge? *Say, you there, why don't you stab your companion to the right."*

The man drew his sword without hesitation and plunged it into the other man's chest. A burst of viscera poured out of the wound, coating the ground in crimson. He cried out in pain, falling to his knees as the other man lifted a boot and bracing it against the dying man's chest, he pushed and slid the sword out of his body.

The man fell to the ground, his breath ceasing, his body going still as cold stone.

A zing darted down Eric's spine, and he dismissed the notification that lit up his vision.

*"**Miss, would you mind stepping back some and shooting your male companion here in the head, if you please**."*

With a horrified look, the woman moved away, unslung her bow, knocked an arrow and aimed it at the man's eye.

Tears built at the corner of her eyes, and the man looked grim as she unleashed her arrow. The projectile pierced his eye in a sickening squelch as red burst from his face like a crushed rotten fruit.

Eric clapped his hands as the man instantly went still, the arrow coming cleanly out the back of his skull. His body crashed to the ground in a lifeless lump.

Rubbing his hands, Eric regarded the women.

"Now then, how should we deal with you? Hmm. Ah well, I'll make it quick I suppose. ***You, slit her throat***," he pointed at the woman who had killed the man.

Openly sobbing, the woman took out her sword after putting her bow away and walked around the other woman, who was also crying. Eric was the only happy person there, grinning widely as the woman bandit slid the edge of the blade along the other woman's throat, opening up the skin of her throat like a ripe grapefruit.

She emitted a gurgle, and blood sprayed as if from a fountain.

She dropped like a stone, clutching her throat. Eric watched the light leave her eyes as if it was a movie he couldn't tear away from.

He let out a sigh of relief when she finally died.

"I'm sure you think I am a monster. You're absolutely correct, but in this case, I would lay the blame at your feet. After all, you attacked me first. I could let you live, spread what happened here today. A reputation does me good, after all."

Eric rubbed his hands, savoring the pule of hope that lit up in her eyes.

"I could. But I won't. ***Slit your own throat, slowly.***"

The hope died, and inwardly, Eric crowed in delight. She lifted her sword ever so slowly, and being exact as possible, she opened her own throat.

Like all the rest of her friends, she fell to the ground like a sack of bad meat.

Eric tsked at himself, "I forgot to see if I could control their skills. Ah well, it is what it is."

Eric whistled as he continued on his way.

It was a day of travel before he left the forest, finding himself on the open path, surrounded by fields and mountains afar. It was a few more days after that before he entered the forest he was looking for.

It was darker than the last forest, a thick mist hanging over it, and the air would have caused goosebumps to break out over his skin if it wasn't for the fact that he was D-Grade. He heard the howls of wolves in the distance.

Eric was certain he would find monsters here. He wanted to, needed to, in fact. He knew his enemy would not stay idle. He would be progressing. He might even be C-Grade by now.

Eric could not afford to fall too far behind. He wasn't too familiar with gamer vernacular, but he believed he was about to engage in an old time practice of "grinding" as some called it. He would go after monster after monster, and slay them until he reached C-Grade.

As he did so, he would make his way to the heart of the forest.

Where he would find the armor of Loki.

CHAPTER FIFTY-TWO

Ambrose stepped through the realm portal and into Midgard. Noelle walked beside him, her ears twitching as she looked around. They were in a forest, and he could hear the lapping of waves nearby. Air circled through the trees. Sweeping his gaze around him, he scanned for threats.

He found none.

His first priority was to find Eric.

Which was a problem he chewed over. He had no clue where Eric would have went. His best bet was to head to the nearest town and ask around. Noelle was chasing a butterfly, trying to snatch it out of the air with her delicate hands.

He felt his lips tug upward in a gentle smile. Noelle was a predator, a mythical item too, yes, but a predator all the same. But she also had a.. kitten like quality to her. She even moved with a feline grace. Which made sense since she had been a magical tiger.

It took him most of a day to find the town. Surprisingly, he encountered no monsters along the way. Noelle followed, tail moving back and forth as she scanned the forest, eyes wide. Her mouth slightly open.

"It's just a forest, Noelle. We've been in one before."

She cast a glare his way, and tried to speak.

Her short time with Vivienne had proven to be effective, but Noelle still spoke carefully, her voice as light as a feather, with an ever so slight knifes edge to it.

"I didn't really see it before, did I? Spent most of it as a cloak."

Ambrose rubbed the back of his neck, looking away. Noelle huffed in satisfaction.

The town came into view soon after. It was a town made up of many long buildings, entwined planks, and seemingly pulled straight out of a standard fantasy novel.

The town appeared to be very busy, with a large congregate of people gathered at the entrance to a large castle on a hill overlooking the ocean. Noelle's ears waggled as she looked at the group.

Guards were barring the way up the hill, and further on, Ambrose's C-Grade vision could pick out another group at the castle proper. As Ambrose neared, another man appeared. He was dressed in what Ambrose would call a fantasy version of a suit.

A silk black doublet lined with gold, matching pants and polished boots. His features were all sharp angles, his skin like ground coffee and his beard was salt 'n' pepper, groomed perfectly. His milk chocolate eyes had a sharp, but bored edge to them.

His voice, a little nasally, carried far. "Lord Elgin, a forerunner of Midgard, has been killed. An investigation is underway, and the guard promises to update you when we have more information. For now, I will be acting as steward until a new leader is selected."

Murmurs broke out among the crowd as people shared glances, and shuffled uncertainly. Some began to weep at the news. One called out, "What about the Advancement Trial?!"

The man raised a hand to quell the noise before speaking. "The trial will continue as normal. With sign-ups beginning tomorrow."

More murmurs at this, but the crowd soon dispersed a few moments later.

Ambrose and Noelle got a few stares as they made there way to a local tavern. The tavern was busy, with locals clearly discussing the incident,

"I hear someone broke in and assassinated him!"

An older man guffawed, "Pshh! Assassinate Lord Elgin? No way! I heard he killed himself."

Conversation went like that across the room, with different theories being discussed and weighed.

"Get you anythin' sweetheart?"

The blonde waitress was elven, plump, with rosy cheeks and wearing an apron. Her mouth curved into a joyful smile at Noelle, who smiled back in return, tail swishing. Ambrose ordered the special, and a big slab of meat for Noelle who's tail swished harder.

Before the waitress departed, Ambrose smiled at her, "I'm new to town. Would you mind telling me what happened?"

He had no doubt she would know what he meant.

She tapped her notepad. "Lord Elgin, our forerunner, was killed last night. His body was discovered this morning. Don't know much more beyond that, the guard is keepin' it all hush hush."

He nodded, "I see. What is this Advancement Trial?"

She blinked at him, "Ya don't know? It's how you go up an adventurin' rank. Without that, you can't travel through the western gate out of town, which means you can't fight higher level monsters or progress."

Ambrose stroked his beard, "I don't get it. Why would you need to do that? Why restrict travel in such a way?"

He wasn't concerned about asking these questions. There was no reason for him to lie or hide who he was.

"What rock have you been under?" She placed her hands on her hips.

Ambrose told the truth, "I'm from a different world. Newly integrated."

The waitress blinked, and realization dawned. "That makes sense. Okay, well, let me go get your order in, and I'll be back when I can to answer questions, yeah? I can't be seen jabbin' all shift. I'm a waitress, not an information broker."

He nodded, and she went off to get his order in. Noelle looked around, curiosity writ plain on her face.

Do you know anything about this world, Akaroth? He sent his thoughts toward the dragon in axe form.

He felt her mind shake in a negative, *I'm not from here, nor have I ever been here. Every world integrated into the system has a different shade of scales.*

He grunted. *There's something I don't understand. If this world has been integrated for a while, why aren't the people here higher level? I don't get how that forerunner isn't supremely powerful by now.*

Akaroth's mental chuckle reminded him of grinding rocks deep within the earth. *You have merely to look around you to see the answer to that, hatchling.*

He did that, coming up blank. Akaroth explained it, *After worlds have been integrated for a while, survival becomes less of an issue. People transition into living as normal a life as they can. You've already seen it on Avalon, have you not? People there do not want to fight for survival, they do not have a desire to progress. They simply wish to live a simple existence. It is the way of sheep.*

Akaroth seemed to sneer at the end.

He had to admit, that did make sense. Clearly some people did want to move on, due to this trial, whatever that was. However, the rest didn't appear to have any desire to do so. His eyes landed on a couple nearby, laughing, joking and otherwise enjoying eachother.

A pang in his heart caused him to wince just slightly.

What would he have given for that? To have a normal life with Alice at his side, watching his daughter grow. Yes, he could understand why some people wanted to live a normal life.

Eric had taken that from him. Killed that from him.

He needed to get back on the trail. That meant he needed to learn everything he could of relevance about this world, and ask around about Eric.

Because the end game was near.

He could feel it.

Chapter Fifty-Three

The waitress's name was Elayne Mccoy. Ambrose didn't get to talk to her for a while, as things picked up in the dining area, and she became busy.

He could have left and likely pursued the information elsewhere, but he had already promised to wait, and besides that there was the fact that he couldn't leave.

There was no getting beyond the western gate without the appropriate badge, apparently. Yes, Ambrose had a portal skill, but he had to have some idea of where he would portal to for that to work.

Also, he didn't want to have to argue with or fight every single authority figure that demanded to see a badge. No, he didn't want any further obstructions than there had to be.

Noelle ate her food with ferocity.

Ambrose blinked. "Hungry, eh?"

She paused to glare at him, an action that was quickly becoming a habit for her.

"I'm an inanimate object most of the time, thanks to *somebody*, and that means I don't get to eat much."

He grimaced, "Fair point."

Hours went by, filled by Ambrose watching, and the occasional conversation with Noelle. She looked uneasy, and he could feel that something was bothering her.

He asked her about it, and she sighed. Her ears twitched and she poked a fork at her plate. Finally, she put the fork down. "I don't know who I am. That's what's wrong."

As the hours had passed, Noelle quickly grew more confident with the language, Vivienne really had been a good teacher.

Ambrose blinked at her words and leaned back. "What do you mean?"

Her tail curled, swishing in an agitated fashion. "Your ears work fine," she growled.

She was also becoming very short tempered, he noticed. "Yes. They do. But I'd like you to elaborate."

She pointed at Ambrose in an accusatory fashion. "You have a history. Things you like, things you don't. An..." She fumbled, searching her mind for a word she may not even know yet.

"Identity," she exclaimed finally.

The finger reversed course, pointing at herself. "I was nothing but an item for a long time. I had vague feelings, perception and instinct but that was it. This meal?" She tapped her fork on the plate, "It's my favourite meal because I've never had cooked food before this."

He nodded, "I understand."

Noelle's answering growl turned a few heads as her eyes bored into his.

"No. You don't. How could you? You've always had a body, desires, and a consciousness. I look around all the time because everything is new to me. You don't understand."

She sounded defeated at the end.

Ambrose rubbed his face. He considered his words before he spoke, and selected them with care.

"You're right. I don't understand. More importantly, I am likely to blame. I kept you as a cloak whenever possible because I was afraid of losing you. But you were never a child. Even as a cloak, you had an awareness, and I never took that into consideration. How about this-" Ambrose took a breath, "We will find things you like, okay? We can explore who you are together."

Noelle's tail swished again, less agitated and more excited. She nodded, giving him a smile.

"You're the best, Ambrose."

He shook his head, "I don't know about that. But you're my closest friend, and I want you to be happy."

How touching, Akaroth snorted in his mind.

He ignored the dragon.

Elayne was off soon after, settling into the open chair beside them. She had a steaming mug of coffee, which she slurped before speaking, "Man, I'm beat. I hope you two understand how hard waitressing is."

"Of course. Definitely hard."

Elayne stared at him for a moment, trying to determine if he was being sarcastic. Finally, she shrugged, "I think I promised you two some answers, eh? So, let's get to the info dumping. I have a bed callin' my name."

"What does this advancement trial entail?"

It was looking like he was going to have to compete in it if he wanted to move forward, so he decided to get as much information about it as possible.

Elayne sipped coffee, the steam curling around her face as she thought about how best to explain it.

"Well...it changes every year. I can say that much. This year, the rumor is that it's going to be a free for all capture the flag type thing, with monsters thrown in. Capture an opponents flag and kill a monster, you earn your badge."

"That's all?" Noelle questioned.

Elayne shrugged, "That's all you gotta do to earn a badge. But there's also prizes."

His eyebrow raised, and Elayne smiled, taking it as a que to go on. "I don't know the point system, they'll talk about it more tomorrow at the commencement ceremony, which is the tenth hour by the way, but every flag is worth some points and every monster kill is worth some. Top three get prizes."

She sipped some coffee, eyes bright, "I'm hoping for a sword."

"You're taking part then?" Ambrose asked.

She nodded, a wide grin splitting her face, "Sure am. I don't want to spend my whole life waiting tables, you know? There's treasure and adventure out there. I wanna experience it. I *will* experience it."

Her eyes shone with determination.

Ambrose decided to move on. "Have you seen another out-worlder like me come through? He would look like an academic type, with brown eyes and a snake-like presence to him. Maybe he made you uncomfortable."

She pursed her lips, and nodded decisively. "When you put it that way, yep. I remember a guy like that. He was here for a couple days. Didn't speak much, mostly watched. Gave me the absolute creeps."

She shuddered at the memory.

So then, Eric had been here. He was getting closer.

"Is he still in town?" He doubted it, but there was hope.

Which was immediately crushed by a shake of her head. "I haven't seen him. I don't see how he could have left, but if he's still in town, I haven't laid eyes on him in a couple days. A blessing if I ever knew one."

He drummed his fingers on the table in thought. Eric would find a way. Something told him Eric had killed the forerunner and ditched town. Probably took the forerunners badge.

"Is there an inn my companion and I could stay at?"

Elayne nodded, and told him about the Sleeping Pony.

"Did you have other questions?"

He did. "Where does the trial take place?"

She waved a hand in the forests direction. "In the forest. An array is erected around it as a barrier, and monsters are unleashed, then the people go in after random groups are drawn and given a five minute start to get some distance. That's how this kinda trial has been done in the past, anyway."

"You never participated before."

She twirled a finger in a strand of her hair, "No. I didn't."

It didn't sound like a good idea to push, so he didn't.

"Alright. Thanks, Elayne. We'll be off to the inn, now."

She nodded, standing up and smiling at them, "Good luck!"

Ambrose smiled too, before leaving.

It wouldn't be luck he needed.

CHAPTER FIFTY-FOUR

Jenny killed the rabbit by flicking her wrist and sending an orb of viridian power at it. The creatures were not the adorable, fuzzy kind of rabbit that she might have gushed over once, but rather the kind straight out of your nightmares. With a twisted, pale horn, and beady red eyes glowing with malevolent hate. Their fur was matted, ripped out in places, and they would open their mouths in sickening hisses.

Not cute at all.

But they were good experience.

[You have killed a Horned Rabbit Level 15 and have advanced to level 20]

Jenny might have clapped her hands or even smiled at the message once upon a time. Instead, all she felt was a sense of grim satisfaction. She was closer to her goal, but it was a single step upon a path that stretched onward towards the horizon and beyond.

Closer. But still so far away.

She sat down to consolidate her gains, trying to ignore the weight in her heart. Sometimes, in between building, her Dad would take her out to the forest like this to just admire nature. She would ask questions, and he would answer, and then she'd ask to sit on his broad shoulders where she felt safe.

She wouldn't be able to do that anymore.

The days that passed didn't make the pain any easier to bear. People tried to comfort her, particularly Andrea, but she just didn't care. The life had been sucked from her world, and the only way she felt she could get it back was by killing Ambrose.

At the thought, her heart beat like a drum, fire blazed behind her eyes, her fists clenched. It was his fault. She wasn't stupid, she knew that it wasn't entirely Ambrose's fault, but certainly a lot of the blame could be laid at his feet.

He would pay for that.

But it wouldn't be soon. Jenny needed power, first. Which meant training her new class, and skills. She brought it up now, wanting to check her progress.

Name: Jenny Smith
Race: Human [E-Grade]
Class: Witch [Epic]
Level: 25
Skills: [Spell casting-Rare], [Ritualism-Epic], [Inspect-Common]
Constitution:30
Strength: 30
Intellect: 30
Wisdom: 30
Willpower: 25
SC:0
Attributes:0

She was progressing, though progress was slow. Andrea had started something she referred to as the "Tutorial Program," and part of that entailed putting low level creatures in a cordoned off section of the island. An array covered the section, preventing the creatures from escaping, and even if they did somehow get out, the Swords of Avalon were more than capable of dealing with them.

She had expected to have to sneak in, but Andrea was supportive of her coming out here, something about "venting her frustrations." As if she expected her to forgive Ambrose after killing enough monsters.

She snorted, kicking a rock with her shoe. It skipped over the ground, settling on a patch of grass.

Even while he was away, Ambrose's presence could be felt on the island. People talked about him, asked after him, felt safe with him. He was powerful, there was no question about that. He possessed a strength that felt all encompassing, overwhelming.

She wasn't sure she would get enough strength to challenge him, especially because he likely grew stronger by the day. She wouldn't give up, she would keep progressing until she caught up.

No matter the obstacle. Today, that meant bunny monsters. She stood, brushing off her jeans, and looked at the corpse of the bunny. Her ritualism skill required guts from the monsters she killed, but she could create nifty items from them, like hex bags. Hex bags could have a variety of effects, none of them very good.

The skill also allowed her to speak to spirits of the recently departed. She had tried talking to her Dad, but he had been gone for too long.

She had thought about trying to place a hex bag in Ambrose's house, but he was never home, and he was a higher grade than her, so she very much doubted it would work. Part of her worried about her deal with Misaq as she used a knife to skin the bunny, depositing its innards into a bag of holding she had inherited from Dad.

Her Dad hadn't trusted the devil, and so she had been reluctant to. She hadn't forgotten that day after arriving on the island. The devil had caused her to hurt, somehow, but nothing else really mattered to her beyond revenge.

Even her own life.

She spent the next few hours depleting the monster population. Andrea had purchased an array that made them respawn, so she wasn't too worried about that. No other kids came out here.

All the better for her.

After a hard day, she returned to the group home, passing kids that whispered as she passed.

"There's that weird girl. I think her name is Jenny?"

She ignored them as best she could, going up to her room for a shower.

At her desk, she chronicled the day's events, her gains, the items she had collected, and her goals for the next day after school. She briefly considered ditching, but then Andrea would come looking for her, and that wasn't a confrontation she wanted.

People kept trying to get close to her, and she wouldn't allow it. People who got close, died. So long as they thought her an unpleasant, angry little girl that was rude to them, they would leave her alone and live.

It was the best thing she could do for them, really.

After journaling, she did her homework.

Then she would go to bed and begin the process anew tomorrow. It was a grinding existence, but every gain was worth it. No other kids wanted to be doing what she was, and she couldn't understand that. To them, she was the abnormal one, but to her it was the opposite.

This new world was all about strength.

Those with it survived while the weak perished.

She would never be weak again.

Andrea Pender met with Tina in her office. The younger woman looked bored, as if she would rather be fighting something.

But her news was interesting.

"This could really work, if we approach it right." Andrea said.

Tina shrugged, "I will leave the politics to you, just tell me what you need, yeah?"

Andrea nodded, glancing out the window.

Jenny was walking back from the tutorial area. Tina noticed as well, and her bored look transformed into one of sympathy,

"She carries a heavy burden, that child."

Andrea turned to look at Tina. "Something tells me you can relate."

Tina smiled, "That obvious, hmm? I can, indeed."

"What do you think about talking to her?"

Tina was shaking her head before she finished speaking. "She has only one goal in mind. I can see it in her eyes. Talking will do no good at this point."

Andrea frowned, watching Jenny go into the group home.

She sighed, because she had other matters to consider.

Mentally, she wished Jenny would find healing, and then she dismissed the girl from her thoughts.

Business awaited. The pressing kind.

The kind that could cost lives if she didn't attend to it.

CHAPTER FIFTY-FIVE

E layne caught them just outside the tavern.

"Hey, wait up a sec, will ya?"

Ambrose turned, eyebrow raised.

She stopped, shifting her feet. The tips of her pointed ears turned red. "Umm...Listen...what do you think about teaming up for the trial?"

Ambrose wasn't sure how to react to the request. He used [Retributions Gaze] on the elven woman.

[Elayne Mccoy-Level 198 Beast Druid]: She carries some guilt over her brother's death, believing it to be her fault. She has a love for animals, and her choice led her down a druidic path.

No crimes there that stood out. The story behind her brother wasn't his business, so he wasn't going to ask. Her level, however, indicated that she wasn't entirely useless. However, levels were not always the best indicator of strength.

He looked around at everyone going about their evening. Elayne waited on his answer, while Noelle looked thoughtful.

Two roars are louder than one, hatchling. Akaroth added her voice to his considerations.

In all honesty, he liked being alone. When he was alone, the only one who was in danger of dying was himself. Noelle had been with him from close to the beginning, but he could unmanifest her if things got to be too dangerous.

Darren's face flashed through his mind, followed by Jenny's dead eyes.

His fist clenched slightly. He was on the verge of opening his mouth to tell Elayne no thanks, but Noelle flashed him an intense glare, giving him pause.

How long was he going to allow fear of loss to control him? He had tried to make a commitment, more than once, not to do that with Noelle. But it couldn't stop there. It meant nothing if he only dealt with Noelle that way.

He sighed, running fingers through his beard. "Noelle and I were about to get a room for the night. How about you join us so we can talk about your capabilities?"

Elayne beamed, nodding, "You betcha! You won't regret this!"

I hope not, Ambrose thought grimly.

Their room was spacious, but not too large. Two soft beds, a dresser and smooth hardwood floors the color of rich dark chocolate. The bathrooms were surprisingly modern, and Ambrose gratefully took a shower, peeling off his armor.

The hot water soothed his muscles, washing away the tension and stress that had built up.

He was beginning to find his armor useless. Before, it gave him some ability to teleport, and lent him an air of fantasy badassary he supposed, but beyond its appearance, it was functionally useless. He could portal wherever he needed to go now, and he was so attuned with the island, he didn't really need the Key of Avalon.

He felt like he would be better served with lighter armor, maybe half-plate, or even leather.

It was a problem for another day, however. After putting it all back on, he went out to find Noelle bouncing on the bed, ears swiveling, hair bouncing up and down in a wild tangle as her she grinned from ear to ear.

Elayne was laughing.

Ambrose allowed himself a small smile at the sight. But that was all.

"We should talk about your capabilities, now."

Elayne nodded, looking suddenly attentive. "Of course! I could just share my status page if ya like."

Ambrose shook his head. "I don't want to read off a bunch of numbers and skills. Those won't tell me anything, anyway. We need to talk about the things that actually matter."

"Like?"

Noelle settled on the bed, running her hands over the soft material.

"Like spiritual skills. Do you have one?"

Elayne smiled, her ears twitched, "I do, yep! That's fairly common knowledge in Midgard. It's only newly integrated worlds like yours that don't know stuff like that."

Ambrose was learning more and more that the System did not hold your hand. On Avalon, they had a school for the kids, but perhaps he would talk to Andrea about having a library or some such that contained public information packets so people didn't start with the same disadvantages he and others had.

He put the matter behind him for now, bringing himself back to the situation at hand.

"What about an Icon? You're very nearly at the level the System recognizes as C-Grade, Icons are important."

At that, Elayne's ears went reddish pink again. "I've been tryin' but it's hard, ya know?"

Ambrose crossed his arms. "I understand, trust me, but you're going to cripple your advancement if you don't have one."

Elayne looked sheepish, "If I win the trial, there's an amulet their offerin' and it would supply an Icon."

It was Ambrose's turn to look uncertain. "I know some items have a spirit you can use, but I didn't know they could have Icons, too."

Elayne nodded excitedly, "They sure can! There's a legend that Loki's armor gives access to an Icon."

"Loki's armor?"

"Yep! It is apparently in a forest beyond the western gate, past some plains. No one's ever gone after it though, on account of it bein' certain death."

"How so?"

Elayne was happy to explain, "Because it's guarded by Fenrir!"

He blinked. "Like that large wolf, you mean?"

Elayne laughed, "Large? More like gigantic! I've never seen him, of course, but he's supposedly this nightmare wolf with fur like the void itself, and eyes like the lakes of hell itself. It's a legendary top tier C-Grade monster."

Elayne was animated now, hands moving, and her eyes sparkled as she talked about the legendary wolf.

Ambrose, for his part, was thinking about hunting the wolf down. Yes, it sounded dangerous, but he had never been afraid of a little danger. Besides, that was the nature of this new world.

You needed to find ever increasing danger to advance. He also found himself wondering if he could have multiple Icons. He doubted it, items like that tended to be meant for those that hadn't been able to unlock the powers for themselves.

In other words, they were crutches. When you took away a person's crutches, they fell. It was a weakness.

He told Elayne such, and the elf crossed her arms. "What else am I supposed to do, eh? I can't spend my whole life here."

Ambrose borrowed a line from his father, a piece of advice he had often ignored, even recently. "Patience cost you nothing, boy, but it can gain you everything."

Elayne growled in her throat, "I'm not a boy, ya know? What do ya even mean by that?"

He shrugged, "Something my dad used to tell me. It means a lot of things, but mostly it means that being patient can save your life. Rushing is dangerous, it leads to mistakes, it takes away control."

Elayne clutched her ears, puffing in frustration, "I've been waiting my whole life! If I had prioritized growin' stronger earlier, then maybe he wouldn't have-" she cut off, looking away.

Ambrose knew the pain in that voice. He had felt it, continued to feel it in fact. When he spoke, it was like unlocking a piece of himself he hadn't dared share with anyone before. Maybe he saw a kindred soul in the elf, maybe he had to respond to that kind of pain. Either way, he felt himself talking as if he didn't have a choice.

"You're running from it. You feel it every day, and as fast as you run, you can't get away. Part of you doesn't want to. You think that if you can just grow stronger, if you could just reach the next threshold, you might feel better. If only you could reach that goal-" He wasn't looking at her as he spoke, but Elayne stared at him, eyes filling with tears, mouth open.

Noelle watched him, sympathy and love burning in her eyes.

"Then maybe, just maybe, you might feel some relief. Maybe you could finally move on. You tell yourself that's what she would want, for you to be happy again. Except there's no feeling happy, because her presence isn't there. You reach for it, desperate to feel it, but you can't. So you search, you rush for that goal, because maybe, just maybe, you'll feel her again if you achieve it."

Elayne was sobbing now, and almost as if coming out of a trance, Ambrose looked at her. "Yes, Elayne, I'll team up with you. I'll help you, at least a little bit, to reach that goal."

He held out a hand.

She took it.

CHAPTER FIFTY-SIX

Elayne departed not soon after that, the elven waitress had a bounce in her step that Ambrose had not seen just hour before. After that, Ambrose and Noelle settled in for the night. Now that he was C-Grade, he found that he needed little sleep.

Noelle, however, curled her body up into a ball on her bed, tail wrapped around her, soft breaths signalled she was deeply asleep. He couldn't help but find her adorable, and a powerful urge to protect her built up within him.

He had to be careful with that urge. Noelle wanted to take part in the fights ahead, and he couldn't deny her that. Unable to sleep, he settled on the bed, posture straight, and legs crossed. From the window, moonlight bathed the room, and when he closed his eyes and focused, he could hear the creaking of boards and the sounds of the people in the inn.

He could feel it when the building and the people within settled in. It was a kind of silence that one struggled to describe, but knew nonetheless.

Focus was key in a lot of what he did. You needed it in combat, but it also needed to be passive.

"It's focusing without focusing, son."

At the time he had nearly pulled his hair out when Raylen had told him that. It hadn't made any sense.

But as the years went by, he got it. There was a kind of art to it. You needed to be focused enough, but not so focused that you lost awareness of your surroundings.

It took practice, discipline, and experience, but he had picked it up, eventually.

None of that focus helped him with his Icon. Not even a little bit.

Focus, at least for him, was being aware of his body and his physical surroundings. Yes, it could help him relax, but it couldn't help him understand himself. Even if it could, taking that understanding and connecting it to an abstract concept like the Forge Icon was something a little beyond what focus could help him with.

He had done well to come as far as he had, in understanding enough of himself to connect it to his Icon, but he had a long way to go. He worked on that now.

Previously, he had figured out that he was forging himself, becoming something new.

Tonight, he wanted to take a different approach. Instead of trying to think about how he was like the Forge Icon, he instead just allowed his mind to drift through his life. Almost like spinning a wheel, he wanted to see where he would land.

He found himself thinking back to when he had just lost his hundredth spar with his father.

"I don't get why I have to keep doing this! It's pointless! All I do is lose!"

His father wiped a towel over his face, regarding his son who was sprawled on the floor. "Have you ever heard the phrase 'Iron sharpens iron,' boy?"

Ambrose shook his head.

Raylen nodded, expecting that. He was his son's teacher after all. "It means a lot of things, but mostly it means we improve through challenge, through hardship. Especially with one another."

Raylen went to the wall where a rack of weapons stood, looked it over for a moment and selected an axe. He hefted it, turning towards his son. "See this? Do you know how it was made?"

Once again, Ambrose shook his head no.

"With fire and blows from a hammer. In other words, under intense pressure and heat it becomes something newer, better and more dangerous than it was before."

His father returned the weapon to the rack, gesturing at him.

"You think I abuse you. You think I hurt you. In a way, you're right. I am going to bring you heat, I am going to pressure you. Because that's how you'll change, that's how you'll become dangerous. Get up. We go again."

They had fought three more times that night, and Ambrose lost every time.

He felt it when his connection with his Icon deepened, not quite putting another piece of the puzzle together, but beginning to understand it. It was almost like he was on the cusp of working out a problem but needed a little more to fully solve it.

He spent the rest of the night trying to do so to no avail.

When morning came, he and Noelle checked out and headed for the town square, where the announcement for the advancement trial would begin. When they reached the square, they found Elayne looking out for them.

She beamed when she saw them, waving them over.

The Elven druid was dressed in leathers of forest green and browns. She looked quite good in them, the leather form fitting. She had a staff in her hands that looked to be carved from an ancient oak tree. The same man from when Ambrose first arrived in town appeared, addressing the crowd.

Ambrose began to listen, but soon tuned him out when he delivered information he had already heard.

"Flags will be worth two points, killing others is worth one and killing monsters is worth three! Top three participants will earn a prize, whilst anyone who possessed one flag not their own and kills one monster will be awarded their badge, and will be free to move on to the next zone."

"Zones?" Ambrose questioned.

Elaine supplied the answer. "Midgard is separated into zones. Beyond the next western gate is zone two. Ya need a bronze badge to be in that zone. Advancements like this prevent needless death because it means ya actually can defend yerself. Plus, it's a mark of distinction."

Ambrose nodded.

"Teams are allowed, but each person must have a flag and kill one monster for each team mate."

"So three flags and three monsters then," he muttered to himself.

He heard Elayne curse softly, and he looked up.

A man strode towards them.

And Elayne didn't look happy about it.

He was blonde, elven, and wore duelist leathers with a sword strapped to his hip. He moved with the confidence of a stalking leopard. His eyes were burnished gold, flashing in the morning light.

His strong features held a smug grin. "Trying again this year, Elayne? Tsk tsk. When will you learn?"

Elayne's ears went hot pink, and her fists clenched as she put them on her hips. "Leave me alone Stroud."

"But if I did that then how would you know to stay in your place, lowborn?"

Elayne blew out a breath, and Ambrose actually saw her bite back a retort.

He was tempted to step in, but he wouldn't be doing Elayne any favors if he did. He knew bullies when he saw one, and this Stroud character fit the bill.

He would stand down if Ambrose intervened, but as soon as his back was turned, he'd be back. Ambrose couldn't be by Elayne's side all the time.

There was also the fact that she hadn't yet indicated that she needed his help. Elayne was no delicate flower, and he wasn't about to treat her as such.

No, this was something she needed to do on her own.

Iron sharpens iron.

Chapter Fifty-Seven

E layne snorted, "Really, Stroud? Sinkin' to that level? That war has been over for a long time ya know?"

Stroud winced, "You should really keep that mouth shut, lowborn. Your bumpkin, lowborn accent offends my ears."

Ambrose leashed the sudden heat that suffused his chest, reining it in. Elayne had to defend herself, getting involved would not help her.

She shrugged, "Ya came to talk to me, kin fucker. I suggest ya leave me alone if ya don't want to hear my dulcet tones."

Some people, when angry, got loud. Their body tightened, their face became an angry scowl and they let you hear their anger. Maybe they attempted to break something, or do you harm. Perhaps they devolved into insults or incoherent screaming.

Some had more control than that, like Ambrose, and showed you nothing of their emotions unless they wanted you to see it. Inwardly, Ambrose wanted to test out his new portal abilities and use this elf as an experiment. Noelle was glaring, ears almost flat on her skull, and if it weren't for Ambrose sending her mental waves of calm, she'd be growling.

Stroud was neither of those people. He was the kind who just went blank. His whole face went neutral, his eyes becoming chips of ice. He swept that icy gaze over Ambrose and Noelle.

He sniffed once. "I hope you keep an eye on each other in the forest. Advancement Trials can be...dangerous."

He turned and walked away. Ambrose almost used **[Retributions Gaze]** on him but chose not to. He had a nagging feeling he'd get his chance, and he didn't want to chance that the elf would be alerted. Best to wait.

"What was that about? There were some slurs there that suggest...history."

Elayne nodded, her body slumping slightly as she leaned on her staff. "It's an old score between the high elves and us regular-" she put finger quotes around the next words, "Lowborn elves."

"I couldn't see much of a difference other than he's male."

She smiled slightly, "That's the trick, there is no difference. Biologically we are the same race. It's a class thing."

"Ah, I see. A certain group saw themselves as being elitist, oppressed yours and then your group rebelled?"

Elayne waggled her hand. "It's not that simple. We oppressed them, actually."

Ambrose blinked. "I guess I shouldn't have assumed."

She laughed, "I see why ya did. Short version is that his 'group' as ya put it rebelled against mine, and rightfully so, but they didn't stop there. The oppressed became the oppressors. It spawned a big ol' war, we almost went extinct. Now we have the Emerald Conclave Concord, or the ECC. But there's still a lot of bad blood as ya can plainly see."

She turned away from Ambrose as the steward began to say something new.

"Each team will enter at the same time, and be teleported to different areas of the forest. The trial begins in one hour, good luck participants!"

Ambrose was still chewing over the interaction with Stroud. He was going to be a problem, he was certain of it. That kind of grudge bred a burning hatred that urged action. He knew it well, and so too, did Elayne.

"We'll see him again," Ambrose said.

Elayne ground her staff into the ground, blowing a strand of her out of her face with a puff of breath.

"Yeah, we will. I'm sorry. Ya don't deserve to be pulled into my problems."

Ambrose waved a hand, "We're a team."

Noelle nodded firmly, face firm, and determined.

"You've participated in this trial before? Stroud seemed to imply that you have."

Her ears went pink again, "Yeah, I have. Sometimes they do different things, but last year was the same trial."

Ambrose stroked his beard, "Since you have the most experience, what do you suggest our plan of attack be?"

Elayne studied him, "Ya know I failed last year, right? Yer really askin' me?"

Ambrose nodded, "I am."

Elayne stood a little straighter then, and she considered for a moment, lowering her head. Moments later, she spoke, "Well then, if things go like last year, then the first thing we should do is establish a base."

"Why?"

"Because people are gonna fight by just stumblin' into one another, and its chaotic. Random chance is not a good way to win this. If we establish a good area, we can scout from there, and plan our attacks. In the meantime, people will whittle each-other down."

Ambrose pursed his lips and shook his head once. "Establishing a base isn't a horrible idea, I'll give you that, but you're wrong."

Elayne looked offended for a moment, but Ambrose held up a hand to stop her.

"I'm not trying to be insulting. I understand why you have that thought, but there's something you've missed. In order for us to achieve top three, we need to get as many flags, kill as many people and as many monsters as we can. Sitting back while people kill each other off and waiting for them to come to us isn't going to accomplish that. We have to be aggressive, we have to go after them, there is no other option if we want to win. This is as much a race as it is a trial."

Elayne digested that for a moment, clearly unhappy that her plan wasn't good enough. Her face looked briefly like a lemon, but she finally sighed and nodded.

"Yer right. I'm not good at this."

"If you just wanted to pass the trial, it's not a bad plan at all. It doesn't make you bad at this, it just doesn't fit with our goal is all."

Elayne squirmed, her hand tightening on her staff. "I don't feel good about killing folks."

"I understand, but you're going to need to come to terms with it," he pointed in the direction Stroud went. "That guy is going to try to kill you. He has a burning hatred in his heart anyone can see. Others will too. I admit, I don't know much about Midgard, but I do know the System and what it did to my world. The weak will not go far unless sheltered by the strong. You can either be weak, or be strong. I'm not saying become an unfeeling psychopath, but you have to be willing to kill."

Elayne looked uncertain as she pursed her lips. She said nothing in response.

"Everyone! It is time to enter the forest! Merely line up and touch the orb and you'll be teleported to a random location in the forest."

The crowd quickly oriented itself into a line, with each person touching a silver, glowing orb and vanishing.

He, Noelle and Elayne waited in line until it was there turn. As one, they touched the orb and there was a flash of silver light that faded away. It was replaced by the familiar sight of the forest outside of the town.

"Why do I always end up fighting in a forest?" Ambrose muttered to himself.

First Avalon, now Midgard. It was beginning to become a pattern.

Tree's swayed, and with it came a subtle signal.

The trial had begun.

Chapter Fifty-Eight

The party wandered a little while, and it didn't take long for them to run into trouble. A bellowing roar shook the very tree's as they parted to reveal a massive, ugly monster. Its skin was like mold on cheese, its hair like smeared feces, and it had an oversized, bulbous and elongated nose.

Large ears tapered to a point, and its jaw looked like a rotting mashed potato. It was hanging open as the creature bellowed, revealing cracked green and yellow teeth. It was fat, and had huge shovel-like hands with giant skewers for fingers.

Elayne shouted, "Troll!"

As she rolled away to create distance.

Ambrose tossed a **[Retributions Gaze]** at it.

[Forest Troll Level 208]: Forest Trolls are a plague upon anyone travelling the forest. They are fiercely territorial and hate humanoids with a passion. Contrary to popular belief, trolls do not have a weakness to fire. Trolls that have reached C-Grade usually have a connection with the Strength Icon.

Elayne raised her staff, and dark green vines erupted from the earth, wrapping around the troll's legs. Noelle sent a burst of lightning at the monster, which caused it to let loose a guttural cry of pain. Noelle's ears flattened against her head, and she growled as she bounded away.

The troll tried to lash out, but the vines rose up, and its attempt to move caused it to fall like a great tree crashing into the ground, sending out a reverberation all around them. Ambrose thought it over right there, before he even engaged himself, but the troll flexed and he felt a *pressure* billow forth from the troll.

It wasn't like spiritual pressure, but something more potent than that. It was as if the troll was exuding a strength beyond itself, a strength of not just a mortal body or mind, but of reality.

The vines snapped as easily as twigs in a storm.

Then troll attempted to stand, and Ambrose, for the first time since upgrading to his new class, engaged in combat.

Ever since he had become an Infernal Crusader, he had felt a connection to his [Hellfire Manipulation] skill that went beyond what he normally felt with a skill. It was a connection that gave him plans. Blueprints for how to use his portals in new and unique ways.

First, he attempted to open a portal up between the troll's neck, hoping to outright decapitate it outright. He frowned, because the portal would not open. He realised the problem moments later. In order for the portal to work, he needed to have line of sight, and he needed to know where he was opening a portal to.

He couldn't see the inside of the troll, and thus he could not open up a portal inside of its neck.

That was fine. What he could do was open up a portal that originated on the outside of the troll's neck and opened length wise. The result should have done the trick in beheading the troll.

But the edges of the portal did not cut through its skin. Something resisted him. Ambrose frowned, because he knew what it was. The Strength Icon was making the troll's skin far stronger than it had any right being.

He couldn't complain. Not really. Since the Forge Icon did something similar for him. Getting to its feet, the monster roared again, slashing out at Noelle with its skewering claws. Like the tiger she once was, she was too quick, and easily evaded the attack.

Elayne twirled her staff, and nature responded. Vines, acting like whips, cracked against the troll, but his Icon flared, and that same pressure filled the air, leaving the troll unharmed.

With its Icon, it would have been an impossible foe for Noelle and Elayne to beat. Even with Noelle's constant assault of lightning, her weaving around the troll and Elayne's use of summoned foliage, it did nothing. With its Icon, the troll was in a league of its own.

As it had many times previously, it struck him how easy it was to ruin your advancement, your chances of ever being one of the truly strong. If Ambrose hadn't had Vivienne, he likely would have never progressed to the point he was at now.

He had several options for dealing with the troll that didn't involve his portals. He was sure he could keep walloping the monster with Akaroth, and along with Noelle and Elayne's help, the monster would eventually be too tired to call upon its Icon, or else they would overcome it at the strength it was at now.

He was reasonably sure he could also bring his own icon to bear and overcome the troll that way.

He decided to handle it in a different way. He had access to a Word of Power now, and while he couldn't be sure how Icons interacted with it, he was sure that they were supremely powerful.

Looking at the troll, he focused on what he wanted to happen. Visualising it in his mind, he uttered the Word of Power.

"BREAK."

He didn't shout nor even raise his voice a little when he spoke the word. Yet it echoed as if being shouted by a god. He felt the Word resonate within the world, as if he were inputting a command into reality itself.

The troll shattered. Like a sledgehammer taken to rock, its body simply broke apart into chunks of wet, red and green moldy flesh that squelched as it hit the ground. It was as if some invisible being was ripping the troll into pieces like shredding paper.

It was over in a few moments. There was no resistance from the Icon. Ambrose immediately slumped, a wave of exhaustion passing over him as his mind fluttered, like he had just taken a blow to the head.

Noelle rushed to his side as he staggered, while Elayne merely stared at the bits of troll on the forest floor, mouth wide open.

Ambrose grimaced, "I'm okay. I just..wow. Yeah, I won't be doing that again for a minute."

He held his head with one hand as Elayne turned to him. "What was that?"

She didn't even attempt to hide the awe in her voice.

He smiled slightly at her expression. That...was a Word of Power."

Elayne slowly shook her head, "I've never even...how do you get that kind of power?"

He shrugged, "I got it by closing all the Incursions on my world. Do you have Incursions here you can close?"

Slowly, she shook her head, hand tightening on her staff.

"There's one person who was said to be around during the Incursion period, but I wasn't alive then. Is there no other way?"

Another shrug, "Hard to say. It comes from the System, not me."

She nodded, looking thoughtful. "Well, that's one part of the trial complete. Now then, we just need to find some people," Ambrose stated.

Elayne pointed to the north, "I think that way is as good as any other direction."

Noelle was still looking at him with concern, and he stood straighter.

Gesturing, he said, "Lead on then. We have a trial to complete don't we, everyone?"

Elayne laughed, and the group began to walk in the direction she had pointed, not seeing the man who materialised behind them, watching them go.

Chapter Fifty-Nine

Elayne Mccoy did not know what to make of Ambrose Severen. He was powerful, she saw that much. He killed that troll with a *word*. She still remembered how it felt, the world itself thrumming in response to it. The troll just ripped apart from some unseen force.

He had looked exhausted after he had spoken that word, so there was a cost at least. She was used to skills and the power that came from them. Skills had been a part of her world since she was born, after all. She even knew of Icons, and spirit, but that word he had spoken, its power? No, she hadn't heard of that.

As she walked with the group, with Noelle looking like a curious kitten seeing the world for the first time, and Ambrose scanning the area for threats, she felt like she might actually have a chance at succeeding this time.

After failing so much, it was nice to have a bit of hope.

As she so often did, Elayne turned her thoughts to her brother. They had been inseparable as children, and that bond only grew as they got older. They only had each other since their dad died in a dungeon. Adventurers were what so many people aspired to be on Midgard, because it offered a chance at power.

She longed to escape the confines of the small town. Not just for herself, but for her brother. She still remembered that day, him bleeding out on the ground, her hand clasped in his.

"Promise...promise me you'll succeed."

"I promise, Z. I promise I'll become the greatest adventure Midgard has ever seen."

She carried her brother's dream in her heart.

When Ambrose had shown her that he understood, that he knew the pain she held, she saw within him a kindred spirit.

These thoughts swam through her head as they walked, and so she did not feel it, nor did she see it when the leaves rustled beside her. Suddenly, pain blossomed on her skull as her hair was yanked back, her body pressed against someone, and she was so surprised she dropped her staff.

She felt a cool, sharp blade press to her throat, and a male voice she knew well spoke into the forest air.

"Now, now, don't act so hasty, hmm human?"

Ambrose and Noelle had whirled around to face her. Ambrose's expression was one of utter calm, like a meadow on a cool day. She imagined that she could see the calculations running through his mind already. Noelle growled, her cats ears flattening, lightning sparked between her hands.

"Stroud," Elayne choked out, her throat undulating against the edge of the blade. A trickle of blood appeared, running down her throat.

"Shh. I wouldn't speak just now, lowborn. You might get more than just a small nick."

Stroud turned his attention to the Infernal Crusader before him.

"I don't know you two, and I certainly have nothing against you. Here's my proposal, you stay right there, don't get in my way while I take this filthy lowborn here with me, and all will be well. Try to use a skill against me, follow me, or attack me in any way, and I'll slit her throat first thing. Maybe you think you're fast, hmm? Maybe you think your skills are enough to get me first, but I assure you, that is not so. Barely any pressure at all, and I'll open her throat up lickity split."

Ambrose said nothing, merely stood and watched. Noelle flicked her gaze to his, some sort of silent communication passing between them, and she did nothing.

Stroud nodded, "Good boy. I knew you'd see it my way."

Slowly, Stroud began to back up, dragging her with him. She felt the subtle power of a skill being activated, and shadows engulfed them.

Ambrose did not follow.

She worried about that for a minute. Did he simply not care? He could kill Stroud with a word! Why wasn't he saving her? But she calmed her mind with a mental breath, as she felt a literal one would be hazardous to her health at the moment.

Ambrose had said he would help her, and he didn't strike her as a liar when it came to such a thing. Stroud had him over a barrel, perhaps he was merely afraid of him killing her before he had a chance to do anything. Still, it stung her anyway, because he hadn't even spoken! Just stared, letting Stroud cart her off as if she was just some object.

No, again, that was unfair. He was thinking, she could see that much. What would speaking have done for her? No, instead of focusing on casting blame, she tried to get her surroundings.

Hard to do since her surroundings was utter darkness.

Before long, however, the darkness faded. They were in a different part of the forest now, but before her was a simple camp. Over thirty people were engaged in various activities across the camp. Setting up tents, cooking, storing supplies, it was all being done.

She couldn't believe so many were working together.

"Welcome to my little band of merry men, eh? I'd let you in on my plans, but I don't think you will need to worry about that much before long."

Stroud took her to a pole, and tied her to it with rope.

"It's enchanted rope, designed to resist skill effects, so I wouldn't entertain any ideas of escape."

"What are you going to do with me?"

Stroud shrugged, "Nothing good, I'll tell you that."

He grinned at her.

Elayne swallowed.

Hours had gone by with nothing much happening. Elayne was uncomfortable, but not overly so. Being D-Grade meant that nature didn't call nearly so often, and the rope wasn't hurting her. It was just awkward. Though the sense of fear she felt alleviated the boredom.

She spent the time observing, and what Stroud was doing made no sense.

He was drawing strange symbols in the dirt, setting up candles, placing crystals and other weird things within the symbols. More than once he would look at her and grin a crazy grin.

Whatever he was doing, she knew it was nothing good.

She never dabbled in the occult, but she suspected he was going to attempt a summoning. That was usually what strange symbols, weird items, and a kidnapped elven woman in the woods meant.

Please come soon, Ambrose. She pleaded to herself. Things were not looking good for her. Stroud was now drawing out a huge circle over the symbols, leaving a wide gap in the middle. An ornate knife was placed in the center.

That could only mean a few things. A tingle crawled up her spine, like a creeping spider over her skin. She swallowed, trying to dislodge the lump that had formed in her throat. Her eyes were glued to the knife as moonlight bathed its silver edge, causing shadows to dance around it.

Candles flickered as a slight breeze played over the area like a mischievous kid.

Suddenly he was certain she knew what her role was going to be in Stroud's plan.

She was going to be the sacrifice.

CHAPTER SIXTY

When Elayne was taken, Ambrose calmed his mind and heart. Some people often panic in situations like that, and because of that, they lose control. That and giving into anger. Noelle raised an eyebrow at him at the thought, and he scowled.

"No, the irony is not lost on me. Come on, we need to follow."

It wouldn't be hard to follow Stroud. If he had used **[Retributions Gaze]** on him, the skill would have allowed him to track him that way. Except he hadn't used the skill on Stroud. It didn't matter much anyway; he could track Stroud without it. Whatever skill Stroud had used to hide his departure did not hide his tracks.

Ambrose wasn't the best tracker. His father had been really unhappy about that fact, but he had picked up enough that he could easily pick out the path that Stroud had taken.

Even when he had trouble, Noelle's nose twitched, and she would point out a direction. *It was nice to have options*, he snorted. After walking for a while, he paused. Ahead, the clearing opened up, and he looked at Noelle, nodding. Stroud was ahead, and what was more, he could hear ominous chanting.

"Ominous chanting in the dark, foreboding woods? Yeah, nothing good has ever come from that." Ambrose muttered to himself.

There was nothing for it, though, but to push forward. Besides, he would surely need to stop whatever was going on. When he walked into the clearing, he immediately took stock of the area and situation. He found Elayne instantly. She was in the middle of a huge occult-like circle, with candles and other items at the edges.

Stroud stood over the kneeling Elayne, a ritual athame in his hand. He was wearing a pitch-black robe, with the hood pooling around his shoulders like a pillow of black silk. Others stood around the circle, hoods pulled up, looking every inch like dark cult members attempting to summon a dark god. For all he knew, they likely were.

Stroud paused, but the others kept chanting. He patted Elayne on the head, and her face twisted into a wrathful scowl. Ambrose saw her try to move, but the inner circle flared with terrible light, and her scowl turned into an expression of pain.

Stroud stepped out of the circle, walking confidently toward Ambrose.

"Ah, the outworldler. You're going to attempt to interrupt our little ritual here, aren't you?"

Ambrose shrugged, "I've got nothing better to do. Look, I know you're going to resist. You think you're powerful enough to stop me. You're not. Let Elayne go. Stop whatever profane thing you've got going, and that will be that. We'll go our separate ways." He hardened his voice into brimstone. "Don't, and I'll scatter your ashes across this forest."

Stroud threw his head back, and cold, mocking laughter filled the air.

"Well, aren't you just full of yourself! I don't think there's much more to be said, is there?"

With a flash of a gleaming knife, Stroud flowed forward, shrouded in liquid darkness.

Only to be met with crackling lightning raking across him with arching power. Stroud was blasted backward, his form shattering into black glass before flowing back together.

Ambrose's eyepatch flared, trying to catch any illusions, but he saw nothing. He had to conclude it was a different sort of skill.

Drawing on the power of [**Hellfire Manipulation**] he crafted a portal, sending it spinning like a blazing shuriken of fire toward Stroud. As he did this, he spun up another portal, summoned Akaroth to his hands, and fell through the portal.

His spinning portal sliced through Stroud's reconstructed form like he was paper, and once again, he burst apart into a shard of dark glass. When he reformed again, Ambrose was there, and with a slash of Akaroth, he decapitated Stroud.

"We could do this all day, big guy."

Stroud had not reappeared in the same way as before this time. Instead, his decapitated form merely melted like black wax. Ambrose whipped his head around as Noelle growled, held out her hand and sent a bolt of lightning at Stroud, who was now standing yet again by Elayne with a nasty grin on his face.

The grin wasn't relevant.

No, it was the blade jutting out from Elayne's chest that demanded his attention. The elven woman's mouth was open in a little 'O' and her skin was going pale as blood flowed like water from her wound. It was swirling as if it had a will of its own, seeping into the circle. A faint sanguine glow like that of dying light emanated from the circle.

As Elayne's lifeblood drained out of her, the circle itself lifted off the ground. It was rotating, glowing, and thrumming with power while draining Elayne's life force by the second. Ambrose did not wait, he attacked the circle, raising Akaroth high.

The dragon roared in his mind as lightning wreathed the blade. At his strike, thunder boomed, lightning pulsed, and he was blasted back in a flare of a sanguine blue explosion. His feet skidded against the dirt, and he gritted his teeth, furrowing his eyebrows in a scowl as a clawed hand burst out of the circle's middle.

Elayne fell to the ground, life draining from her eyes as she stared at Ambrose. Her face calmed, and a little smile curved her lips. She mouthed her final words, "Thank you."

Then she died.

Heat blossomed like a rose in his chest that intensified as his body quivered.

Anger was a tide of fire within him, and he roared as Stroud's mocking laughter filled the air.

He raised his hands, crying out as a demonic form tore itself free from the vortex in the air.

Its skin was as red as the blood that had fueled the portal it came from. Sickly yellow eyes blinked slowly, and ebony horns curled in a horrific fashion from its bald skull. Gleaming claws were its hands and webbed; leathery wings unfurled from its back.

It floated in the air, and Ambrose could feel the spiritual pressure coming from it like an invisible pillow attempting to smother him.

She had thanked him. His nails dug into his palms, and Akaroth shook in his hand.

Her final words. The last thing she would ever say.

She had thanked him.

Ambrose could not care less about the devil that hovered in the air. His own spirit was countering the devils, so it was no obstacle for him at all in preventing him from raising Akaroth at Stroud.

"I am going to kill you." He said calmly.

Stroud grinned but turned away from Ambrose to kneel before the demonic entity.

"My lord Wrath, we have broken the spell that sealed you in Muspelheim. This world is ready for you to take."

Ambrose raised Akaroth to strike out at Stroud, but the entity spoke.

"How many eons has it been? No matter...I am hungry."

Almost casually, his forked tail lazily swishing behind it, the entity lashed out with a claw, piercing Stroud through the chest and lifting him high.

With his other clawed hand, he decapitated Stroud, blood bubbling from his stump; the demonic being lifted Stroud's body up, and like a bottle of soda on a summer day, he drank him.

The being's throat moved up and down as he drank Stroud's blood before tossing his corpse aside like a discarded bottle in an alley.

"So good to be free."

Chapter Sixty-One

Ambrose did not bother talking. Instead, he tossed a **[Retribu-tions Gaze]** at the summoned devil. He received a message in return that he had not seen in a long time.

[???]

"Huh."

"You thought you'd get more than just question marks. How interesting. You're more powerful than this rabble that I can see."

Ambrose did not talk to the entity. Instead, he noted his nonchalance and hefted Akaroth.

Do you know anything about this thing? He queried the dragon axe.

Akaroth's growling words drifted through his mind, *I only know that it is a devil and not to be trifled with, hatchling.*

Ambrose tugged his lips into a frown. He had met devils before, notably Misaq. Of course, there was also the devil that guarded Merlin's Grimoire, and neither looked like what he had expected devils to look like. That wasn't surprising, as his expectations were formed by media.

This one? It met every expectation—the personification of stereotypical evil. He calmed his mind, thinking through the situation. Honestly, he wanted to retreat. It wasn't cowardice; it was training. The smart thing to do was to retreat, gather more information, and then deal with the foe after he was better equipped.

Except it would cost lives if he did that. The people here signed up to face monsters that were supposed to be more or less their level. They were unprepared for a devil far beyond them in level and strength. Normally, that wouldn't be his problem, but he had to be better than that, a mantra he had been repeating to himself lately. Then there was Elayne. Yes, it was Stroud that killed her, but ultimately it was in service to the monster before him.

He lifted Akaroth, and the devil laughed, "You intend to fight, I see. I could use a little warm-up, even against a roach."

The devil flicked a finger almost lazily, and a fireball larger than a man's head flew his way, scorching the air as it flew. Ambrose raised Akaroth, slashing through the fireball with a burst of lightning.

"Oh, how interesting. You have a toy. Alright, let's amp it up just slightly."

This time, the fireball was doubled in size and flew even faster. Ambrose still cut it down. He sent a thought toward Noelle, *I need to fight this guy at full power, and I don't think anything you can do will affect him.*

She wasn't happy, her ears flattening, but she nodded, seeing that he was right. Her form brightened, flowing towards him until she was a cloak around his neck again.

The devil was scratching his pointed chin. "I may have to put a little effort into this. How interesting, indeed!"

This time, the devil shot multiple fireballs at him from different angles as he floated around counterclockwise, the bored look never leaving his face.

Ambrose tapped his mana and called upon [**Hellfire Manipulation**], creating portals that swallowed up the fireballs, spitting them right back out at the devil and detonating in an explosion of crimson fury.

When the fire faded, the devil stood, smiling slightly and utterly unharmed.

"Ah, so you use portals. I'd say you're at C-Grade and a sage. Your foundation is solid, and you should be proud. You're not at a level where you can effectively beat me. I tell you what: I'm in a whimsy mood. I call it a full stomach. I want to see how powerful you get. Meet me in a world called Xanalia; you'll know it when you reach that level and go to the arena of wrath. I'll be waiting. Ta!"

A portal not unlike the one Ambrose made tore through reality behind the devil, who floated through it, a grin on his face. It closed moments later.

Ambrose tightened his grip on Akaroth, staring at where the devil had vanished. Only when he was absolutely certain the threat had passed did he relax, putting Akaroth into his infernal realm. He looked around, and found most of the cult members who had assisted in the summoning were gone.

There was one laying on the ground, but he was dead. Ambrose could tell because the body looked like a grey, lifeless husk. Whatever ritual had been used to summon the devil, it had exacted a terrible price.

Mana death. Akaroth's voice sounded interested in his head. He had never heard the term before.

What's that?

With a flick of her mind, Akaroth twitched in his hands towards the corpse.

That. It is what happens when there is not enough mana within your core to power a skill or spell. This ritual instead drew on their life force.

It was a reminder to be careful not to go too far. Ambrose didn't feel like he had ever gotten close to the point of drawing on his own life force, but it was good to know what would happen if he ever pushed it.

Ignoring the husk, he went to the where the ritual circle had been, standing over Elayne's corpse. He hadn't known her for long, and her death certainly didn't hit him as hard as his wife's...but it was something else he put on his shoulders.

He manifested Noelle at her prodding, and she too stared mutely down at the once determined young woman now a corpse. He gritted his teeth.

He had gotten overconfident. All of his progress made him believe he would have no problems in this world. Made him think he would be able to steamroll every challenge.

His father had taught him better, and yet he continued to make the same mistakes. Sure, he deliberately ignored some of his father's teaching, because at the time he had been rebelling against what he felt was an unseen leash around his throat.

He had to be better, or he would keep losing people. Elayne had dreams, she had goals, a life ahead of her.

"All gone, now." He looked up into the night sky.

He didn't vow revenge, he was already on that path. He didn't make a promise to her.

But he did grieve for her.

Using portals he transferred dirt until he had a deep hole in the ground. Picking up Elayne's corpse, he buried her.

Even with portals, it took him a while.

After she was covered, buried beneath the ground, Ambrose stood for a while.

"Is there anything you'd like to say?"

Noelle's expression was somewhere between sad and fierce. "She was a friend," was all she said.

Ambrose nodded, placing a hand on her shoulder. "Yes, she was."

Ambrose would never forget her, and though he wouldn't rage down a path of vengeance for her as he was doing for his wife, he would take the devil up on his offer. After he dealt with Eric, he had a list of items to take care of. Now, he could include finding that world and that arena on it.

Noelle tucked herself into his side, small tears rolling down her cheeks. Almost awkwardly, he put an arm around her, trying to send her comforting thoughts. Sometimes, if he wasn't careful, it was easy to see Noelle as a child, and not a mythical being with her own mind and emotions.

They stood there for some time with nothing but each other and a gentle wind for company.

Chapter Sixty-Two

Ambrose Severen fell from a portal he had opened just behind the mage's head and cleaved the unfortunate spellcaster in two with Akaroth. Elayne was dead, and while he mourned her, time waited for no one.

He had a goal, and that meant he couldn't afford to take too many breaks. Even if that weren't true, this was a trial he still needed to pass. He wouldn't admit it to himself, but he also had a competitive streak, and it wasn't in him to lose an event he had set out to win.

As the two halves of the mage fell to the ground in a bloody heap, Ambrose stood up. Noelle was digging fingers wreathed in lightning into the throat of a warrior, who died moments later. Her ears were flat against her skull, her face twisted into the intimidating snarl of a predator. In a way, it was cute.

That makes ten.

Since leaving Elayne's new grave and wandering the forest, he had run into several people, none of them particularly powerful enough to harm him. It reminded him of when he saw Alice playing an epic fantasy game where the character absorbed dragon souls.

"This game looks super easy," he had said to her.

She threw him a grin. "I'm just over-leveled, that's all. It's what happens when you do a bunch of side quests before taking on the main story. I almost forgot this game had a main plot!"

The memory faded away, leaving behind the ghost of a smile on his face. That's exactly what he was feeling here. He was over-leveled for these people. That was fine with him. He set his mouth into a grim line. It meant he was ready to face Eric.

"Wow, you really did a number on him!"

Ambrose turned to find a red-headed woman with bright green eyes staring at him. She was...barely dressed. Her shirt was cut off, showing an impressively muscled midriff. Her bare biceps bulged, and Ambrose thought she might have broader shoulders than his own.

Resting on her shoulder was a massive bastard sword, the grip of which she held in one hand. Along the blade were glowing green runes, and he felt a pressure emanating from her, attempting to bear down on him like an invisible predator.

His own spirit repelled the oppressive, predatory force, but Ambrose had a feeling this foe was not like the rest of the under-leveled rabble he had faced so far.

She did have on what appeared to be sweats, like the kind you might wear to exercise. However, her feet were bare.

Ambrose used [**Retributions Gaze**] on the woman, not caring if she thought him rude.

[**Susanna Borreat Level 215 Arcane Berzerker**]: **Susanna is a fierce warrior from a world known as Davalice. She was exiled from her tribe for being considered too weak.**

"Didn't anyone ever tell you that it's rude to analyze a girl without asking first? I mean, come on big guy, at least buy me dinner."

Ambrose raised an eyebrow. Her words sounded almost flirty, but the way she said them was anything but.

"Seeing as you're an enemy likely going to attempt to kill me at any moment, I don't care whether it's rude or not."

Susanna pursed her lips, blinked a few times, nodded, and then said, "Yeah, that's fair."

Then she hefted her sword and tried to kill him.

Ambrose opened a portal right in front of her at the very last second. The result was the red-headed warrior woman rushing head-long into a fifty foot drop because Ambrose had crafted the second portal that high up in the air.

He didn't think that would end the fight, but he had been hoping. Using the time wisely, he created distance, raising Akaroth to be at the ready.

When the woman crashed into the ground, there was a burst of destructive purple light and an explosion of dirt as a crater formed at her impact. After the dirt settled, Susanna stood up, a wild grin on her face and a wild light in her eyes.

"Oohh, do that again!"

She blurred toward him like a crimson bullet. As she moved, her bastard sword flashed, knocking away the lightning Noelle sent her way.

As fast as she was, Ambrose had created considerable distance between them, and he used that distance well. First, he formed small portals, and willed them to rotate between open and shut, at the same time he fused more hellfire into the portals, creating spinning portals of hellish flame and death.

He sent those right at the warrior woman.

That was when he felt her Icon.

The feeling that swept over the area was like an open challenge, a defiance cast into the teeth of an oppressor.

His portals vanished.

Just like that.

Then she was on him, and he didn't have time to think about what had happened.

Fending off a bastard sword with an axe was not a great idea, and so Ambrose found himself ducking and weaving around her blows. It was easy to avoid them because Noelle was hounding the woman, blasting her with lightning or rushing in attempting to scratch her with claws.

Irritation blossomed in Susanna's eyes, and finally she whirled around at the last second, lashing out with a vicious kick at Noelle that landed on her chest.

Noelle cried out in pain as she was spun away from the woman with incredible force.

"Now then, where were we?"

Ambrose unmanifested Noelle who flowed around him, a cloak once more. She was in pain, but alive, and being in cloak form would help her heal.

After that, he went on the offensive. He dropped through portal after portal, using hit and run tactics against the woman.

Whose flesh repelled his attacks as effectively as if she were wearing heavy plate mail.

What succeeded in impressing him was that she did not grow overconfident. She didn't just let him rain attacks on her body, she fended him off as best she could, that same mad grin on her face the entire time.

Kicking off, she flew backward away from him, resting the huge sword on her shoulder once more.

"You're good. Your foundation is about as good as mine, if not better. This is fun. Who are you?"

He wasn't interested in exchanging pleasantries, so he fed Akaroth mana, and the axe lifted into the air, taking her large dragon form, and roaring her fury at the warrior as dark clouds gathered overhead. He never understood the desire to talk in fights like this. It was a waste of breath, and often pointless. He didn't feel a need to brag, or taunt, only to end the fight as the victor.

Her eyes widened a bit at that, and widened even more as Akaroth sent a beam of destructive lightning directly for her. Thunder boomed, rolling across the sky in a wave of potent fury.

She raised her sword, her grin never wavering, as she prepared to meet the destructive power head on. He could already feel her gathering her Icons power.

He didn't want a drawn out conflict. No, he hoped to end this here and now.

CHAPTER SIXTY-THREE

Susanna had to admit the red-headed man before her was good. She raised *Avulain*, flooding it with arcane mana to withstand the lightning, and slashed straight through the dragon's destructive beam. That was one thing she had not been expecting at all from the fight, a freaking dragon to appear.

The axe-wielding warrior's green eye was filled with a cold calmness like grass frozen in the winter. So far, he hadn't reacted with surprise or even uncertainty. He defended when he needed to, assaulted when he should, exploited openings he saw, and otherwise acted like a fucking machine.

It was glorious, and Susanna could not keep the mad grin from her face.

"This is amazing! Even if I should fall today, I will rest easy for our battle has been legendary!"

The lightning attack faded, and Susanna exerted the lion Icon. She wanted to put pressure on him but found that no easy task. The man's foundation was beyond excellent, and she felt resistance. His Icon was a weight beyond hers, like great chains bolted to the earth.

This was no prey for the lion to feed upon. She felt like being in the presence of a smith of all things—a craftsman, not a powerful warrior.

She decided to take a precious second to analyze him. Normally, she didn't bother with such things. Battle was a language, and it usually told her all she needed to know about her foes. Yet, this man, she would make an exception for.

[Ambrose Severen, Infernal Crusader Level 225]: You stand at a simple grave, and a man kneels over it, head bowed. Clouds gather overhead, and his shadow is a banner of wrath. Chains shackle him to the ground; they are an invisible weight. A ghost of a little girl stands at his side, pointing accusingly.

Her [Soul Read] analyze skill always involved metaphorical images of the person or being she was analyzing. This was supposed to give her an idea of who she was dealing with or what.

She snorted. "You're a real sad bean, aren't you?"

She hoped the taunt would make him slip up and give her an edge.

Instead, he dropped lava on her.

He did it by opening one of those portal things above her head, and wherever he connected it to, it must have been a volcano or something because the liquid fire poured out from it like a waterfall.

At the same time, he held out a hand, and the dragon morphed into a cloud that shifted back into an axe.

She had been ready for an attack and used her defensive [Arcane Armour] skill to wreathe herself in a thin shield that could tank most every attack she had come across.

She hadn't tested it against fucking lava, however. It hissed, spitting like a living snake.

She gritted her teeth, pulling on her spirit to fortify her skill further. Her spirit came from her spiritual skill, [Arcane Rage], and she was close to activating that one.

Ambrose wouldn't wait there to see if the lava did her in. She couldn't just wait until he got tired of attacking her.

So she moved, kicking off to the side, moving out from underneath the lava.

"Alright, big boy, looks like I need to pull out the big guns for you."

He didn't answer her. Rather, he did something with his axe, wreathing the edge in a hellish fire. She could see a place within that edge, maybe trees.

Did he open a portal on the edge of his axe? She didn't have time to think it over as Ambrose blurred toward her with all the speed and precision she expected from a deadly combatant.

She activated **[Arcane Rage]**, and violet power erupted around her as if she were turned into a bomb. She roared with it, spreading her arms, *Avulain* shaking in her grip.

All thought fled her mind. Nothing remained except the rage.

With every movement, a detonation of violet mana; with every slash, a hurricane of power.

But Ambrose Severen dealt with it all with a calm, focused demeanor that defied normalcy.

He portaled around her, seeking an opening. He found several and exploited them.

Whatever power he had put into his axe, it cut through her mana like it was butter instead of a magical force. She was too angry to feel shock at him getting through her defenses. She ignored the wound, lashing out with her blade, power booming from her like a thunderclap.

It should have blasted him backward, but his Icon was keeping him grounded, and he must have had a defensive skill of his own.

A cloak of violet mana surrounded her. She clenched her fists, thrusting her arms outward. The veins starkly against her skin pulsated with power.

She was faster than a speeding bullet and could leap tall buildings in a single bound.

She was power incarnate.

"I'm a fucking super woman, you fuck!" She screamed her fury and rage, her sword blurring with such ferocity and speed that the human eye could not track it.

Though she could not see it now, the air around them began to warp with the mana pouring out of her.

"Fucking die!"

But he wouldn't. No, the bastard merely portaled or parried her attacks. He did it as calmly as one might take out the trash or perform a menial task. It infuriated her, and her skill reacted like an insane beast, thrashing, striking wildly.

His calmness did not waver. His green eye held that same glacial light as if someone had carved a winter crystal from the deepest depths of a winter cave into an eye and placed it in his socket.

His eyepatch burned with the fires of hades.

And then, like a match burning too quickly, she was spent.

Her strikes grew weaker; her mana bottomed out like a fuel tank on E.

Only then did the fucker speak like a teacher correcting an overeager student.

"My father told me once that when you had two fighters of equal skill, the one who tired out first loses. He said a fight like that was all about resource management, with your stamina being the recourse. I have a bad habit of ignoring my father's excellent advice. Call it father issues, I guess."

Suddenly, he blurred forward, a flash of white and black, and *Avulain* flew out of her hands. Her feet were swept out from under her just as her mana sputtered.

She had nothing left in the tank, and her skills vanished. No more defenses.

She still had her spirit and her Icon, but they wouldn't be enough to protect her—not when he had his own.

Ambrose nodded, satisfied that what he had expected to happen had.

"Now we come to it."

He raised his horrible blade, and her eyes widened. She could see the shadow of a great dragon looming over her, eyes glittering with lightning.

He paused before delivering the death blow.

"Come on! Finish it!" She screamed at him.

She was no longer grinning.

"This is just a contest. I've already killed more than enough to win this. There's no reason for you to die, too."

She pounded on the ground, "Don't you do that! I don't want your pity! End this!"

Ambrose cocked his head and then lowered his axe.

"See you around, warrior."

Then he walked away from her.

She didn't have the strength to follow.

Chapter Sixty-Four

A mbrose stood in the town square with Noelle at his side. She had been hurt, but a purchased healing potion helped make her healthy again. She hadn't been a fan of him sparing the red-headed female warrior, but that was to be expected. Despite current appearances, Noelle was a predator.

She had a hard time understanding concepts like mercy when it came to taking on enemies. But killing the woman just hadn't felt right.

No, that's not the correct feeling. It hadn't been honorable.

Ambrose rubbed his thumb and forefinger together. *When did I start caring about honor?*

His father had always told him that honor was for fools and the dead. He taught Ambrose to be ruthless, to exploit every weakness, to cheat and to lie in order to win.

But Alice had shown him a different path.

He took a breath, closing his eye briefly, sending his thoughts out like a net, trying to wrap around the memory of her. Every day he felt like a piece of her was fading from his mind. It wasn't that he couldn't remember her, but rather that the memories from that night, from when Eric killed her in front of him, were overpowering the others.

He didn't want that. Yes, he wanted to keep his goals in mind, and he wanted that rage to fuel him.

But he didn't want to forget the good things, either. In their Dungeons and Dragons games his wife had always told the party not to be

"Murder hobos," in that they didn't need to kill every person they came across.

Ambrose had killed plenty of people in that forest. Enough that he was about to be announced as the winner of this trial, slash competition. He didn't need to kill her.

Yet everything raged at him to do so. For one thing, leaving threats behind was a bad idea. He had no doubt Susanna would pursue him at a later time. That one struck him as the grudge-holding type. It would have been far smarter to kill her to prevent her from coming back later when it was less convenient and she was more powerful.

Noelle nodded her head at his thoughts, and he suppressed a chuckle.

But it had felt like that would have been a murder-hobo decision, and Alice would want him to be better than that.

Some might say she'd want him to give up his crusade of revenge, too. Those people didn't know his wife. She was a good person, but she could be vindictive if she wanted to be. She would want Eric to pay for what he did, and he would.

The announcer, or whatever he was, Ambrose didn't care, was walking onto the stage that had been set up for the event.

"Here are the results of the trial! In third place we have..."

In the end, Ambrose had won first place, just as he thought.

He walked up to the quartermasters desk in a small building in the town square to receive his winnings, and his badge.

It was a small, shiny bronze badge with the words "Bronze Adventurer" stamped into the metal. A simple thing, but he had to put a little mana into it in order to bind it to him.

"It's so's people can't fake it, ya see?"

Ambrose didn't respond. The quartermaster, a portly man with olive skin and a grey beard, grunted and produced his reward for the competition part of the trial.

Set in a small black silk lined box was a glimmering red stone. It was small, and oddly shaped, like a tear-drop. There appeared to be a flame inside of it, hungrily pressing against the stone, trying to free itself.

He used **[Retributions Gaze]** to see what it was.

[???-Unique]

"What is this?"

The portly man shrugged, "No's clue."

"No one can identify it?"

The quartermaster shook his head.

Ambrose got it. "Ah, I see. No one can identify it, and you can't sell it precisely because of that, so you offer it as a reward. That way, if it's something worthless, there's no harm done. If it is valuable, you still win out because it was a legitimate prize, thus earning positive public opinion."

The man scratched at his beard, looking confused.

Ambrose sighed, throwing the item in his infernal dimension. It didn't really matter.

"I was also supposed to be able to have custom items made?"

Paperwork was produced and handed over to Ambrose. He read it over, and found it was a purchase order for 'to be determined' custom work by the townsmith, and enchanter. It said the town would pay for the service up to ten thousand gold.

Now *that* was a prize.

"What da ya be wantin' made then?"

That was the question. Ambrose sat with the townsmith and Noelle at a table in the smith.

"Well, before we get to that, what are your capabilities?"

The smith puffed up, "Ya be lookin' at a C-Grade Craftsman, young man!"

"Okay...what does that mean?"

The smith's brown eyes narrowed. "Yar not pullin' my leg, are ya?"

He shook his head. "Hmph. It *means* that I can make up to legendary gear in the C-Grade. Armour, weapons, jewellery, robes, all of it. I can even enchant it all."

The smith smirked at him as if he had just let Ambrose know that he had won the lottery in getting his services. Ambrose stroked his beard, thinking.

"Before we get to discussing my order, what's your name? I'm Ambrose."

The smith stuck out his hand. "Bori Snugerson at yar service."

Bori's eyes glittered like a snake's, likely waiting to see if Ambrose would make fun of his name.

He didn't. He merely shook the smith's hand firmly. In truth, he didn't care about being polite. He just didn't want to keep calling him 'The smith' in his head. Plus, his father had always told him to treat people handling his gear well.

"Last thing you want is some tinkerer deciding to sabotage your weapons because you were an asshole. Good way to find yourself in an early grave, kid."

Ambrose waved away his old man's words with a mental hand.

"Now then, back ta' my original question. What is it ya be wantin'?"

Ambrose sighed.

It was a question he had been considering for some time now. He just had no idea what to ask for. At this point, he was beginning to think he didn't need armor. The plate mail he wore now was practically useless except for making mana more efficient.

Everything else about it was redundant, except for looking cool.

He explained this to the smith, who stroked his own beard.

"Hmm. Impressive array o' skills ya got, young man. I could at least make ya somethin' a little less bulky."

Ambrose gestured for him to continue.

"Half-plate would probably suit yar needs a little better. Ya don't need all the bulk with yar skills."

"Sounds fine. But that doesn't answer the question of what it should do."

Bori shrugged, "Could do lots o' things. I can include mana efficiency easy enough for ya. But that leaves a whole lotta o' room for other effects."

Ambrose sat back.

He had some thinking to do.

Chapter Sixty-Five

He thought of and discarded many different ideas. Bori had left him to it, getting to work on other orders while he thought. The smith was not interested in helping him decide.

"It's yar armour, just know that if the System says what ya want is beyond legendary ranked, I won't be able to do it."

What he needed was utility. He didn't want any new offensive or defensive skills, he had that in plenty. His eyepatch allowed him to pierce illusions, and that was something none of his skills did for him.

Awareness was the most useful thing you could have in a battle. If you don't see it coming, you're dead. His recent trouble with the now deceased Stroud supported that fact.

He hadn't seen him coming. The elf had gotten the drop on him and it had allowed him to capture Elayne. If he had known the enemy was there, he could have done something about it. That's why he was always scanning the area, to be on the look-out for threats.

But when those threats were invisible, it didn't matter if he were looking. His eyepatch was great, but he was sure it had limits.

With an idea in mind, he called the smith over, and Ambrose went over his thoughts with the man.

Bori nodded, fingers combing his beard, "I could do that, yes...Okay then. Sit tight!"

After that it was just a matter of waiting. Noelle kicked her feet under the table, and he looked over at her.

"You okay?"

She swiveled her head around to look at him directly.

Her tail swished, and her ears twitched. Then she shrugged, her blue eyes lowering.

"Miss Elayne?"

Noelle nodded, ears lowering.

Ambrose put a hand on her head, and she looked up at him, mouth open slightly.

He smiled a little awkwardly at her. "I don't always check in with you. You must feel like you're not my priority, and that isn't true. I am sorry, and I will try to do better, okay?"

Noelle beamed, tail wriggling happily. She launched herself into his arms, and he let out a little breath.

He tried to ingrain the feeling into his memory.

"Got yar order right here!" Bori exclaimed, setting out the chest piece of the half-plate.

Ambrose blinked.

It didn't look like his current plate mail. It was simpler. The armor was carved from the void, but occasionally, lines of sanguine red and iridescent green light pulse along it.

"I took what ya already had goin' on as inspiration. O'course I had to add my own spin, yeh? This right here would scare a Kraken back into the sea if I do say so."

Ambrose used [**Retributions Gaze**] on the armor:

[**Infernal Crusaders Half-Plate-Legendary**]: Crafted by the C-Grade craftsman Bori Snugerson. This armor is enchanted to provide the wearer with multiple benefits. The first is a mild

awareness of everything around you, up to one hundred feet in every direction. The armor integrates with your senses, making this ability easy to use. Secondly, the armor has been attuned to your Infernal Realm, allowing you to retrieve anything within it instantly.

He almost whistled. It was exactly what he had asked for. Bori tapped the armor with a finger, a proud grin curling his lips, beard jiggling.

"I'm proud o'this. I won't lie about that. Took a considerable amount o'ingrediants, too. May it serve you well!"

He wasted no time putting it on before putting his plate mail in his infernal realm. Instantly, his senses expanded. It was like he had just uploaded his mind to a high-definition camera with an eagle's eye view. He could see and hear everything going on around him.

The people bustling about outside, the old man sleeping in the house near the shop, the child crying to his mother, all of it filtered to him. He almost clutched his head, but a second later, it all toned down to a mild background noise. With some experimentation, he realized he could prioritize what he heard and saw.

If people or things weren't dangerous, they were grayed out and muted. If their level was near his, and there was hardly any of those, they were highlighted, and he heard them like they were on a television screen in front of him.

Noelle cocked her head as she watched his lips tug upward into a smile.

He looked at her. "Nothing like what happened with Elayne will happen again. With this armor? I will at least have a chance to stop it."

Noelle smiled, tail curling around her shoulder.

Ambrose tried to thank Bori, but the smith just waved at him to leave.

Shrugging, he did so.

He had places to be and people to hunt, after all.

He had decisions to make. Firstly, he needed to find Eric. However, he had no idea where Eric had gone. However, it wasn't a huge leap in logic to put together where he may have gone. Eric had been after a spear, and he was reasonably certain his foe had gotten it from the forerunner in this city.

He had needed the spear to get access to spirit. So why wouldn't he go after an item that gave him access to an Icon? It felt right. If not that, Eric would likely want to control Fenrir. Having such a powerful creature under his control would appeal to him.

He hoped to have surprise on his side, but he doubted he did. Eric had a healthy paranoia, and he would expect Ambrose to follow after him. He would prepare for it.

It was the only lead Ambrose had, however, so he had little choice but to follow it. Which is how he found himself on the path to yet another great forest beyond the western gate. Once again he found it somewhat amusing that he kept ending up in forests.

Were there no other settings that one could find mythical monsters to fight? Noelle skipped along beside him, the dirt smooshing beneath her feet.

You go into the dragon's lair, hatchling. Beware its claws.

Ambrose acknowledged the dragon's words with a thought. She was right that he should be aware of traps or even an ambush. It was possible that Eric had surrounded himself with flunkies, or other such minions. It was better that he prepared for that.

His awareness wasn't quite precognition, but with his training, he would be able to use it almost like it was. Eric would be prepared for a powerful opponent in Ambrose and likely would expect him to have tricks he wasn't aware of.

He wouldn't think of Ambrose having this kind of awareness, though. There was no way he could predict that kind of thing. It was a card he would surprise the bastard with.

He passed a few others on his path. Signs warned travelers that the forest was dangerous and to go around. The path even wound around the forest itself. He ignored the signs, heading straight for the foreboding opening into the forest ahead of him.

He could practically feel the danger from it, like it was a living, sinister thing, beckoning him forth.

Ambrose entered its embrace, ready to face what came.

Chapter Sixty-Six

The monster thought it was hiding. It was doing a good job, admittedly. His awareness ability, which his new armor granted him, showed the monster lurking in the shadows against a large tree. Its dark brown-green fur allowed it to blend in with the tree and foliage surrounding it.

Its eyes were the color of fresh dung on the ground during a rainy night. Its dark claws trembled against the bark of the tree. Its whole body shivered with anticipation. Ambrose walked right past it, and it slunk forward on silent, padded paws.

"Now, Noelle," Ambrose stated calmly.

She spun immediately, lightning-wreathed claws tearing out the thing's throat, its eyes wide with surprise. It died in a fountain of blood, lightning crackling around his body.

Ambrose wasn't surprised when dozens of the creatures appeared, dark eyes glittering with hate.

That was when a voice emanated from the group of creatures. A voice he knew very well.

"I knew you'd find me, eventually. To avenge poor, poor Alice."

A mocking laughter portended the attack that came. Claws flashing, the monsters rushed forward, their bodies moving through the air being the only sound they made.

Noelle flashed into action, lightning burning baby blue in the night, reflecting off their dark eyes and highlighting the swaying leaves of the trees around them.

She killed scores of them, but the vicious creatures kept coming. Ambrose sent forth spinning portals that cut the monsters in half as neatly as one of those laser swords in those movies Alice loved.

When only a few remained, the rest scattered, dismembered, broken parts, the voice returned.

"I must say, I didn't expect you to bring a friend. You wound me, Mr. Severen. I thought this dance was just for you and me."

Ambrose ground his teeth, jaw clenching, and his fist tightened on Akaroth. Like the axe that could summon a storm in the sky, one brewed in his chest.

Ambrose believed in leashing his emotions, but he allowed a bit of the storm to rage freely as he cut down the rest of the creatures, the dark chuckle fading away into the night like a lost, insidious whisper.

He didn't gain any experience from the monsters. He wondered about that a bit. This area was supposed to be more dangerous, and though he didn't analyze any of the monsters, he was reasonably sure they were mid D-Grade at the absolute best.

As they walked, the voice Ambrose knew to be Eric spoke up, "It truly is wonderful to see you again, old friend. I've gained control of these forest monsters, and let me tell you, there was a lot. I did it on a whim, thinking it would be nice to have a bunch of bloodthirsty minions on my side. What a good idea that was, eh Mr. Severen?"

As he spoke, a huge monster, not unlike the other creatures, lumbered calmly out of the forest.

"This one looks like an honest to god big-foot to me! Let's see how you handle this big guy, Mr. Severen."

Ambrose tossed a **[Retributions Gaze]** at it. He didn't think it was very powerful but thought and know for sure were two different things.

[Grendalkin Level 195]: Grendalkin stalk forests near towns and prey on hunters, gatherers or forest creatures.

With a roar that shook the leaves, the creature ripped off a low-hanging branch with a resounding crack that thundered through the forest. It swung the branch low at Noelle, who dodged with feline grace, lashing out with claws that dug into its fur.

It roared, lashing out with a foot that would have knocked Noelle in the head if Ambrose hadn't opened up a portal beneath her. She dropped through and came out above the monster, claws of hissing electricity raking down its back.

This time, the ground shook as the big foot look-alike bellowed, whirling and stomping. It swung the branch, desperate now to land a blow on Noelle.

However, it had made a fatal mistake, turning its back on another, far more dangerous foe. Ambrose hefted Akaroth, and, much as he had done back on Avalon when it was cursed, threw the axe into the grendalkin's back.

Blood burst as if from an angry blister. Akaroth flared with power, lightning piercing its body. It quivered, falling to the ground. Ambrose recalled his axe, and sent a spinning portal forward toward its neck.

The severed head plopped to the ground like an apple from a tree, its bloody stump squirting out more blood.

Attacks continued from various monsters as Ambrose and Noelle traveled through the forest.

"You sure are cutting a bloody swathe through all these monsters. Ah, well, they're just cannon fodder. Up ahead, you'll find the entrance to the main event!"

His knuckle popped, and Noelle hissed, her ears flattening. He took a breath. It wouldn't help him to lose composure.

They continued their walk, coming across a cave set in a mountainside.

He paused before entering, reaching his hand to the top of the cave entrance. He brushed aside some of the dust and frowned. A small glyph in the form of a wolf's head had been engraved into the rock.

Fenrir, he thought.

It was possible they would have to fight the legendary monster. Alice, the nerd she was, likely would have known all about him. He smiled sadly, steeled himself, and turned to Noelle.

"I think you should go cloak form from here on out."

She frowned, ears swiveling. She shook her head, "I want to help," she mewed out.

He crossed his arms. "This isn't an enemy you're ready for. You could easily be killed."

She put fists on her hips, tail shaking in annoyance. "You promised."

He sighed, "I know. But it's different this time."

"Why?" She flexed her claws.

"Because, we aren't about to face a monster near your level. You don't have the skills or experience needed."

Noelle hissed, tail lashing.

"No. I will fight. You promised."

Ambrose stroked his beard, closing his eyes.

Noelle had been with him from the start of this journey. It was right to have her here, at the end of it. He had promised, but he didn't want to sacrifice her. It would hurt no matter what, but if she died against a foe relative to her strength, at least he could say they had a reasonable shot of surviving.

But this foe? He didn't know much about Fenrir, but he was a being out of mythology. A nightmare, demi-god wolf that Ambrose felt sure he would need all of his strength to beat.

"Noelle, how about a compromise?"

Her nose wrinkled, but she gestured for him to go on.

"You go in as a cloak, but if its an enemy I think you can reasonably fight, I'll manifest you. Deal?"

Noelle shook her head, not even considering it. "Not this. Too important. I fight with you, Ambrose."

Ambrose rubbed his face, suddenly feeling tired for the first time in a long time. At the end of the day, Noelle had her own mind. Even if she was a mythical item. He had to respect her choices, even if he felt they were poor ones.

"Fine. You win. Let's go."

It was time to finally end Eric.

Chapter Sixty-Seven

It wasn't a cave filled with monsters like he had expected. He didn't even sense any traps, nor were there puzzles. It was entirely possible there *were* traps and his awareness offered by his armor didn't pick them up.

He was careful not to be complacent. His awareness ability was powerful, and he would use it. However, he wasn't about to let it replace his own good sense and training.

Mostly, what he noticed as they walked were murals. Carved into the stone were depictions of a great battle.

Do you know anything about what these are, Akaroth?

Frankly, the only reason he cared was because information on his potential opponent was a weapon all in its own. Another nugget of wisdom from his old man.

It certainly wasn't because he had much interest in the lore. Akaroth's voice filtered through his mind.

I was not present for it, but this was the battle between the Aesir, Loki and his son Fenrir. The clash of mana that day was felt across all the multiverse.

Ambrose paused next to a mural, studying it. A hooded figure and a man with an axe that looked a little like him were wrapping great chains around a dark wolf deep within the earth.

"The artists did an excellent job, they even included the glyphs on the chains."

It didn't take a genius to put together that he was headed straight for where Fenrir had been chained up.

In another mural, the chains appeared to be sapping something from Fenrir.

The glyphs are weakening him. Taking his strength, his skills, and locking them away somewhere. Akaroth sounded like she was impressed. *Whomever worked the enchantments did so like a dragon weaves flight.*

Deeper and deeper the smooth path wound. He never once felt like he was losing air, nor did the cave grow darker. A faint green light illuminated the entire path from a source he couldn't determine.

Before long Ambrose and Noelle stood before a great door. Broken glyphs sputtering with dying light were emblazoned upon it.

Ambrose had no idea what they did. He assumed they were warding glyphs, and someone had managed to break them.

Eric couldn't have done it. He was positive of that much. He was a one trick pony, and pretty much always had been.

Which meant the glyphs had to have been broken for a *while*.

With a shove, he pushed open the stone doors, the scraping as they moved echoed like growling thunder.

Beyond the doors was a massive cavern, so big you could probably fit several football stadiums within.

But that's not what drew his attention.

It was the massive wolf out of nightmares and legends that demanded his focus.

Great chains of wrought silver, red and black metal wrapped around its great form, engraved glyphs pulsing a toxic light, seeming to suck in vitality from the wolf.

Its fur was the color of a painted horror from the deepest recesses of a dark, twisted mind. Its eyes were a dark, polished amber.

There was no hatred there, no madness, no wild light.

Just deadness.

Whatever had been done to the wolf had broken it so utterly that it was beyond even madness.

Rattling metal blanked and echoed like a detonation as the great wolf rose up. Its maw opened up, revealing fangs the size of glaciers and shining like forged moonlight.

Its great tongue was a living flame, and Ambrose knew that this monster's only desire was to kill. To kill and to devour until itself had met the same fate.

Ambrose took a mental leash, wrapping it around the pulse of cold fear that settled over his heart like some icy hand. He jerked the cold hand back, tucking it in a neat cell constructed with thought and mental discipline honed over a lifetime of training.

He used **[Retributions Gaze]** on the wolf. Already knowing part of what he'd get back.

[Fenrir, The World-Eater Level 250]: The son of the Aesir god of magic, Loki, Fenrir is destined to end Asgard, the world of the Aesir. Fearing this, the pantheon chained Fenrir in a forgotten world in an ancient forest. They seeded the forest with deadly monsters. The chains were designed to sap the monster's power, locking it away somewhere else. However, the enchantments were so powerful it weakened the entire forest. Fenrir is now beyond mortal madness and desires only to kill.

"Magnificent, isn't he?"

Ambrose looked past the great monster, finding Eric in the middle of a circle of glyphs. He was grinning and dressed in the same academic-like attire as on the day he came to his house. He waved a hand enthusiastically at him.

He threw Akaroth right at him, but the great wolf raised a massive paw and, with an ease and quickness of movement that defied his size, batted the weapon out of the air, showing unconcern with the lightning that exploded against it in a flash of iridescent blue.

Eric's mocking laughter boomed throughout the massive cave as if he held a loudspeaker.

"I must say, I am so grateful to whoever chained this great beast up. If they hadn't designed them to sap its strength, I would have never been able to control it. Isn't he such a good boy? Yes, he is!" Eric laughed again, throwing his head back as Fenrir let loose with a stone-shattering roar that shook the very cave itself.

Ambrose closed his eyes as its force washed over him. He recalled Akaroth, and his grip on it was firm.

Beside him, Noelle was tense, ready to spring into action.

A calmness, a single moment of utter focus descended on him.

This was it. He could feel it like the sounding of a great bell or morning dawning.

The path ended here.

Here, he would destroy Eric, or he would die trying. It had been a long road, paved with obstacle after obstacle, but finally, *finally,* it would end one way or another. Either he would die and face whatever journey lay beyond the doors of death, or he would send Eric straight to hell.

All of his skills and training will be used at this moment. Alice would have said now was the time for boss music.

What seemed like an age ago, Ambrose and Alice had been trying to find a good song for her paladin character. She had wanted something epic, and it had to be just right. They had spent hours combing the internet. Finally, they had settled on one song that even Ambrose had enjoyed.

It was a song called "I'm So Close I Can Taste It," and the music filled his mind now. The claps, the beats of the music, the memory of Alice dancing to it, and a grin on her face all rushed through his body.

Ambrose was calm, and he tried to control his emotions in every fight he had ever had. It was usually the best practice because if he didn't do it, he paid for it.

Darren's death was a perfect example of that.

But here, now, in this moment, in this place?

Ambrose raised his arms, unleashing the storm in his chest, giving voice to it in time with his thundering heart, "COME ON THEN! LET'S SEE WHAT YOU GOT! I AM THE STORM!"

CHAPTER SIXTY-EIGHT

Ambrose rode the storm, focusing and harnessing it. He drew on his core and spun out deadly portals. Fenrir opened his maw and crouched low. When the portals got close, he *ate* them. The dark wolf's amber eyes glowed, and he pulled on his chains, the grinding metal giving him enough slack to allow him to bound forward.

Fenrir, the world eater, a level 250 C-Grade legendary monster, unleashed hell from its maw. Black fire thick with hunger bathed the area in an attempt to devour Ambrose's life.

Using the Forge Icon, he reinforced his **[Infernal Aegis]** and felt his mana drain as the skill exerted considerable effort to protect him from the void fire that wanted to eat him.

Ambrose dropped through a portal, raising Akaroth high. He slashed at the beast's flank, poured infernal mana into the dragon axe, and, at the same time, called lightning.

Noelle rushed the wolf as Ambrose's axe bit deep into its body.

Dark golden blood gushed from the wound, but Fenrir gave no reaction. The wolf lashed out to the side just as Ambrose vanished through a portal. However, as Fenrir's claws hit the portal, Ambrose felt the power of an Icon flare, and his portal was ripped to shreds with the passage of Fenrir's claws.

Like a ball a large dog had gotten a hold of, Fenrir's great paws batted Ambrose, and it felt like being smashed by an industrial-sized hammer.

He flew through the air for a second, but before impact, he formed another portal into existence.

Flying through it, he skidded on the ground.

Noelle reached Fenrir at that exact moment.

Her wreathed lightning was about to dig into one of the wolf's legs, but that terrible Icon blazed, and that same black fire from before erupted around the legendary monster like a cloak of horrific dark flame.

Amber eyes, once dead, filled with a terrible hunger, and the lightning meant to burn and shock, were instead devoured by the black.

He didn't piece it all together, but he knew now that Fenrir's Icon allowed him to devour magic.

There was a reason Ambrose hadn't wanted to bring Noelle along. He meant it when he said she wasn't ready for this fight. But he had resolved to give her more agency, to respect her desire to fight alongside him.

Her inexperience cost her. Seconds meant everything in a fight. You had to know when you could afford to decide your next course of action and when you needed to act immediately.

Noelle should have created distance to gauge this new power and to avoid being hit by any possible attack or effects.

Instead, she paused. It was just a moment, a mere blip of time, and her blue eyes looked uncertain.

The fire rushed out from Fenrir's body in a black, raging tide, and its sound was every dark whisper, every horrible thought that lurked in the forgotten corners of the mind.

It said a single thing.

Hungry.

Noelle screamed, her body locking up as the fire washed over her.

Ambrose was already acting, dropping through a portal as the fire reached him. He appeared by Noelle's side, and yanking on his Icon, he made sure his shield covered him as he lifted her. He went through another portal and appeared as far back away from Fenrir as possible.

Noelle was twitching, and small whimpers were causing shudders to run through her body.

He tried to unmanifest her, turn her back into a cloak...only for nothing to happen.

"What?"

Akaroth, what is this?

The dragon sounded sepulchral.

I do not know, hatchling.

Eric's laughter was filled with condescending scorn.

"Always failing to protect those you care about. Perhaps I should put those words on your gravestone after your corpse is buried. If Fenrir leaves anything left of you, Mr. Severen."

"What is happening to her, you sick bastard?"

"Oh? Doesn't 'the storm' know? Fenrir is the devourer, Mr. Severen. He was meant to eat entire worlds, all of its life, gone with one snap of his jaws. I'm sure you can fit the pieces together, Mr. Severen."

He stared down at Noelle's face, Fenrir straining in his chains to get to him. It was pale and growing slightly paler by the moment.

"He's devouring her life...those flames."

"Ding ding! Winner winner, chicken dinner. Give the man a prize. One of Loki's names was also Loki Firestarter. He granted his furry progeny a similar way with fire. Fenrir's flames, though? They do not burn. They eat. Ah, it gives me so much pleasure to see yet another person you care about die before your eyes, Mr. Severen. It is all the sweeter knowing it will be a slow, agonizing death."

Desperately, he retrieved a health potion from his infernal realm, his armor making the red bottle appear instantly in his hand with a mere thought.

He poured it into her mouth, watching her swallow.

"Please..." He whispered, watching her skin, hoping it would work.

"As if a healing potion would stop Fenrir's flames. Please, Mr. Severen. This is a legendary monster. That attack is powered by an Icon whose power strains the bounds of the C-Grade limits to which those chains have drained Fenrir down to."

Noelle quivered, eyes full of utter pain, and reached out a shaking hand.

"Not...fault."

Ambrose closed his eye, taking her hand in his.

"How can you say that? I could have made you turn back into a cloak. It's not like you ever really had a choice. Not really."

Noelle smiled then, a weak smile, but one nonetheless.

"My...friend...stubborn,"

Then her hand slipped out of his, falling to the ground as her eyes closed. She was still alive, just too weak to remain conscious any longer.

"How touching. Hey, you should be happy. At least you got a goodbye. Not even dear, sweet Alice got that, did she?"

Ambrose stood up. Noelle's still form encapsulates the whole of his vision.

He couldn't do anything for her. All of his skills, all of his power, were meant to do one thing and one thing only.

Kill.

Alice had called him a knight in tarnished armor. He had liked that vision she had of him because it meant that maybe, somewhere deep down, there was some shred of light in him.

Vivienne called him the Knight of Avalon. The island's great protector, its avatar of justice.

Avalon's people certainly thought of him that way, and it was an image he had cultivated.

Maybe he was all of those things, or maybe he just wanted to be.

But before all of that, Ambrose Severen had been one thing.

A killer.

His father had trained him, and Ambrose had honed that training for many years. He was a surgeon of violence, a brutal machine as unfeeling as a winter storm.

He turned, facing the great wolf. With a thought, he dismissed Akaroth from his infernal realm. He couldn't do anything for Noelle. She would be one casualty amongst the many that were on his shoulders. Just one more punishment for all of his many wrongs.

But what he could do was be what he was.

Ambrose Severen had once been a killer of men.

Now, he would be a killer of monsters.

CHAPTER SIXTY-NINE

Ambrose allowed his mind to go cold. He often lapsed into an analytical state when searching for solutions in a fight. His thoughts were faster than lightning as he ran down the problems and possible solutions. The main problem was that he couldn't use his skills. Fenrir devoured all magic, or in other words, mana-powered skills. Possible solutions included relying on sheer stats, attacking physically, and hoping that was enough.

He discarded this approach. Fenrir's cloak of black fire would merely get in the way, and it would drain his shield.

His shield.

Why hadn't Fenrir devoured it? Every other skill had been devoured by the black fire, after all. He called up the very recent memories, like reviewing camera footage. Yes, Fenrir had bathed him in that hungry black fire. Yet he had not ended up like Noelle.

[Infernal Aegis] had held.

Why? He thought.

His Icon, of course. He reinforced his ability with the Forge Icon, and that was a power on the same playing field as Fenrir's own. Yes, the Nightmare Wolf's Icon was more developed, but it couldn't consume another Icon. If it could, Ambrose would have died in that initial fire at the start of the fight.

The Forge Icon didn't just reinforce; it enhanced, and it made things sharper.

Ambrose walked forward, and when he was close to the demon wolf, it leaped at him, mouth open to swallow him whole.

Ambrose Severen opened mini portals over his fists, wreathing them in infernal mana. As he did, he brought the Forge Icon to bear, enforcing his skills.

So when his fist slugged the demigod wolf in the snout, it felt it.

His fists were backed by his C-Grade strength and enhanced with his skills.

Fenrir was knocked back as if hit by a speeding semi, hellfire blowing up in shards of brilliant flame and eldritch green light.

Ambrose held the cloak in his hands, feeling that mental connection with Noelle, that bond he knew would be with him all his days.

His eye settled on the chain length that crashed into the ground as Fenrir fell.

Fenrir did not devour the magic of the chains.

The enchantments upon it drew power from the legendary wolf monster. Did so in such a way that a once godly beast was now a C-grade being.

He could only assume it was because an Icon had been used when crafting the enchantments. He wasn't sure if that assumption was correct, but it didn't matter. All that mattered was that the chains affected the wolf, giving him a plan.

Using **[Infernal Sanctuary]** for the first time in a long time, he sent out chains forged seemingly from ghost light, moonbeams, and the infernal fires of hell itself.

He wrapped the chains around Fenrir's back legs, and the Forge Icon met the full pressure of Fenrir's own.

There was no way Ambrose was going to win out in that fight. His Icon would soon be overwhelmed, and his chains would be devoured.

Seconds mattered in a fight, as Noelle's indecision had shown. While that benefited Fenrir then, Ambrose had no such inexperience, and he knew how to capitalize on a second.

He was already at work, kicking off his back foot in a run; he grabbed one of Fenrir's heavy chains.

If he hadn't possessed C-Grade strength backed by his Icon, he never would have been able to lift the chain.

But because he did, it was easy. Holding onto it, he rushed to the side of the wolf's huge neck, the dragging of the great chain echoing all around.

Fenrir tried to move, but Ambrose hopped over the great wolf in a great leap, bringing the chain over his neck and yanking downward; Fenrir stumbled, letting out a great yelping growl as he crashed back into the ground.

Ambrose picked up the opposite chain as his infernal chains from infernal sanctuary burst apart.

Now holding both of Fenrir's chains around the monster wolf's neck, he pulled hard on them, tightening them around its neck.

He knew Fenrir would not allow himself to be choked, and Ambrose had prepared for that.

I hope this works, he thought grimly.

If it didn't, he would have to find another way to kill the wolf. But he did not allow the doubt to bother him, merely sparing a thought before shoving it in a mental hole.

It was easy to pull on his spirit. He had control of his Icon in the sense that he could call upon it, but now he took it and forced it onto his spirit.

The two forces pushed together like combining two different colors of play-dough.

And then Ambrose brought that combined force down upon the wolf like a descending meteor.

The hammer of his combined spirit, reinforced by the Force Icon pounded Fenrir into the ground.

Ambrose tightened the chains around Fenrir.

The wolf burst forth with that cloak of black fire, but with Ambrose's combined spirit and Icon, he felt confident in being shielded from it.

Then his awareness flared, and Ambrose looked up to see a blazing spear flying toward him, Eric smiling viciously.

Ambrose was going to ignore it, but Fenrir shuddered, and the wolf's spirit pulsed. The wolf bucked just as the spear took Ambrose in the shoulder.

His Icon seemed to shake, the tip of the spear clanging against his armor as Ambrose lost his grip on the chains, and he was sent flying backward. He crashed into the ground as Fenrir rose, shaking off the chains.

"How do you like Gungnir? It's supposed to repel Icons and pierce magical protections, so look at that! It worked!"

Ambrose gritted his teeth and began to weave a portal, but Fenrir bathed him in stygian flame, and the portal was devoured. Then the massive wolf leaped onto Ambrose, pushing him down with a paw, that tartarian flame coating his form.

Its great maw was dripping thick, moist saliva that would have gotten him wet were it not for his **[Infernal Aegis]** skill. It may have failed to keep the spear from piercing it, but it wasn't failing with the black fire.

If he didn't do something soon, he was going to die.

Fenrir leaned forward.

Ambrose tried to portal away, but that devouring flame ate his skill.

He looked into the monster's dead eyes.

And he knew he was going to die.

Alice's smiling face, her hand on her pregnant stomach, flashed through his mind.

Memories of them rolling dice and laughing while they played Dungeons and Dragons played like an old movie across his mind's eye, and from there, it rolled like a film reel.

He and Alice are making love for the first time, her smoldering eyes never leaving his as they connect on the most intimate level one can.

Her showing him the positive pregnancy test, and him smiling.

Her grave and his vow of vengeance.

Noelle's twitching cat ears as she ran through the forest.

And suddenly, Ambrose wanted it all to be worth it.

I will not die here, not without ending that smug bastard first.

Ambrose looked into what may have been the last pair of eyes he'd ever see and used his last card.

But instead of targeting Fenrir's outer body, he went deeper. He stared into the wolf's eyes as his jaw was full of razor-sharp teeth meant to devour worlds closed around him.

Through its eyes, he stared past the dead light, past the hunger, the long-dead pain, past its spirit, and found its heart.

He uttered one word.

"BREAK!"

CHAPTER SEVENTY

Like a great strumming guitar, the Word of Power thrummed. Its power was said to transcend even the System. As Ambrose felt a wave of utter, bone-deep exhaustion overcome him, Fenrir paused in trying to eat him as the Word went to work.

The great wolf began to vibrate, moving backward on its great paws.

Its dead eyes widened, and for the first time, Ambrose saw real emotion within them.

Fear.

To Fenrir's credit, it tried to attack him again, to fight through it, but the Word was simply beyond it. Perhaps, at one time, it wouldn't have been. Maybe, before his captivity, Loki's child would have been able to do something.

But the chains that had bound him had done their work well. Over the eons, the chains had drained Fenrir's power, much like Mordred's curse had drained his, but for far longer.

Ultimately, it wasn't Fenrir's heart shredding itself apart and bursting forth from its chest in a spectacularly horrific detonation that killed him.

It had been the chains themselves that had done it.

He dismissed the notification as soon as he had gotten it and warily stood up. Fenrir lay on his side, chest open, and a mess of dark golden blood, bone, and bits and pieces of a crimson heart coating the ground around him.

His eyes were bleached white, devoid of all life in truth now.

"I wasn't expecting that," Eric said dryly.

Ambrose was weak as if he had just finished a marathon beyond his skill.

Slowly, he limped towards Eric, who hefted Gungnir, and adjusted his tie.

"You won't be able to break through this circle, Mr. Severen."

Ambrose said nothing. He just kept walking. Holding his hand to his side, his armor enchantments allowed him to summon Akaroth with a thought.

Eric laughed, "I've always admired that determination of yours. It's what made you such an effective employee. But you're wasting your time, Mr. Severen. You cannot break through the wards."

He lifted Akaroth, and with his muscles screaming their protest, swung it at Eric.

Glyphs flared, and light pulsed, Akaroth was knocked away.

"You see? It's futile." Eric grinned at him, his viper eyes glittering like dark crystals.

Ambrose lifted Akaroth again, and again, he smashed the axe into the circle.

Light flared, repeating what had happened before.

Ambrose hit it again.

Then again.

And again.

One might have said that Ambrose knew only one way to solve a problem, but the truth was that what he was doing was effective.

With the wards the fire giants had used, he couldn't have been expected to break through. There were too many, and he would have needed a much larger assault force to have a chance.

But with time and enough people, and if the fire giants had been courteous enough to let them sit there pounding at their wards unopposed, they would have gotten through eventually.

Eric was using a personally contained circle. Ambrose didn't need an entire assault for this.

He just needed himself.

So he kept slashing, and as he did, his strength slowly began to return. The Words effects always faded after a time, though he wouldn't risk using it again for a while. If he used it too many times, he was afraid he wouldn't have enough mana in his core. If that happened, it would be his life force that was drawn instead.

"Mr. Severen, this will not work. Cease this pointless attack."

Ambrose did not speak. However, he did note the slight anxiety in Eric's voice as he hacked away at the circle.

"Ambrose, I know it hurts, but you won't make it through this circle. You have other friends, other people on your island relying on you. Go, turn back. Leave me alone, and I'll do the same."

Eric's voice was calm now, but there was a pleading edge. He could see as well as Ambrose could that the light was growing dimmer with every slash.

He ignored the bubbling fury that built in him. With a final, mighty slash, Akaroth bit into the circle.

The glyphs exploded apart into glass shards of crystalline light.

Eric Delrosa swore and rolled away from Ambrose's follow-up.

"You stupid ape! You think I'm helpless?"

At his words, Eric's clothing began to ripple, and with it, his skin. He grew, elongated, and in the span of a second, Ambrose was looking at a massive silverback gorilla.

It raised its fists and brought it down on Ambrose, and he let them connect. **[Infernal Aegis]** held, and the fists did not end up connecting.

Dismissing Akaroth, Ambrose punched the gorilla in the face, and it flew back, its form morphing back into Eric's human shape as it did.

"You can change your form, but no matter what shape you're in, you still lack the experience necessary to be effective."

Eric snarled, and Ambrose's awareness let him know that Gungnir was flying his way from behind him.

Without looking, he brought a portal into existence, and the spear flew through it.

Right into the back of Eric's left shoulder, spinning him around.

Eric cried out as he hit the ground. Gritting his teeth, he lifted his face and spoke, **"Stop and kill yourself!"**

Ambrose felt the words settle over him, and he did stop.

Eric laughed, standing up, hand grasping at his bloody wound where the spearhead poked out of.

"I should have ended it this way from the start! Silly me, thinking you had the willpower to resist."

Ambrose brought the force of his thoughts, backed by the Forge Icon, against the compulsion like a hammer.

The Forge Icon wasn't just some mystical force of reality. Yes, it was that, but to have an Icon, to make an Icon work for you, one had to meditate on how they fit within it.

In other words, when the Forge Icon backed up his thoughts or enforced anything he did, it did so by bringing all he was and all he had the potential to be into the equation.

He was who he was not because of his personality but because of the people who had influenced his life.

His father, who had trained him, raised him.

Andrea, Thom, and all those on Avalon who supported him. Believed in him.

Darren, who had died because of him.

Alice, who had loved him.

His daughter, who would never know him.

They *forged* him.

All of that influence, those people who made him who he was, came to bear in the Icon he called forth to support his bladed thoughts.

Eric's voice was a skill, nothing more.

It could not hold against such a thing.

As Eric raised his spear for the killing blow, his eyes widened in shock and fear when it was batted away.

Ambrose's spirit flared, and he saw Eric's spear shine in response, sending forth its own spirit to counter his.

At that moment, he could have laughed. All of that effort to get the spear, the armor that surely allowed him to shapeshift, all of it was for not because he knew the flaw in using these items.

If you didn't have the item, you didn't have its effects.

Ambrose spun a portal into existence.

Right near the shaft of the spear.

His portals would cut through almost everything; though Gungnir was a powerful weapon, it was ultimately a tool.

Tools could be broken.

The broken spear fell out of Eric's hands as he stared in open-mouthed horror.

Like an extinguished match, the spear's spirit vanished, and breaking from the dam that had held it back, Ambrose's spirit slammed down onto Eric like a crashing wave.

Eric was slammed to the ground, groaning.

"You're a manipulator, Eric. That's what you are at your core. A serpent hissing lies into people's ears to control them. I've learned something about the System, you see. It takes note of your choices, and the skills, classes, and rewards it offers are directly related to those choices."

Almost idly, he formed a portal above his palm and stared at it. Like a miniature gate to hell, the infernal portal slowly spun, its edges sharper than any mortal blade.

He flicked his hand, the portal zipped forward, and cut Eric's left hand off.

He would have screamed, but Ambrose's spirit was smothering him.

"Alice couldn't talk that night, remember? She couldn't say anything to me as you killed her. So you don't get to talk."

He cut off Eric's other hand, calmly watching Eric's silent scream of agony as blood poured out of his stumps.

"Some people say there are worse things than death. I could cripple you, take your tongue, and then let you live. That might be worse," Ambrose shook his head.

"I won't be doing that. You're going to die here, Eric. In this cave. Forgotten."

He cut off a knee, Eric's leg falling to the ground like a broken branch, sanguine liquid gushing as if from a broken pipe, bits of bone glistening in the light.

This was justice. This was the fulfillment of a long road.

It's also torture and makes you no better than him.

Ambrose almost scoffed, but he knew that voice in his mind.

It was what Alice would have said.

Her memory was the one light inside him he didn't want to extinguish.

Fingernails digging into his palm, Ambrose flicked a hand.

A portal of hellfire ended Eric Delrosa's life while an expression of agony and fear was etched onto his features.

His head plopped on the ground like a discarded melon.

That was it.

Journey over.

Ambrose had avenged his dead wife and daughter.

So why didn't he feel better?

Epilogue

Ambrose sat by Noelle's body. He looked down at her, and he balled his hands into fists.

"I did it, Noelle. Eric is dead. After all this time, my wife and daughter have been avenged."

He lifted his head to look at the cavern ceiling, the many stalactites and rough rocks reflecting the light that had no source.

"Yet I don't feel at peace. Alice is still gone. I'll still never know my daughter."

He gritted his teeth. "The pain is *still* there. It isn't any less. It should be. She can be at peace now. By all rights, by every measurement, I should be happy with that."

He punched the ground, his heart beating out a furious beat.

"But I'm not. It's still there, Noelle. Like a branding iron on my soul, its burn never fading."

It should have abated, or at least he should have felt *something*.

But no, Eric's death brought him nothing.

Nothing of substance anyway. There was satisfaction, yes. He was glad the fucker was dead. He had done the multiverse a favor. But there was no peace, no closure.

Just the same pain that he had carried on his heart with him all this time.

A notification lit up in his mind, and he didn't read it.

He knew what it would say. He could feel it.

Noelle had died, the final bit of her life ebbing away.

But, as promptly as the first, another notification lit up, and this one...this one felt more insistent.

He looked at this one.

[Would you like to use 'Phoenix Tear-Mythic' on 'Noelle?' Y/N?

He did not recall possessing such an item, but he sent forth a resounding yes with his mind.

Appearing from his infernal realm, the tear shaped stone he had won from the competition and received from the quartermaster, floated just above Noelle's heart.

It slowly began to spin, turning into a small glowing molten drop that fell just like any tear would.

Right onto Noelle's heart.

A glow of warm firelight from a hearth surrounded Noelle. Ambrose stared, a little flutter of hope blooming in his heart.

The glow receded into her.

Slowly, as if waking from a deep, deep sleep, her eyes fluttered.

Then they opened.

Ambrose shouted, scooping up Noelle in his arms, practically crushing her to his chest.

"You're alive! Thank god, you're alive!!"

Noelle mewed weakly, pushing against him.

"Oh, sorry." Ambrose sat her down, rubbing the back of his neck.

Noelle smiled. She still looked pale, and he was sure she was a little weak.

But she was alive.

"Did you?" Her voice trailed off.

Ambrose pointed, and Noelle turned to look, blue eyes landing on Eric's severed head.

The System has blinked a notification in his mind, so he knew Eric was dead. He didn't look at what he had earned, not feeling like checking out his progression at the moment.

Noelle laughed, beaming as she turned to him, hugging him again, tail swishing wildly back and forth.

Ambrose stood, holding out a hand.

She took it.

"Let's go."

***

Ambrose and Noelle stood over Alice's grave. His house was no longer there, a scattered, broken building, surrounded by other, scattered broken buildings.

He held Noelle's hand in his own.

Gently taking his hand out of hers, he knelt, rubbing his hand over the grass of his wife's grave, feeling the wetness on his fingers.

There was so much he could say, so much that came to mind.

But he said what was in his heart first and foremost.

"I miss you, Alice."

With his words came a gentle wind, brushing over his hand in its passing.

"I miss your smile. I miss your laugh. I miss playing D&D with you. I miss watching movies in bed, and waking up to your beautiful green eyes. I miss your touch, and the way you lit up seeing me."

He clenched the grass, imagining himself clenching her shirt in his fist.

He didn't know he was crying.

"I miss the future we were supposed to have together. I miss the daughter we were meant to hold, to raise."

He took a deep, shuddering breath.

"It was my fault, Alice. Sure, maybe Eric was determined to kill you, maybe that's true. But I *knew* he was in town. I *knew* what he was like, and I *provoked him*. We could have moved, could have had a fresh start, but I didn't want to seem like a coward. I didn't want to run. I prioritized myself image over you."

Ambrose's voice shook, thick with emotion as he said the next words, "I am sorry. I am so fucking sorry, Alice, Jenny."

He collapsed onto both knees, hanging his head.

He stayed there for a long while, the wind tousling his hair.

Suddenly, he felt a weight lift from his shoulders. A weight that he almost hadn't realized he was carrying.

It was...it was if he had been forgiven.

Which was absurd since his wife was dead and could not forgive him.

Nonetheless, he felt it. Like the ghost of a hug, wind combing his hair like invisible feminine fingers trailing his scalp.

He sighed, and as he did, finally, he felt it.

What he had been searching for.

Peace.

The pain was still there, but along with it was the peace, easing it and making it tolerable.

He stood, wiping his eye with a knuckle. Then he threw his head back and laughed.

His laughter carried throughout the air, startling birds in a nearby tree.

"Someone's in a good mood," a wry voice cut through his laughter at the right moment.

Ambrose and Noelle whirled around. Her ears flat, Noelle hissed at Misaq, who tipped his fedora at her.

"Careful, kitty, you'll cough up a hairball doing that. Been a long time, Ambrose."

"Not long enough," he growled.

Misaq put a hand on his chest. "Tsk! You wound me, Ambrose. Why would you do that to me? Haven't I been a good friend, hmm? Here you are, triumphant after all this time. The villain slain, peace restored, a once dead companion brought back to life, and none of it possible without that little deal I've offered you."

Ambrose shrugged, "What do you want, Misaq?"

"A little acknowledgment might be nice," Misaq stated with a grin.

Ambrose said nothing, and Noelle narrowed her eyes at the devil.

"Oh poo, you're no fun, you know? Very well, I am here to...change the terms of our agreement."

"No deal, fuck off."

Ambrose didn't trust the devil, and if he wanted to change their deal, it wouldn't be anything good.

"Such a vulgar tongue! Just listen, eh? Instead of a bunch of bad people taken to the Tree of Eden, I want you to bring one."

He narrowed his eyes at Misaq. "What are you playing at, devil? That deal sounds skewed in my favor."

Misaq gave a flamboyant bow, "Indeed it is! You might not think so after I tell you who I want you to retrieve, but I shall sweeten the pot further. Should you accept my wondrous deal, I will consider your obligation to me completely fulfilled. I will no longer consider Avalon my base of operations here, I will even go so far as to never contact you or yours ever again should you wish it."

Ambrose didn't trust it. He was making the deal too good. Whomever he wanted, he wanted badly enough to make the deal too good.

Things that looked too good on the surface were often false.

Misaq's eyes glittered, and before Ambrose could reply, he spoke again. This time there was a hint of venom in his tone.

"You humans have interesting ways of convincing each other. I've always been fascinated by them, You have even named the ways! The way

I just offered you was the carrot. It's supposed to entice you, motivate you to take my desired course of action because you want it. That tasty, tasty carrot. But there is another way, Ambrose. You know it as the stick."

There was a little pop of fire, and Misaq held a wooden stick in his hand. He brandished it at Ambrose, eyes swirling with menacing light.

"If you don't help me out this way, Ambrose, I'm afraid you'll leave me no choice but to use the stick."

Ambrose crossed his arms, lowering his own voice. "It isn't a good idea to threaten me, devil."

Misaq's laughter was light-hearted, and his grin was boyish. "I would much prefer not to, friend. In fact, my stick is no threat at all. Shall I tell you what it is?"

Ambrose grunted, interested now. "I shall come to live with you on Avalon."

"Uhh, what?"

Misaq's smile grew, "You heard me. Our deal means Avalon is my base of operations as well as your home. I will reside there, and trust me when I say this, Ambrose, I am a *terrible* roommate. I have this affliction, you see. All kinds of monsters just keep popping up around me. If I'm around people, the situation gets awfully... bloody."

Ambrose gritted his teeth, stepping forward.

Misaq wagged a finger, "Now, now, let me expand on the carrot, mm? Not only will I release your obligation, you will have an opportunity to unlock a most amazing secret about the grimoire in your possession."

Ambrose blinked.

Misaq pointed at his face, "See? That's got you hooked. Possibly laying your hands on more power means you could defend Avalon better. Plus, there's your precious tree, yes? You've been sorely neglecting it, and it could use a little watering. The person I want you to get would greatly increase the tree's energy."

Noelle tugged at his sleeve, and he looked down at her, raising an eyebrow.

"Can we talk?" Noelle's voice was low.

Misaq waved a hand. "By all means. Go, discuss it. I shall wait here for your answer. Just remember my stick."

They walked some distance away, turning towards one another when they thought Misaq would not hear him.

"What is it?" He asked Noelle.

She bit her lip, ears moving uncertainly. Finally, she blew out a breath, blowing a strand of white hair our of her face.

"I want to go away," she started.

"What?!" He almost yelled.

Noelle put her hands on her hips, tail moving in annoyance.

Ambrose tried to look apologetic, and she continued.

"I was a burden. In that fight."

He started to interrupt her again, but her look of annoyance caused him to shut his mouth.

"I was, I want to get stronger. I want to train. Get used to this form, master my senses. I want time to find out who I am apart from you, Ambrose." Her eyes filled with tears as she said this, knowing it would hurt him.

She was right, as he felt her statement like a sword point in his heart.

But it was tempered by the love and support that flooded their bond. He knew she needed this.

"Very well, Noelle. If that's what you want."

She nodded, "Take his deal, Ambrose. You can't endanger Avalon."

He nodded, sighing. "You're right. He has me over a barrel. Even his carrot would be enough reason. I wouldn't care about the stick, except its directed at Avalon, not me."

Noelle hugged him, and when they parted, he turned and walked back towards Misaq.

"Okay, Misaq. You win. Who do you want me to hunt down?"

Misaq grinned, spreading his hands.

"Why none other than Merlin himself, of course."

The End of Rise of The Infernal Paladin, Book Two:
WORLD EATER

Thank You For Reading

Dear Reader,

Thank you for sharing this adventure with me.

If you have enjoyed this story, I'd be truly grateful if you'd leave a review on Amazon.com. It truly helps.

And, for updates and more adventures, you're invited to join my mailing list at ShadowLightPress.com/

If you'd like to read ahead on this and other stories, hop onto my Patreon at https://patreon.com/EmrysAmbrosiusand stop by Noveliz ing.comand say hi.

Come hang out with the author on discord at Immersive Ink.

More Incredible Stories by Emrys Ambrosius
Rise of the Infernal Paladin: Book Three

Wyrmhaven: A Progression Fantasy Academy Novel
Bloodfyre
Nexus Awakening

You might also enjoy...
Terra Mythica: A LitRPG Epic Adventure by John Stax, available now on Amazon.

The world is dying, and everyone knows it. But is the alternative worse?

In rust-choked streets and hollowed-out cities, there is only one way out—Terra Mythica, a virtual world so immersive that time warps, hunger vanishes, and even the most broken can live like kings.

Jace wasn't supposed to make it in. He cheated death, and now it's catching up to him. As the reluctant protégé of Hades, Jace finds himself thrust into Mount Olympus University, where gods manipulate Travelers, and the line between real and digital blurs with every step.

Declan Dark, Book One: Dark Daze, A GameLitRPG Vampire Noir, System Earth Series by Declan Darkmor Available now on Amazon.

He's blind. Thirsty. And in over his head.

Declan Dark never signed up to be a vampire -let alone a blind one with a mysterious System whispering in his skull.

After one disastrous bachelor party, he's plunged into Sin City's secret supernatural underworld, where every shadow conceals a predator, and even his allies might be out for his blood.

With uncanny abilities, a reluctant shifter sidekick, and no roadmap home, Declan must chase down the truth of his curse before the underworld's hidden dangers pop him off the menu.

*Think capricious vampire noir meets GameLitRPG adventure
-where leveling up fast might just save your un-life.*
Sink your teeth into Dark Daze.

**Return of the Wing Mage by Dominick Ruiz, available now
on Amazon.**

What would you do if you had the chance to rewrite your greatest
failures?

After eight years of brutal war, victory is finally in sight.

The forces of North America stand united, one final enemy stronghold left to conquer.

Santiago Silva - Santi to those who know him - leads the charge, his
magic commanding the winds.

But just as the end seems near, a desperate enemy ritual goes awry,
flinging Santi back in time.

Acknowledgements

As always, I have a lot of people to thank. As always, everyone at Shadow Light is amazing for making this happen. I know how hard you all work, and I am very appreciative.

I have to thank every member of my family. I love you guys.

Everyone at Immersive Ink deserves a heartfelt thank you as well. Seriously, you all rock!

Thanks for reading!

ABOUT THE AUTHOR

Emrys Ambrosius has been a fan of reading since he was five. Escaping to fantasy worlds with dragons, like in Eragon or the works of Tolkien, that passion for reading only grew to encompass all things "nerd." His passions include D&D and video games like Oblivion, Skyrim, and The Witcher, especially The Witcher 3.

He began writing when he was thirteen years old... and never finished anything he started. A peek at his Google Docs would find dozens and dozens of half-finished projects. It wasn't until he was 29, married, and with two kids that he was finally driven enough to finish a book. By this time, he had discovered a way to turn his love of D&D and video games into stories on the page.

When reading his books, you can expect well-written action and, hopefully, a few solid punches to the feels.

GROUPS AND COMMUNITIES

Join the news letter at Shadow Light Press
Hang out with us on Discord at Immersive Ink
Author Facebook group at Immersive Ink
LitRPG Facebook group by Magic Dome Books
Hang out with us on Facebook at Shadow Light Press